PRAISE FOR JOHN P. MURPHY

"John P. Murphy's Claudius Rex is a particular standout. A cyber-noir-humor mystery, the novella combines flawless plotting with provocative technical speculation to introduce a pair of detectives whose snappy banter and dauntless verve will remain with you long after you've turned over the last page."

Ken Liu, *author of* The Dandelion Dynasty *series*

"John P. Murphy's Red Noise is a snarky, grungy, hyperkinetic space romp that reads like a Neal Stephenson novel collided with a VHS copy of A Fistful of Dollars at high speed. The pacing is taut, the characters are vivid, bad-ass, and zany, the dialogue is razor-sharp, and the whole thing is just plain fun."

Marko Kloos, *author of the* Frontline *series*

"Stylish, funny, action-packed, cinematic, Red Noise is the wise-cracking, gravity-defying, bullet-lasering Yojimbo-in-space you've been waiting for. John Murphy is a master of tight plots and unforgettable characters."

Ken Liu, award-winning author of *The Grace of Kings*

"Murphy skillfully transports spaghetti western tropes to a lawless space station in this action-packed debut… This fast, fun space western is pure entertainment."

Publishers Weekly

D0168479

BY THE SAME AUTHOR

The Liar

John P. Murphy

RED NOISE

ANGRY
ROBOT

ANGRY ROBOT
An imprint of Watkins Media Ltd

Unit 11, Shepperton House
89 Shepperton Road
London N1 3DF
UK

angryrobotbooks.com
twitter.com/angryrobotbooks
Tick Tick Boom

An Angry Robot paperback original, 2020

Cover by Kieryn Tyler
Edited by Eleanor Teasdale and Paul Simpson
Set in Meridien

ISBN 978 0 85766 847 9
Ebook ISBN 978 0 85766 852 3

Printed and bound in the United Kingdom by TJ International.

9 8 7 6 5 4 3 2 1

To everyone who just wants to be left alone

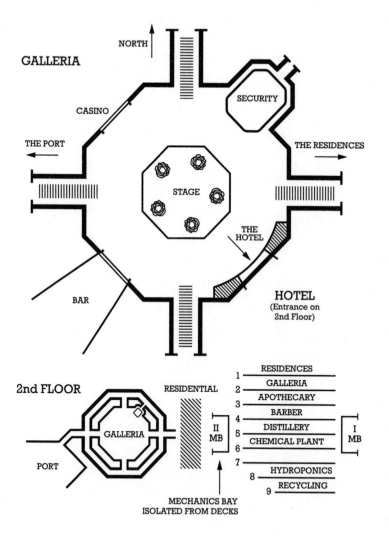

GALLERIA

NORTH

CASINO

THE PORT

SECURITY

THE RESIDENCES

STAGE

THE HOTEL

BAR

HOTEL
(Entrance on
2nd Floor)

2nd FLOOR

RESIDENTIAL

GALLERIA

II
MB

PORT

MECHANICS BAY
ISOLATED FROM DECKS

1 RESIDENCES
2 GALLERIA
3 APOTHECARY
4 BARBER
5 DISTILLERY
6 CHEMICAL PLANT
7
8 HYDROPONICS
9 RECYCLING

I
MB

THE MINER

Station 35 was a dot on the nav screen. It meant ore buyers and fuel sellers, necessary transactions and unwelcome human contact. The Miner needed the first and dreaded the second, but cash meant freedom and she couldn't eat rock. So she set her course, made sure her dwindling fuel would get her there, and then thought no more about it.

She laid eyes on Station 35 a week later, loaded with ore and low on everything. It was big and ugly and damn near deserted.

She first met one of its inhabitants in orbit, a vacuum-mummified corpse tethered to an orbital path marker and clutching a sign that read, "NO FIREARMS. WE MEAN IT."

So it was that kind of place, then.

She'd been waiting patiently in a holding orbit for five hours, listening for the OK to dock. At least, she'd waited as patiently as anyone could as her fuel burned down below the one percent mark, past the point where the engineers who'd built her spacecraft expected any sane person would still be operating it. The station crew knew she was there; they'd scanned her half a dozen times. They just hadn't given the OK. Or signaled why they wouldn't. Or said anything at all. She tapped her fingers on the pilot's console, had the computer run another radio equipment diagnostic, cranked down the gravity and temperature control a little more, and that all still counted as patient, in her opinion.

There had been plenty of opportunities for her to curse herself over the fuel squeeze, and she'd made use of them efficiently on the long trip from her claim. Even with a hold full of asteroidal nickel-iron to sell, it had been so easy to stay one more day, and then another. No people in a million clicks, just silence and work, her plants and her books. She'd stayed too long, and then she was low on fuel, low on water, low on cash to pay her claim fees. Another week and the government would seize it for non-payment. Of course, long before then the fuel would run out, and when the life support, power, and grav plating all ground to a halt in turn she'd asphyxiate, floating, in the dark.

The station looked abandoned. It was a big gray monstrous thing, chunky and ugly. Burrowed into the side of an asteroid, it looked like a giant spider clutching its bloated egg sac. The big round hab complex had a set of windows that glowed with a venomous green light that flickered red. It had been military once; most of them had. All along its gray steel skin, wherever some rating with a paint nozzle had found room, it bore the number 35 at all angles and configurations, except for the one spot with a 53. Converted to commercial use, someone had at least been bright enough to remove the great big sub-C cannons, leaving flat round patches where the emplacement had once wielded armament capable of flinging mass hard and fast enough to obliterate even the best-armored cruiser. There were probably still some junky little lasers for zapping trash and other projectiles, but she couldn't see them from so far out.

The comm light blinked, and she slapped it before she could register that it wasn't the dockmaster. A big round face filled the small comm screen, unshaven and with a swollen red nose that had been broken for him pretty thoroughly, leaving bruises rimming bloodshot eyes.

"Mining ship *Cincinnatus*," she said automatically. It was redundant, since he could see her identifier on his screen just as clearly as she could see "Transport ship *Cassandra*" below his beat-up face. She just didn't feel like saying "Hi."

"Hey," said the trucker, his voice muffled for obvious reasons. "Glad I caught ya. You ain't aiming to dock here, are you?"

She bit back a remark proposing an alternate reason she might have sat in a docking orbit for five hours. "I am."

He was already shaking his head. "I'd push on to the next station if I were you. Ain't far to 36."

"What's the matter, is the place abandoned?" She felt her hand tighten involuntarily on the arm rest. There might be fuel and water in an abandoned station, and there might not, but there wouldn't be money to pay the patch fees.

"Might as well be. Anyone decent up and left a long time ago. All that's left is the assholes who did this." His hand flicked into view to indicate his broken nose.

She glanced at the ad beacon, which still offered ore-buying as a station service. She frowned.

"They still buying ore and selling supplies?"

He blinked like she'd flicked him in the face. "Yeah; I mean, I guess. The provisioner's open, anyway."

Her shoulders released some of their tension, and she sat back in the pilot's chair. "Then I'll be fine, thanks." When it looked like he was about to say something, she interrupted, "Is there something wrong with the port? Almost all the berths are open, but I've been waiting for the clear to dock for hours."

He shook his head. "Portmaster's crooked as hell; probably playing chicken. He got me with a two hundred credit fine for docking without permission, when I thought my radio was busted."

She winced.

"Listen," he said. "This place is bad news."

She sighed, hopefully not too obviously. People. "Thanks for the concern, but I don't have the food or fuel to make it to 36. I'll keep my eyes open, don't worry."

He looked skeptical. "Hell, if it's fuel you need, I can spot you some. I'm about at the last marker buoy, I can stick around–"

"No thanks," she said, and tried to make it sound polite. There was no way. Either she'd have to kill a would-be pirate using fuel as bait, or worse: she'd be in debt to a stranger.

"I just don't want blood on my conscience."

"If there's blood, it won't be mine."

They stared at each other until he looked away. "Your call. Just keep an eye out for their 'welcoming committee', goddamn little shits."

"Will do." The faint memory of manners tugged at her conscience. "Thanks for the warning. Safe flight."

"Safe flight." He nodded and the picture blinked out.

The Miner rubbed her face with both hands and glared at the comm system, which still showed her dock request pending.

"Ship, auto-accept dock permission," she said aloud. "Notify me immediately."

"OK, boss!" the ship computer's chipper voice replied, and she was up and out of her chair.

She went to the plant room, the bunk she'd converted. Two plastic shelves of orchids and another with three bonsai trees filled the small space with a heady, earthy atmosphere.

She closed her eyes and breathed it in. It was warm and humid with the ship's cooling systems cranked down to save power. It felt nice, even as a trickle of sweat crept down her neck. The hatch closed behind her, leaving her in the dim light of plant room night – she was so far out of daytime sync with them it wasn't even funny – but she didn't mind. She couldn't make out greens and purples and pinks in the low light, but she knew they were there. That was the point; wherever she was, whatever she was doing, she knew they were there. She had a center.

"Hey boss, the fuel level is down to zero point five percent. You instructed me to–"

"I know," she interrupted, and then swore. Two hundred credits was a lot of money to her just then. Her whole cargo would only go for maybe thirty, thirty-five grand. But a tow could be much more expensive, assuming they even had a working tugbot.

She pulled the hatch open and stepped into the upper corridor of her small ship, glanced into the opposite hatch and thought again about selling her service rifle that hung uselessly above her bunk. She couldn't fire it onboard without risking a hull breach. There was really no point to keeping it. Nor the sword that hung beneath it. Or any of the other mementos.

"Docking permission accepted, boss."

The Miner snapped out of her musings. It took some doing to maneuver her heavily-loaded ship, but she wrestled it around to its final approach. Then she collapsed in her seat, feeling the weight of the last few sleepless nights and the stress of the low fuel gauge.

A half-empty station wasn't so bad. Ideal, in some ways. Sell the ore. Pay the debt. Don't attract attention. Get the hell out of there. No problem.

The Welcoming Committee

Screwball and Ditz stood outside the main port hatch feeling exposed and foolish. At least, Screwball did. He stuffed his hands in his pockets to grip the brass knuckles he'd had printed, glad for their reassuring weight. Shithead Preston, taking his best pistol away. He leaned against the wall under the big Welcome sign and glared at Ditz, who was waving his hands around like some kung fu shit and saying "ha!" and "wa!" and otherwise living up to his nickname.

"What the fuck are you doing?" He finally got fed up and embarrassed enough to ask.

"Getting my head in the game, Screwy man. Psyching my fine self up. Ha!"

Ditz flailed his leg up in a way Screwball figured was meant to be a high kick.

"You're gonna hurt yourself."

Ditz spun with his fist up suddenly and Screwball froze as that fist came to a halt right in front of his nose. The rings on Ditz's jacket jangled loudly and their eyes met. Ditz's pupils were blown.

"In the game," Ditz whispered, staring into his eyes. His wet breath stank. He turned after a long silent moment and started flailing again.

"I knew you weren't going to hit me," Screwball lied.

"Uh-huh. Ha!" Ditz punched the air hard, lunging like with one of those skinny fencing swords.

"How long's it take to dock a stupid spaceship, anyway?"

"They got to scan it first," Ditz said matter-of-factly, not looking at him. "Checking for you-know-who. Make sure the old man doesn't sneak him back."

"Nah," Screwball said. "Nuke's dead. He's got to be."

"Says you. Anyway, Preston looks for contraband and shit, too."

"So he can take a cut, you mean, or see if there's anything worth stealing." Screwball still felt sore about losing his gun. Not just feeling defenseless – that was an expensive pistol and it ate him to think of that scrawny asshole hoarding it or selling it. This place was supposed to be a fucking goldmine for a guy who wasn't afraid of a fight, but instead he just got stolen from and paid shit and made to hang out and try to recruit anyone else dumb enough to dock at the universe's asshole.

Ditz punched the air one more time, then turned and shrugged. He was breathing hard. "I don't tell the old man how to run his… Shit!"

Screwball spun to see where Ditz was looking: at a tall, good-looking dude with a shaved head and an easy grin, almost a leer. He squinted before realizing that the bald head wasn't painted at the temples but gene-modded with some sick-looking scales, all shimmery in the light.

He took his hands out of his pockets and folded his arms, intending to look tough but forgetting the brass knuckles. "The fuck are you?" he managed.

"The fuck am I?" The bald guy turned to a bony chick who Screwball didn't know either. "I don't know. Shit, Ditz, who the fuck am I?" If the bald guy wasn't intimidated, that worthless jerk Ditz sure was. He ran his hand over his yellow-dyed hair.

"Come on, Raj, he's new. He doesn't mean anything."

"Well I guess I'm Raj then, brother," the bald guy said to Screwball. "So if I'm Raj, then who. The fuck." Screwball backed into the wall and Raj poked him hard in the chest. "Are you?"

Screwball resisted the urge to rub his sore sternum. "I'm the guy who's, uh, asking who the fuck you are."

Raj stared hard at him. His breath stank, too. "Never mind. I think if I knew your name I'd lose an IQ point." The girl behind him laughed. He stepped back and lazily waved a hand. "Now push off, brothers, I have work to do."

Ditz gave Screwball a worried look. "Hey, Raj, sorry for the disrespect and all. You know I like you, man, but they agreed, dude. This is Feeney's patch. We're the welcoming committee, right?"

"New arrangement," Raj said. He folded his arms and looked pleased with himself while his pal leaned against the wall where Screwball had been, looking pleased with herself, too.

"What new arrangement?" Screwball was getting pissed off. He'd been promised money, drugs, and ass when he came to this godforsaken station, and all he'd gotten was a lot of bullshit.

Raj uncrossed his arms, gave Screwball an appraising look, then punched him right in the face. Screwball staggered at the sudden stinging pain and flailed his arms out. Adrenaline and shock fought, and for a moment all he saw was red.

"The new arrangement, my brother, is I punch you until you fuck off, savvy?"

Screwball's rage pushed him through the fog, and he

fumbled in his pocket for his knuckles, twisted in the lining. Raj stepped neatly and dealt him a second rabbit punch, and he reeled. Ditz was gone. Blood streamed hot down his face and his shirt felt warm. He swung at Raj, but, angry and pain-muddled, only managed a slap, barely catching the guy's chin.

"Shit!" Raj rubbed his face with his fingers. "If you get blood on me I'll kill you."

Screwball hadn't been watching Raj's pal, and he realized his oversight when she elbowed him in the side of the head. He hit the far bulkhead and saw stars, while she reeled off-balance.

The thought "two on one" made it through his skull to part of his brain that could do some good, and he fumbled to back away. They let him go, which he counted as a miracle. Distracted when the hatch to the dock made a noise, they left themselves open for Screwball to hurl his brass knuckles at Raj's head.

"Welcome to Station 35," he yelled at the opening hatch, breaking into a run and technically fulfilling his role as welcoming committee, if not the point. "Hope you like assholes!"

He laughed his idiot head off as a pissed-off Raj pursued.

Dockmaster's Tour

The dockmaster, whose name tag read "Preston", was rail-thin and had an expression like he'd just smelled something nasty. If his black jumpsuit was a uniform, it was hard to tell given its shapelessness and obvious stains. He didn't bother to hide his effort to crane his neck to see into the Miner's ship behind her before he refocused his eyes on her and grudgingly offered a hand.

"Welcome to Station 35," he said, and disengaged from the handshake like dropping a dead frog. "You never been here before, that right?"

"That's right."

He nodded. "Gotta inspect your ship and give you a scan before you come aboard."

The Miner frowned at him. "You've scanned my ship eight times already."

"And now I'll do it again," he said, smug.

She couldn't even pretend to be surprised. Every pissant little pseudo-authority out there had their own way to get their kicks. He didn't have the spit-and-polish look of the guys who love to give fines. Spit maybe, but no polish. She guessed he was looking to confiscate contraband, or "contraband", and sell it off, probably right back to her. Well, he could knock himself out.

A few minutes of peering and poking, accompanied by

disappointed grunts at each promising – and empty – hiding spot, confirmed that theory.

"Just selling ore?" he asked when he apparently got tired of prying in the cargo hold.

"Only thing of value on this heap."

"Let me see your claim docs," he said, but didn't sound hopeful. She pulled them up on the cargo area display, showing the orbital path of the loose cluster of rubble she called a living. The dockmaster peered at it skeptically, then punched the numbers into his wrist-mounted gadget.

"You've been in range of the station for four months now," he said, and gave her an accusing look.

"I've been in the field for six," she said. "Hit a good seam, didn't want to leave." Didn't want to deal with self-important jackasses. Didn't want to talk to anyone or explain herself. Didn't want to get in any fights.

Uninvited, he stuck his finger into the display and dragged. Station 35's own orbital path showed up green, slower than her patch. "Another six month stretch like that'll take you out to 34 next," he said.

That's the plan, she thought, unless she could make it seven months. "Just passing through, I guess," she said aloud. "I'll be out of your hair in no time."

She was confused for a second by a flash of hostility before she noticed the thinning hair on top of his head. He didn't say anything, just shut all that down and went on to the galley, peering around her mostly unused cabinets and clean cooking gadgets. He frowned, suspicious. "What've you been eating?"

"Emergency rations."

"Christ, why the hell would you do that?"

"They're cheap, last forever, and I like them."

"Weirdo."

He poked around further, apparently trying to prove that she had some secret source of nutrition, but seemed to get bored and walked straight out again. He spent a couple of disappointed minutes tapping at pipes, then wandered to the upper deck.

After the macabre warning sign, the Miner had expected some pushback when he saw the rifle over her bunk. He looked at it speculatively.

"Looks military," he said.

"It is."

He eyed it a while longer, ran a finger along the barrel like he was checking for dust, but finally just said in a bored tone, "Don't take it off your ship. Don't sell it to nobody here, neither. Try either one, and it's mine." He peered at the beat-up old sword that hung beneath the rifle in a black canvas-wrapped scabbard. He pulled it a little way out to look at its gleaming sharp edge, then let the magnetic catches resheathe it with a click. He didn't find the more dubious stuff behind well-hidden panels, and she didn't offer to show him.

The plant rooms were more interesting to him; he positively woke up. He craned his neck this way and that, sniffing around. The Miner tensed every time he stuck his nose in a bloom and snorted.

"The hell are they?"

"Flowers," she said, and when he turned an annoyed eye on her, amended that to, "Orchids."

"What, do you get high on them? Eat the petals?"

"No. They look nice."

"Hallucinate, you mean."

"No, they just look nice. Don't you think so?"

He grunted and shrugged. Philistine. "There's import restrictions," he said. "Can't risk the hydroponics. Diseases, you know. Might have to impound to quarantine."

She bit the inside of her lip. "I'm not taking them off the ship. No danger to the hydroponics from here."

"Can't be too careful with hydroponics," he said, warming to his subject. "Never know what *diseases* plants might carry. Critters. Viruses. Could wipe out our food supply."

She let that hang in the air, waiting for him to come out with the bribe demand or make her offer it.

"Last station had a test," she lied. "I gave them a leaf and they had a fifty credit testing fee."

He wrinkled his nose and mulled it over. "They must have had fancier equipment than mine," he said. "The fee's a hundred here."

She gritted her teeth and ignored the bilious surge of disgust rising in her. "Any kind of discount for paying that directly? Save you the time of tacking it onto the invoice."

He grinned, all yellow and streaks. "That *is* the discount, lady," he said, and then dawdled, fondling the leaves and blossoms proprietarily until she paid his damn bribe. He didn't even bother taking a leaf.

Apparently satisfied at finally extracting a bit of graft without too much effort, the inspection was unceremoniously over. The Miner had to walk fast to keep up with the little toad on his way out.

They stopped just outside the airlock, the first step she'd taken onto the station, and she put her thumbprint and signature on the inspection report. It had a lot about the state of her ship's engines, thrusters, and reactor – miscounting the number of thrusters and getting flat wrong her reactor type – and a biological analysis of her ship's air and water, none of which he'd done. It had the wrong date, too. The two hundred credit fee was right, though. She winced, but paid.

"You staying long?" There was a look in his eye, like there was a wrong answer to that question.

"No," she said. "Just long enough to sell off the metal and pick up supplies: O2, water, and fuel. When my business is done, I'll go."

He nodded, and she figured she'd given the right answer. "Fuel and air you'll get from me. Ore you'll sell to the Company. Everything else you can find off the galleria if you're not choosy."

"Don't care who I buy from," she said, finishing the process of shutting the hatch and setting the lock, "but I prefer bids for the ore."

"And I'd prefer not living in the ass-hairs of the solar system. We don't get our 'prefers' out here. You sell it to the Company or you haul it away with you. Just make up your mind before I unload it for the assay."

"What company's that anyway?"

"Anaconda Consolidated. This is their station."

The Miner took a look around the cavernous port, with its doubly-reinforced bulkheads, two armored guard shacks, and a scar on the floor from where a big steel baffle had once blocked direct access to the inner hatch. "Looks military to me."

"Anaconda leases it, I mean. They run it." He eyed her sourly. "It's theirs in every way that matters, and don't forget it."

"Don't worry. I've got a good memory."

"See that you do. You want me to do the assay or what?"

She'd dealt with Anaconda before, a couple stations back. They'd been all right, not especially more corrupt or inept than anyone else, but she'd still rather have bids. And she'd really rather have a different company do the composition assay the price would be based on. Still, even with a good whack off the sale price from this single-buyer bullshit, it had to be cheaper than the fuel costs to haul it to the next station. And with the patch fees coming due on her claim, she needed cash sooner than she could reach another station. No wonder indie miners were so few and far between.

"Yeah, all right." She gave his pad her thumbprint, and that was that.

They dickered about mass and carbon. She was keeping most of the biomass for plant fertilizer, and he didn't want to bother buying the rest. But it was stupid to dump it, and legally he had to take it, so they settled for ten credits off the fuel bill, which usually ran to three thousand. The Miner reminded herself that she was literally selling shit and stale air, but she still felt cheated as she thumbprinted the pad again.

They were done then, but he lingered, giving her that appraising look again. "It'll be a while before I'm finished. If you're bored or looking for some extra cash, old man Feeney can always use someone who isn't planning to stay long."

Someone who might be willing to beat someone else up or maybe shed some blood, and then be gone before the law came looking. "Thanks for the tip," she said, since "fuck you" or "die in a fire" might have offended the guy assaying her cargo.

"Tell him I sent you if you do. Just you remember," he called after her, "no firearms."

She nodded, remembering the colorful warning outside and wondering if that was his handwriting.

THE SUBSTITUTE WELCOMING COMMITTEE

The dock main exit released a stale smell of old rubber gaskets and the faint whiff of urine as it opened onto a wide passage that took a right turn. The walls were streaked where condensation had dripped from vents, and a faded sign high on the interior wall pointed down the hallway with a big blue arrow and friendly lettering that read, "Welcome to Cpt John Wayne Koganusan Station (#35)! This way to our Famous Galleria!"

Under the sign stood a scrubby kid, probably in her twenties if the Miner could still judge, gawking down the passageway.

"Hope you like assholes!" someone was yelling, chased by a taller bald kid in leathers.

The kid under the sign stooped to pick up what looked like metal knuckles, made a punching gesture at the fleeing one, and seemed to notice the Miner. "Hey lady!" Her grin showed a broken front tooth.

"Ow! Fuck! Ow!" came from away down the corridor.

"Nice place you got here," said the Miner. The kid looked at her like she was stupid.

"It's a shit pile," said the kid. "But listen, right, we've got everything you could want, right. I know all the best places to get booze and drugs, or get laid. I know where to have fun, right?"

The Miner glanced at her, and believed she knew all the places to get drugs. "Pass."

The kid's eyes went wide, showing intricate tattoos on the sclera. She'd had money at some point, to get those done, but looked to have pissed it away. "Whoa, whoa. Not so hasty, right? I bet you're here for a fight, ri–"

"Wrong."

"Come on, where'd you get those scars, then? Don't go work for Feeney, he's a tool. Come on and work for Angelica! Punch bozos, it's fun!"

"I'm not here to fight, kid. I don't punch anyone I'm not willing to kill."

The kid looked skeptical but pressed on. "So you're what, a trucker? A miner? Mining sucks! I can get you rich, lady, all you need's a little luck and you'll make bank at Lady Angelica's casino. You want to be rich, don't you? I'm good luck, I am."

"Not a gambler."

"Looking for company, then? I bet it gets lonely out there…"

The Miner gave her a level look and bit back a remark. "Pass."

Taking a step in the direction of the "famous" galleria, the Miner felt a tightness in her joints as old augmentation implants reacted to the first whiff of adrenaline, before she consciously registered the characteristic *snik!* of an old-fashioned switchblade.

"Don't be like that," the kid was saying, quieter now. "I've been helpful, right? At the very least you ought to give me a tip, lady."

The Miner turned slowly and saw the kid standing in what she probably considered a fighter's stance, holding the switchblade like a screwdriver. The Miner took the knife away from her. *"Pass."*

The girl's expression flashed from shocked to angry, and she showed her teeth.

"Don't start something you can't finish," the Miner said mildly.

"Give that back," the kid growled.

The Miner grasped the blade with both hands, poised to snap it, but the kid threw up her palms in surrender.

"Hang on, hang on! That was my grandma's knife; she used that to shiv Rudy Houston, right?"

The Miner stared, her brain refusing to engage with that sentence. "I'm going to go that way," she said. "If nobody follows me, I'll leave it on the deck at the next hatch. Right?"

The kid nodded mutely, and amazingly didn't follow.

Welcome to the Galleria

The galleria wasn't entirely the rathole the Miner had imagined. It was a tall atrium in the middle of the station, and its overhead windows had been the eyes of the spider she'd observed from orbit. Back when this had been a military outpost, it would have been two connected decks: a lower area for assembling and organizing, and an upper area for support. She could close her eyes and picture it, complete with navy ratings and Marines milling around.

The upper decking had been sawn away to clear out a big central area like a park under the trio of sun lamps arranged around the windows. The remains of the second floor ringed the space with a deckway and storefronts. Neon lights and animated signs flickered and sent shadows like campfire at the entrances to shuttered businesses, most closed with no more care than turning off the lights. There'd been a tattooist and gene-modder, VR rigger, a Fitz's Drugs, and a lawyer. The open doors showed that everything not bolted down had been taken, though a number of stripped bolts protruded from the decking, too. The Lady Luck casino, a bar called Ama no Gawa, and the security station remained dubiously open on the first deck, and there was a big sign for a hotel called Ad Astra on the deck above.

The space in the middle had scattered tables and chairs, a bunch of raised beds hosting some sickly-looking palm trees, and a stage in the center. In some designer's fevered mind, and maybe even recently, it had probably bustled with shoppers and loungers and young people having loud and picturesque fun. The Miner could only make out two people, one asleep at a table and clutching a bottle, and the other in a black uniform, dozing in a chair in front of the security station. It was 1100 station time and the day lights were on, so either the place was seriously nightshifted or just dead.

She contacted her ship and asked for a heads-up map.

"Sorry, boss, they don't have one in the usual place. There's a directory listing, though."

"Send it," she said, ignoring the sinking feeling and bringing the text up on her heads-up display. Green text floated up her retina, lazily showing a list that was either vastly out of date or just bullshit. Three ore buyers, wouldn't that have been nice. Even being bogus, though, the listings helped her orient herself a bit. The galleria had the two rings she could see, full of the ghosts of shops, and then straight stubby alleys nominally at compass points with west leading to the port. North, just clockwise from the casino's big neon-lit windows, had a provisioner under the name Anaconda, and she ambled over that way past the drunk.

Heads popped up like meerkats' as she approached the casino, then settled down again as she passed. She didn't like the odds that they were actually ignoring her, and she walked slowly so she could hear if anyone approached.

The provisioner – *Anaconda Supplies* – bore a sign in the window that claimed to have been "Rated highly in a customer satisfaction survey!" which was just vague and sad enough to be true. The shop inside was tiny, practically a closet. All the actual goods, if they had any, would be tucked away somewhere in the bowels of the station or maybe even in a parking orbit around the rock. The walls were instead coated in ads, a lot of them real paper, for various brands of yeast feed, entomo-protein bricks, Real*Chikken (which the Miner had to admit was actually pretty good) and so on. There was even a big animated ad for *France!* brand oxygen/nitrogen blend ("Avec that *je ne sais quoi* that makes Paris smell like Paree!") which she stared at for a while to be sure wasn't a joke, and then still wasn't sure.

There was a terminal at the counter facing the shop, and the Miner spent a few minutes typing in her short order. It asked for a water order in milliliters, which was laughable – if any station had ever filled a water order to within ten liters, she'd have been shocked. The provisioner herself appeared from a back room. She was short and skinny, and looked at the Miner like she might steal the ads off the walls but for the provisioner's own vigilance. Still, she said hello gracefully enough, and put on a pair of reading glasses to examine the order.

The provisioner stared and frowned, then peered at the Miner over the top of her glasses. "You've made a mistake."

The Miner peered back at her, trying not to loom but failing thanks to her enormous height advantage. "What do you mean?"

"This order you entered... this says six person-months of emergency rations."

"That's right."

"How many people on your ship? There's not much water, and there's nothing else–"

"Just me. It's what I eat."

The provisioner's frown turned into an outright horrified

stare. "You're not supposed to live on them. They're for emergencies. They're… it's right in the name."

"So? No law against it."

"They're–" The provisioner stopped herself, then obviously took a moment to compose and restart. "They're not intended for everyday consumption. They have a bitterant."

"I know, I've been living on them. I like it. It's like coffee."

The provisioner massaged the bridge of her nose like she was getting a headache. The Miner was used to that. "I don't keep much on hand," she managed. "And I'm not going to sell you my whole stock. Someone who isn't insane might need a brick or two," she muttered, poking into the air at an interface only she could see.

"I can sell you three person-months," she finally announced. "That's the limit. I know it's not enough calories for a six-month span, but I've got flour blends, cricket flour, mealworm flour, lentils, and if you really are a culinary masochist there's nutrient powder. But you'll need extra water." She frowned at the list. "You should carry more water than this anyway."

"Got any of that bitterant?"

"Has anyone told you there's something really wrong with you?"

The Miner grinned. "All the time."

The provisioner reset the pad to a catalog, and the Miner spent some time poking through the rest of the stock, filtering out anything that wasn't stable for at least six months at standard ship storage temperature and pressure, leaving most of their in-stock catalog. Not a lot of turnover, she figured. There was wheat flour, but it was exorbitant and probably rancid. The millet/cricket blend was cheap, but she mostly remembered it for making the shittiest beer she'd ever had, and decided she wasn't that hard up. There was straight-up jiminy, too, but pure cricket flour wasn't good for much on its own, and she might as well get it premixed rather than to try to do it herself and have to replace the ship's air filters.

It took almost an hour of haggling and poring through the catalog to put together a tentative order. She declined a free 50ml sample of *France! Air*, then declined to accept three credits to take a free 50ml sample of *France! Air*, then put the whole order on hold while the provisioner finally agreed to see if she could lay hands on more emergency rations.

"Just make up your mind soon," the provisioner said when they'd finished. "In eight hours I'm out."

"Off-duty?"

She shook her head. "Out. I put in my resignation and I've got a berth rented on that last freighter. I don't mind telling you, this place has gone to shit."

"Who'll do provisions?"

"Not my problem."

"Then why don't you just sell me your whole stock of emergency rations?"

She shook her head. "The people staying here might need them. I owe them that much at least, poor jerks."

The Miner considered the doorway and the goons in the casino. "Is there a back way out of here? I was getting some looks when I came through."

The provisioner looked grim. "Yeah, there's a service entrance. Hook a right to head clockwise; there's an outer ring that goes all the way around, and you'll get to the eastern spur. That'll take you back to the galleria. Listen... I can't promise it'll be any safer that way."

The Miner shrugged. "I'm not avoiding a fight for my sake."

She slipped out the back entrance and heard a heavy metal *ker-chunk* behind her as the provisioner locked it. The long curving corridor had unmarked hatchways on either side, lit poorly. It smelled of piss and mold here and there, and occasionally she caught the whiff of blood on the warm humid air. The place was dead – no footsteps or voices, just the low whirr of the air movers, growing to a hiss and fading again as she walked past vents.

The remains of a cleaning robot lay against the inner wall as she got to the intersection. It looked like it had been kicked to pieces, with its plastic chassis crumpled, wheels all askew, and the contents of its compartments strewn a little ways. She'd never been the type to romanticize robots – or anything, really – but she felt a pang of something looking at it. Not sadness, exactly, or at least not for the bot. The whole station was starting to grind on her.

The eastern spur led right back to the galleria, as promised, past a sleazy-looking clinic. Sure enough, three morons stood just at the entrance to the northern spur where she'd have come out. She stood and watched them for a moment, almost mesmerized by the stupidity, and half-wishing she'd come back that way and taught them a lesson. The thought of it made her implants buzz and warm up. She decided she'd rather have a drink, and took a chance on that bar.

The sign by the door said "Kenichi Takata, Proprietor" and it was dark inside, but comfortable dark, not "closed for business" dark. An old guy with wild white hair and a big white beard sat in a corner booth with an empty glass, openly staring at her but not saying anything. The Miner wove through the tables and crossed to the two meter-long stained wood bar and picked the red stool on the far end from which she could see the exits. The taps didn't have any brands she recognized, though she had a dim recollection that the one with the blue diamonds was popular.

The back wall should have had dozens of full bottles of liquor, but didn't. There were a few upside-down pint glasses and a baseball bat. There was a doorway behind the bar to some kind of back room, with a split blue-and-red curtain with fish printed on it hanging halfway to the floor.

She planned to give it a minute before calling out for service, but the old guy in the corner booth beat her to it. "Hey Takata! Customer!" He was staring down into his glass by the time she looked, already bored with her.

Another old guy with his iron-gray hair pulled back in a ponytail and a fierce mustache poked his head out from the back room. He looked square at the Miner and said, "Shit." He disappeared, saying, "No beer. No whiskey. All out."

"I'll have what he's having," she called after him.

"He brings his own. Beat him up for it."

The guy in the corner either laughed or wheezed; she couldn't tell which.

"How about a water, then?"

"Tap's busted."

"Then I'll have a glass full of air. You have that, don't you?"

That was answered with silence and then a sigh.

"Look," said Takata when he reappeared. "It's nothing personal, but I gotta stay neutral. No side. That means I don't serve your kind. Nothing personal, OK?"

"You don't serve miners?"

"Of course I don't… Oh. Hell, you're no miner. Either kind."

She was amused, despite herself. "Yeah? Where'd I get that thirteen tons of nickel-iron, then? Did I beat up an asteroid?"

He had the good grace to look sheepish, at least. "No shit?"

"They haven't finished the assay yet."

Takata shuffled over to the taps and filled a glass without asking. He stuck it in front of her with a dull thud that splashed the head over the side, then put the side of his hand in his mouth to taste where it had run over. "Sorry lady. But you got to admit, you got 'tough guy' written all over you. No offense."

"None taken. I've been getting a lot of that here."

"Welcome to Poisonville," he said, waving to take in the empty galleria outside. "Population: stupid."

The Miner hadn't had a beer in six months. She didn't keep alcohol on the ship anymore even when she was flush with cash, and she hadn't been. The amber liquid caught the low light, and all she could smell were citrusy hops. "Mind starting a tab?"

"Shit."

"I'm good for it. Just have to sell that bunch of ore."

"You selling to Anaconda?"

"Nobody else."

"That fucker Preston doing the assay?"

She thought back, failed to remember the dockmaster's name, and figured the answer was, "Yup."

Takata's face twisted in a way that made his mustache bristle. "Ah, hell. It's on the house. I suppose you want something to eat, too."

"Truly, your hospitality is legendary." She thought about Preston, and mentally adjusted down her expected profit from the trip. If she had any other options, she'd consider canceling and moving on. As it was... at least there was beer.

Takata disappeared into the back again, muttering something from which she only caught the word "asshole." She took a long drink from her beer, cold and bitter, and enjoyed the feel of the icy glass in her hand and the faintly sour aftertaste. Civilization had its uses. She heard scraping of utensils on a plate, and Takata reappeared with a plate of rice and some kind of stew or curry.

"I didn't mean for you to give me your lunch."

He shrugged. "Beats turning on the griddle. Just eat it, it's good."

It *was* good. There were a few chunks of meat – she couldn't tell what and had learned not to be picky – and potatoes and carrots, with little flecks of ginger. The aromatic steam in the dry station air flooded the space around her, reminded her of busy mess halls full of banging trays and clattering tableware.

She found herself eating fast and forced herself to stop and sip the beer so she wasn't wolfing. Takata just leaned against the back wall and watched her eat, a kind of bemused but satisfied look on his face. He cleared away the plate the moment she finished.

"Best meal I've had in ages," she said truthfully, tossing off the rest of her beer in one swallow.

He kind of ducked his head and shrugged, acknowledging the compliment, but she could tell it pleased him.

"Hey, how about some for me?" called the old guy in the corner.

"Shut up, Herrera. Pay your tab," said Takata without malice in his tone. Herrera just cackled.

Takata returned to cleaning in the back while the Miner sat and cooled her heels. No word yet on the assay, so she sat and watched the empty galleria. The vacancy grated on her somehow. She hated crowds, but there ought to have been one. *There's a comfortable emptiness*, she decided, *and then there's abandonment*, and this was the latter.

A short wiry guy, pale and balding, appeared from the eastern spur, peering around and then hustling straight across the galleria, weaving his way between the empty tables and making straight for Takata's bar. He was clutching a cardboard bottle under one arm and not really paying attention to where he was going.

When he got to the restaurant entrance he kind of hopped through the door like it might spring shut on him. He started for the bar, then noticed the Miner and stood stock still. She was reminded of nothing so much as a startled lizard.

"Howdy," she said, nodding and breaking the staring contest.

"Hi!" he blurted out. Herrera raised his head in brief interest, then huffed and looked back down at his glass. "Hi, hi, how are you? Nice to meet you. Didn't know you had customers, Mr Takata."

Takata had come from the back room, and groaned. "Finn."

"Heya, Mr Takata. Listen. I know you've got a slump going on, and I wanted you to know something." He scuttled forward and leaned in like he was sharing a secret. Eyes wide, he said, "I have a tequila now."

Takata groaned. "No tequila, Finn. Look, your vodka's decent. Your white whiskey's good. Let's stick to those. If you're hard up I could stand some more vodka."

Finn drew himself up to his full height, looking offended. "No, no, no. I have to diversify, that's all."

"Why?"

"People get tired of vodka."

"Nobody gets tired of vodka."

"I get tired of vodka," Finn said, then rubbed the back of his bald head. "Making it, anyway. I guess drinking it's all right." The Miner wondered just how much of his own supply he drank, and whether he'd gotten all the methanol out.

"Look. Finn. Remember the gin?"

"Come on–"

Takata planted both palms on the bar. "Remember the gin?"

"That's not fair."

"It's entirely fair."

Finn looked like he wanted to argue the point, but instead waved the cardboard bottle. "You won't try the tequila?"

Takata opened his mouth, then gave half a smile. "All right, Finn. She'll try the tequila."

"Wait, what?" The Miner didn't like the looks either of them were giving her. Takata already had a shot glass out on the bar, and Finn got to filling it.

"Try it! Free tequila, just like your free beer and free lunch. Tell me how it is and I'll call it even."

"What was wrong with the gin?"

"Just drink the damn tequila."

Finn held it out with both hands. The glass was full of an oily liquid with a faint yellow tinge. She took it and got it too close to her nose.

"Jesus, is that benzene?"

Finn answered too slowly, "Nnnno. No, no, it's definitely not benzene."

She frowned, her eyes watering. Takata said, "Drink it. What do you have to live for anyway?"

She sipped. The taste of pure alcohol numbed her lips, and the tip of her tongue burned. There was a whisper of flavor there that she might eventually have guessed was supposed to be agave, but which she would otherwise have thought was a yeast vat with a bacterial infection. Or maybe scotch made by burning rubber gaskets instead of peat. Keeping her face still, she swallowed the sip and suppressed a cough as the back of her throat caught fire. The vapors crawled up into her sinuses and burned those too. It wasn't the foulest thing she'd ever drank, but that wasn't saying much. Staring it down, she picked up the shot glass again and tossed the rest back.

It took her a second to trust herself to speak. "Not bad," she said cheerily, her voice husky. She slid the shot glass down the bar, and Finn eagerly refilled it, splashing. "Give it a try."

Takata looked suspicious, but did. The coughing and spluttering fit was just as entertaining as she'd hoped, and if the look of betrayed injury on his face hadn't started her laughing, Finn's utterly crestfallen expression would have. At least she didn't fall off her bar stool.

Herrera hooted and laughed, and clapped twice. Finn just stood and looked uncomfortable. He plucked the shot glass from the bar between thumb and forefinger, sniffed delicately, and drank it. "So, uh. Back to the, uh, back to the drawing board?"

"Don't pour that shit in the septic system," Takata coughed. "You'll burn a hole in it and we'll all die."

Finn winced but took it with grace. "So, three liters of vodka?"

He had to wait for Takata to stop wheezing and rub the tears from his eyes. "Four," he croaked, showing the count on his fingers, "and two of the white whiskey."

Finn snapped a half-decent salute, and fled.

Takata poured himself a half glass of water from under the bar and drank it all in one go. When the Miner finally let out the cough she'd been suppressing, he gave her a venomous glare.

"'Not bad'," he said, his voice dripping sarcasm.

"Didn't say it was good."

She met his level gaze for a few seconds until he cracked up. "What was wrong with the gin?"

Takata made a face. "Real gin needs aromatics, or it's just

vodka. Trouble is, there's not much in the way of aromatics on a space station, especially juniper. Finn's not the kind of guy to let an obstacle like reality get in his way, so he... improvised."

"What did he use?"

"I asked. He said, 'If I tell you, you'll just be prejudiced.'"

"Oh."

Belly full and feeling the pleasant edge of a buzz, the Miner swiveled on her stool to look out the door. The security guard was still asleep, though the drunk had apparently stumbled off at some point. "So what's the deal here?" She waved with one hand to take in that scene.

"No deal. The place is dying, and I'm only still here to watch it die because I'm vindictive, stubborn, and lazy. Plus if I break the lease on this piece of shit restaurant space it'll cost me what's left of my credit. I was dumb enough to renew it seven months ago, right before it really all went to hell."

"What's killing it?"

"Greed. Stupidity. Gangsters." He looked like he wanted to spit. "You can still get supplies, though. And you can get gone. Around here those are the only things worth getting."

On the Shit List

Screwball didn't want to take the ice pack away from his face, but if he didn't then Ditz couldn't tell that he was staring daggers. So he peeled it off and gave him the full measure of his righteous irritation. It didn't help. Dude was off in his own muddled stoned-but-pissed-off little world.

"I can't believe Raj pushed us off like that, man. What the hell, man?"

"Pushed *me* off," Screwball corrected him. "You fucking ran away, you asshole."

Raj had been enthusiastic in revenging himself, and Ditz had been nowhere in sight.

"Maaaaaan," Ditz said. "Don't be like that. I was going for help. Calling in the cavalry!"

They'd slunk back to the hotel to report Raj running them off the dock, and old man Feeney had gone redline. Screwball should have ratted Ditz out as a coward, but didn't for some reason, so now the worthless little eggfart thought they were friends again. Fucking asshole. Ditz had stolen some ice from the kitchen for him, about the only food in the place, and now they were kicking around the service entrance. In theory, they were on guard duty, but mostly they didn't want the old man to see them while he was still angry. Feeney couldn't take it out on Angelica – if he could, they wouldn't be in that mess – so he'd take it out on them or anyone who looked at him funny. Which meant that in turn, by all rights, Screwball ought to take it out on somebody lower down the pecking order than himself, except nobody actually *was* lower down than him. Even Ditz had some kind of connections. So that just left him to sit and stew.

The hotel's service entrance backed out onto the outer corridors of the station in a ring that went all the way around to Angelica's home base in the casino. Guarding the service entrance was nice and quiet, usually the kind of thing people volunteered for when they wanted to get stoned in peace. After all, it would be stupid of any of her fighters to come around the hotel, just like it would be stupid of Ditz and Screwball to go around the casino. But it would also be stupid to assume they wouldn't, because pretty much everyone involved was stupid.

"That hurt?" Ditz peered at Screwball's face, getting close enough that Screwball shoved him away.

"How high are you, anyway?"

Ditz considered that, then raised his hand palm-down and made a seesaw motion.

"We can't let them get away with this, Ditz." His voice was muffled by the ice, and by not being able to feel his lips, but he didn't care. "If we don't fight back they'll just 'cycle us. In the chute and flush, the whole lot of us. The old man isn't bringing in any money, you know. How the hell's he going to pay us if this drags on, huh?"

"Man, lighten up. You're new here, right? Look. They push us around, we slap them around. It's all good. You can't take it too personal. A couple months ago, with the real fighting, yeah, that sucked. People actually died. This is nothing. We'll make some extra cash while the old man and the witch blow off steam, then they'll make up and we'll all be buds again."

Screwball started to object, but Ditz looked him in the eye, his blown pupils eerie. "Seriously. He who kicks your ass today, is just gonna owe you a beer tomorrow. Be cool."

Doc Mills

After working her budget this way and that, and getting increasingly impatient with the assay, the Miner decided that she had the time and money for an overdue visit to the sawbones. There was a doctor's office right off the galleria, she'd passed it when she returned along the eastern spur, but the bartender Takata told her to skip him. "He's for the gangs," he'd said, "and these days he's usually drunk or stoned out of his gourd." He'd given her directions down into the back bowels of the station and promised to message ahead. There were stairs at the end of the southern spur; she took those instead of the elevator on principle.

As she navigated the corridors she thought back to the same spaces on other stations long ago. She'd worn a uniform then, and fewer scars. Carved into the rock of the asteroid it clung to, Station 35 was divided into hundreds of little squared-off reconfigurable spaces. Not exactly a maze, but not easy to find one's way through without directions. She could tell it had been designed for floor-to-floor fighting, meaning they expected their enemy wouldn't want to seriously damage the infrastructure.

The usual plan for taking a space station was simple: make a couple nice big punctures to evacuate atmo, and then be patient while all the little pockets ran out of food, water, heat, and air. Accept the surrender or clear out the corpses, then spend weeks bringing it up to working condition again without the benefit of schematics or working knowledge of the systems. Station 35 had been valuable once; the designers had known that an attacker couldn't afford to be patient, couldn't afford downtime. The Miner stopped and rested a hand on an access panel: thin plastic, as cheap as it looked, intended to deter invaders from throwing a lot of lead. Make some greedy commander order hand-to-hand fighting, an ugly, bloody rush against defenders who knew they could fix these systems ten times as fast.

Yeah, the place had been something special once, some critical hub. She felt strangely sad at how irrelevant it was now, discarded and loaned out to scum like Anaconda so someone could else pay to keep the air on. Maybe it had drifted out of a useful location, or probably the political universe had just moved on without it. It had seen fighting recently, but pathetic street brawls, nothing serious. In a way, that made it sadder. She stopped once on her tortuous route to stare at a brownish-red handprint that someone had failed to scrub off the wall, barely bothered trying. Charming.

The place was spooky empty. A couple times she caught a glimpse of someone, always just stepping around a corner. Once or twice a head poked out of a hatchway that closed again. But that was maybe six or seven people on a long walk. Maybe just one or two keeping tabs on the stranger in their midst.

She found her destination down in what must have been the old command structure space, embedded deep in the rock in the belly of a poorly-oiled machine, part of a block that had been divvied up into offices and apartments. The seismic rumble of the air movers was palpable down there, thrumming the decking under her feet, only interrupted by the periodic rush of gurgling fluids. The doctor's door just said "A. Mills, MD" and "NO CREDIT", which she found oddly endearing.

Mills answered the door by intercom, and only when told "Takata sent me," did he open it. He was like every other doctor on every other station, if heavier and hairier than average. He was brusque and businesslike, which was fine by her, and didn't ask her name. She paid in advance to be stripped, poked, measured, and prodded, told she had high blood pressure for her age, that her false eye needed to be recalibrated, and reminded that her facial scars could be removed for a fee – same as every other doctor on every other station. When she gave him the list of compounds she'd been exposed to over the years, he drew blood and ran the usual tests for the interesting diseases they caused, and thankfully got the same results as always. He also told her that she ought to get her augmentation implants taken out before they screwed up her joints, but unlike most of the other sawbones he didn't offer to sell them for her, so she figured Takata had the guy right.

She lingered after dressing slowly, and finally admitted, "I'd like a supply of sleeping pills, too."

He frowned so hard his mouth disappeared into his curly black beard. "Aren't you flying solo?"

He was shaking his head already before she finished saying "Yup."

"I really shouldn't sell you any kind of sedative. It's not safe for solo spacecraft operation. You know as well as I do how often emergencies crop up."

"Oh, that's no problem. It's not for me, it's for my ship."

"Your… ship."

"Yeah. See, it gets anxiety real bad."

"Your ship gets anxiety." He had a pretty good level stare, she had to admit.

"Sure," she said, grinning. "It gets this crazy idea that I'm going to pilot into a rock or something while I'm strung out on lack of sleep. Nuts, right?"

Mills stared at her a long time, maybe wondering if he should prescribe an anti-psychotic. "You having trouble getting to sleep, or trouble staying asleep?"

"Both. And yes, I've tried cutting out bright light and blue light, and taking melatonin, and I've got a white noise generator, and a pink noise generator, and a brown noise generator. Think of something and I've tried it. Drugs work."

He pursed his lips and studied her face for a while. His mouth moved like he was chewing his lower lip. "You were in the service, and you've obviously seen action."

"Not relevant."

If he was skeptical, he didn't show it.

"Don't pry, doc. We've been getting along." She gave him a wry smile and raised an eyebrow.

"Mmm." He didn't return the smile. "I'd rather give you a sleep replacement."

The Miner considered mentioning that she'd spent the better part of two years on the damn things. She owed a couple scars to the hallucinations they gave her. "They don't work for me."

He chewed a corner of his mustache for a while, then sighed and ran her bank chip again. He gave her a curious look for a moment, but if he was going to ask anything he was interrupted when the auto-pharm started chugging. It spat pills into the tin like a slot machine paying out. "One, and *only* one, right before bed. It acts fast, but nothing's instant. Don't

take it with alcohol, and please, please take them sparingly."
She reached for the tin. "Not yet, I'm not done."

He punched a second order in and the auto-pharm started
vomiting again. "This is the antagonist. It's not safe to rely
on, but it's better than nothing, and it works quick. Keep
it by your bed. Get some sugar pills or something to train
yourself to take one when an emergency alarm wakes you
up. Don't start taking the other ones until you're confident
you're drilled enough to take the antagonist in an emergency.
Got it?"

The Miner bit back the urge to snark. The guy was trying to
do her a favor. At least, he was trying to keep her alive, and
figured that was doing her a favor. Still. "Got it. It's starting to
get a little expensive…"

"The antagonist's on me, then. I'll feel better if I think
you're not sleeping your way through a collision or raid."

"Asleep" seemed like the best way to experience those
catastrophic events, the Miner thought, but said, "Thanks, doc."

"You want to thank me, stay alive. Repeat business, that's
the actual sincerest form of flattery."

She grinned and thanked him again, and then noticed that
she had a message waiting: the assay was done, and the buyer
was ready to meet with her.

You Can't Win

The Miner had only been sitting in the black faux-leather chair in front of the buyer's enormous faux-wood desk, staring at the rosy-cheeked little man in his too-big suit, for about forty seconds before she realized that she was about to get screwed a lot harder than she'd expected. He looked like Santa Claus, but sure as hell wasn't talking like him.

"...Arsenic isn't necessarily a bad thing in an ore haul, but it's something we'll have to process out, especially in these quantities. Your onboard refinery is new, I know, but it's not configured the way we prefer," he was saying. He'd been talking in that vein for a while and looked very pleased with himself. "Plus, while nickel-iron is in demand, as you say, just like any of a thousand iron ores, the particular isotopic iron you've brought me isn't quite as–"

"How much?" she cut in, her voice hoarse. She hadn't lost her temper, not yet. She hadn't lost her temper in years, and this piddly little backwater cheat wouldn't be the one to break that streak. The longer he spewed bullshit, though, the less confidence she had in that. She'd be patient like she'd been trained, but patient only went so far.

"Well." The buyer had an incredibly punchable face, especially with that poor attempt at an understanding expression. Everything that had come out of his mouth had been complete horseshit. He knew it, she knew it, and the smug little son of a bitch knew that she knew it. What he was deciding now was just how little she'd accept without making a fuss. When she'd finally broken off from her patch with thirteen tons of metal, she'd calculated the value of her haul at well over thirty grand. He'd probably offer less than twenty, the little cheat, and damn her, she'd even take fifteen.

"I think I could see fit to pay ten thousand for the load."

She stared at him blankly, and did the only thing she could think of: she laughed. He didn't.

"I'm afraid I don't see the humor, ma'am."

"Try again," she said.

He eyeballed her, and she could practically see the wheels turning. First timer at Station 35, didn't usually do business with Anaconda, and she'd made the rookie mistake of letting it be known she didn't intend to come back. He was the only buyer in a million clicks for the only company buying. He didn't know she was too broke to push on to the next station, maybe, but who out there wasn't? And since Anaconda did the assay, he held the cards and he had possession. Shit, shit, shit. Stupid. She almost couldn't blame him for taking such an easy mark.

"I'm afraid ten thousand is the best I can do."

"Thirteen. A thousand a ton is still cheap."

"Mmm. Not for this particular isotope."

"At least give me back the arsenic. They paid for it at the last station, I can sell it at the next one."

He shook his head. "The refining process makes that very inconvenient for this particular form of arsenic. I could do it, but I'd have to pay you less for the nickel-iron."

"Let me see the assay."

"I'm sorry, we paid for the assay and so it's confidential."

"Bullshit." Her heartbeat quickened and her augmentation implants warmed up, tickled by adrenaline and ready for a fight.

She heard the door slide open behind her and two sets of footsteps. Heavy guys judging by the sound and the tenor of the mouth-breathing. Just two of them, what passes for muscle on a nasty corrupt little... She shook her head forcefully, and the buyer squinted at her. He'd misunderstood the gesture, but she didn't feel like explaining it.

"Are you saying we have a dispute, Ms..." He glanced down at his pad, frowned. "Ma'am?"

"Damn ri–" She stopped herself. Something about that phrasing... Disputed transactions resulted in the seizure of the disputed goods until the dispute was resolved in arbitration. Seized, in this case, by Anaconda Consolidated. To be arbitrated by Anaconda Consolidated. Son of a bitch.

He cocked an eyebrow, daring her to finish that sentence. She took a breath, reminded herself that she wasn't going to lose her temper, that she'd gladly pay 20,000 credits to keep her temper and self-respect, and then shook her head *no* because she didn't trust herself to answer right if she opened her clenched teeth.

"All right then," he said, voice all oily smooth. Such a punchable face, Santa Claus-looking or no.

Her fuel bill would be about three grand on top of twice that much in supplies. Ten grand would leave her a measly two K profit, less than she'd have made selling her blood plasma for six months. The patch fees would eat that and her savings both. Repairs and updates to the ship could wait. She could limp back to a paid-for claim on that, and just pretend the last six months had never happened. And that her bank account had evaporated.

She thought back to the plant room on her ship, put herself there for a moment, just a moment. The thought of tending the orchids, carefully trimming the bonsai, calmed her down. She wouldn't lose her ship, and the plants, and her freedom, just because she lost her temper.

"Your claim doesn't seem to be doing you much good. Anaconda Consolidated has a very generous buyout program if you think you might be better suited to a different line of work."

Taking her answer from her expression he said, "You don't have to accept my offer. I can return the load to your ship for a modest lading fee. Seven hundred credits would cover it, I think. Plus you'd have to reimburse us for the assay."

Which left her deep in the red. Unable to pay the patch fees, she'd lose her claim. Unable to pay for loaded fuel, they'd impound the ship. She hated herself, but she had to ask. "Ten thousand's the best you can do?"

"I suppose I could go higher." He folded his hands on his desk, looked her in the eye, and smiled. "But I don't see any reason to."

For a brief moment, she visualized herself demonstrating a very good reason. She took a deep breath, decided she'd rather lose it all than make a spectacle of herself like that, and said, "All right."

He transferred the ten thousand credits, and handed back her bank chip.

"That's an unusual name you have," he said conversationally.

"Yes it is," she managed, and was up and out of her chair. The muscle had slunk away, probably once it had become clear that they wouldn't be needed, that she'd knuckled under, clearly in fear of them. But the door still closed very quickly behind her and when she heard it latch she barked out a single bitter laugh.

A message came in while she was storming down the passageway, from the dockmaster. The fuel bill. She swore and opened it–

"Five thousand credits!"

She stumbled to a stop and put her hand on the wall. That wasn't the only item. Five thousand for the fuel, and another line item below it: a five hundred credit charge for the assay.

You Can't Break Even

Takata had actual honest-to-God customers in the bar when the Miner stormed in, so instead of launching into the stream of invective she intended to deliver to anyone with ears, she sat herself in the booth in front of Herrera's and sank into an angry funk. In the walk down from the posh offices and residences upstairs she'd crossed over from being angry at that sonofabitch buyer to being angry at herself. She'd been stupid and naïve and it had cost her dearly.

The customers looked and sounded too damn cheerful. Must have come in on that science ship she'd seen approaching. Five of them, obviously not related, but all looking well-off. Nice clothes, well groomed, expensive smiles. A kid who looked barely out of his teens sported the most ridiculous white fez she'd ever seen. He wore it at a cocky angle and kept finding excuses to tilt his head or turn abruptly so that the gold tassel swung around. The girl he kept making eye contact with obviously found it hilarious.

"You keep looking like that, you'll sour all my beer," Takata said. He plunked a pint down in front of her and cut her off. "You can't pay, I know. It's on me. Or maybe on them if they get drunk enough they can't keep count."

"Thanks," she muttered.

"That bad, huh?"

"Bastards got me coming and going. Paid less than a third what the load's worth, then charged me five percent for the privilege. And they're gouging me on the fuel."

Takata winced. "Shit. They're getting greedy. Not enough miners coming through anymore to just skim a little. If he wants to keep Feeney happy, he's got to really put the screws in. Or he's just a bastard, I don't know."

He bounded off to take care of the paying customers, and the Miner didn't blame him. She sipped her beer and scowled. It was good beer, and somehow that made it worse. The customers laughed and chattered, and one of them offered a toast, "To science!"

Left alone with her free beer – "Cheers," she murmured to her unwitting patrons before she took a gulp, cold and bitter and lovely – the Miner buckled down to her finances to see just how badly she was hurt.

She did the math three different ways. The fuel bill was non-negotiable and non-returnable, damn that little rat. But she hadn't finished provisioning thanks to the emergency rations, and she could alter that. The water wasn't just to drink, it was radiation shielding and she'd already sold off the used gray water, so that couldn't be cut. Much. There was room to reduce caloric intake for a couple months and shorten her stay at the patch, maybe supplement nutrition by growing lettuce or something and keeping mealworms. There was plenty of potting soil and leaf litter in the plant room. She'd eaten worse, probably.

Even cutting to the bone, though, the math just didn't work. She'd dipped into savings to pay for the fuel, and that didn't leave enough to both pay the patch fees and also get back out to it to do any mining. She'd have to go straight out and straight back, and she'd lose on fuel even if Station 34 didn't screw her at all, and what were the chances of that? She had to make up her mind on the provisions in a couple hours, and being late on the patch fees was a non-starter: she'd lose her claim in an automated flash, probably to Anaconda, those dirty, scheming sons of…

The Miner bit down on that thought and sat staring into her empty beer glass. Her chest was tight, she felt acid in her throat, that familiar tingling in her augmented joints, and caught herself getting swept up in the maelstrom of fury and sick dread. She closed her eyes and breathed and put her mind back to the plant room. She pictured each orchid and each bonsai, walked her mind through the chores that needed to be done, and her plans to finally trim the ficus into shape. She needed to be calm and deliberate. Losing her head wouldn't help, just make her feel better, and if she was in this to feel better then why did she go into mining asteroids in the first place? She might be miserable, but she was free.

She sent a message to the provisioner canceling the entire order. No food, no water. Then she stared at the word "Sent!" for a long time. She'd burned out on anger; now she was just tired. She could make the payment. That was all right: she'd keep her patch. It would still be there for her.

She just couldn't go there.

You Can't Quit the Game

The celebrating customers left before too long, or at least before the Miner got grumpy enough to go sulk in her ship. They wandered out one by one over the course of an hour. The last one, the kid with the fez, stopped outside the restaurant to chat drunkenly with a tall, good-looking bald dude with some kind of iridescent gene mod at his temples. He looked familiar, but she couldn't place him. He smiled too much to be a local, but hadn't been at the party. They wandered off, leaving the bar empty except for Takata, herself, and the old guy Herrera asleep in his booth in the corner. Takata hummed to himself as he tidied, and when he finished wiping down the tables he joined him at the bar.

"Get a lot of business like that?"

He shook his head, his pleased expression turning rueful. "Never a lot, but used to be more. They're the first smiling faces in here in months. Some kind of research team, I think. They said they stopped in for fuel and water on their way out to the outer belt with all sorts of fancy new equipment. Something about watching a comet hit something big? Scientists, I don't know about them. I have to admire their enthusiasm, though. Even this miserable pig sty rat hole can't drag them down." He tapped his finger on the bar top. "I just hope they're careful."

"How so?"

"They talked a lot about their expensive gear and their new ship. I liked to hear it, but around this place that's not so smart."

He poured her a glass of water without asking and put it in front of her. She acknowledged it with a nod.

"There a lot of piracy around here?"

"Not... exactly? I don't know. Angelica's crew does a lot of salvage, and who knows how much of it is really 'salvage'. You know, if you're looking to make some money, you could do worse than to offer those people a hand. They're academics. Ivory tower types. You know, stupid. They could use someone who's been around."

She grudgingly considered it. She also remembered the way they'd looked at her: uneasiness about the scarred stranger, pity at the poor disheveled drunk. She hated the idea of being in close contact with people long enough for a trip to the outer belt and back, especially people that young. *She'd* never been that young.

"What would I do, tell them they ought to pay me to come along? The best advice I could give them is, don't take strangers on your ship."

"Take your own ship and caravan. Any pirates, they'll maybe think twice about attacking two ships."

"Pirates barely think once," she said. She didn't mention that she couldn't leave dock without food or water. And the second best advice she could give was, don't pay a stranger up-front.

"Look, I'm no babysitter," she said, cutting off his reply. "The kind of money I need, there's nothing I could do for them that would justify it. What were you saying before, about that pig fucker buyer needing to keep Feeney happy?"

Takata's face darkened. He got back to wiping the bar, finding a spot that required him to face away from her. "Forget it. You want to change the subject, fine, but take pity on me and pick something else."

"The dockmaster mentioned Feeney too. Said he could always use someone who wasn't planning to stay too long."

Takata snorted and seemed to concentrate on that stubborn spot that the Miner couldn't see. She was about to ask again when he said, "It's not Feeney, or it's not just Feeney. I'll tell you if you promise to have nothing to do with him."

"I just want to know. I'm stuck here awhile and I don't know the lay of the land."

"Don't get sucked in. They do that, they suck people in. They chew them up and spit them out. Go babysit instead, it's healthier."

"Tell me about it."

He twisted the rag in his hands, staring down as he wrung it this way and that. "Old man Feeney – John Feeney – he runs the Hotel Astra on the upper level up there." He pointed off to his right. "It's a front. He's a crooked old gangster. Smuggling, drugs, gambling, porno VRs, he's got his fingers in everything. That buyer, Gordonson? Feeney owns him. Dockmaster, too. The two of them screw over the miners and traders, and Feeney gives them cover and launders the cash, gets a big piece in return. He's a mean old bastard."

The Miner grimaced, remembering the muscle in the buyer's office. "Sucks. Hardly unusual, though. Half of these far-out stations have organized crime running things, and the rest are just disorganized. Never been screwed like that before. Never seen a place this dead before."

Takata shook his head sadly. "It didn't used to be this bad, not when it was just him. He's a bastard and he skimmed and strong-armed, but he knew what side his bread was buttered, and that was keeping things running. Keep everything profitable so there's plenty to skim and nobody minds much."

"Someone new horn in?"

He made a face. "Not exactly. He screwed up. Long story, but about six or seven months ago one of his lieutenants, a real piece of work named Angelica del Rio, she and her brother got a bunch of his goons together and tried to rub him out and take over. Everything went to shit. He was tougher than she thought, and had more friends than she thought. Feeney and his granddaughter fought her off, but couldn't put her down either."

The Miner considered that. Aborted coups usually left both sides weak, made everything worse.

"Angelica pushed out Mr Shine and took over the gambling operation, which was a big hit to the old man. Anyway, it was open war there for a while. Bunch of people killed. Drove away all the sane people and most of the business. After that this place has been a magnet for every lowlife pissant crook in a billion clicks who's looking for a fight and some cash."

"Who's this Mr Shine?"

"Big guy, liked to walk around in a tux. Can you picture that, a tuxedo in this dump? He ran off belowdecks, tries to keep the fighting away from the water and air so we don't all die. Bunch of people went down there with him, call themselves 'Morlocks' because they keep stuff running, more or less. He's corrupt as hell, don't get me wrong, but he's got sense enough to keep his head down. He's got some kind of, I don't know, some kind of black market going." He looked bashful for a moment, glancing in Herrera's direction, and the

Miner guessed he had more direct knowledge of that than he let on.

The Miner scowled. "Why doesn't the station master do something about these assholes?"

"I dunno. Hey Herrera, why don't you do something about these assholes?"

"Go shit yourself."

"See, that's why."

The Miner did a doubletake. Herrera was awake in the corner, stock still and staring at a point on the table just past his glass. He had a nice suit on, she suddenly noticed, or at least it had been a nice suit months ago before being rumpled and spilled on and slept in. Shave that crazy beard and cut that unruly ball of hair and he'd look a lot younger, maybe mid-fifties.

"Ah, it's not his fault," Takata said softly, a pained look in his eyes. "Anaconda runs this place, and their lousy Company Rep. Herrera got shipped out here by the government to keep an eye on their property, but he can't actually do anything. The government doesn't give a damn as long as the station's in one piece. He fired the dockmaster, but the Company Rep has to approve a replacement, which she won't, so the acting dockmaster keeps right on ripping people off. Every couple weeks Herrera fires him again, on principle like, and the evil bastard just laughs."

"Corrupt thieving son of a hemorrhaging leech!" Herrera contributed. "Whoremongering shitwhistle! Just... Fuck that guy."

"Herrera!" Takata scowled at the Miner. "See? You get him all worked up and he starts saying the 'fuck' word."

She offered an apologetic shrug.

"Oh, and it gets better! When the fighting got real bad – I'm

talking people getting killed right in the galleria here, the old
security chief getting her head blown off – Herrera tried to get
Anaconda's contract yanked, bring the government in to clean
house. So the Company Rep brought in private security: this
shithead Tom McMasters came in with a bunch of ex-soldiers.
He knocked heads for a while and threatened to space anyone
who showed a gun, that was good. Then he decided all that
was for chumps, and he made deals with both sides. They
pay him off and keep their fights quiet so there's no excuse
to kick Anaconda out, and he doesn't pick sides. That's his
headquarters right on the galleria. Lazy jerks barely even patrol
anymore. I don't serve any of those sons of bitches either."

"Who do you serve?"

"Shut up."

The Miner craned her head to see a black-armored figure
sleeping in a chair out front. Maybe the same guy, maybe
different shift. There was a stun baton dangling from his
hip; apparently they were serious about the "no firearms"
thing. Or maybe he was a feckless idiot who'd shoot his
toes off.

"It's the goddamn Augean stables," Herrera growled. "A
festering abscess full of villains and coprophiles."

Takata gave him a dirty look, but didn't seem to find fault
with that assessment.

"So you got Feeney up there," the Miner mused aloud.
"And Angelica over there. And McMasters in the middle
pretending to keep the peace. All nice and balanced."

Takata snorted. "We're all royally boned, sure, but we're
balanced."

The Miner looked at the down-and-out station master.
She'd never seen a more despondent expression in her life.
"You want me to do something about it?"

Herrera turned his blood-shot eyes to her and stared hard.

"Don't toy with him," Takata muttered. "He doesn't deserve that shit."

Herrera heaved himself shakily out of his booth. He pointed at her as he advanced, stumbling, glaring from under the stringy mass of wild salt-and-pepper hair. "I'll pay you," he rasped. "I'll pay you a hundred thousand America Bank credits if you kill every last one of those filthy motherfuckers."

"Herrera! Don't listen, you, he doesn't have a hundred thousand credits. He doesn't even pay his tab."

The Miner scratched her nose, staring out into the neon-flickering galleria. She saw the lights had a pattern if she watched them long enough. Left, right, center. Back and forth went the red glow, like a dancing flame. "Guess I better go introduce myself."

SCREWBALL SPIES RAJ

Screwball sat out on the decking in front of the hotel, drinking incredibly shitty vodka out of a cardboard bottle and feeling increasingly morbid. He'd had these awesome plans when he bought passage to this shithole. This old guy was hiring an army, they told him. You could make some serious money, they told him. So he'd spent all his money on a gun and passage, and look where he'd landed. His gun got taken by that prick at the dock – who worked for Feeney, so what the hell was that about? – and the first guy he met turned out to be a fucking curse.

He tried to kick Ditz in the chair next to him, but his legs were too far away. He tried again, but missed by a mile.

"Wha?" Ditz wasn't asleep, just stoned. Guy spent more time stoned than anyone Screwball had ever met. "Whassup?"

"Fuck you."

"Oh. Cool, cool." Ditz yawned and stretched. "Hey, is that Raj? What's he up to?"

Screwball sat bolt upright in his chair and looked down at the galleria. Yeah, there was Raj talking to some dipshit in a fez, all smiling and laughing. He couldn't hear their conversation, but it looked like Raj was trying to schmooze the guy, acting like the dude was hilarious or something.

"Talking up some tourist." He realized something and his eyes went wide. He grabbed Ditz's arm. "Ditz! Ditz, look at that. It's just him and that kid. He doesn't have any backup."

"So?"

"So let's go take him. I owe that motherfucker."

"Woah. Hang on."

Screwball got himself out of the chair and crept to the railing, then backed away. "Yeah," he hissed. "Come on. Son of a bitch has it coming."

"Wait, man. That's Angelica's brother, man. She'll shit a brick."

"So? Aren't we at war with those assholes?"

"Yeah, but it's not, like, war-war."

"We're not gonna kill him," Screwball said, already creeping toward the stairs. "Just rough him up a bit. Save him from owing me a beer, right?"

Ditz gave him an expression like a dog trying to do calculus.

"You owe me, Ditz. Come on."

They crept inexpertly down the steps across the galleria from Raj and the kid in the fez, then weaved through the tables to hide by the scrappy-looking potted trees, close enough to hear.

"...really appreciate your help," Fez was saying. He looked like a teenager wearing fancy expensive clothes. "I'm really glad we ran into you when we got here, and your Welcoming Committee."

Screwball swore again, under his breath. If Feeney found out Angelica had landed a rich moron after running him and Ditz off port duty, he'd be livid.

"No problem, kid," Raj was saying. He had an easy grin, and almost looked trustworthy. "I'm always up for a bit of adventure, and this comet thing sounds cool. You ready?"

Raj and the kid turned toward the west spur, which went toward the port. Keeping low, and trying to keep Ditz low, Screwball slunk along the line of potted trees in the middle of the big room and on. His quarry seemed to have no idea they were being followed – overconfident, Screwball thought. Just because they kept the fighting out of the galleria itself didn't make it safe for jerks to just hang out in.

They went into the west spur, through the big steel doors that Screwball had never seen closed, past the shuttered storefronts where the loan shark and the pawn shop used to be and straight through the intersection toward the port instead of clockwise for the casino. Screwball grinned and relished getting his revenge at the site of his earlier humiliation. Ditz stayed quiet, even seemed to sober up a little, and obsessively checked behind them as they walked, but nobody followed. He hung back a bit as they got closer to the port, in case there was a hostile welcoming committee, but the metal corridors were empty.

Screwball hesitated when Raj and the kid actually went into the port, talking all the while without a care in the world, but he screwed up his courage and went to follow.

Ditz clapped a hand on his shoulder, and he about jumped out of his skin. "Woah, man. Hold up. That's neutral territory, we're not supposed to go in there."

"Why not? Preston works for the old man, doesn't he?"

"Yeah… but he doesn't, like, *work*-work for Feeney. A lot of the station staff are on the take. Kind of a quid… thing. They do stuff for him, he does stuff for them. Lot of money laundering. He's got a stick up his ass about the port, though. We go in there and fight, there'll be trouble."

Screwball ground his teeth and stared at the big double-wide port hatch, and the red "open" button next to it. He pictured himself getting his ass chewed by Feeney or his granddaughter for fucking up their relationship with Preston. "All right, are there other exits?"

Ditz scratched his head. "Yeah, there's a back entrance for maintenance."

"Would Raj use it?"

"Probably not…"

"All right," Screwball said, and relaxed a little. "We'll hang out here, and jump him when he comes out. I know this isn't neutral ground, because you let him punch me in the face here."

Ditz visibly struggled with that, but kept his mouth shut. Screwball thought about texting some of the other guys for backup, or just to keep an eye out and make sure there wasn't company coming, but he didn't trust any of those assholes. He got the little baton he'd printed out of his pocket and practiced whipping it out. It made a nice sinister *snik!* noise, and it'd sound real satisfying against Raj's ugly face.

"Woah, woah, hang on," Ditz said, waving his hands at the baton. "Seriously, man, this is Raj del Rio here. He gets hurt, Angelica will fucking flip."

"So what, he can just beat me up and nothing happens?"

"Well, kinda–"

"Can he beat you up? The whole damn crew? Can he walk into the hotel lobby and nobody's allowed to touch him? I didn't hear anything about him being untouchable. Did Feeney say he's untouchable, and he can just jump me and I can't do shit about it?"

Ditz's face drooped. He looked tired and miserable. "No, man, it's just, man, this'll escalate shit. I just want it to all go back to normal."

"What, Angelica and Feeney best friends again? You want Nuke back, is that it?"

Ditz's hangdog look just deepened, and he stared down at his shoes. "No, man, but shit, Nuke was a friend of mine. I know he's gone and he's got to be gone, but he just made a mistake, that's all."

"Some mistake, Jesus."

"Look, you weren't here. You don't know."

Screwball felt bad for him, so he didn't push. He didn't know much about Nuke, but from what he had heard, the guy was a vicious psycho. "OK, sorry. Look, I'm putting the baton away. We'll beat up Raj a little but not too bad, and–"

The door slid open as Screwball was fumbling to collapse the cheaply-printed baton. He dropped it and planted his feet to fight, then relaxed when he saw that rangy jerk Preston standing there.

"What are you two morons doing here?"

"We're the welcoming committee," Screwball said, and grinned evilly.

Preston gave him a contemptuous look. "There's no ship due in. Push off."

"We're waiting for someone who just went in."

Ditz craned his neck to peer into the port behind Preston, but Screwball couldn't see.

"Who?"

Screwball pursed his lips and started to say something cagey, but Ditz said, "Raj."

Preston snorted. "Knock yourselves out, then. It'll be three weeks."

Screwball stared at him, and the dockmaster met his stare with obvious contempt. "Huh? What'll be three weeks?"

"Until his ship gets back," Preston said, "Assuming nothing 'happens' to it."

"He got on a ship?" Ditz asked.

"Jesus Christ, you're even dumber than I tell people. Yes. He got on a space ship. The space ship is leaving. The space ship will be back in three fucking weeks. Now get the fuck out of here, I gotta take a piss."

They stepped aside and let him past, not being able to figure out anything different to say or do.

"He just left?" Ditz said. He seemed even more depressed about Raj leaving than when Screwball had been proposing to ambush and beat him up. Screwball himself, suddenly relieved from the not-too-remote possibility that he'd have been beat up again himself, stood tall and grinned.

"Ain't that something," he said.

"Yeah," Ditz said unhappily.

"You know what that is? That's intel. The old man'll love it."

Ditz's "Yeah" sounded like a funeral bell.

McMasters Gets a Shot

The Miner walked across the galleria to where an unshaven guard sat sleeping in a chair, snoring gently. Taking the direct route from Takata's restaurant meant weaving through the empty tables and stepping over a little cleaning robot as it burbled along looking for something to pick up among the unused furniture. She stood awhile with arms folded in front of the snoring guard, looked up into the big window labeled SECURITY and saw nobody behind it.

She returned to the tables and picked up a half a plastic poker chip from one of them. Examining it carefully, she walked back and flicked it at the sleeping guard, hitting him between the eyes and clattering to the ground to make some robot happy. When he snorted and coughed awake, she said, "I want to talk to Captain McMasters."

The guard – a kid, really, no older than most of the punks – gave her a funny look. "Why?"

"I want to compliment him on the diligence of his crew. Is he here?"

The kid looked to struggle with that one. "Maybe?"

She glanced at the door behind him. "Through there, then?"

"You can't go in there, that's the security station."

She cocked her head. "Yeah? What'll you do if I go in anyway?"

"I'll arrest you, that's what."

She waited a bit to see if he'd catch on, but the look of belligerent stupidity didn't waver.

"And where will you take me?"

"To the—" Enlightenment dawned, and he got mad. "What are you, a smartass?"

"I just figure I'm going in there either way, so it'd be nicer of me to let you sleep in."

He stood up and put his hand impressively on the handle of his stun baton, mashing it down in a way that would make it harder to draw. "What the hell's that supposed to mean?"

The Miner scratched under her chin. "Pretty much what you think it does."

She sidestepped an awkward punch, and the door opened. A man with a crisply-pressed black uniform and an impressive blonde mustache stood in the door and gaped as his goon staggered off-balance, recovering poorly from failing to land the blow. The newcomer looked to be in his forties, and inclined to pudginess. The Miner looked at the new guy and immediately thought "Colonel", even though his uniform sleeve showed gold captain's bars. He wore a sidearm, which she thought interesting. Cheap little flechette job, from the looks of it, all threatening black plastic angles and no stopping power, but still.

"What," he started in crisp, acid tones, "the hell are you doing?"

The Miner didn't wait for him to answer. "Are you Captain McMasters?"

"Yes," he said, not looking at her.

"She thinks she can walk right in and talk to you," protested the kid.

"She's right, you idiot." McMasters scowled. "Go back to sl–" He stopped himself. "As you were, Ellsworth."

Ellsworth didn't have as good a scowl, but he deployed it anyway and resumed his chair with all the dignity of an emperor.

The Miner followed McMasters into the dark security station, through a small empty front room with a vacant sergeant's desk and on into the back. It smelled of cheap whiskey and stale sweat. Two more black-uniformed guards sat hunched in the back corner, playing some kind of game, but other than that the place was empty. Desks bore dirty dishes and a broken-down stun baton laid out on a grease-streaked towel. The inner walls bore dozens of projected squares showing video feeds from all angles around the station, many of them moving. The Miner guessed those were lapel cameras. The rest were too few to cover any kind of real acreage, and there was a lot of bare wall to project onto.

"Well," McMasters drawled. "That's the tour. No charge. Did you have something to say to me?"

She eyed him up and down, not too obviously. Herrera had given some sketchy details about the guy, enough to know she wouldn't like him much but could maybe get along. "Heard you were a military man. Served on the *Kaftan Lay*, that right?"

His thin blonde eyebrows went up, hardly visible in the dim light. "That's right."

"Nice ship," she said. "Well run."

"Thank you," he said, and smiled. He looked a little taller and puffed-up than he'd been before. "Time of my life, I had on that ship. Were you in the service yourself?"

She nodded. "Intel corps."

His smile looked a little frozen. "I didn't catch your name."

"I was passing through, and heard you could maybe use another pair of hands around here," she said, turning to take in the surroundings. "Since I could use some cash, I figured we could help each other out."

He gave her a knowing look, which she didn't much like. "I see. A little place to kick back, maybe take out some aggression now and again? Well…"

She shook her head. "I'm not looking to stay. Seems to me the place could use a house-cleaning, is all."

He laughed. "Seems to you, does it?"

"Seems to me," she said, smiling, keeping it friendly. "I figure five thousand will cover it, then I'll get out of your hair."

"Five thousand credits?" He stared. "And what would that buy me, Ms…"

"I'll tidy up. Take care of Feeney and del Rio, give you a clean slate."

One of the goons in the corner seemed to lose her game, judging by her opponent's cheer. Distracted, apparently.

"Are you out of your mind?"

"Maybe," she admitted. "But I'm trained and qualified in hand-to-hand, zero-G, long guns, and sidearms. I'm no stranger to wet work. I'm cheap at five-k, but what the hell. I need the cash, and the folks on the *Lay* treated me nice." They'd left her the hell alone as an Intel corps spook, which suited everyone fine.

McMasters seemed to notice his mouth was still open, and fixed that. "What's your name?"

"No names," she said, shaking her head. "You can pay me when I'm done. No risk to you, just let me bend that firearms rule for a little while."

"I'm not risking my crew in some insane–"

"I don't recall asking for help."

In the quiet she could practically hear the two game-players straining to listen. McMasters stared hard at her, and she decided he was trying to find a way to say no that let him save face in front of them. Some combination of fear and greed would keep him from rocking the boat, she could see it in his eyes.

"A lot of folks here are hurting," she tried anyway. "The ones who are left."

"The situation on this station is quite under control," he finally managed. "I won't have some amateur scurrying around stirring up trouble."

"They pay that well, huh?" She shouldn't have said that, she knew. She'd been alone too long, forgot how there ought to be a filter between her brain and her tongue. Not that there ever really was.

His face went red, and then redder when one of the goons in back couldn't suppress a snort.

Before he could squeak out a reply, she said quietly, "Sorry about the crack, but every gravy train stops, friend. I can do a lot of good here, and you'd look good if you let me."

"I think we're done here," he said through his teeth.

"Guess so," the Miner said. "Just remember: I offered."

Job Application

The entrance to the Hotel Astra was big, all glass retro-future with lots of chrome and a subtle blue glow that seemed to come from nowhere and everywhere. Tasteful furniture was laid out in a huge lobby, a luxurious waste of space. Comfortable so that tired travelers would feel welcome, but not so comfortable that they'd loiter and spoil the ambiance. At least, that was the intent once upon a time. The effect was currently entirely spoiled by a series of stains and tears, plus the rough-looking drunk sleeping on the big couch. The carpet had seen better times, too. The Miner figured it had either started out crimson and faded under foot travel, or started out white and then been the scene of a large number of improbably well-spaced fights.

She stepped through the front doors and surveyed the lobby with her hands on her hips. Two more toughs played cards off to her left. They slowly, stupidly looked up at her. The one facing her, whose mohawk would have been improved by shaving the sides of her skull more than once a month, tilted her head like a puzzled dog.

"Who the hell are you?"

The Miner scratched the back of her neck and continued her look around the place. It didn't improve under further scrutiny. She'd never actually seen rats in space, but this would be the place to look.

"I said—"

"I heard Feeney's hiring. He worth working for?"

"If you're good," said the other card-player, who had a fat lip and a black eye. The Miner idly wondered if he'd gotten it from Angelica's gang or from his opponent.

"I'm good."

They laughed.

"You laughing at me?"

They kept on, but their laughing gained a brittle quality. The Miner shrugged. "I don't see what's so funny about being good. Maybe you'd like a demonstration."

They flinched like she'd threatened them, but instead she turned on her heel and walked slowly out. A hurried conversation, louder for being hushed, took place and chairs scraped against tile. The Miner walked down the sweeping curved stairs to the galleria floor, in no hurry but not wanting her stumbling followers to get bored or lost. The guard called Ellsworth had left, which was fine by her.

Angelica's casino, which used to be Feeney's casino, was named Lady Luck. Big neon-colored dice rolled in the window and came up seven. Reflected in the mirrored columns out front that held up the walkway above, the only ones decorated like that, the Miner could see her two followers slow down and exchange nervous looks. A couple of the opposing gang's toughs glanced up lazily in the window, their meerkat routine again, then they snapped to attention.

Four of them shoved through the doors, looking around at each other and at the Miner. They were armed, sort of. The ones on either side had knives out, and one fumbled to put her fingers through brass knuckles. The tallest one, in the middle, carried a big steel rod slung over his shoulder. He ambled to a halt a few feet from the Miner and loomed over her, not really looking at her. Through the thicket of metal rings in his lips he managed to say to the toughs behind her, "The fuck are you doing here? You wanna die or something?"

"They're with me," the Miner said. The two knife-wielders walked around either side of her, keeping their distance the way Rings with the metal rod wasn't. They had it exactly backward, of course, but that didn't stop the jolt of adrenaline. Her elbows and knees felt warm as her implants sensed it and tightened up.

"Who the fuck are you?" Rings looked down at her like she was a particularly insignificant bug, and leaned way over so that he loomed more. "So Feeney's feebs are helping old ladies cross the street, izzit? What do you want, old lady? Trying to get laid? You're too ugly, and even I ain't that broke. What the hell happened to your face?"

"They're just helping me find something I lost, that's all. Good Samaritans." She smiled broadly in a friendly, slightly stupid way. She could see in the mirror that her Good Samaritans had backed away and held up various gadgets to record what they probably expected to be her imminent and entertaining demise. "In fact..." She studied his face. "Yep, there it is."

Her augments engaged and her arm darted up into the tall tough's face. She snatched at a ring in the center of his lower lip, faster than he could react, and she yanked hard as she took a step back.

Rings screamed and clutched his hands to his face.

The Miner looked down at the ring as his companions reacted with shock. "Never mind, wrong one."

Blood pouring down the front of his chin, face contorted with rage, Rings roared and sprang for her. Too close for a proper charge and way too close for his weapon, he couldn't get his steel rod up. She took it from him left-handed, sweeping his leg as she sidestepped. He crashed to the ground, sending chairs and a table sliding. His buddies reacted too slowly; she went for the closer knife-jockey, driving the rod into her midsection hard.

As the kid went down puking, the Miner turned and had the rod up to parry a swipe from her pal on the left. A good knife-fighter could recover from that fast, but this guy wasn't; she brought the rod down on his collarbone, and while he was howling she turned and delivered a quick boot to Rings' ribs. He fell hard and she stepped neatly out of flailing range.

That left her staring down the familiar-looking skinny girl who'd managed to get her brass knuckles on, and had apparently left Grandma's knife safely at home. She was standing well out of punching range, but easily within "getting hit in the face with a steel rod" range. A brain cell fired somewhere, and she ran.

Rings made it to his feet in time for the Miner to whack his right forearm with his own weapon, then she stepped into him and shoved. He tripped over a fallen chair and went hard to the ground in a tangle of cheap furniture and limbs.

She looked down at the ring and tossed it onto his heaving chest. "My mistake, sorry." The rod followed it with a soft thump.

Still filming, Feeney's toughs hurried to catch up with her as she walked away from the carnage. Behind her she could hear the commotion spreading through the casino, but she didn't want to ruin the scene by rushing, and anyway she could see up ahead that a mangy-looking crowd had spilled out of the Astra. She tried not to glance too obviously at Takata and Herrera standing gobsmacked in the doorway to the bar, and felt a flush of shame. She hadn't killed anybody, but if she were being honest with herself, the fight felt good.

Off to her left, there was motion in the security office. The two black-armored game-players stood in their doorway looking lost, and after a moment of gawping they went back inside. McMasters didn't show himself, but she hadn't figured he would.

A pale old man had come to the front of the hotel crowd overlooking the galleria by the time she'd mounted the stairs. He was gaunt but well-tailored in black and red. His slicked-back clean white hair gleamed under the lights, and his hard blue eyes, deep set in their sockets, saw nothing but her. She wasn't even breathing hard, not like the guy behind her filming. "That was fucking awesome!" someone said, and the old man put up an indulgent hand to slowly motion for silence, not taking his eyes off her.

"Am I to understand that to be a job application?"

The Miner shrugged. She felt dozens of stares, but didn't take her eyes off him, either. "Not my best work. I let them get too close, even if I did need to borrow a weapon. I'd have been better off sticking closer to the pillar to use that as cover." She gave him a lopsided grin. "Looked cool, though."

"Looked cool," he said thoughtfully. "Why don't you come up and have a drink. Thirsty work, fighting."

Job Interview

"There are some good fighters," the man who introduced himself as Liam John Feeney said almost apologetically as they entered his sumptuously-appointed office. Real leather chairs, plush. The big banker's desk was real wood, and the walls were lined with cabinets full of books – or at least the spines of books – and fronted with glass doors. The Miner stopped trying to calculate the cost of hauling that out to a backwater station.

A big window overlooked the galleria; they must have been up against the outer hull. This had probably been the commandant's office once upon a time, maybe even the original furnishings. It had sure come down in the world.

"Most of them are shite," Feeney continued, "but a few are good. I had one who was really something, but... Ah well, spilt milk, crying, et cetera. Whiskey?" He held up a crystal decanter, probably shaped-diamond by the way it caught the light. He seemed to be holding it expressly so that it would catch the light that way.

"Don't mind if I do," said the Miner, and received a glass that fit neatly in her hand. No ice or water was offered or asked for. She sipped and suppressed the burning sensation in her throat. It tasted of smoke and malt, a clean sting. It'd been years. "Nice stuff."

"From home. I bring it out for special occasions."

He put it back on the sideboard and pulled another decanter closer to the front. The next drink would be the cheap stuff, apparently.

"Is this a special occasion?"

"I hope so." He took a longer drink from his own glass, seemed to have to stop himself from draining it. He wasn't a drunk, the Miner decided, but he wasn't far from it. "You're strong," he said. "Talented. I need someone like you."

"That so?"

"Yes, it's so. I've had some setbacks lately, it's no secret. That backstabbing witch Angelica, and Rat Bastard McMasters. I was here before them and I'll be here after them, you hear me? This is my station."

His face grew red as he talked, and she wasn't sure if it was the booze or the speech.

"I don't come cheap," she said. "What do you need me for? Seems pretty quiet around here, I thought there'd be more action."

He gave her a sly look. "I knew you'd come looking for an opportunity. Preston said you shut him down, not to bother, but I had a feeling you just wanted the lay of the land." He slapped his hand on his chair arm. "Well, by damn I'm just glad you came to me first. I'll pay you ten thousand credits, and I'd like to see that troll squatting in my casino match it."

"Ten thousand..." she said, swirling the whiskey in her glass and watching it drain to the bottom in little columns.

"To start," he added when she'd been quiet too long. "That's just the salary, you see. There are benefits. A man like me has lots of resources, not just money. You want to enjoy yourself, I can make sure that happens." He studied her bored expression, and she pretended not to notice.

"Hmm," she said, and took a sip from her glass. It was very good stuff. She breathed in over the sip and felt the numbing smoky sensation roll over her tongue.

"They'll need a new chief of security when we've pushed McMasters out," he added. "Nice cushy job, that, if you're loyal."

"I'm not keen on cushy."

He slapped his armrest again and made a little fist-pump gesture. "I like that. By God I do. You remind me of me when I was younger. It's money you want, it's money you'll get. You'll swim in it. There'll be profits like you've never seen when we take down the traitors, mark my words."

"So you want me to fight? I didn't come here to cool my heels and talk about jam tomorrow."

He actually rubbed his hands together. She'd never seen anyone do that before. "Oh, yes, I want you to fight. My boys and girls downstairs have heart, but not much skill. Someone like you can rouse them, maybe teach them."

"Teaching's boring. An open fight sounds better."

"Well…" He stopped rubbing his hands and picked up his whiskey glass for a tiny sip. "That's delicate. If we push too hard, McMasters will take the traitor's side. Even with you on board, I can't afford that. We're in a good position. We can be subtle."

The Miner scratched behind her ear. "Subtle sounds boring, too. I'd rather bust heads."

"Oho! Plenty of that, plenty of that, I promise you. Little fights, what you did just now, as often as you want to do that, I'll be pleased as punch."

"McMasters won't give you trouble over it?"

He waved that away in a grand gesture. "I'll handle him. You can't make an omelet without breaking eggs."

She pretended to mull it over. She swirled the remaining

whiskey in the glass, enjoying the sharp earthy aroma that stung her nose. "The ten thousand's up front, of course."

His face went wooden, and he struggled visibly to smile before he succeeded. "Yes, of course. You won't see the traitor pay up front, by the way."

She wagged her head back and forth like listening to music. "All right."

Feeney slapped his thigh hard. "Splendid! Fantastic!" His enthusiasm dampened when she pushed her bank chip across the desk to him, but he took it in stride. He pulled from the top drawer a pad clad in brass and black leather, and did a double-take when he saw what came up.

"Hah!" he said, then repeated it. "Cagey to the end, eh? Well, from one mick to another, I like it. What do I call you, anyhow?"

She lazily scanned the titles on the shelf, and didn't bother to hide it. "Jane works."

He smirked. "Austen or Eyre?"

"Suit yourself." He handed back the bank chip, holding it carefully like it contained the money he'd just transferred, marked "services to be rendered". She put the chip in her pocket. "So who all works for you here? Whose heads shouldn't I bash?"

"Well, stay away from the Company Rep, of course. She's expensive enough as it is, and she can cause more harm than I care to think about if she got bloody-minded about it. She's not even on the station much these days anymore, just orbiting in her yacht. Mr Shine's neutral–" He said the word like it was painful. The Miner perked up at the name, but he just continued on, "and I'd prefer him that way than teaming up with the witch. Most of the station employees are hiding under his petticoats, so leave them be. The dockmaster's mine, though. That's Preston, you met him. And Gordonson, the ore buyer, he's mine."

The Miner looked up. "Gordonson? Really?"

"Oh. You've met him too, eh? That's right, they said you showed up with a shipful of ore. He didn't drive too hard a bargain, I hope?"

The Miner forced herself to laugh. "Nah, the miner I stole it all from might have objected to the price I got, but he's in no position to complain." Feeney joined her in another laugh, and she didn't punch him. Instead she leaned forward, with her best worried expression. "No, the thing is… One of those kids I taught a lesson to just now, the one with the brass knuckles, I recognized her. She was hanging out in Gordonson's office. I don't mean to criticize, if you let him do business with Angelica, that's your call. It just seems strange to me."

Feeney's face went hard. "You sure about that?"

The Miner was all surprise and fluster. "Seeing the kid you mean? Yeah. She was playing with a switchblade, though, not knuckles–"

"That was her," he said curtly. He struck the chair arm with his fist and swore. "Whip, she's called. My grandson used to walk out with her. It's her grandmother's blade." He cursed again under his breath, then hit the armrest twice more, his face getting bright red, even showing red on his scalp beneath his thinning white hair.

The Miner gave him a thoughtful look. "How fast does word get around here?"

"Fast."

"You think he knows you've hired me yet?" She continued on without waiting for a response. "Only, I could go back and suss him out. Pretend I'm threatening to rat him out to you. See what he does. If he's on the level he'll just throw me out, right?"

Feeney started nodded before she'd finished talking.

"Do it. Go see him. If he's dirty, then by God I want to know it."

The Miner tossed back the rest of the whiskey and coughed. It'd been too long since she'd been a serious drinker; she couldn't do that anymore. She grimaced and slammed the glass down onto the big wooden banker's desk. Her voice came out husky. "Consider it done."

Angelica's Crew Have a Plan

"We're gonna grab 'em and we're gonna kick their asses, that's what 'the plan' is." Carter was still pissed off, as he'd repeatedly told everyone in the casino until Bex was ready to strangle him. That crazy chick who joined Feeney had broken his collarbone, and his attempts to make his sling look badass with black faux-leather and metal studs and a skull imprint all mostly just made it look stupid, which pissed him off even more. Bex was sick of listening to him whine, and anyway she'd got hurt too; she had this giant bruise on her stomach where that chick had hit her, so that it hurt to stand up or sit down. But Raj was off doing God-knows-what, and Angelica was sulking in her office overlooking the casino floor after yelling at them, so in Carter's tiny little brain he figured that meant he was kind of in charge.

"That's not a plan," Whip retorted, playing with her new brass knuckles by twirling them on her pinky. She sat cross-legged on her stool in front of one of the working slot machines. "That's just a goal, right. The plan's how you make the goal happen." She'd been embarrassed to not have gotten beat up with Chuckie, Carter, and Bex – as well she should have been, cutting and running like that – so Bex figured all this "I'm so smart" shit was just bravado to keep them from ragging on her. Carter glared at her and she rolled her eyes.

"We'll play it by ear," Carter said, jutting his chin like it substituted for an actual argument.

Whip rolled her eyes again on cue. "What about you, Chuckie? Are you in on this 'play it by ear and magically kick their asses' plan?"

Chuckie took the ice pack away from his swollen bottom lip and its ugly new black stitches with the ends sticking out like cactus spines. "I'm good," he said, his voice thick and hard to understand. He didn't look at them when he talked, just kept staring out the front windows into the galleria. "I got my own plan."

He didn't elaborate, just got up and left by the back. The others silently watched him weave through the short rows of slot machines and the roulette tables covered in junk.

"Jesus fuck, that had to hurt," Bex said, craning her head around the machines to make sure he couldn't hear. "She just fucking ripped it out, man."

"That's why we gotta get revenge," Carter said, warming again to his favorite topic. "We let Feeney's feebs roll us like that, they're gonna think they can do that whenever they want."

"This new one's not so feeble," Whip said. "I met her right off the ship, right? And she took my grandma's knife right off me."

"You never said," Bex accused.

"Well I wouldn't, would I? Fucking Raj…" She glanced up at Angelica's office overhead, but didn't see the black-clad woman in her usual window. She lowered her voice anyway. "Fucking Raj abandoned me, right? What was I supposed to do?"

"Guys, guys, guys," Carter talked over her before she got going on that again. "Shut up. We're not going after the new chick. Whoever she is, she's actually good. We go after the morons, and make it clear that she's why. Let them deal with her."

Silence descended on the three of them, leaving only the faint binging and whirring of the slot machines. Bex and Whip looked thoughtful.

"That's not," Bex said slowly, "actually, if you think about it, completely fucking stupid."

"Gee," Carter started to say, when he was cut off.

"No, it isn't stupid."

All three of them jumped at the sound of Angelica's voice. Whip cursed herself for being surprised; this was a casino after all, and casinos were always rigged for surveillance.

"Just be careful," Angelica continued. "McMasters is already angry at the old man for that little display, and I would like him to stay angry. At the old man. Use the back passages. Stay away from Mr Shine."

"Yes, ma'am!" they said together.

"Have fun. And Whip, dear? My brother did not 'abandon' you. If you can't be trusted to do a job alone, just say so."

Whip flushed, and hurried out.

PORCUPINE

The Miner found her own way back down from Feeney's office. It wasn't hard – the upper level was small and connected to the rest of the hotel by the top of the grand staircase. The hotel was wide and squat rather than tall, with curved hallways stretching out either way from the lobby. The staircase continued down to the big space behind the storefronts. The galley had already been pointed out to her, and she was lured by the sound of voices from the hotel bar.

She knew the tone of gossip when she heard it, and figured – rightly – that she knew the topic too. Walking softly, she took up a spot outside the door where she could hear but not be seen.

"Still, that was something else!" someone was saying. "I've never seen anybody fight like that, not even Nuke!"

"Nuke didn't have to fight."

"Whatever. You don't have to lick his ass anymore, he's long gone. This chick is amazing. That was some serious special forces shit she pulled out there!"

"Who's licking whose ass now?"

Someone else grumbled loud enough to be heard over their ensuing argument, "You ask me, she should have killed them."

A drunk kid stumbled out of the door. She wobbled, straightened up, and then stared at the Miner, first in incomprehension and then with wide panicked eyes. The Miner lifted a finger to her lips and said, "Shhh!" The drunk giggled and crouched behind the wall on the other side of the door. They both leaned in to listen.

"And those scars," said a female voice dripping scorn. "What's up with those? It's gross."

"She looks like she was fucking tortured or something," said a male voice.

"She looks like she went down on a porcupine."

The drunk went wide-eyed again, and gave the Miner a panicked look. Then she mashed her finger to her own lips and lurched away down the hall toward the galley. The Miner herself chose that moment to make her entrance, enjoying the abrupt halt in laughter and the flustered looks and hurried attempts to seem to be talking and laughing about anything but her. The eight or so hired toughs filling the tiny bar looked rangy and stringy instead of lean and hungry. Most of the faces were adorned with tattoos, spikes, rings, or genemods, all mostly the work of lesser artists, though the mod behind the spiral horns on the guy in the back must have had some talent. Dozens of weapons littered tables, bar, and belts, outnumbering the toughs: knives, mostly, some tasers, and stun batons. A couple rods and pipes, some with printed heads to make maces. A few more interesting weapons, like the cutlass-looking thing on the bar, or the pair of metal nunchucks nestled in cloth loops on that guy's belt. The Miner had yet to see anyone successfully use nunchucks to hurt anyone but themselves, and she didn't expect that weedy-looking bruised punk to break her streak.

She talked to nobody in particular, and they stared into glasses of pale liquor, but the hush that descended on the room made it clear they were listening. "This one's a bullet wound," she said, pointing to the faint groove dug into the side of her right cheek where the cheekbone wasn't as prominent as on the other side. "Incendiary round, hurt like a sonofabitch. This one's where my lower jaw was broken in six places and replaced pretty much whole." She brushed her fingers against the left side, still not looking at anyone, just out into space like she was reminiscing out loud. Her hand went up to her left temple. "These are from buckshot, which got the eye, too." She made the iris dilate and contract.

"These were a flamethrower accident," she said, flexing her left hand so that it was obvious that the pinky and ring fingers didn't move much. She moved her right hand back up to her face and pointed with the middle finger at a spot on her left cheekbone, aimed at a trio of beet-red faces.

"And that was the porcupine."

Dead silence loomed as the faces reddened further, their owners looking like they wanted to shrivel up and die. The Miner twitched the corner of her mouth up, and the room erupted in raucous, relieved laughter.

Supplies

The Miner strolled back to the dock, taking the rear exit from the hotel. The back passage looked about the same as the one she'd taken before, but with more random trash and a stronger urine smell. She nodded politely to the dockmaster sitting staring at something in his shack; even if she hadn't guessed what he was so absorbed by, the fact he leapt from his chair and stood at a ridiculous semblance of attention clued her in that he'd gained a newfound respect for her.

"Afternoon," she said nonchalantly. "Thanks for the tip."

When he looked at sea for a moment she added, "Feeney. Looking for people. Thanks. It turned out all right for me."

"Oh, uh. Yeah! Any time, ma'am."

Ma'am. Wasn't that something. She turned to go, but he cleared his throat. He glanced down at his hands. "Uh... Just thought you should know, Mr Feeney asked me to make sure the docking clamps were nice and tight on your ship. Make sure your, uh, property doesn't get damaged if there's a gravity glitch or something."

It was bullshit, and she could tell by his goldfish expression that he knew it was bullshit that put him between a rock and a hard place. She looked at him just long enough to unnerve before nodding a half inch.

"Obliged, I'm sure," she said. The dockmaster couldn't seem to smile without smirking, but he looked to be trying his best.

The Miner strolled on to the berth holding her ship and opened the station side of the airlock. Ship side stayed closed.

"Hey ship," she said, standing right in front of the camera. "It's me. Open up."

There was a slight pause, just enough to make her frown. "Hi, boss! Welcome home!" The inside hatch opened for her, and she closed it afterward.

It took her a moment to readjust to the higher gravity on her ship. Waste of energy, but it helped keep her in shape. She took the steps up to the main deck at a sprint, passing the strapped-down and covered mining equipment that she probably wouldn't get back to using for a while. She stopped and looked, considering her options for ad-hoc weapons, but decided that she didn't want them to know that she really was a miner: too much incentive to wreck her equipment or cause other kinds of trouble if things went south.

"Ship, let me know the moment the docking clamps are released."

"Got it, boss."

"Ship…" She bit her lip. "What do you think about all this?"

"I think you're full of shit, boss."

The Miner laughed. That was a canned response to the question "what do you think?", one of eight she'd preprogrammed. She could ask again and get a different answer, but that defeated the purpose. Anyway, she had a sneaking suspicion that the ship put its digital finger on the scales somehow, that the answers weren't as random as they could be. For one thing, she hadn't heard "I think it's brilliant, boss!" in a long time.

She went to the printer terminal and with a few key presses brought up a menu with a few secret options, stuff from the old days. After some consideration, she set it to printing some surveillance gear – nothing fancy, she didn't have a lot of time, or for that matter a lot of raw materials for electronics.

While she waited, she went up to the plant room and got started setting up the watering rig. She didn't want to have to come back here too regularly, in case someone got the bright idea to set up an ambush. Unpredictability and orchid care rarely went hand-in-hand. Tiny drip tubes were run already, but had to be purged of air and checked for kinks and blockages so that she wouldn't come back to find dead flowers, or worse a dead bonsai. The spiky pink *Dendrobium ceraula* was coming along nicely, finally, and she'd hate to lose that progress.

The red maple was badly in need of a trimming. She took a moment to sweep away a few of its tiny crimson leaves, collect them carefully, and put them in the digester. She eyed the row of different-sized shears stuck magnetically to the wall, and had her first feelings of misgiving. A delicate task like that would have to wait: it needed calm, and she'd be lacking in calm for a while. She absentmindedly brushed her hand over the top of the little tree, feeling its tiny leaves and the prick of miniature limbs. The scents from the orchids had been collecting in the small space, mixing with earthy soil funk and a faint sour note from the digester, and she breathed it all in with her eyes closed. She could just run. She had Feeney's money, bled off a portion of what she'd been cheated out of. That was some measure of revenge. But she had no supplies. And there were the docking clamps, which were designed to do serious damage to any ship trying to leave without clearance. And anyway, with an hour's work she'd have even more. She could bribe the dockmaster to have "forgotten" to set the clamps, and be gone.

She pocketed the branch shears and took them to the head. Watching in the spit-spattered mirror, she maneuvered the shears awkwardly behind her skull, then using her left hand she pulled her ponytail taut.

With a slow, firm squeeze, she cut close to the base of her head, felt the mass of hair fall strand by strand until the whole handful came free. She held it up in front of her, looked without emotion at the white streaks among the black, more than she pictured when she pictured herself. The shears went back in the plant room, and her hair went in the digester. It wasn't the best haircut she'd ever had – it looked terrible, if she were being honest – but she considered long hair a liability in a fight, and she needed to put her head in the right place for one. Peering at herself in the mirror, she was ten years younger and readier, looking an awful lot like someone she hadn't ever wanted to be again.

Her bunk presented decisions that she hadn't fully thought through yet. She pulled out the top drawer of the dresser, tugging twice against the catch in just the right way that the false back opened. That was the stuff that customs shouldn't find. She'd kept it more to maybe sell in a pinch than because she ever expected to need it: a couple concussion grenades, some of the more interesting pharmaceuticals from the old days, a few different kinds of plastic explosive. Her old combat knife, kept there mostly to be out of the way. She put the knife on the bed and reassembled the false compartment.

From under the bunk she pulled a long bag, which she laid on top of the knife. She unsealed it and stared down at her old dress uniform. How much fuel had she wasted over the years hauling this dead weight around? Underneath it was what she was after: two ghostly-gray garments like long silk underwear. Woven diamond fiber was itchy and prone to make her sweat and get blisters. It was wrinkled from being balled-up, stained in a few places, and more expensive than her ship. It was also technically stolen, but what the hell. These morons were lucky to find the pointy ends of their knives, but sooner or later it would come to shooting. Besides, she had to admit that she was out of practice, and anyone could get lucky. She stripped down out of her dirty jumpsuit and shivered at the cool, smooth touch of the thin armor as she pulled it up her legs and down over her head. A clean jumpsuit went on over it, and a look in the mirror told her that it wasn't too obvious underneath. She strapped the knife to her thigh over that.

She considered real armament. The rifle would be easiest, but that would definitely be the hard way. She didn't plan to make friends, but stepping off the ship with her service rifle in hand would be declaring war on everybody. She might win, but probably not.

The flechette pistol was attractive, being small and relatively powerful, but she wasn't sure if it would fall under the firearms rule. It wouldn't blow a hole in the bulkhead or ricochet much, but she didn't feel like arguing the matter, and anyway McMasters would probably be happy for an excuse to toss her off the station, or just out an airlock. The shotgun was tempting too, and definitely wouldn't cause a decompression – which is why she had it handy on her little ship – but again she wanted to stay on the right side of their law, such as it was, at least for the moment.

That left one option. She took the sword down off the wall gently, with both hands. Its black canvas-covered sheath, its textured silicone grip, felt familiar like a childhood song.

She'd picked it up before, of course, when it fell or to clean it, but taking it up to use again was altogether different. It felt light and heavy at the same time, and she had a feeling of rapidly sobering up. This… escalated things. Maybe not like the rifle, but she hadn't really considered that. If she didn't pull off her plan fast, this would guarantee that things got messy. But she reminded herself that looking impressive and acting decisively would make sure she could pull it off. Half-measures result in more bloodshed, cadet, not less.

She pushed with her thumb to disengage the magnetic clasp and the blade sprang free an inch from its sheath. The metal gleamed in the soft blue-tinted light of her cabin.

She hung the sword at her hip, and in twenty seconds the familiar weight had been there all along.

Killing Rings

"Oi!"

The Miner froze in mid-stride when the hoarse voice came from behind her. She had her hand on her sword hilt before even thinking about it, pulling gently against the clasp.

She recognized him by the bandage on his lip where she'd pulled the ring out. He'd ditched the steel bar in favor of a heavy fire axe, and he held it like he'd swung it before. The edge and the spike both had shiny streaks where they'd been sharpened recently. He stood in the middle of the passage with his feet planted and looked pissed. Either he'd been following her all the way from the port or she'd walked right by him without even noticing; whichever way she cursed herself for a lucky idiot.

"You think you're so good," Rings growled. His fingers whitened where he gripped the axe. "I'd like to see what you can do when you're not sucker-punching a guy, eh?"

"I can kill you," she said flatly. Her heart raced and her implants warmed up fast. "I'm not just some bruiser, kid. I've been trained, and you haven't."

He'd picked a decent spot for his confrontation, in a place where the last security camera she'd noticed had been defaced. Probably a dead angle in the surveillance, and not a lot of foot traffic. They'd have privacy, which cut both ways.

"I'm not going to lose to some fucked-up old lady," he sneered. "You caught me by surprise last time, that's all."

"Sorry for embarrassing you," she said quietly. She let her posture relax a little bit, made herself come out of the crouch and look less concerned. Her own advice from earlier came back to her, don't punch someone you're not willing to kill. "It wasn't personal."

"Sorry? Shit, you're not sorry yet, not like you're gonna be."

He's psyching himself up, she thought. She knew she ought to de-escalate, but that had never exactly been in her core skill set. It was one thing to know that she should give him an out, a way to save face, it was another thing to know how to do it when her blood was up.

"There's nobody watching, kid. Back off."

He was stupid, and he rushed her. Without time to think, she whipped her sword out and up. He'd been close, but she was faster than him and she cut deeply across his midsection as she stepped hard into his swing. She felt hot blood and his arm came down limply; she heard the axe clatter and tumble. Continuing the turn, she planted her foot and watched him fall.

Blood flowed freely onto the deck and dripped from her lowered blade. Rings gasped wetly and pushed with his feet until his back hit the wall. He kept kicking feebly, then stopped.

The Miner stood awhile, feeling suddenly very tired. Well, what the hell had she expected, anyway. She took out a scrap of cloth, wiped down her sword blade, and sheathed it. The closest doctor was two decks away, and that wound was too big to put pressure on.

Looking down at her dying assailant, she saw something she'd missed before – a small camera pinned to his shirt. She swore at herself, stooped to pick it off him, then dropped it on the deck away from the quickly-spreading pool and stomped it. If he could be saved, if anyone cared to, his friends knew where he was. If not, they didn't need to watch him die, and they didn't need to hear her say, "I'm sorry," before she left.

GETTING EVEN

The two goons in the buyer's outer office sprang to their feet when the Miner came in the door. They stared at the sword on her belt and the spattered blood on her face and clothes. Her mood hadn't been improved by the fight, nor by the time she'd spent in bitter self-recriminations.

"Relax," she said. They declined to relax. "Mr Feeney sent me to have a little chat with our friend in there. I need to talk to him alone. Check with the old man if you need to, but don't breathe a word to Gordonson."

She didn't make a hostile move, just waited while they huddled around a small comm screen. When they looked up and nodded, she told them to stand guard in the hallway and they did.

Gordonson looked up when the door to his inner office opened, and she enjoyed the look of terror on his face when he saw her. "Relax," she said again. He also declined. She sat down in the same chair as before. "Haven't you heard? I'm working for Feeney now. We're on the same side."

He didn't seem to find that particularly soothing. She passed him a comm screen with a video loaded up on it. The dockmaster had graciously given her a copy, and she in turn strongly urged the buyer to watch. Two minutes later, she was still smiling and he had lost all the color in his cheeks. It took him two tries to slide the screen back across the desk to her.

"Well," he said at last in a thin voice. He coughed. "Well. I'm glad you're on our side."

"So am I," she said. She leaned forward and put her elbows on his desk, showing bloodstains on her sleeves. "It's just, I got to thinking about our earlier conversation. You said something pretty funny. I asked if you could go higher, and you said something like, 'I don't see any reason to.' Was that it?"

"Ah." His voice sounded strangled.

"Ah." Hers didn't.

"Well, obviously matters have changed some. Situations have changed. I… made a mistake, possibly."

The Miner leaned back into her chair again and crossed her legs, seemingly oblivious to the way it made her sword clatter against the chair's side. "I think, possibly, you did. Let's have a second look at that assay."

He seemed about to repeat that it was confidential, and then appeared to think better of it. In his evident panic, she realized that they probably hadn't actually done one. She smiled. "Or whatever you think is fair, Mr Gordonson. You're the expert."

Visibly uncomfortable, he fumbled to operate his pad, and when he finally succeeded he hurriedly scrolled through something she couldn't see. She wondered what it might be, since it probably wasn't a materials composition assay. Maybe a romance novel. Or a spy thriller – he seemed the type.

"Ah," he said. "I think, yes, I think I may have underestimated the value of that particular, um, isotope. And of course, arsenic processing is an advancing field, it's not as expensive as it once was. Naturally, we can buy the extracted arsenic, which I had been planning to have the refinery credit you for later, of course, maybe I forgot to say that."

"Maybe."

"Would you say, twenty thousand?"

"Hmm." She stroked her chin, feeling the scar along her jawline. "On top of the ten thousand you already paid, that does seem fair."

He winced, but nodded and tried to smile. "Quite fair, yes. Are we agreed?"

"I think so," she said, and passed her bank chip over. He accessed it again and after a last moment of hesitation, transferred another twenty thousand credits.

"I..." He stared down at his pad. "This is a real account, isn't it?"

"It is."

"I'm just curious. I mean, I have to ask..." She raised an eyebrow and he blurted out, "How the hell did you get a legitimate account at a major accredited bank under the name 'Mickey Fucking Mouse'?"

She grinned. "I guess I'm just really persuasive."

He stared at her, hollow-eyed and unbelieving. "Say hello to Mr Feeney for me," he said.

"Oh, I will."

MAYBE MORE THAN EVEN

The Miner waited while Feeney's face cycled through an impressive array of colors, and for a moment thought he'd have a stroke.

"Son of a bitch," he managed. "Disloyal little toad! I've made him rich, that ingrate! I've given him protection, I've given him cover, kickbacks, laundered his money, and this is how he repays me?"

He swept the glassware off the desk so hard it all shattered against the wall. The Miner slowly but pointedly reclaimed her bank chip showing the "proof" that had sent Feeney into a steaming rage: twenty thousand credits' worth of hush money paid by Gordonson when she'd confronted him with his treachery. She bent to rescue a glass off the floor that had merely chipped, and then languidly stood and filled it from the decanter on the sideboard – the cheap stuff, she noted.

"I'm too loyal," Feeney was saying. "I'm too goddamned loyal, Jane, that's my problem. Loyal to Gordonson, loyal to Angelica. They all told me to cut Wilfred loose, and by God I know I should have, but I'm too goddamned loyal, and they all take advantage of me. Now look at me."

He rounded on her, planting both hands on his desk and

leaning forward. "They're bleeding me, my good Mick. I'm telling you, they're bleeding me like two dozen leeches. Business has been shite since this damn fighting started, since that ingrate Angelica cut my feet out from under me. Instead of running my operations I've been paying out for these lousy cut-rate gangsters. Why? Because otherwise she'll hire them and overrun me. Nobody stays at this hotel who pays. Nobody gambles at my casino she's squatting in either. Nobody comes to this damn station at all except lunatics who come for a fight and to suck me dry."

"He can't have been at it long," the Miner offered after a sip of rescued whiskey. It wasn't nearly as good as the good stuff. "After all, your guards keeping an eye on him would have noticed before too long."

Feeney stopped ranting and went completely still. He started tapping his fingers on his desk, then sat heavily in his chair. The Miner watched him make a call and speak in low, angry tones. While he talked, she pretended to scratch herself behind the neck and retrieved the bug she'd printed on her ship, tucked in her collar. She shifted in her chair and dropped it between the cushion and the arm.

Feeney cut the call and smiled grimly. "Well, those two can earn their pay, at least."

The Miner nodded. "By the way," she said offhandedly, "I had to kill one of Angelica's people."

Feeney stared. "What, now?"

"No big deal. One of those I beat up earlier took a run at me in the back passages. Now he's dead."

Feeney ran his hands through his thin white hair. "Well, these things happen," he said, seemingly more to himself than to her. "As long as nobody saw it–"

"I'm pretty sure he was streaming video when he attacked

me," the Miner interrupted. "Probably got the whole thing. Don't know if anyone was watching."

He flushed and she got a glimpse of a very ugly expression before he mastered himself. Still red in the face, he gave her a strained smile. "You do work fast, Jane, I have to hand you that. You do work fast."

"Is there a problem? I didn't think you'd mind me breaking some eggs."

"No, no," he protested. "Not at all. Only... maybe you'd better lie low for a little while."

She took that as a dismissal and stood. He'd just suffered a couple of blows: he'd paid her out a lot of money and lost a major asset, and if his situation was as precarious as she hoped, he was teetering. "McMasters going to be a problem over this?"

He waved it away, but he wasn't very convincing. "He's my problem, not yours."

That was definitely a dismissal, and she took it gladly. Getting Feeney teetering was one thing, but the question was whether she'd strengthened Angelica. She considered that on the walk down from Feeney's office, around the bend and down the stairs.

There was a commotion in the lobby, cries of pain and anger. She strolled down the steps, hand resting lazily on her sword, watching as two of Feeney's gang were carried in by five of their fellows. They were dumped onto the couches, leaving smears of blood down the back cushions. They weren't dead – they were swearing loudly enough that she could be sure of that even through the mashed noses, blackened eyes, and broken limbs.

"Ambushed." A young woman covered in spikes came up to the Miner from behind. "Coming back from checking up on the old man's interests down below, and some of the witch's crew jumped them."

"Anybody killed?"

"Naw. This is revenge for what you did." She really did have a lot of spikes. Through her ears, implanted around her neck, stubby little ones in a line along her cheekbones with tattoo swirls exploring them like raked lines in a Zen garden. The Miner wondered how she slept without shredding the pillow.

"They need to get their eyes checked to mistake those kids for me."

That earned a snort from Spikes. "They don't have the guts to go after you."

"That so?"

She nodded at the Miner's sword. "You know how to use that thing?"

"Yup."

"You ever killed anybody?"

The Miner glanced sideways at her, but couldn't read anything but idle curiosity. "Some."

"How come?"

She shrugged. "You can't like everybody."

"Huh." That earned her a long side eye. "You know, we got it pretty good here. Place is a dump and it'd be better without the fighting, but it is what it is. Just don't go psycho on them, and they'll return the favor."

"That so?"

"I'm just saying, don't fuck it up."

The Miner just rubbed her chin and nodded, thinking that she didn't have to.

"I keep hearing this name Nuke," she said, watching as some idiot kid tried entirely the wrong way to set a broken arm. It was kind of entertaining. "Who is he?"

Spikes gave her a suspicious look. "Why? He's not here anymore, so what do you care?"

"I heard something about a doublecross. Not the kind of thing you want to hear when you start a gig."

She looked angry. "Wasn't a doublecross. He was balls-out crazy."

"Mmm," the Miner said.

"It *wasn't* a doublecross. I was here. He had to go, everyone agreed. Eventually."

If she intended to say more, she was stopped when the hotel doors slid open and McMasters strode in like he owned the place. Puffed up in his black uniform and with his neat little pencil mustache newly-waxed, he walked stiffly with his black cap under his arm like he was inspecting the troops at a parade ground. He looked like a swagger stick would be the best birthday present anyone could ever give him.

He strode through the middle of the room, pausing only briefly to inspect the groaning bodies on the couch and sniff in disdain. He made for the stairwell just past the Miner and Spikes, up to the old man's office. Spikes raised her middle finger like she was scratching under her chin with it, and the Miner saw McMasters' fleeting indecision of whether to scowl or pretend he hadn't seen it, with the latter unconvincingly winning. He looked daggers at the Miner, but said nothing as he passed.

"Going to bitch about the fighting," Spikes predicted. "And try to get his kickback early. You're getting to be expensive."

"Is it getting around how much Feeney's paying me?" She hoped so; it would sow discontent in the ranks on both sides.

"Not yet, but it will."

The Miner nodded at that, and thought. She turned to Spikes. "I don't believe we've been introduced."

"Mary Feeney."

"Huh." She considered the likeness under the tattoos and spikes. "Your granddad calls me Jane."

They didn't shake hands.

"I didn't agree with hiring you," Mary said. "I think you're trouble."

The Miner didn't answer. She agreed, after all. A pair of scruffy-looking toughs came in the front door and peered at the injured on the couch. One was tall and dark, with white tribal tattoos on his forearms and a busted lip. He had an intense, excited look on his face, in contrast to the laid-back shorter guy with a bit of a pot belly and a dopey smile.

"Excuse me," Mary said, and went down to join them.

Four's Kind Of a Lot

Screwball marveled at how beat-up Marko and Cassie were, and how miserable they looked, bleeding on the couches in the main lobby of the old man's hotel. "Dang," Ditz said, scratching himself.

Mary was up on the stairs to Feeney's office, standing off to the side with the new chick who had a sword now, and a pretty aggressive haircut. She looked dangerous as hell, he thought, and was glad when Mary shook her loose to come down.

"Well?"

"Hey, Mary," Ditz said. "How's it going?"

She favored him with a smile; she seemed to like the dumbass for some reason, and when he talked about her, Ditz implied that they used to be friends. He'd been the one to insist that they talk to her first instead of the old man, and that chafed Screwball, but he had to admit Ditz just knew the politics better than he did. So they'd hid out for a little while until she came back from whatever she'd been doing down in the lower decks.

"Could be better," Mary said. "What did you want to talk about?"

Screwball suggested they stand away from the annoying cries of the wounded, and the new fighter's eyes were on them as they walked towards the little tables and stools off to the side. In low tones he explained to Mary that they'd followed Raj out to the port, and that Preston had told them he'd gotten on a ship and left. She looked stunned.

"What ship?"

Screwball shrugged. "Couldn't get it out of the guy at the docks," he said, and that was technically true, since you couldn't succeed at something you hadn't thought to try. "Only three ships are in, though," he said. "Some kind of science thing, a freighter, and hers." He gestured at the lady with the sword, who was watching them from the stairs. His stint on the welcoming committee hadn't exactly been distinguished, but at least he paid attention, mostly.

Mary considered that, running the backs of her knuckles along the edge of the spikes along her collarbone. He tried not to stare, so it didn't look like he was staring down her shirt again.

"Thanks," she said at last, still looking thoughtful. "Three weeks, you said?"

They both nodded.

"Thanks," she repeated. "That's… interesting. Don't mention it to anyone, all right? I don't want it to get back to Angelica that we know."

Ditz pointed up the stairs. "So who's the new person?"

They all turned to look at the lady with the sword, who had been mobbed by admirers. One of them, some douchebag whose name Screwball didn't know, had his hands up in some kind of karate stance and looked like he thought he was some kind of funny shit, while the lady looked at him like he was just shit.

"Just someone Granddad hired," Mary said.

"I heard she took down like eight of Angelica's dudes," Ditz said.

"Four," was her absentminded reply. "She took them by surprise, but still: four."

"Four's kind of a lot," Ditz said, and she nodded.

"Who is she?" Screwball asked. "What's her name?"

"Don't know. She has some kind of hacked bank account, so even Granddad doesn't know her real name."

Screwball thought Feeney had only a hazy idea what anyone's real name was, but kept that to himself.

"Do me a favor, you two," she said, again acting like he and Ditz were best buds or something. "Keep an eye on her. I don't trust her. If she's really that good, then what the hell is she doing here?"

"Causing trouble, Ms Feeney."

Screwball jumped. He hadn't seen that security guy with the blonde mustache approach. The guy moved like a cat. Mary rolled her eyes and turned. She didn't say anything to him, just gave him a look like she was happy to wait until he left.

"Your grandfather won't see reason," the security guy went on. He had an annoying voice, kind of nasal. "I hope you will. I won't like to interfere in your business, but I won't tolerate a move against your rivals."

"You mean you won't tolerate anyone disrupting the status quo and cutting off your payments," she said.

His face got ugly, fast. He put his finger in her face and snarled. "Watch it," he said. "Your family's little circus only operates on this station because I let it."

Mary looked like she had something to say to that, but smiled sweetly instead. "Well, I guess that's just really nice of you," she said. The security guy stared, didn't seem to have any kind of reply to that, and left with his little hat up in his armpit.

"Jackass," Mary murmured, but she was staring up at the new woman and her sword when she said it.

Listening In

An hour later, out on the balcony in front of the hotel overlooking the galleria, with the sun lamps turned down to simulate evening, the Miner stood and rested her elbows on the railing. She'd managed to get her order in before the provisioner closed up shop; a bit of a rush job, but it would do. It might get back to Feeney, but to hell with it. She hadn't left the station, and couldn't really explain why. Preston would take a bribe to release those clamps, she was sure. The look Takata had given her from the front of his restaurant before pulling the shutter made her think maybe she should just leave.

Across the way in the casino, a handful of Angelica's toughs stared right back at her. Crazy, she thought. Two gangs headquartered right across a damn mall food court from each other. Off to her left whirred a little laser anti-artillery gadget, which would probably knock a bullet or two out of the air if anyone decided to take a potshot, but that wasn't much. It was a stupid, tidy little war, and she was embarrassed to be part of it.

She queued up the lousy audio playback from the bug in Feeney's office, checking once over her shoulder to make sure nobody was coming out to join her before she got distracted.

"So, Tom," she heard Feeney say after some murmuring and clinking of glassware. "To what do I owe the pleasure?"

"Mr Feeney, you seem to have forgotten our agreement. There was an altercation in the galleria today involving one of your soldiers."

"Ah, but that's where you're wrong, Tom my boy, though I see where you might have made your mistake. Jane is one of my people, yes. And yes, she had an altercation today, a regrettable thing. A misunderstanding."

"She walked out," McMasters interrupted, "started a fight, ended a fight – rather brutally – and walked back again. What's to misunderstand?"

"Namely, this: she didn't work for me then. She didn't know how things go around here, you see. So, none of my people were involved while they were my people, and four of Angelica's were. Getting your ass kicked in public is still fighting, you know. Being bad at fighting is a poor excuse. But never you mind that, Tom, I'm willing to overlook Angelica's breach, and I've taken this Jane under my wing. I'm showing her the ropes and I'll keep her out of trouble, never fear."

There was silence on the bug, long enough that the Miner wondered if its juice had run out. Stupid printed batteries never lasted long, especially the little ones, and she hadn't had any manufactured ones to use. That worked in her favor, anyway: if Feeney found a dead bug, it could have been there forever, while a live one only had a few possibilities.

"Mr Feeney," McMasters said at last. "That woman, Jane you called her? You should know that she came to me first."

"Is that so?"

"She offered to take on you and Angelica both, to 'clean up this station.'"

Another silence. The Miner put her hand on her sword instinctively, then felt incredibly foolish for it. Still, she was relieved to hear Feeney say, "Well, what of it? She certainly has an inflated view of herself, but maybe she *could* take us both on. Makes me all the more glad she's on my side, doesn't it?"

"Are you sure she's on your side? She was very moralistic about it, very nasty. Holier-than-thou."

"And she offered to do this for free, did she?"

"No, she demanded a ridiculously high fee."

Feeney hooted. "You see, there, Tom? I daresay you're good at knocking heads and I appreciate how reasonable you are, but you're no businessman. You can't tell a sales pitch when you hear one. She's just another mercenary. Out of curiosity, how much did she ask?"

"Mr Feeney, I don't think you're taking me seriously. I'm not joking."

"I know, Tom, I know. And I appreciate the warning. You know as well as I do that I've had to learn to cut my losses when it comes to troublemakers. For Chrissakes, I cut loose my own grandson, Tom. Don't you think I've gone soft now."

"See that you don't. That woman is trouble."

"All women are trouble. Now see, you've barely touched your drink, Tom. Would you prefer the Balmoor? Maybe the Glencallan?"

The Miner waited through small talk and clinking glasses and those irritating little chuckles men like that made when they thought they were being sophisticated.

"Oh by the way, Tom," Feeney eventually said in a faux-off-handed way. "Talking of fighting, it was brought to my attention that one of Angelica's little goons has got hisself killed."

"What?"

"You should tell her to keep a tighter rein on them."

"Damn it, Feeney!"

"She attacked one of my people, Tom, and I can't help it if they can defend themselves. She should know better than to let her little trolls out if she can't control them."

More silence.

"When was this?"

"This afternoon some time. I only learned of it a little while ago, and here I am telling you to your face forthrightly."

"I told you no killing, damn it! Keep the fighting down, and don't bloody kill each other. How goddamn hard is that? Who did it?"

"I told you, Tom. Deal or no, I wouldn't let that woman run me out of my business. I didn't agree to any suicide pact. I didn't agree to tell my people to turn the other cheek like little saints. Anyhow, what's done is done. She'll be mad, maybe, but it's nobody's fault but hers."

The Miner listened to the sounds of rustling and breathing. McMasters was in the chair she'd bugged, and while the microphone filtered out the worst of the noises, she could tell he was squirming. "Yes, well. I wouldn't mind a show of good faith here, Mr Feeney."

"I thought it might come to that," Feeney said brightly, and the conversation turned circumspectly to money. After a lengthy dancing around, a thousand credits changed hands and McMasters finally bade him a good evening. She had seen him leave, though at the time she'd been mobbed by a little crowd of Feeney's toughs who had wanted to know where she'd learned "that special forces shit."

Feeney talked to himself, the Miner had already discovered, but didn't say anything interesting. He reiterated parts of the conversation, repeating bits that he'd said and hooting in obvious pride. She was about to turn off the recording, when there was a knock and Feeney called "Come in."

"Hello, Granddad," came a woman's voice.

"Mary! Come give your old granddad a kiss, girl."

The Miner hadn't noticed Mary slip past her, and made a mental note that there could be a back way up to Feeney's office.

"I've just met your new bruiser."

"What do you think of her? She's cracking, isn't she?"

"She's dangerous, Granddad."

"You're the second person to tell me that. Nobody seems to think the old man can take care of himself anymore. I tell you, I'll outlive all those sons of bitches, mark my words."

"I'm serious. She's a real fighter. That sword of hers is military issue. Why's she hooking up with us?"

"Because I pay, child. She already touched McMasters, and when he couldn't afford her she came to me. She's not cheap, either, she cost me eleven thousand credits already."

"Eleven thousand! We don't have–"

"I know. It cuts to the bone. But! She flushed out a rat and she killed one of Angelica's morons already. That's her first day."

"Killed! When?"

"Just this afternoon. And let me tell you, was McMasters steamed!" He hooted.

"This isn't funny, Granddad. Who did she kill?"

"I haven't the faintest."

"Raj has gone missing."

"Has he now." The merriment went out of his voice.

"Ditz and his buddy think he got on a ship and left. What if they're wrong?"

"Then we'll finally have that fight with Angelica I've been wanting."

"And if McMasters teams up with her?"

"You worry too much. Tom's a wimp. When things get tight, I'll deal with him. And don't you worry, I'll deal with this Jane woman too. I don't intend to finally knock down Angelica just to replace her with someone twice as dangerous. She's got a ship I could sell off, make back that ten thousand plus a tidy profit."

"You're treating this like a game, Granddad. This is serious."

"Damn right this is serious, child. For months now – months! – I've sat here and let Angelica lord it up over there in my casino. Squatting there where I can see her. Every damn day I look out my window and it stabs me in the fecking heart to see it. That's my property she's squatting in, and the salvage port I fixed up for Sparks, that greasy ingrate. So I'm paying off that puffed-up hall monitor so he won't team up with the traitor, and I'm paying an army of incompetent layabouts, and what the devil do I have to show for all that paying, Mary? What do I have to show?"

Mary made a frustrated noise and sat heavily in the bugged chair. The Miner jumped at the sound.

"Don't think I don't know you wanted to join up with the del Rios, girl." Feeney said it conversationally, but there was malice in it. "Blood is thicker than water, but that's not 'thick' as in 'stupid'."

"I've always been up front with you, Granddad."

"Surely, and I appreciate it. You've got spirit, and I guess that just cuts both ways, doesn't it? I built this all up for your father, and when he passed on I kept building it for you and your brother. When I'm gone, you'll have it and can do what you like with it, but not until then, Goddamn it. And if I haven't killed that snake Angelica by the time I go, then I hope to God you finish the job. You'll feel differently about her when you're in charge, I know you will."

"So you've said."

"So I have." There was another long pause in the audio, and then Feeney said from far away, "How did your talk with Mr Shine go, any…"

The audio trailed off and went dead again, and stayed dead. The Miner cursed her luck with nano-cap power supplies, then she just stood at the railing. Angelica's goons had lost interest at some point and slunk away, leaving the casino windows dark. Nobody bothered her. Nobody went out into the galleria at all. The space was designed for night life, she thought. Lots of hidden alcove lights cast dramatic shadows on the trees, the casino and restaurants and bars. It was supposed to be the kind of place she hated, full of laughing, carousing people. Instead it was peaceful, dark, and silent except for someone quietly retching off in a side passage.

After a while there was movement below, and the Miner stood still. A moment later she watched as the buyer, Gordonson, beaten badly and limping, slunk out of the far shadows. He carried a bag over his back, which made him look more like Santa Claus than before.

He turned and looked up at the hotel, locked his eyes on her. She looked back impassively. He'd cheated a lot of people, that little snake, and she'd spent three thousand credits buying him passage on the last freighter out of there. It left in half an hour. If he pissed away that chance by joining Angelica, she washed her hands of him.

He let his bag sink onto his right elbow, then down to the ground with a muffled thump. He dug in one pocket and pulled out a small angular shape that he held out in front of him in both hands, arms outstretched. She sat still as he aimed the pistol up at the hotel, didn't flinch when he fired.

The anti-artillery laser clicked and whirred like a disgruntled pigeon. She barely noticed it move in her peripheral vision, only saw the bullet flare phosphorous-white in the air in a bright sharp arc down to the deck.

The loud retort echoed in the big space and for a while Gordonson stood with the pistol up, panting and staring. She couldn't tell if he was looking at her, or at Feeney's window up above, didn't know where he'd aimed. Who did he hate more, she wondered.

She waved, and broke the spell. He started like he'd been the one to get shot, then hurriedly stuffed the gun back in his pocket.

There was a noise from the security station, and muffled voices behind her. Gordonson stooped to snatch his bag, and ran – to the port, not the casino.

The Miner sighed, and walked back into the hotel through the emerging crowd of gawking misfits and assholes.

Angelica Pays Attention

Angelica del Rio paused when she heard the gunshot. She listened a moment, then turned off her book and got up from her desk to go peer at the monitors. The wall showed a dozen angles of the casino, where thugs and morons roused themselves from drunken or stoned reveries in among the slot machines, roulette wheels, card tables, AI fight rings, and all the other flashy garbage Mr Shine had crammed into the place. Her people all looked sluggish and stupid, not alarmed; by the time she'd navigated to the outside cameras, someone in dark clothes was running away with a bag. Older guy, not one of her crew.

She waved her hands, expanding the view to the full wall, then swimming back in time to watch as he pried a gun from his pocket and held it up at Feeney's hotel. A burning projectile leapt back into his gun barrel, which he shoved in a bag that crept up his arm back onto his shoulder. Only when he turned back did she get his face, recognizing him a moment after the system painted "Nils Gordonson" above him in friendly green letters.

"Well, well." So Feeney had pissed off Anaconda's buyer. He had that effect on people.

She returned to her desk, and to the absolutely fascinating transmission her antennas had intercepted. Either the old man had left an unsecured radio active in his office, or – intriguingly – someone had planted a bug in it. She'd seen Tom McMasters go in, and caught the tail end of a conversation between him and Feeney. She'd swept her own operation from top to bottom and found nothing operating on that frequency, so if McMasters was bugging the old man, he was *only* bugging the old man, and that was interesting.

The death had been easy enough to follow up: Chuckie hadn't come back after leaving base, and they'd found him dead not far from Gordonson's office. The cleaning robots had been at him, and had left a smear of blood down two corridors to where they'd jammed him ineffectually in a too-small trash chute.

She dug up Chuckie's video log, which she then locked down. Most of it consisted of his dubious sexual exploits, fistfights with Feeney's people, and his use of little improvised explosives to blow up trinkets he stole from the locals. In one of them he'd balanced a little cleaning robot on a bucket, and he and his unfilmed buddies had guffawed at its distress beeps before they chortled out a "guilty" verdict for something, and blew it up. Chuckie had been that kind of man, and had been useful to have around. The last video, the reason she'd locked down the log, chilled her.

Angelica steepled her fingers and watched again. The woman on the video was nothing much to look at: average height, badly-cropped black hair with white streaks, a face that looked like she'd stuck it in a running engine. That sword, though, and the knife strapped to her gray jumpsuited thigh… those were something to look at, something military if she made her guess. Whose military, she couldn't say, and didn't really care. Anaconda had hired ex-mil before, the wonderfully, pompously feckless Thomas R. McMasters.

But then, who knew what Feeney might be doing with his dwindling pile of credits.

She ran it through again, watched the woman draw her sword with nearly inhuman speed. Angelica had priced out second-hand combat implants once, and only once. Whoever this woman was, she – or her patrons – had money. The sword whipped toward the camera's field of view, and disappeared. The view went dark, then light again but with a red film over the picture.

Angelica pushed her chair back from her desk and exhaled the breath she hadn't noticed herself holding. She'd seen death, though not very much until the trouble with Wilfred "Nuke" Feeney started. But this felt like a gut-punch in a way that even the fights she'd been in hadn't. Those had been adrenaline-fueled, and followed by relieved joking and bragging among the survivors. This was private, almost an execution.

She saved a selection from it, editing out the woman's half-hearted attempts to de-escalate. "Back off"? Chuckie? Not likely. That was nothing that McMasters needed to see, if and when Angelica saw fit to share it with him. He was mollified now, fat with Feeney's cash, but sooner or later the old man would piss him off again, and this would be a useful bit of ammunition.

The wall still showed the paused views from the galleria. The swordswoman stood frozen on the balcony in front of the old man's hotel, one hand up in a lazy wave. The system's green text above her read, "Unknown".

A Tour of the Facilities

The Miner didn't want to go back to her ship, or bring any kind of attention to it at all, so she took Feeney up on the offer of a hotel room. "Finest accommodations in a million kilometers! Clean linens – thread, mind you, not plastics – and the same mattress I sleep on my own self. It's luxury, I'm telling you." Luxury wasn't free, but she'd taken ten thousand off him and twenty off Gordonson, so giving back a hundred a night didn't sting too bad.

And as space station hotel rooms went, it was positively swanky: a good quarter meter on all sides of a bed in which she could lay out both arms with only her hands falling over the sides. The ceiling was painted with a video screen, there were VR rig hookups, and the washroom door could be closed so that the head doubled as a gravity shower, which the panel cheerfully informed her could be activated for a mere fifty credits. The commode flushed for free – a good tactical decision, given the number of one-night stays – but the bidet cost three per use. The sink cost the same, though the UV sterilizer was free. The Miner watched the UV flicker and mentally reviewed her day to recall if she'd shaken hands with anyone.

She sat on the bed a while, staring at the door and deciding how best to handle it. After a while, she went and banged on the wall for a couple minutes until she was reasonably sure there was either nobody next door or they were too polite to complain; either would suit her purpose. She left the room again and with the aid of a few tools, unlocked the door of the neighboring room. Satisfied she could get in and out without trouble, she left a little light sensor in the old room, closed the door, and went to the new room where she could finally relax.

The hard mattress had lumps like ribs running from head to foot, and whatever thread the sheets were made of was apparently trying very hard to be as plastic-like as possible. Softer than her bunk, but too unfamiliar to be comfortable, and with a faint smell like rubber. She whiled away the time by checking in on her ship. The plants were doing fine; humidity and temperature were in good shape, and the sun lamps had gone off for the night, but the last still picture showed only two fallen leaves from the bonsai and no visible wilting in the orchids. The outside cameras showed two ships leaving: that slick private ship filled with academics, and the freighter that was carrying the provisioner and Gordonson away. That reminded her to check, and she saw that the fuel, air, and water had actually been delivered, and the provisions had been loaded into external hatch B. That had been a good investment, little airlocks with one-time access codes so that she didn't have to let deliveries come in through the main airlock and get access to the whole ship.

She tried to call up a book, but without a proper reader she couldn't concentrate, and anyway she wasn't in the mood for the mystery novel she'd been working through. Life was complicated enough. After double-checking the sensors and the lock, she turned off the lights and set her communicator to produce background noise, what the ship called "pink noise".

That was the beginning of a lengthy staring into darkness, of her active mind reminding her of her problems and anxieties. She'd planned for it, mentally tallying the things she needed to think through in the long hours, and added to that list when she'd felt the uncomfortable mattress. There were always the sleeping pills if necessary.

She dropped off to sleep at some point, though, and woke to her alarm instead of an hour before it. For a moment she assumed that she'd set it wrong, but it was 0600 station time. More sleep than usual, an unexpected bonus.

She hadn't undressed, and only needed time to wash as cheaply as possible before slipping out the door and down the hall. Here and there, people slept on the floors, and she found the bar full of snoring toughs. There was an impressive kitchen behind the bar, though: four prep tables, two big induction grills and two gas stoves, a couple combo ovens, and sinks with faucets that ran freely. The place was a disaster and smelled of mold, but the equipment still functioned. The Miner threw together a scrounged breakfast of some kind of off-brand artificial egg cooked in a pan that might have been clean, then she wandered out into the lobby eating straight from the pan with a fork. The nice thing about living on emergency rations was that pretty much any edible food tasted good.

She finished half the pan, walking between the sleepers as she ate. The galleria's day lights were coming up gradually, and she could see the scraggly-looking palm trees through the big windows like great big spidery shadows. A cleaning robot buzzed and bumped merrily among the tables, but otherwise she was the only moving thing around. The place was peaceful, almost pleasant.

It was while returning to the kitchen to replace the dirty pan that the Miner heard arguing.

"No way. Just three of us?"

"It'll be fine. As soon as Blue gets back from the can we'll head out."

"They're going around in fours now. I don't want to be outnumbered, I want to outnumber them."

The Miner set the pan gently on the floor and stood with arms folded against the wall next to the door.

"We don't have time. Feeney said to relieve the guys watching the cooks, OK? And he said don't back down from a fight."

"Yeah, cool, fine, but I don't want to get my ass kicked, all right? Let's wake up a couple more guys, see if they can watch our backs."

"Shiiiit. I told you that'll take forever, and that fucker McMasters said he'd arrest groups that are too big."

"So what?"

"So they have stun batons and they fucking hurt, that's what."

"Getting fucking stabbed fucking hurts too."

The Miner waited until she heard a third voice saying, "I'm back, what's wrong with you assholes?" before she turned the corner and the conversation stopped dead.

"I heard you looking for a fourth," she said off-handedly. She rested her hand on the hilt of her sword and yawned. "I could use some exercise."

They fell over themselves to invite her along. None of the three of them looked like much of a fighter, the Miner thought. The girl they'd been waiting on, Blue, looked like a nervous scarecrow with fractal-style blue tattoos and gene-modded hair resembling teal-painted aluminum. She had a kind of makeshift cutlass at her hip, and a couple of knives strapped to her jacket and pants in ways that would make them a pain to draw in a fight, probably literally. The big guy, Khan, saw the Miner looking, made a wrong guess, and confided with a waggle of his thick unibrow, "Rumor is if you get her clothes off she's got bits that glow. Guess what color." Khan was tall and wide but really just big, not muscular. He wore black from head to toe, and fingered a structural spar that had been sharpened down like a heavy machete. A little cartoon cat head on a chain grinned up at her in its pendulum swing. They hurried to explain that Feeney wanted someone to check in on the "cooks", who the Miner took to be making drugs down below on deck six, away from where people lived.

"They don't exactly work for the old man," the heavy-set guy with all the bright red-dyed scars, Scratch, explained as they made for the door. He had some kind of cudgel with faint ridges like they might have come out of a printer, and it only took a few minutes of watching him apparently search for fleas to understand his nickname. "But they agreed to only sell through him."

The Miner nodded thoughtfully. "So the four of us go check on them and make sure Angelica's not horning in. Maybe have some fun if they are."

"Yeah, yeah."

"Make that five," came a voice behind the Miner. Mary Feeney crossed her arms and made clear that five was the right number for that bit of fun. "I want to make sure we're getting our money's worth."

"More the merrier," the Miner said, and wondered whether Mary was keeping tabs on her for her grandfather, or out of her own suspicions.

They set off through the hotel back passages, downstairs and to the door for laundry and deliveries. The Miner let the original three, now comforted and psyched by their honor guard, prattle on about how much ass they were going to kick and how sweet this was all going to be.

"What kind of fighters does Angelica have?" the Miner wondered aloud.

The chorus of response indicated that the other side was so feeble it was amazing they hadn't all blown away with the first really bad fake egg fart. The Miner bit back the question about why old man Feeney was having such a hard time beating them. Instead she thought about some of the rumors. "I heard del Rio's brother's something."

"Raj?" Scratch looked uncomfortable. "Yeah, he's pretty tough, I guess. Not as tough as you, lady. Or you, Mary!"

Mary looked troubled, and stared at the deck as they walked. "Don't go gunning for the brass," she muttered. "Assassination's off-limits. That's from the old man himself."

"All right," the Miner said. "I'll steer clear. Where should I steer clear *of*, just to be sure?"

She snorted. "Transparent. Just don't fight him if you see him. Him or Angelica."

"You'll have to kill Angelica eventually, you know. This two-party thing isn't stable."

"I'm sure you're so sad about that."

The Miner shrugged. "I got paid in advance," she said. "I want you to win so I look good, but I don't actually care."

"Well I care. I fucking live here."

"So do they. Someone's gonna be unhappy."

The three stooges had long since gone quiet, realizing too late that this wasn't going to be as fun an outing with their side's two toughest fighters as they thought.

"Well, Granddad's paying you, so it better not be us."

The Miner yawned. They'd descended a staircase, having independently decided that being stuck in an elevator was a bad idea, and came to a T intersection. They stopped when they heard the hallmark of bad ambushes everywhere: the excited whisper "Here they come!" followed by multiple voices going "shhhhh!" They exchanged looks: the three stooges nervous, Mary cautious, and the Miner exasperated.

"Ours?" Khan murmured. Mary shook her head, no.

"I expected a better class of idiot," the Miner said, not whispering. She popped her sword's magnetic clasps with her thumb, and the *click* echoed down the empty passage.

There was another long silence. A head poked out around the corner and ducked back. Hurried whispering drifted down the hallway, too confused to be made out over the low drone of the ventilation fans, but the syllable "shit!" figured prominently. Then the five of them heard running.

"That was fun," said Mary.

"Ish," said the Miner.

The stooges came down from their adrenaline highs with whoops and laughs, jeering down the passageway at their fleeing foes and slapping each other on the back.

Their party continued on toward hydroponics, or so the Miner assumed as they followed a series of turns that left her disoriented, but which the other four seemed to know well enough to not even pause at the splits. The old military layout was designed to be hard to navigate for anyone not wearing a keyed-in personal nav. She wondered if the others had one, but there were no signs of them listening to sub-audible instructions. They passed old blood stains a couple times, and then a relatively fresh pool, stinking badly. Two trails led from it up the passageway for a long way before fading. The Miner wondered if their janitorial staff had any humans left, and if so how long it would take before they snapped and killed everybody just to have time to catch up. Small bits of trash and other clutter collected in corners and along the walls.

"We're keeping the bots busy," said Blue, probably thinking along the same lines as they passed the clotted dark puddle. "You guess that was one of theirs or ours?"

"Can't tell you apart by the smell of your blood yet," the Miner said.

Ten more steps down the hall, Mary said, "She's joking." The stooges dutifully laughed.

The second ambush was much better. The Miner heard a faint buzzing noise as they entered an intersection with a cross-hallway, and two groups descended on them from both sides.

She'd been walking with her hand resting on her sword; she had it out of her sheath the moment a buzzer sounded, and up in time to deflect a blow from a sledgehammer by way of its bearer's exposed wrist, then to step into the person swinging it down over his head and slice up the length of his torso. One step to the right away from the gout of blood put her in view of three other attackers arrayed behind him. There was a brief moment where they stared each other down. A crackling and buzzing stun baton and two knives waved uncertainly in the air as their hammer-wielding comrade gurgled and whined in pain as he fell to one knee against the wall. The baton-holder immediately behind him made a move, just a twitch, and the Miner lashed out with the tip of her sword, a single stroke up the forearm to tear it open and send the buzzing weapon flying and its wielder stumbling away.

Her combat augments hummed from the exertion, keeping her muscles taut and flushing their cells with micro dose painkillers and nutrients. She had her sword up and looked between the two intact fighters, each holding their knives like they were life rafts. She realized abruptly that she was grinning as she prepared to cut them down.

"Scram!" she yelled, and they turned and ran pell-mell away. The dropped baton spun into the pool of spreading blood where it sizzled and crackled. A hot iron smell assaulted her, humid and cloying.

She turned and surveyed the fight that had commenced behind her, four-on-four. Mary was a competent knife fighter, lean and nimble. The Miner studied her and filed the knowledge away for future reference: she knew when to engage, had a feel for the enemy's reach, and wasn't afraid to get in close when it made her enemies movements more awkward. Definitely one to watch when things got to their inevitable endgame.

The other three were about what she'd expected: enthusiastic amateurs who did a lot of darting forward and backward, waving their weapons like a single touch would wound. Blue had already been tagged and was bleeding from her left shoulder, but was keeping her opponent off by virtue of standing between the taller Khan and the wall, and waving her makeshift cutlass like a feather duster. The Miner watched for a little while, then waded in sword-first.

"Coming in behind," she warned, and did just that, gently elbowing aside two of the fighters so as to step neatly between them and take out their opponents with a single V-shaped stroke from left to right, down across a torso and up against a thigh and upper arm. The flashing blade and resulting screams were enough to let the other two overwhelm their foes; Mary's enemy got the picture and fled, unchased.

"Good," Mary said, and turned to see the body on the floor

behind her and the blood on the deck and wall. She looked a question at the Miner, who swung her sword up once to shake the blood from it in a wide arc spray along the wall, then grabbed a handful of Mary's jacket to wipe off the rest.

"The hell!"

"Didn't bring a hankie," the Miner said, sheathing her weapon. The magnets caught it with a *click* that made the stooges flinch. She looked down at her gray-green jumpsuit, flecked with blood but not badly stained. It'd come out in the wash. The two she'd cut down last lay groaning on the deck, and the guy with the sledgehammer had gone still. "Should we let someone know about these?"

"Angelica already knows, I promise," said Mary. "She can deal with her own dead, but we'd better push on before she does. How's your arm, Blue?"

The scarecrow girl put on a show of toughness, but was weaving from blood loss and pain. The Miner made an impatient noise and poked at the wound, eliciting a high-pitched gasp from between the fighter's clenched teeth. It wasn't deep, but it was bleeding freely. They managed to scavenge cloth from Sledgehammer's shirt to tie it up tight, then they hustled away from the intersection before the survivors could bring in reinforcements. Once they were well away from the sight of bodies and smell of blood, the two unwounded stooges started in on how awesome that was, and precisely how much ass it had kicked. Blue walked woodenly, but quietly kept up.

"What all's down here, anyway?"

Mary glanced at the Miner, suspicious. "Big hydroponics operation. Soy and beans pretty much, and algae and fish. Yeast tanks and bioreactors below that, and reclamation."

"Your grandfather got a hand in it?"

She shook her head. "It's neutral ground. Company Rep and McMasters would shit if we made a move, and anyway, there's no money in it. We pulled out most of what we had in the lower decks, but the geeks down here cooking are too tied into utilities, so we have to keep guards."

"Seems easy to overrun."

"Nah, Mr Shine wouldn't stand for any real fighting. This is just maintaining a presence."

"Who's Mr Shine?"

She ignored her. Khan glanced back with a wary look on his face, but then pretended he hadn't heard.

"What are they cooking, anyway? Amphetamines?" Damn popular among the miners and transport navigators, the kind of people for whom every hour alert and awake meant money.

"All kindsa shit," Scratch contributed, suddenly enthusiastic. "Meth, smack, reds, dust."

"Acid," said Blue.

"Acid," agreed Scratch. "Coke. Crack."

"Roofies," said Khan.

"Roofies. Redeye. Molly. Lizard. Fenty. Thic. All kindsa stuff, and it's all really cheap right now, on account of the old man can't move it after Sparks went for Angelica."

Mary glared at Scratch, but he didn't see it, then she turned her glare on the Miner. "You don't need to know details, just don't get ideas: the geeks down here are ours. You'll probably pull a protection shift if there's trouble, but so far Angelica hasn't touched anyone but the fighters."

"So the passageways are fair game?"

She gave the Miner a distrustful look, but nodded once.

"But," the Miner said, "she won't hit the lab."

"Right."

"Because Mr Shine won't stand for it."

Again the distrustful look. "Right."

"And–"

"Where the fuck have you been?" A scruffy woman in leathers leaned out of a hatchway. "You're fucking la–" She cut herself off and stood up straight when she saw Mary and the Miner trailing the three stooges. "Trouble?"

"Nothing we couldn't handle," said Khan. He grinned. "We pissed 'em off pretty good, though, so, you know, you'll probably all die on the way back."

The leather-clad woman gave them a worried look, but Mary shook her head. "Come back with us. We've got to meet with the reinforcements."

The Miner raised an eyebrow, and wondered what passed for "reinforcements" on Station 35.

REINFORCEMENTS

Geronimo Rommel stamped back and forth in his tiny shared cabin on the rickety old transport ship he'd spent over a week in, crammed practically shoulder to shoulder with all the lowlifes, misfits, and dimwits Station 32 had coughed up. All the idiots who'd been given a choice between a ticket and the brig, who needed to skip town while something else cooled off, or who just wanted a good old-fashioned fight or some cash. Rommel himself was a professional; he did his fighting for money, thank you, and he had three offers to do just that, which he thought was out-fucking-standing. The trouble was, the transport ship's captain had just come on the horn and said they were putting into a boarding orbit on Station 35, and he still hadn't picked one.

"Fuck," he said aloud.

His two bunkmates had been ignoring him for hours, no matter how much noise he made, and he found that irritating. They were not impressed by his three offers, and he found that even more irritating. Eight days in a tiny cabin with a couple of stuck-up assholes who didn't recognize their betters just irritated a man. Here he was, a natural leader of men, fresh off yet another lucrative job, with his hand offered in friendship to his fellow mercenaries, and the idiots just snubbed him. He hadn't even managed to bang any of them, and that irritated him, too.

He pulled his duffel down from the foot of his bunk, the second one up the bulkhead, and slapped it noisily on the communal table. He unzipped it and rummaged to no real purpose, but it gave those jerks a nice view of what he'd brought: an electro-slug rifle, broken down but still pretty obvious; a sawed-off repeating shotgun with bespoke gold inlay on the barrel that read "Gilgamesh" in calligraphic script; two serrated combat knives – he nonchalantly placed one on the table while he rummaged; and a short military-issue tanto blade with a custom embossed gold dragon on the side that looked pretty goddamn wicked. His pad was down at the bottom, where he'd put it before, wrapped in a black shirt. All his clothes were black.

He left the bag ostentatiously gaping as he leaned against the bulkhead, idly swiping through his messages on the gunmetal gray pad. "Three thousand from someone named John Feeney," he mused half-aloud. "That's not bad. Or two thousand from Angelica del Rio, with some interesting perks. Hmmm. Or," he added almost as an afterthought, "thirty-five hundred from some law guy, Thomas McMasters. That's a tough decision, mates."

He happened to glance up at the other two guys in the cabin, each lying on their own bunks. The guy on the bottom bunk, Ng, was curled up with his back to the cabin and a pillow wrapped around his head. The guy up on the top bunk, called himself the Bastard, was watching porn again. Morons.

Rommel zipped up his bag, thumbed the lock, then heaved it up onto the middle bunk again. He stuck the knife in his pocket and grabbed the pad and wandered out into the gangway. The transport ship wasn't that big, and it didn't take long to reach the galley, passing five more cabins full of assholes. He wondered again how much the captain made on this trip. Twenty-two passengers paying two hundred credits apiece plus meals – at least, he assumed they all paid the same fare; they all got on at Station 32 anyway. He frowned, wondering if anyone else had gotten a cheaper fare than him, whether anyone had gotten more invitations to the captain's bunk than he had and shaved some credits off, maybe. Didn't matter, he was getting distracted. Call it forty thousand credits and whatever salable stuff people forgot, or "forgot", when they got off. There was the captain, an engineer, and a cook who was also a pilot. The ship was former military – while it didn't smell like cabbage and washed-away puke, its origin was unmistakable – which meant expensive but reliable. He kept trying to do the math in his head for how much profit a guy could make each trip, and how much he'd need to start off, but all the "maybes" and "ballparks" piled up and in the end he wasn't sure if the captain was a millionaire or deep in debt. He shook his head. A soldier of fortune like himself ought to have a retirement plan, but better not to obsess over it. Be loose, flexible, see what drops in your lap, that was the way to do it.

"I'm thinking Feeney," said Artemis, a buff chick with no hair anywhere on her, and a fondness for knives. "The guy with the hotel. The del Rio woman with the casino sounds stingy as hell, and I haven't slept on a proper bed in ages."

Rommel went for the coffee dispenser, pretending not to listen to the conversation around the galley table. There were a couple of "me too"s.

"Nix," came the first dissent, a gangly gunman named Huey with some really interesting implants that gave tiny electric shocks. "Ever seen how casinos are built? Cameras and stuff everywhere, those places are locked down tighter than prisons. Maybe it pays less, but I call that a safe gig, me."

"Then we ain't supposed to 'fraternize' anymore," Artemis said, waggling her forehead where her eyebrows would've been.

"Didn't sign nothing yet," Huey said with a leer. "You want to go… counter-offer?"

Rommel lost track of that conversation when a couple more people going for Angelica del Rio started to explain themselves too, all at the same time.

"Anyone going for this McMasters guy?" he called out.

Two cautious hands went up, a guy and a girl he didn't know by name. He studied their sheepish faces and just grunted.

Nobody asked him in turn as he poured his lousy coffee, and that was just as well since he didn't really have an answer yet anyway. The slow realization that they'd all, or almost all, gotten three offers annoyed him. He tried casually to peer over shoulders at pads, wristmons, and ink on hands, and at least he'd been offered more than them. A lot more than some of them. A few probably wouldn't even make back the cost of the trip.

He stood back, sipped the thin mud pissed out by the machine and frowned at the room. They'd spent the whole week boasting about their fighting skills, and as someone who had actually seen combat he had mostly considered it idle chatter. But now that the ship full of miscellaneous mercenaries was actually at its destination he gave them a second look and wasn't sure what he saw. They were amateurs, most of them. A few had unit or platoon tats, but none of them looked authentic. Still, they were all pretty athletic, and looked like scrappers. Some wiry, some beefy.

He could take them down if he had to or wanted to, but some of them would go down hard, he had to admit. Trouble was, there was no telling where they'd go to, or who he'd wind up fighting. No rhyme or reason to who got offers from the gangs or from security. Hell of a place, this Station 35.

Something else bothered him. He'd gotten desperately bored enough to look at the telescope view of the station, and he recognized a beat-up old mining ship that he was pretty sure belonged to a beat-up old intelligence corps officer who flipped the 'verse two birds at the end of her last mission and went off to work the remotest patch she could find. He didn't want to cross her path if he could avoid it, that was a lethal kind of mistake even for a badass like him. Probably she wasn't involved, but if she was, who was she in with? Security, probably, knowing her. Probably. He remembered something else about her: she'd taught him about this guy Sun Tzu, who said, "if you know your enemy and you know yourself, you have nothing to worry about." Or something like that. With all these "probablys" stacking up, though, he was starting to feel like he didn't know shit.

No two ways about it, all his instincts told him this was a bad job.

"Hey." The captain showed up in the hatchway. She had a worried look on her face, and her eyes were scanning the room. "Just so you know. Chief of Security on this station just gave me a heads-up that there's a blanket firearms ban on Station 35. Anything that shoots, gets confiscated. Anyone who tries to smuggle onboard anything that shoots, gets spaced."

She put her hands up like she could quell the shouts of outrage. Rommel frowned hard. Gilgamesh had set him back two whole jobs' worth of profits, and it was worth a lot more than that after his mods. It had saved his sorry ass on at least three occasions.

"Don't bitch at me, it's not my rule. Take it up with McMustard or whoever he is. What?"

"What if we go to work for McMasters?" some kid asked. "He's the security guy right? Or is that Feeney?"

"He didn't say. Ask him yourself; we're on the station network now, so there's no comm fees." She folded her arms and unfolded them again. "Look, I'm no arms dealer and I don't want to be. But anything you want to sell me, I'll try to pay a fair price. It's that or take your chances, that's as good as I can give you, all right?"

Rommel watched the groaning crowd and caught the arm of a good-looking tough guy with no neck. Fergus, was that what he called himself? Looked and talked like he might plausibly have been ex-military, too. "Hey," Rommel murmured. "Did I hear you say you hadn't gotten an offer from McMasters?"

"What's it to you?" the guy rumbled.

"I think that stinks," Rommel said, keeping his voice low and his smile friendly. "And I got a proposition for you."

MURDER, MAYBE?

Mary led the way back and didn't seem to notice or mind that the Miner lagged behind. She watched Feeney's granddaughter, flanked by three tired toughs, as she navigated back passages through a circuitous route that would probably avoid trouble. Deck six was down deep in the station, close to what she thought was Mr Shine's territory, him and his people who called themselves Morlocks, but she didn't see much evidence that anyone still lived or worked there.

The Miner mused as she walked, decided one option was to come back that night. 3am station time, maybe, if everyone was asleep. Explosives would do the trick. Nice empty corner of the station. Relieve the guards – they'd believe Feeney would send just her to relieve three of them, at least they'd believe it long enough for her to take care of them. Take care of the chem geeks. Set the explosives somewhere impressive but safe. Safe-ish. Work of an hour, and she'd be back at the hotel ready to help the enraged old man get his revenge on "that witch".

The Miner didn't ask what route they were taking, and Mary didn't explain. She played the good little bodyguard, watching the boss's granddaughter because the others were too tired, stupid, and feckless to. She found herself tempted.

Off Mary Feeney, and it would drive John Feeney spare. From idle talk she'd gathered that his family was his one major weakness. If he thought Angelica's goons had done her, or grabbed her, whatever peace there was would be over. Herrera would have his excuse pretty damn fast. It might solve the McMasters problem, too: either the mustachioed twerp would get steamrolled, or he'd sense the change in the wind and do his damn job.

She liked the idea, liked it a lot, and yet somehow found herself not murdering anyone. The five of them walked briskly but quietly, and all seemed to keep breathing.

Her first rationalization was that Feeney going spare might go way over the top. Might even flat-out win. But that was nonsense; she could handle him, if by no other way than through switching sides.

Her second rationalization was that despite herself, she liked Mary Feeney. The kid was too clever by half, and even kind of fun when she had a drink and loosened up. But she was also an enthusiastic and capable part of a criminal gang that had destroyed a lot of lives and livelihoods. She was more serious than her blustering and fickle grandfather, which made her dangerous as hell. Anyway, the Miner had met a lot of corrupt SOBs in her time behind enemy lines. She'd liked them too, and knew not to get sentimental. Besides, she also liked Takata and Herrera, and this was their home, too.

Her third rationalization, probably the real one, was harder to express to herself. She'd killed in cold blood before, sure. She'd killed for flag and country and other bullshit; she'd killed to survive and for advantage. And then she'd bought a ship and some mining equipment, and set herself to a life alone with plants, books, and rocks. Yeah, it was also before getting ripped off by some little toads and coming face to face with a lot of people who really had it coming. But if she wanted to just kill people, she could make a hell of a lot more money just doing that. She was giving the toads a chance, at least. It might not be a fair fight, but it never was.

She continued to ponder her ethical position, until Mary stopped abruptly with one finger in the air. All it would take is a couple more steps, pretend to not be paying attention, to be caught up short, then have her sword out and cut them down before they knew what was happening. Her sword stayed sheathed, and she halted in her tracks.

"Good news," Mary said. She turned and smiled. "Transport ship's in, and we managed to hire about half the crop."

The Miner frowned. "What do you mean?"

"We made offers to everyone aboard, crew included. A bunch of them signed up."

"How many?"

Mary smirked. "Afraid of the competition? Too many and not enough. You want to count them, get moving." She paused, giving the Miner a speculative look. "Why don't you take the lead."

Geronimo Rommels

The transport ship airlock finished its cycle while the assemblage of aspiring goons loitered with duffle bags slung over shoulders and bored looks masking varying stages of anxiety. Gases whooshed through tubes and vents, heavy metal doors slammed together and squealed as unlubricated areas dragged. When the massive doors finally opened, light poured in from the dock to frame a mustachioed blonde man in a black uniform with his hands behind his back.

Black-uniformed guards rushed up to them and began a hurried search. Patdowns, detector wands, straight-up opening and rifling bags. Knives, swords, drugs, were left alone. The new arrivals snarled and grumbled, but they'd been warned to expect it, and at least it went fast. Security moved from front to back haphazardly, searching some people twice and others not at all, and more than one of the fighters kicked themselves for not trying to smuggle their guns through.

"Welcome to Captain John Wayne Koganusan Station," the man barked in a less than welcoming manner as his crew retreated behind him. Rommel recognized the clear signs of stick-up-ass syndrome. "I cannot by Anaconda Consolidated policy prevent you from boarding this station, but I can damn well make sure you know and obey my rules."

At that point, every attention wandered, and nobody – including the man's own fidgeting, nose-picking honor guard – heard his lengthy lecture about fighting, gunplay, and getting spaced. They'd each gotten their own instructions, anyway, which had included (from Feeney) "don't piss off McMasters, just smile and nod until he finally shuts up, don't bring a gun aboard, and get yourself to my hotel as soon as you can." Or (from Angelica) "Ignore the lecture from station security. Sell your firearms before boarding the station if you can; otherwise write them off as a loss. Come singly or in pairs to the Lady Luck Casino without attracting undue attention." The few who had gained employment with McMasters himself were told, "I will provide an edifying lecture on station security rules and procedures; you need not attend to it yourself, as it does not apply to you, but pay close attention to make sure the others do."

Geronimo Rommel scratched his ass while he listened to the more-interesting drone of a ventilation fan with a bad bearing that kind of had an off-kilter on-again off-again rattle a little like a tiny drum solo. He hefted a duffle bag that barely concealed a stolen fire axe, wrapped in his underwear so that he figured nobody would investigate too closely. He was pretty sure that was a genius move, the most recent of several, and congratulated himself on it again as he walked as nonchalantly as a badass like him could with the group heading for the Ad Astra hotel. Three thousand credits, here he came.

Geronimo Rommel, meanwhile, grinned like an idiot and shuffled his way toward the casino through the galleria, glancing up at all the other fighters trying – and failing, ha! – to look inconspicuous as they moseyed out with him toward del Rio's meeting point. He glanced over at that McMasters guy, who kinda fumed and tried to glare in every direction at once.

Finally, only two toughs remained standing in the port. A rough-looking woman with a shotgun openly displayed on her shoulder. Despite a natural disinclination to hard thinking, Rommel was carefully considering his position. He ran his hand over his head in a sheepish gesture, then on an impulse offered it to McMasters to shake. "Geronimo," he rumbled, talking slowly as though unfamiliar with the shape of the word. "At your service. Only, I go by Fergus Capper, if you don't mind. A guy like me can't be too careful with his real name."

McMasters hesitated before taking it, then pumped it with some enthusiasm. "Of course, of course, Mr 'Capper'. I got your message, I merely forgot. Good to have another military man on the crew." He stopped and stepped back to get a better look at them, his face reflecting conflicted thoughts. "Two's enough," he said aloud, and obviously didn't believe it. "The cream of the crop, anyway. You must be Sinthia, then? Welcome, both of you. Let's get you into uniform and on the roster."

Rommel lay back on his bunk, the only bunk in one of the transport ship's few private cabins. He counted his credits again and reminded himself that two thousand profit for doing nothing but staying on board a ship for a couple weeks without risking his hide or his guns, that was worth some cabin fever. Let those other three jerks take the risks, if they were so keen to get their fight on. That Sun Tzu guy said to fight if circumstances were favorable, and if they weren't... well, all right, he didn't explicitly say to sell your identity three times and run away if circumstances sucked, but Rommel felt that the old buzzard would have approved.

He just had a single moment of doubt, wondering what would happen when his old friend on the mining ship got wind he'd been in the area. Might have been friendly to say hi, maybe. But he had to grin at the idea of her stumbling on one of those chumps wearing his own illustrious name. He wondered which one it would be.

The docking clamps finally released with hull-shaking thumps. His smile broadened as he listened to the chatter of a handful of voices relieved at getting the hell off Station 35. They sounded tense. Unhappy. In need of some relaxation. They needed a good solid dose of Vitamin R, of which he, Geronimo Rommel, was the universe's only source.

A JOB

"Jane!" Feeney leaned over the stairway to loom above the small crowd. The newcomers had shuffled in full of anxious bravado and been introduced around. Looked like a half-dozen new fighters, bedraggled and lean from the long spaceflight. The dregs and leftovers of the grimiest stations, washed out of some navy or merchant fleet, or on the run. Bloodshot dark-ringed eyes full of cunning, fingers always straying toward weapons. The Miner had been sitting, bored, as the various goons, new and old, tried their best to impress each other with stories about their martial and sexual prowess on the one hand and pharmaceutical tolerance on the other. One grinning moron crowed that he'd saved up and was having a chainsaw printed.

Feeney located her and fixed his eyes down on her from the railing. "Lend me one of your expensive hands, won't you? One of my generous supporters isn't feeling so forthcoming. Whyn't you take a couple of my new boys and girls and go put this gentleman in the giving mood?"

The Miner scratched her neck, feeling a weight in the pit of her stomach. "Who?"

"Man named Peder Finn, a few decks down. Does some distilling. He used to share his profits like a good little boy, and I always rewarded him with brisk business, very brisk. But lately, not a credit..."

Feeney's smiling face had some tightness behind it, she thought. Angry at something. When she'd stared back at him long enough that he looked like he might say something, she nodded once to acknowledge the order.

That name rang a bell, and the association with booze clinched it. She'd liked Finn, but cover was cover. "You, you, you," she said, pointing out three seedy, rough, and less-than toothy specimens, ones who'd been boasting about busting heads and robbing locals. She had no idea if they were new or not. "Can you beat someone up without killing him?"

They exchanged lazy amused looks. "Probably not," the short pimply one said with a leer.

"Good enough."

The Miner walked so fast they had to jump to keep up. She took the service exit into the back halls, then the back doors into the big circular corridor that Blue, Khan and the others had led her through. She wasn't totally sure of the route, but she mumbled something about avoiding patrols, and that was apparently enough to bluff the three clowns into thinking she knew where she was going. Anyway, she had a map in her heads-up display now, and the roundabout route gave her time to think.

They grumbled about her decision to take an elevator down – Mary had drilled into them that they were ambush risks, and while she admired the tactical thinking, she was firm. "Anyone dumb enough to mess with the four of us, they'll get what's coming." That seemed to mollify them. She wanted time to think and look, and from the back of the elevator she finally got a good view of her three companions.

The biggest and meanest of the three, the guy who'd boasted about being on the run for killing three people, carried a kind of mace-looking weapon that looked like it'd been printed from a medieval recreation catalogue. It had a fat four-sided metal head with sharpened corners. His bare arms had some serious muscle to them, but she thought he looked like a gym rat more than a fighter: strong, but slow.

The skinny nervous-looking one looked to be a knife-fighter, maybe even a good one. She was on some kind of stimulant, judging by the way her eyes darted, pupils narrowed to dots, and she couldn't keep her long nimble fingers off her knives. She kept half-unsheathing them, showing a couple centimeters of scratched and pitted blade, then shoving them back in.

The last one, short and pimply, had a fire axe that reminded her of that punk of Angelica's she'd had to kill. The axe wasn't sharpened and it looked like it hadn't been used, but he fingered its edge with a dreamy look, and she remembered he'd told a story of beating the shit out of a lawyer like it was the funniest thing in the world. The goons had cackled as he'd stumblingly relayed how he'd demanded "the password" off the poor jerk who tried to insist it was some kind of mistake.

Two slow fighters, she decided, with maybe some power behind them, and one quick one.

"Looking forward to a proper fight?" The Miner forced some cheer into her voice.

"Damn right," said the mace-wielder. He spun the weapon in his hand so that the sharpened edges caught the wan industrial light. "All this tiptoeing around, not wanting to make waves around that security fucker who took my guns. Makes me puke."

The other two made approving noises and offered sage observations such as "fuck that guy", and the Miner nodded.

They'd all been on edge, and she could tell her own presence keyed them up worse. The elevator lurched as it halted, making her drop into a crouch, and the doors shuddered open. She tried not to think about how long it had been since it'd seen any kind of maintenance, even before the fighting started. Of course, anything that put it out of commission would knock out gravity too, she was pretty sure. Probably. She ushered her crew out quickly.

The heads-up map showed a couple twists to the corridor, with Finn's compartment taking up a good chunk of reconfigured space well ahead. They walked for a minute before the Miner raised her hand and brought the company to a halt. It was a good spot, without sight lines in most directions thanks to those twists in the corridor and a strangely built-out living compartment. No hatches in sight. They'd passed a few security cameras, most obviously defunct, but there weren't any in view here.

"Something seems off," she said. They looked at her with naked apprehension. She pointed to the guy with the axe. "I don't like it. Go up ahead and check it out. Don't run, don't fight. Just walk out, look, and come right back. Go slow."

He looked relieved when she said "don't fight", and when she finished her instruction he nodded sharply and turned the corner. With him gone, she visibly relaxed and turned to the guy with the mace. "That's a hell of a weapon," she said. "While we're waiting, you mind if I take a swing?"

He grinned broadly, showing gaps and broken teeth and sharing some impressively bad breath. "If you think you can lift it." He hefted it one-handed and she dutifully gave it a dubious look. She eyed it up and down, to his evident amusement.

"Hold this," she told the knife fighter, who had to quickly put her knives away in order to take the Miner's sheathed sword with the clasp locked. Freed of that, the Miner made a show of stretching both hands and accepted the mace. It was heavy enough as it was, but she exaggerated its heft and the two goons laughed as she let it almost hit the deck. She grinned good-naturedly, feeling familiar tightness and warmth in her elbows, wrists, and shoulders as her augments gave her a little extra strength. Not much, just a notice that they'd been engaged, a friendly warning that if she overdid it they'd tear her muscles, stretch her tendons, and snap her ligaments like forgotten dock tethers.

The mace's owner chuckled as she visibly struggled to lift the weapon upright, and she showed her genuine appreciation for the craft that went into the weapon. It was newly printed, she saw, and well-balanced. She raised it unsteadily, then turned and smashed the knife fighter on the top of her head, bringing it down as hard as her augments could manage, then spun and slammed the butt of the weapon into its owner's gut.

Tossing the mace, she pulled the knife from its scabbard on her thigh, and drove the blade into the man's throat. They died with a clatter but no other noise, and she had to step back fast from the rapidly-spreading blood. She grabbed her sword back and after a moment plucked the mace one-handed from the path of the blood, marveling at the impressive dent it had put in the deck. Then she stood at the corner.

She waited, heart pounding and listening hard until she heard faint steps. When the punk turned the corner, she brained him too.

After taking a moment to breathe and collect herself, the Miner leaned over the blood to put the mace next to its owner's hand, swapped out the knife in his neck for one off the knife-fighter's jacket, then sprinted for the elevator. She hated to put herself in that contraption again, but it gave her a minute to examine herself, wipe some blood spatter from her face and hands, clean and sheathe the knife, and put on a properly bored expression. She got into her computer's messaging system and dictated a few quick alterations. By then the doors opened and she needed to start walking.

She didn't hurry back to the hotel despite the overwhelming urge to run. She tossed the bloodied cloth in a corner, checked that it hadn't re-soiled her fingers. The rear doors opened for her and the couple of toughs hanging out there perked up but let her pass. She went straight through the still-milling crowd of toughs and soldiers awkwardly chatting each other up, to Feeney's office. She knocked once and let herself in.

Feeney looked up from his desk, surprised and blinking.

"Well?" she said, sounding impatient. "What's up?"

"I... Done already? By God, you do fast work–"

She frowned. "No, I'm not done. You called me back. What's up?"

"I did no such thing."

"'Come back. Just you. Trouble. F.'" She read from her message screen. "It's from you, or at least it says it is. You didn't send it?"

He stood, wide-eyed and alarmed. "No!"

The Miner swore loudly and turned to run.

They're All Dead

Screwball tried not to look at the bodies on the floor and tried not to step in the blood and tried not to laugh at Ditz, stoned and pathetically fighting off the cleaning robot with poorly placed kicks.

"What the hell are you doing? Stop that, you idiot," Feeney snapped, and then paid Ditz no more mind. He went back to staring down at the three dead people on the deck and the huge pool of stinking blood. That was one of the new guys right off the transport ship. Duff, Screwball was pretty sure he'd been called, when he forced himself to look. And the chick was Siobhan. Shiv. He'd slept with her once. Feeney had collected Screwball and Ditz and three more of them, plus the lady with the sword, and brought them straight to this carnage. He'd made them go through the bodies' pockets for credit chips, and then had just began staring.

"Well?" the old man finally snapped at the swordswoman, Jane. "What is this?"

She looked at him blankly. "They're dead."

"Brilliant, Holmes. Any other deductions?"

She stared down at the bodies, and looked as blank and dumbfounded as Screwball felt. The old man had been giving the corpses a suspicious look. After a long uncomfortable silence, Feeney clucked his tongue against his teeth.

"I'm disappointed, my dear Mick. I really am. Hand me your sword, will you?"

Screwball saw her hesitation even if the old man didn't. She fiddled with the release at her belt while looking up at Feeney and the rest of them with an expression that made him want to be elsewhere. Then, after another moment where he wasn't sure he was breathing, the sword was up and away from her hip, still sheathed.

Feeney took it without really looking at her, and instead examined the weapon in its black fabric sheath. He weighed it in his hands, then used it as a stick to lift Duff's arm away from the mace and drop it again, and then to nudge the knife still embedded in the poor bastard's throat. It made his whole head wiggle.

"I'm getting tired of traitors," Feeney said in a mild tone, almost conversationally. Screwball felt a chill go down his spine, and even Ditz seemed to sober up. He kicked the cleaning robot again, but didn't put much spirit into it. Feeney stared down at the bodies, his face pale and his lips pursed tightly so that they were white. He didn't look up to see the effect his words were having on his bodyguards. He ignored them all, poking his dead soldiers with the sheathed sword.

He stood a long while with the sword wedged under Shiv's arm. Screwball found himself staring into the reflection of the overhead lights in the dark glistening blood, and he jumped when the old man let the woman's dead arm fall. He returned the sword to its owner without comment, and she hung it on her belt.

"This fellow killed the others," Feeney said, louder than before, and confident. "Got the drop on that one, what did you call him, Squealer? Must've figured he couldn't take you and them together, Jane, even if he got the jump on you."

"He wouldn't have got the jump on me," she said, and from the look on her face, Screwball believed her.

Feeney went on like he hadn't heard her. "If he'd pulled this off he could have hidden the bodies and we'd have assumed all three of them dead, and you the last to see them. He'd have gotten a nice bonus from that witch." He sneered.

"Witch?" The swordswoman looked confused. "Angelica?"

"Of course Angelica! My God. All these new people, it must have been only too easy to bribe one to pretend to join up. I should have tried it myself. Damn. Not a brilliant plan, mind, but not bad. No, not bad."

She gave him a wary look that Screwball couldn't quite understand. It looked like she was reacting to unexpected good news, almost. "So she was trying to frame me for this?"

Feeney sighed. "Well, I didn't hire you for your brains, did I. She was trying to frame you, surely. Homicidal witch must have thought she could set me against you and kill two good soldiers in one stroke. But for this fine lass..." He nodded his chin at Shiv, then let out another great sigh. "There'll be a reckoning for this, believe you me. The witch's little spies want to play rough? Well, I was playing the hard game before she was born, winning it. Let the robots have them," he barked, turning on his heels. "We've no use for corpses. Come on."

A Visit to Finn

The Miner finally let herself relax. "Homicidal witch must have thought she could set me against you and kill two good soldiers in one stroke," Feeney went on. "But for this fine lass..." He nodded at the twitchy little knife fighter, who seemed to have become a heroine in death just like the guy with the mace had become a villain. The Miner wondered what they'd have made of their posthumous roles. Probably preferred they not be posthumous.

"Let the robots have them," Feeney said, snapping her out of her thoughts. "We've no use for corpses. Come on."

The five bodyguards he'd brought seemed all too glad to step away from the blood and the stink. The stoned one grudgingly let the cleaning robot get by him, and it gleefully plunged into the mess, splashing and guzzling into some internal tank. The Miner stayed put.

"I'll be along in a bit," she said. "I still need to talk to Peder Finn about his donations."

Feeney looked at her with a kind of wonder. "Aye," he said finally. "That you do. I'm glad someone's got their eye on the bottom line. Why don't you take two..." He looked nervous then, and glanced up around them. They all seemed to have felt suddenly very aware of how far they were from the hotel. Feeney looked relieved when she shook her head.

"I'll do it on my own this time. If he's not feeling generous I'll drag him out here for some inspiration."

Feeney raised his eyebrows at her. The bodyguards looked a little put off, themselves. "You're a cold one, my girl," he said, and it sounded like respect. "Don't kill him."

Big white tanks lined the walls of the enormous space the map marked as Finn's place. They hung from the ceiling, looming metal cylinders that tapered down to tapped points, each with a readout and controls, and each big enough to shove a person into. They dripped and the place stank of malt and alcohol, a heavy molasses fug that was oppressive in the humidity. The low hum she'd heard in the passageway had grown to a rumble as she got closer, and inside the room she felt it through the floor.

She walked softly, peering in and around the various tanks, looking for labels but finding none. The tanks were numbered, but that meant nothing. The smell grew strong enough that she wondered whether she was getting a contact buzz just from inhaling the fumes. A dozen steps into the long room and she stopped. She took her sheathed sword from her belt and rapped the hilt against one of the pipes. Droplets of blood flew and splattered the walls. The deep clanging echoed, and a moment later a familiar short wiry guy poked his head in from a side door, his bald dome beading sweat. His eyes went wide on seeing her.

"Hello, hello," he said, looking like he was about to bolt. "I didn't, ah, I didn't hear you come in."

"I'm quiet," she said, raising her voice to be heard over the low rumble. "We met earlier, at Takata's bar."

His expression took a moment to register recognition, like he was on a time delay, but then his nervous face split into a crooked-toothed grin. "Yes, yes, yes. Hi! Did he send you?"

"No," she said casually. "Feeney did."

The brief relaxation turned to obvious panic. She held up a hand to calm him, the one not holding the sword.

"I don't care what he wants," she said, keeping her tone friendly. "I'm not going to do anything to you. But I'm curious why you stopped paying him off."

"Well..." He still looked like he wanted to jump and run. He looked around the room instead of answering her, like goons might spring out from between the tanks. "Truth is, truth is I'm broke."

She frowned. "Didn't Takata just buy some vodka off you?"

"He did. He did. Good stuff. But 'buy' isn't the right word. Barter, you see, barter. He'll make me dinner sometimes, give me some beer. I really do get tired of vodka, even drinking it. I tried mixing it with a bunch of stuff, but it never comes out very good."

"Like the gin?"

He made a face full of resentment, but didn't dispute it.

"So Feeney won't take payment in booze?"

He looked surprised. "It never came up. He buys it back off me with the credits he makes me cough up."

The Miner rubbed her chin. "Lot of people bartering these days?"

"Everyone, everyone. If you keep too many credits on-hand, Angelica or Feeney come tax you. I think the security guy tips them off. The Company Rep's letting us pay our rent a little at a time, and she doesn't know how much space I'm using now. If we ever have too much money, we can buy stuff off Mr Shine." He turned and waved at a shelf full of electronics and tools. The Miner frowned at it.

"What do you need a radiation-hardened multimeter for?"

"Nothing. Nothing. But Mr Shine'll buy it back, pretty much same price. And he won't tell, probably because of the chicken pox."

She blinked. "...chicken pox?"

"Yeah, yeah, he said Feeney and Angelica had chicken pox. It was weird. I thought it was weird."

She tilted her head and looked at the little man. If he was having her on, he had a damn fine poker face. "Do you mean he said, 'A pox on both your houses'?"

"That's it. Yup, yup. So he won't let on when I have cash."

"So why aren't you under his protection?"

Finn looked bashful all of a sudden. He scratched the back of his head. "It's complicated. Complicated, you know."

"You used to work for Feeney, too." The flinch told her she'd scored. "And you and this guy Shine didn't get along."

"That might be, it might." He gave her a hard look. "So you're collecting for Feeney, that it?"

She shrugged. "Yes and no. I can't go back empty-handed."

"So what, you're going to beat me up again?"

She shook her head. "Nah. I was more thinking... What happened to that batch of gin?"

He looked horrified for a second, then grinned.

"But I do have a price," she said. "I want to talk to this Mr Shine."

SHINY

The Miner stayed at the back of the hotel lobby and watched the newcomers mixing awkwardly. She was curious what Feeney meant when he had promised to "show them the ropes," and was only a little disappointed that it turned out to be mostly Feeney waving away complaints that their fancy guns had been taken away, and making grand promises. Then pretty much everyone got drunk.

The evening wound on and got drunker and rowdier. They toasted their fallen heroic comrade, whose name turned out to be Siobhan, and booed the makeshift villain, whose name turned out to be Dopp or something. She never did find out the other poor jerk's name. Some twitchy little creep was trying to get people interested in helping him get the printers to make him a chainsaw. A few patrol shifts staggered out, in bigger groups now and heavily armed; they came back blooded and thirsty. The Miner wasn't offered many drinks; she took a few to be friendly and poured them out into the fake plants without making much effort to not be seen. Nobody seemed to care. The acrid odors of various pharmaceuticals afire crossed her nostrils and she moved a couple times to avoid a contact high or worse. They pretty much left her alone, and she was fine with that.

When she judged them at about the right spot for it, she unveiled the gin. Feeney had groaned, but accepted her earnest explanation that Finn had no cash, and when she pretended to be proud of herself he didn't have the booze-soaked heart to not write off the debt. Mary stood by and smirked, a nice bonus.

The welcome party wound down when Feeney went upstairs out of exasperation with the sudden uptick in puking; pairs and trios gave each other suggestive looks as they wandered off to dark corners, a few fistfights broke out and ended in mutual exhausted collapse, and others just passed out wherever they happened to be. The Miner wasn't tired – her implants could keep her up for days if she let them – and anyway she had finally gotten the ping from Finn.

She slipped out the back without too much trouble. There were guards asleep in easy chairs at the service entrance, behind makeshift barricades of tables and gym mats. There was another watch point by the stairs, that was new. It was also abandoned already. She thought she knew which directions the patrols went, but didn't put it past Mary to hide some of them. So she went quietly, but maintained an air that she had every right to be where she was.

Feeney's crew had simply destroyed the cameras around their territory; the Miner had pieced together that the alternative was to be spied on by either del Rio or McMasters or both. It was six flights down before she saw one intact and with a lit power indicator. She stopped and watched it a while, thinking. Feeney wouldn't know about her visit, but who else would? In the end, she decided that this close to Shine's territory it was here with his blessing, so destroying it might cause complications. She willed her legs back into movement, and continued her descent.

Down in the bottom decks the pipes were bigger and louder, and the conduits were as thick as her leg. Outside of the stairwells and in the maze of passageways, the Miner felt like she was in the digestive system of a giant, an unpleasant sensation not helped by humidity so high water beaded on the cold water and gas pipes, or by the various smells like combustion and fermentation. Finn's instructions hadn't been the best, but it was hard to get too lost: *just go down, and they'll find you.*

She could hear footsteps on the other side of the pipes as she walked. Scurrying movements, sudden. She kept walking, pretending to pay them no heed even as a chill ran down her back. Whispering from ahead. A white-haired head poked out briefly, then ducked back behind the ductwork.

"You lost?"

She turned, cursing herself for not having heard someone come up behind her. He was a big guy, heavyset and middle-aged but in good shape. He wore dirty coveralls and had a badly-shaved head that left little tufts here and there in the hard-to-reach places. His broad stubbled chin jutted out like he was about to object to something. He held a good-sized shotgun in his thick-fingered hands. Something about his heavy frame, his level incurious gaze, and the way he carried himself reminded her of a bull. He'd worn a tuxedo before, and was the guy she'd come looking for.

"You're Mr Shine," she said, only partly a question. Behind him, people began filling the corridor. They came from hatches she hadn't seen, in the walls, in the deck, in the ceiling. Lined faces, some gray or thin hair. Grim expressions, and hands holding wrenches and pipes and guns. She could hear them shuffling in behind her, too.

"I'm the SOB they call that," Shine rumbled. "I hate that nickname."

"Sorry. That's what Takata called you."

He frowned, and moved his jaw forward even further. "Kenichi Takata?"

She bit back the impulse to ask if there was another one. "That's him. What do I call you?"

"My name is Mohammed Shinagawa, but I think that ship has flown. Shine'll do. From what I've been hearing and the vids they've been sharing round, you must be Mick. Or Jane."

She nodded, and continued looking him over. The shotgun hadn't wavered while they were talking, not that she was necessarily planning to take it away from him. The pipes vented something humid and effluent, but it didn't seem to bother him so she didn't let it bother her. She'd come looking for him, but having found him, he had the look of someone who had something to say.

"You're a pain in my ass," he said after ruminating on it, cocking his head. "A shit-stirrer. I don't like you." Some of the faces behind him nodded, but she mentally filed away the fact that some didn't; some looked troubled when he said it.

"I didn't ask you to like me."

He snorted and the tip of the shotgun's barrel dipped and rose a finger's breadth. "You came within arm's reach. That's asking me to like you."

"Fair enough," she said. "You going to shoot me?"

He looked surprised, then faintly sheepish. "Not planning to, just... I don't know, making conversation. Keeps things friendly. What do you want?"

The Miner folded her arms and studied the man. He cleaned up well, she knew that from the pictures around the hotel. He was pretty imposing in person. Maybe he still had the tux. "You ever think about running this station?"

He raised his eyebrows. "That's a dangerous question."

"There's a dangerous answer to it."

"There aren't any answers to it that aren't dangerous, I'm thinking."

The corner of her mouth lifted. "Then there's no special harm in any one of them." He still looked like he had something to say, but this time she cut him off. "Feeney and Angelica aren't stable, Shine. They both think they're clever." He snorted again at that, but it wasn't disagreement. "They both think they can win. And that's not going to end well. I figured you knew that when you came down here. I figured they knew it." She pointed with her chin at the small grimy crowd behind him, and they seemed taken aback at being acknowledged. "So let me be blunt. I can clear those two away. But if I leave a power vacuum, will you fill it, or just let things go to hell?"

He didn't answer right away. "I'm a casino man," he said at last. "I understand risk, and I'm comfortable with it. They're not. Del Rio thinks risk is something to be stamped out. John thinks you grab hold of the most interesting risk and go along for the ride. Neither one's right."

"She's too cautious, he's too incautious. I've noticed."

"I bet you have. Me, I know that risk is something to be evened out. You've got to lay your bets if you want to get ahead, but you don't have to go all in. You just have to see things for what they are. For example, I don't trust a hired gun who uses words like 'incautious'." He grinned to show he was kidding, or to pretend he was. "A brain behind a trigger is another risk to my mind, maybe a big one."

"She might notice you didn't answer her dangerous question, maybe?"

He lapsed back into silence. "Do I ever think about running this station? I do run this station. We do. We keep the children from playing the games that might get too dangerous. They'll stab each other and shoot each other, but they won't get into the air or water, they won't destroy the food supply. Tom McMasters won't touch us. Even the Company Rep and the station master don't bother us."

"You're helping it grind on," she said, aware now that she wasn't just addressing him. "If it grinds on long enough, this place'll die."

"No it won't. Some powerful people don't want it to. *We* don't want it to." He leaned the shotgun back against his shoulder and jutted his chin out. "What you're really asking is, do I want to run the fun bits? Not just the casino, but the long games and the salvage ops, the light touches and the old man's other little enterprises. You want to know if I want to be called 'boss', is that right? Balls to that. I just want my casino back. And I'll get it back if I'm patient. Fortunately for you, being patient means not shooting one of Feeney's people, even if I think she has it coming."

If the Miner didn't understand herself to be dismissed, she got the message when he turned and left. He didn't have to shoulder his way through the Morlocks, but they closed ranks behind him. That wall of grimly-determined bodies, and the noises behind her of the corridor emptying out, made it clear which direction they wanted her to go, and she obliged. Anyway, that was the answer she wanted.

THE SPIDER IN HER WEB

Angelica del Rio sat upright in her bed. By the time she woke all the way up, the jolt of adrenaline was just starting to wear off but still left her heart pounding and muscles tensed. The first thing on her sleep-addled mind when the alarm went off was that her brother was in trouble. When she calmed down enough to shake off the panic and look at the monitor, though, it had been a different alert – someone was in the stairwell behind Feeney's hotel going down to the Morlocks.

She frowned at the image of Feeney's new fighter, alone. Angelica was sure it was the same woman who started the fight in the galleria, wearing the sword she'd killed Chuckie with. Why was Feeney sending her down to talk to Shine in the middle of the night? She'd seen Mary once or twice, obviously going to try to persuade him to switch allegiance. But this woman was a fighter, by all accounts, not a diplomat. Was it an assassination attempt?

Angelica got out of bed and pulled on her robe. She hated that robe. It was nice silk, scavenged from a clothing store left empty when the owner fled, but it wasn't hers. Hers was still over in the hotel where she'd left it six months ago. Hers was warm and fluffy and she'd had it for years. She had the sudden mental image of the old man wearing it himself out of spite, and chuckled without meaning to.

The fighter walked past the stairway camera without acknowledging it; probably didn't know it was there. And then she was gone, down the stairs where Angelica didn't have access to any video feeds. All she had was an unchanging image and a quandary.

"Tea," she said aloud, drumming her fingers on the desk. "I need tea."

It would take someone a couple more minutes to get to the lowest decks by stairs, and a while longer to actually find Shine – unless they were meeting by appointment. She frowned down into her dwindling stash of tea leaves. Not the real stuff, she hadn't had that in months. The bioengineered hydroponics stuff wasn't bad, and it had caffeine, but she was even running out of that. She needed the use of her brain just then, though, so she shook a few leaves into her mug – Mr Shine's mug, really, stolen when she commandeered the casino and still tasting faintly of his coffee and cardamom – and dispensed hot water into it.

The warm steam and gentle grassy aroma relaxed her, helped her to think. She'd promised Shine she wouldn't spy on him, so just contacting him and warning him was out. Anyway, if this wasn't an assassination attempt, he'd resent it. Nor could she simply send people down; he'd see it as an invasion. Doing nothing and waiting didn't sit well with her.

She glanced through the other cameras, looked for the handful of night owls prowling the corridors around her various assets in the lower decks. A crew of four, looking drunk, that was all. An ambush might work, but she'd seen firsthand what had happened to the last group that had come upon that swordswoman. They had probably been sober, too. Some of her crew might flat-out refuse to take the woman on, and if they started refusing her orders, things would go south fast.

Angelica sipped her tea and thought, scanning the monitors idly. The old frustration rose up in her, felt like acid in her throat. All these stupid games, all the wasted money and sleep and opportunity. Shine used to call her "loss averse" and laughed and said he made a lot of money off people like her. But she'd done well so far, damn it all, carved out a lot of territory and kept the old man back on his heels. And let them think she wouldn't take risks – if Raj's little gamble paid off, she might just sweep the table.

A nervous-looking trio caught her attention. Not too far from the swordswoman, and not too far from backup. A seven-on-one fight might...

She frowned. She didn't recognize them. She tapped on the face recognition, but it came up blank: they weren't any of hers. Morlocks? Not seedy-looking armed punks like that, and not so close to her territory. What was Carter's plan? Go for the foot soldiers and get them mad at the new woman? Four drunks and the element of surprise, that could do the job. Nothing major, just a little sucker punch to keep morale up while they waited on Raj.

Angelica pushed the talk button, enjoyed for a moment the look of shock at her disembodied voice on the four tiny faces on her video screen, and rapidly laid out her instructions. Then she let go of the button and watched them hurry out of view. She could watch the fight, maybe, if there happened to be a camera nearby or if one of them had a lapel cam. Watching seemed like the responsible thing to do. Or the thing Raj would do, which was usually the opposite of responsible. She found herself repulsed by the thought of watching, though: some general, she just wanted this damn fight over.

She finished her tea, took a sleeping pill, and went back to bed.

Doc-Blocked

The Miner didn't dawdle heading back to a part of the station she could more easily justify her presence in. Shine had given the answer she'd wanted to hear: nobody who wanted to run Station 35 should by any means be allowed to do it, was her opinion, and he passed that test. She had gotten back to the hotel without too much trouble, and was thinking of returning to her stolen room to read when some kids stumbled through the hotel doors, bloodied and beaten up. Two of them dragged a third between them, and while the two doing the dragging didn't look so hot; the third looked downright bad.

They evicted a snoring drunk from the couch and dumped their buddy on it. She'd been beat up pretty thoroughly. Both eyes were swelled shut and a stream of pink saliva stretched from her mouth. Her black clothes shone with blood, though the Miner couldn't see an obvious wound.

"Why didn't you take her to the doctor?" she asked. Mills wouldn't treat the gangsters – and anyway it was a hell of a walk down to his office – but there was that clinic right off the galleria. One of the girls had gone over the evening before, and Mary had tersely explained "payment" when the Miner gave her an inquisitive look.

The shorter goon grinned at her, his teeth slicked with blood. "He's busy dealing with the damage we did, hey?"

"Angelica's assholes pushed us off," grumbled the taller one as he swabbed gingerly at a bloodied nose. He didn't bother looking at her as he talked. "They've got the door guarded."

The Miner considered that. She was weakening Feeney's side to try to force a confrontation, but she didn't want them so weak they couldn't fight at all. Anyway, she could have need of a sawbones herself.

The girl bleeding on the couch coughed a red spray and groaned. The Miner went back to examining her. After some prodding and some "that hurt?" "shit yes it hurt, motherfucker!" back and forth, she decided the kid had a broken leg, a couple cracked ribs but probably not a collapsed lung, broken teeth, and a concussion. Maybe more than that; that was about the limit of the Miner's dim recollection of field medicine.

"Don't let her sleep," the Miner said. "Keep her awake and don't give her any booze or downers."

"Meth OK?"

She gave him a blank look, started to answer, stopped, then went back to the broken leg. "Get me something long and straight."

"I got something long–" The short goon stopped talking when the taller one slapped him upside the head.

"For the leg, asshole," the taller one said, then walked off muttering. There was a sharp crack and a moment later the Miner was being handed a hollow plastic barstool leg. Its chrome-like finish splintered and crumbled where it had been broken off. She rubbed off the splinters then tied it to the girl's broken limb, tested it gently.

"Fuck! Goddamn it!"

She tested it as gently as she could be bothered to, and after some adjustment pronounced the splint sturdy.

"All right," said the Miner. "She's set for now. Come with me."

She dimly remembered where the other doctor's office was, and walked straight there flanked by the two bruised goons. "Uh," said the shorter one when the office came in sight, just a modest entranceway right off the eastern spur, uncomfortably close to security, but they seemed closed up for the night. "Dr Joff Philippe, MD" read the neat blue letters on the frosted window. The discreet thing to do would be to have her two wingmen stick close and try to be unobtrusive. Finish this quickly before attracting notice, two would be plenty.

"Get backup," she muttered. "Have them hang out just outside the galleria so nobody comes up behind me." That would be indiscreet enough, she decided, but still defensible. Now the second part.

Three of Angelica's soldiers loitered by the open door, looking about as haggard and hungover as Feeney's crew; they noticed the Miner's approach and drew an assortment of makeshift weapons. Only one had a proper weapon, a drawn military-style sword like her own, though chipped and scarred. Second-hand, then, a tidy euphemism for a weapon scavenged from some vet down on their luck or dead. The other two had club-looking things, deadly enough if they could land a solid blow.

"Piss off," growled the swordswoman. She held her sword two-handed with a grip tight enough her knuckles were white.

The Miner shook her head, but didn't draw her weapon. "Doctor's neutral ground."

"Not anymore. Get out of here."

The Miner shook her head again. "Can't."

Someone behind her said "uh", but she couldn't afford to turn and look. She'd just have to trust them to fuck it up.

"Piss. Off."

"Hey doc!" the Miner called out. "You have a patient in there?"

A skinny man in a tatty white lab coat hesitantly poked his head out of the door behind Angelica's goons. His protruding eyes were fried-egg wide, and he stammered a consonant-free reply.

"Shut up, doc," said the swordswoman, not looking at him. She had nerve, the Miner had to admit.

Being shushed seemed to remind the guy he had a few vertebrae, and he used them. "I'm seeing a patient, yes," he managed. "Don't kill each other out here. For God's sake. We'll be done in a few minutes."

"Fine," said the Miner. "When you're finished, these folks will leave, then you've got another one coming. She's next."

"The hell we will," the swordswoman said. "The hell she is."

The Miner put her hand on her sword for the first time, gently resting it on the grip. Angelica's goons tensed like she'd drawn on them, and the doctor fled back inside. "If you don't leave he'll have three more patients. And you'll have to wait your turn."

A club-wielder sneered from his position behind the woman with the sword. "You're pretty goddamn sure of yourself."

"That's right."

She saw the attack coming. The woman might have fenced, probably VR, but wasn't a proper sword fighter. Still, she didn't waste time waving her blade like a stick, and she came in low to use her center of gravity well. The Miner drew with plenty of time; brought her weapon up one-handed, parried by simply slapping the other sword away, and then down two-handed while stepping to the right. Her blade met the other woman's arm as she tried vainly to correct for the Miner's practiced and augmented quickness; the Miner sliced through flesh and struck bone.

It was over before the other goons on either side could react. The Miner held her sword with the point down, dripping blood onto the deck, ready to bring it up if anyone else had bright ideas. The swordswoman shrieked on the ground, her chipped sword forgotten beside her while she clutched at her right forearm, blood gushing between her fingers. Wound like that, fighting style like that, she'd be out of the game for a month at least. Suited the Miner fine.

"Stings, huh? Should have listened."

When someone behind her said "uh" again, she did turn. A group had formed behind her; two groups in fact, maybe four or five goons in each, all trying to watch each other and watch her at the same time.

The doctor reappeared with a dazed, pale, tattooed young man trailing him, and knelt in the blood to administer aid. Angelica's other fighters stood uncertain with their makeshift clubs hovering at the ready but not ready enough to be an obvious threat. The Miner pulled a handkerchief and wiped down her blade with a show of nonchalance.

"If I'd wanted to kill you three, I would have. But this is neutral ground." She raised her voice, not too much, but she wanted to be heard.

"All right," snapped the doctor. "You've made your point. You, I'll treat. The rest of you, get out of here. Will your friend last another half hour?"

The Miner considered then nodded.

"Good, come back in half an hour."

She stepped away, putting some distance between herself and Angelica's goons. That gave her a view of the crowds facing off, and she looked at them speculatively. If she joined Feeney's side in that one, the other side would probably melt away. "Doc?"

"What now?"

"You're going to be busy." She turned and left past his office, walking away from the crowds.

Feeney Watches the Fight

Screwball peered out at the galleria from the hotel windows, squinting against the dim light. He'd been woken up still tipsy and pressganged into helping carry Tara to the doctor to get bandaged up. The doc had been pissed off about something, but Screwball hadn't paid much attention because of all the noise from the galleria – maybe two dozen people were out there yelling and jeering at each other from across the row of trees. He couldn't see Angelica's crew real well, but the fighters from Feeney's side looked hungover and confused, and he decided that "I'd better report back" was the better part of valor.

He hadn't been the only one. It was either too late at night or too early in the morning – it was just the wrong damn time of day for that kind of thing, for his kind of people, and a lot of Feeney's crew stumbled around groggy in the hotel lobby, those who could actually be roused.

"What's going on, eh?" Screwball jumped at the old man's peevish question. He turned and Feeney's unshaven face stared at him with bloodshot eyes.

"Some kind of fight," Screwball ventured.

"I know that. What of it? What's the matter?"

"Tara, Bull, and PJ were coming up from guard duty at the

cookout and got jumped by some of Angelica's gang. Tara's leg got broke, but when they got to the doctor, Angelica's guys were already there and wouldn't let them in."

Feeney made an annoyed sound. "Doctor's neutral ground. Even that traitorous bitch Angelica knows that."

"Yeah, but they got reinforcements or something, and it was really early so nobody else was up. So Bull and PJ got that chick you hired, with the sword, and she pushed them off."

"Did she now?" The annoyance in his voice went away, and he sounded pleased. "Well, someone's earning their pay. What's that got to do with the fracas down there?"

Screwball scratched his head and studied the crowd for a moment. A couple of people had weapons out and waved them unsteadily, but most of them seemed to have wandered in empty-handed. "I think they went out to see what was going on, mostly. But it was some of them and some of us, and none of us are going to be the first ones to leave."

"Damn right," Feeney said distractedly. He elbowed Screwball aside and examined the crowd, frowning. "But what are they going to do?"

"I don't think they've figured that out."

Feeney's frown twisted like he was sucking his teeth. "Where's Mick?"

"Who?"

"That girl I hired, with the sword. Jane. You said she pushed them off from the doctor's, but I don't see her down there."

"Dunno. I never saw her this morning, I just heard she'd chased away Angelica's people."

He made unsatisfied noises. "Well." He went back to scanning the milling crowd below. "What's your name?"

"Corbell," Screwball said. Feeney glanced at him, confused for a second.

"Corbell... Corbell..." The old man frowned, still staring down at the two crows facing off below.

Screwball sighed quietly. "Some of them call me Scre–"

"Oh, Screwball! That's right, yes, yes." Feeney grinned like he'd won a treat and winked. "Senior moment. They say there's nobody so dangerous as an old gangster, but old is old, eh?"

Screwball tried to grin as his mind worked furiously around the trap in that question. "You're still sharp enough to cut, sir."

"Eh, nobody likes a brownnoser." Feeney concentrated on the galleria, and Screwball was glad for the distraction. The crowd had grown and the two sides were slowly moving toward each other. It was like watching waves lap at the sides of a filling waste tank, moving back and forth while inching forward. The crowd grew as wanderers and stragglers from both sides showed up, pushing the front lines toward each other.

"Getting serious," Feeney murmured. "Where the hell's McMasters? Ought to be putting a stop to it. Or Angelica. Rotten traitor ought to know better than to allow a fight in the damned galleria. And where's Jane?"

"Maybe distracting McMasters?"

Feeney didn't respond right away, but he looked worried. "She would," he admitted. "She would at that." He turned around to see a half dozen more of his fighters rubbernecking for a view of the simmering crowd.

"And what the hell are you doing up here? Get down there, what am I paying you for?" They all but fell over each other in their stumbling rush down the stairs. Weapons were out below on both sides. "I don't want a fight right now," Feeney muttered, "but I'll be damned if I lose one. Where's Jane?"

Screwball reluctantly sagged his shoulders and made to join the crowd, but Feeney clamped a cold bony hand on his arm. "Not you, Corbell. Leaving me without a guard up here, what's the matter with you?"

"Sorry sir," he said brightly. "Just eager to help, is all."

Feeney grunted. "I don't want suicidals, boy. No place for a man without common sense."

Screwball bit his lip, couldn't think of an answer that wouldn't get his head bitten off, and stayed quiet. He watched the fighters below menace each other. It was like some kind of ritual dance: forward, wave something sharp and yell, then stumble back again when their counterpart did the same. Shouts of mingled anger and terror filled the galleria. The result wasn't inevitable in its particulars, only in its effect: Yarbles inexpertly swung a nunchuck and hit himself in the face. Screaming and bleeding, he went down, and the battle was joined.

THIRSTY WORK

The lamps had come up to part "sun", making it morning, in theory. A couple more of Feeney's other goons had woken up and had casually drifted toward the little standoff that had slowly formed after the scene at the doctor's. A few heads popped up in the casino windows, and a couple fighters came out even if most of them were just watching. They were itching for a fight, and she could see the guard in front of the security station nervously looking back and forth. She'd woken the place up nicely, the Miner decided, but she needed information. She took the corridor to the back passage before things got too hot, and took the long walk around behind the hotel to the spur next to Ama no Gawa. By the time she got back to the galleria the long way round, things had heated up: not an outright fight yet, but with maybe a dozen wary thugs facing off already. She slipped unnoticed into Ama no Gawa's open door, where she was greeted with a hearty "Fuck off!" from Takata.

"Morning," the Miner replied.

"You're no better than those other hooligans! Get out of my restaurant."

"Hello, Herrera."

"They're still alive," Herrera told his glass mournfully. She wondered if he'd slept in the booth. "You don't get the hundred thousand unless you kill every last one of those bot-fucking syphilis reservoirs."

"Language!" Takata scolded. "See what you do to him? You get his hopes up and he starts swearing. They're going to kill each other out there and knock everything down. Get out of here. Fly off to some other station and do your mischief there."

"Can't. Feeney's got the docking clamps on my ship."

"Eh? Hah! Serves you right, you play with fire like that."

The Miner didn't sit, since she wasn't invited to. She stood with her hands folded on the back of a chair, her sword out of the way. She looked Takata in the eye, and he looked right back. "I'm sorry to bother you. I need information."

"Like what?"

"I have to know about this guy Nuke."

Herrera said something unintelligibly angry into his glass.

"That son of a bitch," Takata spat. "He was a bigger bastard than all of them put together. Crazy fucker, too."

"They're all crazy."

"Not like this guy. You know why they call him Nuke? Old man Feeney scoured this place years ago, stole all the stuff the military left behind. Found a stash of pocket nukes down in the asteroid rock, what they used to blast it out in the first place, figured he could sell them. Except his grandson Wilfred gets hold of one, see? Gets the fucked-up idea to have it implanted in his chest, wired up to his heart. If his heart stops, everything around him gets vaporized."

The Miner stood, stunned. She'd had the misfortune to have to place a couple of those, and they scared the shit out of her. They were the size of a large fist and had a variable yield, around half a ton. They could easily take out armored hulls, especially from the inside.

"It's all messed up and ugly," Takata was saying, "looks like some kind of robot's trying to push out of his chest. He goes bare-chested too so everyone has to stare at the nasty thing."

"Christ," she managed.

Herrera looked up. "What did you call him? It was pretty good." Takata waved him off, irritated. "Yeah, you said he was a 'militant solipsist'. Pretty good, I thought. I think it's funny."

"It's not funny, it's a fucking nightmare. That son of a bitch is what started this whole thing," he told the Miner. "See, Angelica used to be Feeney's lieutenant, like his top soldier, but she freaked out when Nuke got that thing put in his chest. She told the old man his grandson was nuts and she wouldn't stand for it, got a bunch of the others to go along with her. They forced him to deal with the little psycho, eventually, but by then half of them were fed up and revolted." He waved his hand at the galleria. "This is the result."

"How'd they deal with him?"

Takata shrugged.

"Is he dead?"

"No idea. I'm just glad he's gone. Guy scared the crap out of me."

"Is he likely to come back?"

"Wish I knew."

The conversation lulled, so they could hear when the yelling started up. The Miner wandered over to the big window and watched as the two opposing groups finally made tentative steps toward actually fighting. Knives, bars, electrified truncheons all waved uncertainly in the air above two scraggly groups. Maybe a dozen on each side by then. They still weren't fighting yet, just menacing each other. A step forward on one side, a step forward on the other side, then back again, almost choreographed.

She'd barely registered Takata coming up to join her, and shot him a confused look when he pushed a glass of beer into her hand. By way of explanation, he pointed his chin at a red-faced McMasters advancing on the restaurant's front door from behind the crowd of Angelica's goons.

"You did this!" He had his finger already deployed when he walked in the door, his mustache quivering in fury, and he pointed it right in her face. The Miner lifted the glass to her lips and sipped, regarded him coolly. It took every ounce of self-control not to react to the stale, warm, flat liquid. *Touché*, she thought.

"Did what?"

"I saw you watching and conniving and… and… orchestrating this gratuitous display!"

"I don't know how to orchestrate. I'm just having a beer," she said, holding up the proof.

As near she could tell, the first one down knocked himself silly and fell into the plants, but that was all it took. They fell on each other, an ungainly mass of arms and legs and heads, mostly screaming in fury and terror. A tough went down clutching an abdominal wound, and another reeled drunkenly away from the melee bleeding from the scalp. Having met in combat, both sides were busy trying desperately to unmeet again, the panicked jerks on the front lines pushing back against their own comrades pressing forward.

They'd just managed to disengage themselves when a dozen security goons flew out of their station, attempting to look tough but failing as they tried to swarm and pull on their black armor at the same time. They had their stun batons out, though, and had the drop on the terrified gangsters. Twelve batons pumped up and down mechanically, hitting exposed flesh as hard as they could. The Miner figured they did more damage to the fighters than the fighters had done to each other. There wasn't much resistance to it, and they'd timed their arrival so they'd get to bust heads without actually endangering themselves.

"You think I don't know what you're doing?" McMasters yelled over the noise of the melee when he finally managed to break his attention away. "This is deliberate! You're deliberately disturbing the peace on this station, and I won't stand for it. I tell you I won't!"

"Looked to me like you were doing a fine job with the gratuitous display yourself. I noticed your people didn't bother to come bust up the fight until it was already mostly over."

He pursed his lips, making his little blonde mustache bristle. "What are you insinuating?"

The fight was breaking up behind him as fast as it could. McMasters' forces pursued anyone upright, chasing them away as the injured fighters in the middle scrambled in every which direction. One of them made for the bar, but the Miner put her hand on her sword and scared her off.

"I don't know how to insinuate, either," the Miner said. "I just meant that your goon squad's made up of cowards who enjoy beating people up as long as it isn't too hard."

He probably wished he hadn't let his face get so red on the way over, she decided, because there was nowhere left to go from there. He glowered at Takata and Herrera, which had the virtue of letting him ignore her. It gave him time to think, but he still only came up with, "I've got my eye on you." The Miner thought she deserved a better class of cliché, but also decided that Takata didn't deserve blood on his floor.

McMasters looked past her at the bartender. "If you expect my officers to spend money in your bar, you'd better do something about your roach problem."

He stormed back out again and yelled at Mary, who had appeared from somewhere and was busy pulling someone out of the pile. Her rescuee waved a knife and posed more of a harm to his rescuer first and himself second than anyone he might have actually wanted to stab.

"Shitstache thinks I'm behind this," Herrera said, and didn't sound unhappy about it.

"Why?"

"Because if he loses control, I get to try again to cancel Anaconda's lease. Then his pustulous hide and goat-bile mustache are space-bound."

"There'll be others," Takata said. "You knock one down, there's another one waiting to take his place. Maybe her."

The Miner shook her head. "Not my gig," she said.

"Says you."

They were both quiet for a long time.

"Sorry about losing you business," she said without looking away from the melee.

Takata snorted, but she didn't believe the put-on of disdain. He looked uncomfortable. "He thinks he has enough sway to keep his crooked crew of morons from drinking? I'd like to see him try."

She didn't know what to say to that, so kept her mouth shut and thought back to the fight. It had been worthwhile, she thought. The gangsters were too drunk and sleepy to really do each other damage, and it was probably a wash. She'd hoped to see how McMasters' crew deployed themselves in a fight, though, and hadn't been disappointed.

All huddled in their spider hole security station to armor up, they'd poured out of two doors – the kind of deployment that could get stoppered long enough to get a good solid fight underway. They were cowards, it seemed, but bloodthirsty ones. She could work with that.

The trick would be timing. The two hornets' nests could be stirred up pretty fast if they were mostly awake. Middle of the night might be worth trying anyway – Feeney felt most confident when he thought he was pulling something off, and Angelica seemed paranoid down to her bones, enough to keep a sharper watch at night. As for McMasters, she had no idea what his response time in the wee hours looked like, but probably faster than early morning. It would be better, she decided, if the security crew were in their station rather than streaming in from quarters – they'd be right on the scene and ready to organize, but more easily contained. She didn't know enough about their off-duty movements as she liked, and since they weren't usually in Ama no Gawa, she wondered.

"They don't like to pay is the trouble," Takata admitted when she asked. "McMasters pays shit. He's got some kind of deal with Mr Shine or Finn for raw booze, and they drink in their barracks or the security station most of the time. They only come here when they're bored." He looked uncomfortable again.

"Mr Shine. What do you think of him?"

"He's all right. Kind of a coward. Tried to stay neutral when the old man and Angelica really went at it, and look where it got him."

"I'm looking. Where did it get him?"

Takata scowled. "Nobody likes a smartass. It got him kicked out of his casino. He got his claws into the physical plant now, a whole slew of people who were only ever half-heartedly corrupt. Casual like. You know, got the occasional kickback for providing water or power to the drug lab, but never really cared."

The Miner considered that. "He have many of his own fighters, those Morlocks you mentioned?"

"Not what *you'd* call fighters. Dishwashers and blackjack dealers, and the people who ran the machinery. The old man and Angelica leave him alone because they figure he could play kingmaker if he wanted to. They respect him when he tells them to lay off someone like Doc Mills."

"He protect you too?"

He shook his head. "He makes sure I get water and power, but I pay for it." He grinned. "Everyone kinda thinks I'm being protected by someone else, I think. I don't rock the boat."

"That why you let McMasters' goons drink here?"

Takata scowled. "It's because he's a coward!" Herrera contributed.

"Oh, to hell with you, Herrera. You've got a salary no matter who you spite. I've got a business to keep open."

"'Open' you call it. You sell watery expired piss beer to thugs and drifters, and you alternate between ripping 'em off and giving it away."

"I've got the good stuff, too," Takata said. "I never give you the shit, just the people who have it coming."

The Miner looked down at the glass in her hand, at the tiny bubbles rising in the pale yellow liquid. Takata looked defensive. "What, you're going to argue?"

"No."

Takata's defensive look didn't entirely go away, but he added a shade of guilty to the palette. "Look, I gotta get my kicks in where I can."

"Vive la résistance," the Miner said. She drank the rest of the disgusting stale beer in one long go, put the empty glass on the table, and managed a "thanks" on her way out.

Aftermath

Screwball hadn't left the old man's side through the whole fight, and maybe that hadn't been all that long, but it was a couple minutes more attention than he'd ever gotten before, and Feeney had remembered his real name. Plus, even with the fighting over, the old guy seemed kinda loath to send him away. Screwball could picture himself as the bodyguard type. Quiet, menacing, dependable.

"Corbell."

"Sir?" He felt like his voice was deeper than usual, projected kind of a calm competence.

"You're hovering. Piss off. Oh, Mary! Are you all right, my dear?"

Screwball backed away a few steps, right into a pillar, and tried to coolly take his absence. Feeney's granddaughter looked like hell. She had a big blossoming bruise under the row of spikes along her cheekbone, and a dark line on her lip where it had split and just stopped bleeding down the front of her black jacket, which was still wet with it.

"What the hell was that?" Mary demanded. "I went to look in on the cooks, and when I come back you've started a war!"

Feeney waved off her anger with a single thin hand. "You've got it all wrong, child. This was an organic fight,

Angelica's fault. She tried to claim the doctor, and by God we fought back!"

Mary frowned and folded her arms. If she noticed Screwball trying to look insignificant while dying of curiosity, she didn't show it. "Doctor's neutral ground."

"Of course. And we showed her."

"Stupid to fight in the galleria."

Feeney raised his chin. "My soldiers fight where the fight finds them."

Screwball tried not to stare. The last fifteen minutes, the old man had been muttering about how stupid the whole thing was, and why wasn't McMasters breaking the fight up yet. And now he sounded like he'd won some kind of daring victory. Mary just raised an eyebrow. If she was going to say anything, though, it was lost when the old man suddenly went red and shouted, "And just where the hell have you been?"

The new hire slowed and stopped with her left hand resting on the handle of her sword like it was a chair arm. Her gray jumpsuit was spattered and smeared with blood, as was her right hand, which she used to casually guide a lock of salt and pepper hair back behind her ear. She gave Feeney a mild surprised look, like Ditz always did but without the heavy sedatives.

Feeney didn't wait for an answer. "You weren't fighting."

She nodded. "That's right. Except for the doctor's office, I didn't touch them, I promise. I figure the thing with the doctor was a special case, since that's supposed to be neutral ground. But I stayed away after that, honest."

Even Mary looked wrongfooted by that, and Feeney just gaped for a moment. "Well, what were you doing, then?"

"Distracting McMasters. Giving your people a chance to do some damage before he called in the clowns. Proving you hadn't ordered the fight." Her mild look fell into a grin. "If you had, I'd have been in it, right? So he can't blame you for it."

Mary shot the older woman a look of contempt, the kind of look that would have made Screwball shrivel up. It turned to dismay when she saw Feeney puff himself up.

"We did all right, we did all right. Could have used that sword of yours, sure, but I'd say we gave as good as we got."

"Two dead," Mary growled. "Five cut up or beat up bad enough they can't fight."

Feeney hesitated. "Us or them, do you mean?"

"Us!" When he looked the obvious question, she unclenched her teeth enough to say, "I don't know how bad they got it."

"Such an Eeyore," Feeney said. "It looked to me that we knocked down twice as many as all that. I think–"

He was interrupted by groans and cries of pain from the group crowding the entrance. McMasters and eight black-armored security guards muscled their way through with their stun batons crackling. McMasters glared up at Feeney, angrier than Screwball had ever imagined he could be. Everyone looked tense and ready for a fight except that chick Jane, who just leaned against a column looking bored.

"I warned you, John Feeney," McMasters barked. "I warned you, and by God you've put your foot in it. If you think I'm staying neutral in your little fight with del Rio after this, you're bloody well mistaken!"

"Now wait one moment," Feeney stammered. All the blood had gone out of him and he looked like a ghost. All his soldiers fell quiet and listened. "That's just not true. Angelica violated your neutrality–"

"She–" Here he pointed at Jane, who reacted with a single raised eyebrow. "She cut down one of Angelica's soldiers right on Joff's damn doorstep. And *she* works for *you*, Feeney."

"No, I don't."

"And she... What?" Wrongfooted, he whirled on her. "What did you say?"

"I said, I don't work for him." She pushed herself off the column squarely onto both feet, and rested her hand on her sword. "He fired me. I gave his money back. I don't work for him. I can keep rephrasing it, if you're confused."

"Bullshit."

Feeney suddenly looked a little less at sea. He pulled a small pad from his pocket, and seemed to steel himself before looking at it. When he looked back up at McMasters, he smiled like he'd just rolled double-sixes. He handed the pad to McMasters and said, "It's true, see for yourself."

The security man snatched it from him. "Who the blazes is Mickey–" He fell silent. "This was only timestamped two minutes ago!"

"I only agreed to give it back two minutes ago. That way I don't owe him anything." She looked right at the old bird when she said that, and he went pale. "That's what we were talking about when you interrupted us."

Feeney didn't miss a beat. "Well, after all, she started a fight, didn't she? That's not what I was paying for, I only wanted protection from Angelica, that's all I ever hired any of these fine folks to do, not to start a war." The color came back into his face as the bullshit flowed. "She picked a fight in the goddamned galleria, though, and she had to go. Did I do wrong, Tom?"

McMasters' eyes bulged and Screwball thought he'd stroke out. His eight armored guards exchanged glances, and the crowd behind them murmured. "No," he finally managed. He jabbed an accusing finger. "But you damned well better see that she stays fired, do you hear me?" He whirled. "And you, you'd better get the hell off my station."

"Can't," she drawled. "I'm broke now. Are you going to pay for my fuel? It'll cost a few grand."

"The hell it will!"

She shrugged. "Seems to me that you want me to go pretty far away. Takes a lot of fuel."

If McMasters had an answer, she didn't stay to hear it. She started walking toward the hotel entrance, and they stumbled over each other to clear the way for her. Screwball stared as she walked, dumbfounded.

"Well, Tom," Feeney said, the first as usual to find his tongue. "It seems that's settled. I've lost a fine soldier, thank you very much. I hope that settles all this talk of siding with that del Rio woman."

"I'm not promising anything," McMasters snarled as he turned on his heel. The crowd didn't part for him; his own guards barely stepped out of his way as he shoved and pushed his way out of the hotel.

Feeney turned to Mary, who'd worn a look of deep suspicion through the whole thing, and said loudly, "I for one could use a drink. Who's with me?"

Free Agent

"Get out," Takata said when the Miner walked into his bar again. They'd had a nice long quiet afternoon of everyone nursing their wounds and then she'd walked right across the galleria like she owned the place, and stood in his doorway with her arms crossed. He swept the floor in a long pink shop apron that went to his shins, glowering.

"I thought you wanted me to quit Feeney's service."

"I do!" He stopped and leaned the broom against a table. "You did?"

"Paid him back in full." The ten thousand, at least. What was left of the rest, she figured was hers.

His face lit up. "Well. Well! I'll be damned. You listened to me? Nobody ever listens to me. Well!"

"I don't listen to you either," offered Herrera from his usual corner.

Takata ignored him, instead gathering up his shop apron with both hands and practically dancing his way back behind the bar. He beckoned the Miner with one hand as he fiddled with the taps using the other, and then pulled a tall glass of amber beer. The long slow pour headed up and foamed over into the overflow. "So when are you heading out?"

"I'm staying put," she said, and he smoothly pulled back the hand that had been in the process of offering the cold inviting drink.

"Why?" His suspicion was palpable, and he held the glass up against his apron.

She shrugged again. "I'm still pretty broke."

"What, and you think he'll take you back?"

"Or Angelica."

"Oh." He held eye contact as he took a long drink from the glass in his hand, and then set it on the bar behind the taps, well out of her arm's reach. "So that's it."

"You gonna get back to croaking all those flea-ridden pus-bags?" called Herrera from his corner.

She sat on a stool and shrugged. "Nobody's paying me for anything right now," she said.

"Yeah, but you expect that to change," Takata said sourly. He took his apron off and shoved it under the counter.

"It might. It might not."

"I'm cheering for 'might not'."

"Seems to me," the Miner said, "that hurrying things along is the better way to go."

Takata was shaking his head emphatically before she'd finished talking. "No, no, no. You sound like Herrera. The fighting won't stop. They'll keep importing goons. They'll drag it out. Better to keep it at a simmer, so people come back again. All we need is a little peace, get some money coming in, everybody will calm down."

"Bullshit!" Herrera jumped to his feet. "Horse shit! Rat shit, every kind of shit. That's no kind of peace, that's just a ceasefire. It's a fake shitty peace."

"I'll take a ceasefire any damn day of the week!" Takata's face went red and he jabbed a finger at Herrera. "I take too much of your holier-than-thou 'no justice no peace' garbage. You don't have rent to pay, you just have your pride to worry about."

"What about your pride, hey? Don't you have any of that under your pretty pink apron? You want to go back to paying protection money? You want to have Nuke and Raj and them back in here every night stealing your booze and laughing at you? That what you want? There a profit in that?"

"Shut up, Herrera, you don't know."

"I do know! I watched everybody get driven out of this station, my station, everybody I was supposed to be protecting. Where's Cheyenne? Where's Qi? Where's Binyamin and Sven and Arun and Precious? Huh?"

"Arun's still here," Takata said, petulant.

"Hiding out in the lower decks! Everyone else got driven off. You're too stubborn to leave, or you signed a shitty lease, or you like the smell too much, I don't know, but don't pretend this all goes back to normal if Feeney and Angelica kiss and make up. Them and McMasters are a goddamn pus-filled boil, and it's not going to get better on its own. Someone's got to squeeze it." He held his hand up and squeezed three fingers together in front of his contorted expression.

"What, you think that's her? She's your royal pus-squeezer, is she?"

They both stopped and looked at her, suddenly embarrassed.

"Pus squeezer," she deadpanned.

"Eh," Takata said, rubbing the back of his head with one hand. "Forget him, he's drunk."

"I'm not drunk enough for this," Herrera vowed and weaved toward the front door. Then he turned to the Miner. "You stay here tonight. He's got a mattress for drunks, not too full of bugs."

"She's not staying here, she's broke!"

"I'm paying!" He wheeled and overdid it, grasping at a chair to steady himself. "I'm paying. And I'm going to bed now, so go get it and I'll pay."

Takata favored them both with a scowl, then threw his hands up and went into the back. Herrera watched him go, then leaned over to the Miner, his sour whiskey breath strong as a punch in the face. "He's not going to lose this place," he said, staring intently at her like only a drunk can. "I paid the rent, and I'm going to pay it. He needs to remember his goddamn pride, that's what he needs. He needs to remember what it was like to run a good restaurant for real, not a dive bar for gangsters, not a watering hole for broken down old assholes like me. You kill those motherfuckers. You kill them dead. Worth your while."

He slapped her on the shoulder, nodded more to himself than to her, then staggered out the front door. The galleria lights were down for the night, and he weaved out into the darkness among the tables and potted trees, and she watched him go.

"Sentimental old buzzard," Takata groused behind her. He struggled with a thick slab of yellowed foam, hauling it this way and that to free it from the doorway. "All this crap has really hurt him. This used to be a nice station, and he used to do a good job. But he's too wrapped up in the injustice of it all. The perfect's the enemy of the good. Once the fighting dies down and people come back, he'll perk up. People don't care if there's criminals, they only care if there's crime, if they'll get hurt or get robbed. Once it seems calm, it'll be calm, and he'll be all right. He put up with worse and it was all right." He threw the slab of foam out next to the bar, then punched the button to lower the shutters. They creaked and rattled and shut out the remaining light from the galleria.

"Restroom's over there. Don't use too much water, will you? I don't meter it, and he's got no business paying for you. He's too free with his cash, he feels too guilty about it." He paused. "What do I call you, anyway?"

"Jane works."

"That your name?"

She shrugged. "Could be. Forgot my name."

He snorted a laugh. "Sure." Then he looked down at the deck, thoughtful. "Guy named Zhuang Zhou once said that the point of a fish net was to catch a fish. When you catch it, you forget the net. Or whatever you catch fish with, I don't know. And a rabbit trap. Catch the rabbit, forget the trap. And the point of words, he said, the point of words was to catch meaning, so what *he* wanted was to talk to the guy who forgot words, because that's the guy who really understood stuff. So, I just wonder, what would he make of someone who forgot their own name."

"Don't know. Forgot that, too."

They stood a while in the low light, him staring at the deck, her watching him.

"Good night," she said. He looked up at her, surprised, then nodded sharply in reply and went in back.

The lights dimmed on their own, leaving her in the dark with only a few red status lights scattered around the place like sparse constellations. The low rumble of the air movers and the subtle rush of water and coolant, noises that had always been there, suddenly intruded on her senses. All the sounds of an operational space station, just as she'd expect to hear them on any other station. She unstrapped her sword and lay it on the floor. She'd laid low after the fight, walking the abandoned middle decks and thinking. She hadn't gone back to her ship; didn't want to draw attention to it. The walking had tired her out, at least. She settled into the faint boozy-sour smell of the foam mattress for another sleepless night, for her brain's usual recitation of decades' worth of wrongs and lost friends, and she fell fast asleep.

Ditz and Screwball Take a Stroll

"She's just sitting there," Ditz said almost reverently. He was bent at the waist so that he could rest both arms and his chin on the railing, and because his hairy ass stuck out of his pants that way Screwball walked up to the railing so he didn't have to look at it. Jane was still there in the galleria, sitting on a chair in front of the restaurant. She'd been there all morning, or at least since the crack of ten. She sat with both feet on the floor, with her sword across her lap, and she was reading a beat-up paperback book. It looked like she was halfway through already.

"McMasters came out before," Ditz said, and yawned. He looked up and Screwball could see that his pupils were blown. "When there weren't too many people watching. He kinda came up and huffed at her and said, 'How much?' and I think she said fifteen thousand—"

"What!" Screwball looked at him in astonishment.

"That's what I thought she said. Anyway he got all pissed off and huffed and puffed and stomped around, and he said," here Ditz used a high-pitched voice, "'Get off my station!' And she said – get this, man – she said, 'Get out of my light.' I thought that was pretty good, man. Get out of my light."

Screwball looked down at her. She turned a page. Pairs of eyes all around the edge of the galleria were on her. Screwball could see faces in the casino windows and through the big heavy shutters on the security station. She turned another page.

He shook himself away and stood back from the railing. "The old man wants me to go scout around the old repair bay," he said. "See what Sparks is up to, if I can."

"Oh, all right," Ditz said, and heaved himself up off the railing.

"I wasn't– I mean." Screwball stammered. "I was just saying. He wanted me to do it. I wasn't asking you to come along."

"It's cool, we're bros. You don't have to ask."

"Yeah, but." Ditz walked past him, then turned and beckoned. Screwball slumped his shoulders and followed. They cut back through the hotel, and he kept his voice low.

"I was just saying, it was cool that he asked me, you know. He like knows my name and shit now."

"And you want your old pal to help out, it's cool."

"No," he protested, but it fell on deaf ears, or at least stoned ones. "Whatever."

"Me and Sparks go way back," Ditz said as they walked. "She's wicked smart, but kinda high-strung, you know?"

"I don't know who she is."

"Oh! Huh. She, like, runs the repair bay."

"Yeah, I figured that much out."

"Right. She's a mechanic." Screwball made impatient noises. "Oh, and she used to run all the old man's 'salvage' operations." Ditz used his fingers to make quote marks in the air, and stumbled after distracting himself from his walking. "It's a chop shop, see? Pull in wrecked ships that maybe were wrecked on purpose sometimes, scavenge for stuff to sell, and scrap the rest. Used to make good money, I guess. Only she went with Angelica because she was kind of sweet on Raj."

They walked in silence for a few minutes, and took the stairs down.

"I got the feeling," Screwball offered, "that he thinks she's up to something."

"Who?"

"Sparks."

"Sparks is a she, dude."

"Feeney. Feeney thinks that Sparks Laghari is up to something."

"Oh. Probably right. She's wicked smart."

"Why are we going this way? This isn't the way the old man said to go."

Ditz turned and winked. "This is the back way. When me and her used to smoke up I'd come out this way. There's an office one deck up. She doesn't use it much, and it's locked but I know the code... woah."

He clumsily put an arm up in front of Screwball, and they both fell silent. Up ahead and around a corner, Screwball heard raucous laughter and someone swearing a blue streak. He flattened himself against the white plastic bulkhead, felt the deep bass thrum of air flowing through the big conduits overhead.

"Let's go around the other way," Screwball murmured.

"Can't," Ditz said. "That's where we're going."

"That's Sparks's office up ahead?"

"Yeah. Been there a bunch of times, man. Know it like the back of my hand."

Screwball steeled himself. He took a couple deep breaths and balled his fists. "All right. If they're even guarding up here, he's right that she's up to something. I gotta see. Then I gotta report back."

"I dunno, that seems like a bad idea."

"So, stay here. Be ready to run. I'll be right back."

Screwball crept along the wall, and it made squeaky noises where his sweaty palms dragged against the plastic. He tried to breathe deeply but not hyperventilate, but that wasn't working so well.

It seemed like he walked the whole length of the station like that, the laughter and joking growing louder. He could make out individual voices, one guy calling the others "a bunch of assholes" and at least three others all talking at once. They sounded kinda drunk.

He finally made it to the corner and stopped, his damp palms stuck to the side of the plastic, his head and back planted. "On three," he told himself, and on the count of four he forced his head around the corner to peer with his left eye.

Five toughs lounged around an open hatchway, one of them hopping around with his shoe off and staring daggers at the other four who grinned and leered. All five heads seemed to swivel at once in his direction, and he didn't wait for them to move to start running.

"Shit! Run!"

Ditz stood in the middle of the corridor fiddling with his shirt buttons and looking confused. He didn't run as Screwball barreled past him, and when he realized his pal wasn't following, he cursed himself as a softy but skidded to a halt and turned to grab him.

Four of Angelica's goons rounded the corner in hot pursuit, and Ditz put his head on one side like a dog. Then he reached deep into the front of his pants and pulled out an automatic pistol. They barely had time to go wide-eyed before he raised it dreamily and shot all four of them.

Screwball staggered at the eardrum blast, and Ditz winced and rubbed his ear with the palm of his left hand.

"The hell is wrong with you, Ditz? Move!"

He grabbed Ditz's colorful shirt and dragged, almost pulling him over until his brain engaged and he started running. Screwball made the executive decision to pass the closest stairwell, which would be too obvious, and turned the next corner instead. His chest ached and his legs hurt, and he found an open hatch to duck into. He dragged Ditz in behind him and punched the door closed.

In the dim light of the abandoned barber's shop, way away from the windows, he finally let himself collapse, heaving with his hands on both knees. He stood bent over like that while Ditz just lay on the ground, both of them panting. Ditz started to giggle.

"The fuck, Ditz! Where did you get that?"

"My mom gave it to me."

"I mean… I mean…" He swore and caught his breath. "I thought McMasters took them all away! You're going to get fucking spaced, Ditz!"

Ditz took a while to respond, but when he caught his breath and stopped laughing he said, "Naw, man. He only took them off everyone who came off the ships. Feeney and Angelica just promised him they'd take care of it. Feeney didn't give a fuck, though, as long as we didn't get him in hot water."

Screwball stared, then pointed back the way they came. "That! That's hot water, Ditz! That's boiling hot fucking hot water!"

"Aw, don't be like that. It was self-defense, they were coming right for me."

"You think McMasters is going to give a shit?"

"No? He's a tool, man."

"Well, you have to get rid of it, all right?"

Ditz pouted. "Aw, come on, it was a birthday present."

"Not for good. Just, like, hide it in here somewhere. We'll lay low and head back. You can come get it later, OK?"

Ditz grumbled, but looked around the barber shop with a discerning eye. There were two big chairs with a bunch of what looked like brass and wood that was probably plastic and a lot of electronic arms to make them go in a bunch of different directions. The place had been ransacked, pretty much, and all the scissors and razors had been grabbed. Somebody had drawn a pretty respectable dong on the mirror in some kind of red grease; it maybe needed some more curly hairs on the balls, for balance, but was otherwise pretty good. Screwball touched the back of his own head, where he'd had to use borrowed clippers in the mirror, and it looked like ass. Everyone had kind of a shitty haircut, now he thought about it, or had just let their hair grow out. When he looked back, the gun was gone.

"Did you wipe your fingerprints off it?"

Ditz stared at him dully.

"Your fingerprints. They can get your fingerprints off the gun and match–" He stopped talking and waited for Ditz to stop laughing.

"Man. OK, man. I know I'm high, but."

"...But?"

"Huh?"

"You know you're high..."

"Bet your ass."

"Fingerprints. Why are you laughing about fingerprints, Ditz?"

"I was just picturing McMasters or his idiots trying to get fingerprints." He giggled again. "Man, he doesn't give a shit. You know he sucks at his job, right?"

Screwball folded his arms and kicked his legs out. There were no sounds outside the barbershop still. He was pretty sure nobody was looking for them.

"Where'd you learn to shoot like that, anyway?"

He shrugged like it was no big deal, but was obviously pretty proud of himself. "I used to hang with Nuke, man. You gotta be good to hang with Nuke, he didn't have patience for assholes and dimwits."

"Uh. No offense, Ditz, but, uh."

"Pssssh. None taken. I take the go-it-easy stuff now, because what the hell else is there to do. I used to be pretty badass, I have to say."

Screwball looked at the guy, with his slumped shoulders, watery eyes, long shaggy hair, slight pot belly, and red-and-yellow shirt, but also with his muscular hands and arms and the fresh memory of him taking down four dudes with four shots. He believed it.

Feeney and Angelica Drop By

The Miner carefully replaced the ribbon to mark her place in the book she'd borrowed from Takata, closed it with both hands, and placed it on her lap in front of her sheathed sword. She looked calmly up at the fidgeting young man and said, "Now, you were saying. Angelica del Rio would like to see me?"

"Y- Yeah."

She tilted her head and examined him. He had a sword at his hip, slung wrong, and a knife at the other hip which looked like he could actually draw and use it. The scars on his bared forearms looked real, so he either got so many he couldn't afford to have them all removed, or he thought they looked cool. He looked exposed and harried standing in the middle of the galleria among the sea of chintzy plastic furniture, staring her down in her chair from three meters away.

She tentatively waved a hand, and he tensed.

"Can you see me pretty well from there?"

His "yeah" was the epitome of suspicion.

"Then," she said patiently, picking up *Ethan Frome* again, "if Angelica del Rio stands right where you are, she should manage it, too."

He stood a minute, rocking up onto the balls of his feet

then back onto his heels, keenly aware that everyone in and around the galleria was looking at him except the person whose attention he wanted. The Miner opened the book in her left hand, which was a bit awkward, but left her sword more usable in case he had a brilliant idea. She didn't particularly want to cut him down in full view of half the station and all its security personnel, but advertising pays.

"I mean," he tried valiantly in a low voice. "She wants you to go see her."

"That so?" she replied, not bothering to keep her own voice down.

After a while, he turned and left to the sound of snickering and hooting from Feeney's side of the galleria. The Miner ignored them, too, and continued reading.

She got to the end of the book about an hour later, and did her best to mask how stiff she felt when she stood up. She left the chair where it was, tucked the book under her arm, and walked into Takata's restaurant. He was waiting just inside the doorway, apparently trying his best to look disgruntled. He accepted the book gracelessly.

"Thanks," she remarked. "Hadn't read it before."

"You're messing with them," he said. "They won't like it."

She nodded. "There a back door to this place?"

He frowned at her. "Service entrance onto the back hallway. Off the kitchen." He gestured back toward the curtain, and she set off that way.

"Hey, hey, hey," he followed her all the way to the bar. "You can't go back there, that's my kitchen. You're a walking health code violation."

She just grinned. "You can welcome the guests yourself, then, if you want."

"What guests?"

They both heard a hatch click and slide open from behind the bar.

"That's supposed to be locked," Takata said darkly, but didn't object when the Miner followed him into the back.

The kitchen was small but well-appointed. A griddle and four cold gas burners stood along the left interior wall, and a big dry sink and counter along the right wall, which had a doorway that she'd seen before into his tiny bedroom. A shining steel prep counter stood between them, surrounded by stools. Everything was immaculately clean. Steel and plastic tools hung in neat rows around the cooking area, plates were stacked neatly in various spots on the prep counter. Everything was clean, and nothing like a busy working kitchen.

Angelica del Rio stood in the open hatchway. The Miner hadn't seen her up close before, but she was a striking woman: taller than her, and she had presence. Someone used to knocking heads and giving orders, dealing with an army of morons, somewhere between drill sergeant and kindergarten teacher.

"Hello, Mr Takata. Hello... to you as well." Angelica's deep voice was quiet, a nice trick for making people strain to listen. "May I come in?"

The Miner glanced in the passage behind her, but the woman seemed to be alone.

Takata waved his hands in a rudely inviting gesture and looked put upon.

"A bottle of wine, please. Red. My treat."

She sat on a stool at the shined steel prep counter, hiking up her black dress a bit so as to physically manage it, and raising an eyebrow as if to dare anyone to say a word about it. Feeney's former lieutenant and enforcer didn't look particularly dangerous, but the Miner had known lots of extremely dangerous people who worked hard to look perfectly harmless. The Miner shrugged and sat at the opposite end of the counter, stretching her bare forearms out onto the cold metal.

"You look like you want to talk."

"Then you're wrong," Angelica said. "I want to fight, not talk. I want to hire you."

"That so?"

Angelica seemed to grit her teeth, then nodded once.

"Why? To do what?"

The wine came in plastic cups, and neither woman touched hers.

"They're shooting now, four of my people dead. I can't have that." Her face twisted. "I won't have it."

"Who's 'they'?"

"Feeney's psychotic crew. Goddamned maniacs, all of them."

"That so?"

Angelica leaned in, eyes keen. "Did you know his own grandson had a nuclear weapon implanted in his chest? It looked like a giant blinking tumor, and the crazy stupid bastard walked around with his shirt open so everyone could see it. He. Hires. Psychos."

"He hired me."

"And he hired me. But I quit, and you quit," she said, leaning over the table. "Maybe you're a psycho too, but I want you to be my psycho."

"Listen to her! Her psycho, indeed!" Old man Feeney elbowed his way through the open hatch, and the Miner could see bodyguards getting very close to pretending to shove each other behind him. "Listen, Mick. Jane. Whatever. You did me a good turn in quitting, and I think that shows character, by God I do–"

"You!" Angelica whirled on him. "You murdering reckless son of a bitch."

He smiled patronizingly. "Now, Angelica dear–"

The Miner was curious how he intended to end that sentence, but the cup of wine Angelica threw in his face was followed by a competent jab to the nose. The bodyguards tried to elbow their ways past each other and only succeeded in blocking the doorway. Feeney pulled a pistol, holding the sleeve of his right hand to the stream of blood and wine dripping from his face.

"McMasters would love to see that," Angelica said in a low voice.

"And he'd love to see the one you've got squirreled away somewhere too, I'm quite sure," he said in a muffled voice but not sounding too angry.

"You," said Angelica over her shoulder. "Eight thousand credits if you take care of this stupid old man for me."

Feeney hooted. "You always were a cheapskate. The ten thousand offer's still good, Jane. And unlike Angelica, you know I've got it. That casino's seen better days, girl. You could take tips from Mr Shine." He gestured with the pistol, just waving the end enough to make her stand straighter. The small snub-nose palmed in her hand was a bit more obvious when she did that. She didn't have it aimed at him, but it wouldn't take much at that range.

"If you shoot me, you won't leave this room alive. You've always been too afraid to risk your own skin, John, it hurts you."

The Miner looked back and forth between them. All it would take was a bit of noise. She leaned forward, watching the standoff. Slowly, slowly, in the pretext of leaning in, she braced her right arm against the stack of dishes. They whispered against the steel table as she gently pushed them closer to the edge. Feeney and Angelica only had eyes for each other, full of the kind of hatred that she never really saw in war. Closer.

Her arm slipped when the resistance went away. Takata didn't look her in the eye as he swept the stack of dishes up and put them next to the sink. He took her wine, too, and drained half of it in one go.

With that, the spell broke. Feeney shrugged and took a half step back. The Miner hadn't seen Angelica do anything that might have been communications, and her rangy bodyguard didn't look up to the task of avenging her, but apparently the old man either wasn't sure he could pull it off, or just didn't have the appetite for a gunfight. "I think we've both overstayed our welcome, don't you?"

They faced each other down, and Angelica looked like she'd love for him to let down his guard just a little. The Miner sat and watched with a blank face from across the prep table. The two eyed each other and her to see if she'd intervene, and when she didn't, they managed to stand down enough to extract themselves from Takata's kitchen.

"Thanks for the drink," Feeney said as the door slid shut.

"You're too much trouble, goddamn you," Takata grumbled. "They'll be back. They won't take no for an answer."

The Miner didn't respond that that was the idea, and instead asked, "What's the deal with the firearm ban, anyway?"

"Are you kidding me? You want to add guns to all this bullshit?"

"Not especially. But it's not that common."

Takata grunted and got to work mopping up wine and blood. The Miner, reminded, sipped the remaining wine in front of her and wondered if it was fruit juice gone bad. The stuff they used to call "hobo wine" in the service when they made it from ration pack juice powder. Until the brass caught on and started adding nitrates or something.

"Three months or so back they had an explosive decompression. Some kids in a firefight in the other port. Still busted so nobody can use it. Herrera almost got Anaconda kicked out over that, but the Company Rep and McMasters smoothed it over. They were serious for once; they made it plain that if either side didn't cooperate, they were getting taken down, bribes or no bribes. Maybe bigger bribes, I don't know. I hate that guy."

"Confiscated, or just put away?"

He hesitated. "I thought confiscated. Probably they've got little stashes, though. Stuff like Feeney's pea shooter."

That "pea shooter" had been a military-issue Colt that could fire explosive, incendiary, or guided rounds. The Miner didn't trust her diamond-thread suit against it. Nor, for that matter, space station hull sections manufactured by the lowest bidder.

"So," she said. "Both sides probably have halfway decent armories, but they're worried that if bodies start showing up with gunshot wounds, then McMasters will throw in with the other side and crush them. That about the whole of it?"

He stared at her. "I don't know what you're thinking, but I don't like it."

"I'm thinking that Angelica said that Feeney's crew was shooting, and I'm thinking that if that's true, then it makes no damn sense that she'd come to me instead of McMasters. Isn't a bunch of bullet-filled corpses game over for Feeney?"

"They're gangsters! They don't use logic!"

She didn't answer, just finished off the lousy wine. Out from the restaurant they heard Herrera bellow for whiskey. "He's awake," she said.

Takata just muttered under his breath, and in the process of unnecessarily tidying he tripped over the foam mattress. He swore at it in a language she didn't know, then turned on her. "Why are you still here, leading them on like this? Why don't you just leave us to our crapfest?"

She leveled her gaze at him, but he didn't meet it. "Do you want me to go?"

He grunted and set himself to wrestling with the mattress, trying in vain to roll it up and stick it under the counter again. He burst out suddenly, like finishing a sentence that started in his head, "Or you could go work for McMasters, if you really want to clean this place up. Do it legit."

She shook her head slowly. "He doesn't want to clean up, at least not that way. Anyway, I burned that bridge to cinders."

"Go to the Company Rep. She could make him take you. Herrera could get her to make him take you."

"An arrangement like that's a good way to get a bullet in the back."

"Ah, to hell with you." He stormed out to go get Herrera drunk, and didn't speak to her again that night. But he laid out the foam mattress again before he went to bed.

CHANGE OF PLANS

The Miner ate her breakfast, and it tasted better for having paid for it. It wasn't rice exactly, and it wasn't coffee exactly, but the delicately salted leftover tilapia from the belowdecks aquaculture tasted at that moment like the best thing she'd ever had.

Takata stared at his little video screen for a while after breakfast, sitting behind the bar and not bothering to make conversation. The Miner, with his grunted permission, went to borrow another of his dozen ratty paperbacks, and noted with amusement that *The Count of Monte Cristo* had disappeared. From the remainder, she finally selected *The Moonstone* and settled into a booth to read it while Takata, his video ended, shuffled back to bed for a nap.

The Miner read in the quiet of the dark restaurant through the morning, sitting in a booth with one foot propped up on the seat. She could hear Takata's gentle snoring through the curtain. It had been long enough to put the sides on edge, she decided; it was time to make her move and get Mr Shine to step up. She put down the book and contacted her ship.

"Hi boss!"

"Report status."

The ship rattled through a long list of numbers: fuel level, gas mixtures, power generation, battery levels, water purity, and on and on. Everything sounded good. Incident report showed eighteen intrusion attempts, no successful logins. McMasters, she figured. If he really wanted to get in and was willing to have it officially traced to his office, then she couldn't stop him, but he seemed to want to keep it quiet. Could be he realized she'd be an unfortunate enemy. Could be he just didn't see the profit in it yet. Could be he didn't know how. She pulled up video from the plant room, and felt herself relax when it came up, as muscles she didn't know were clenched untensed. The *Phalaenopsis* was starting to droop, but it would be all right for a few more days. The bonsai were in good shape; only a few dropped leaves that she ached to sweep away. She gazed at it awhile in soft focus, until she felt she could almost smell the earthy aroma of the small room.

"I should go," she murmured. To hell with Feeney and Angelica and McMasters. To hell with Shine. Maybe Takata was right, maybe it would be better for one of them to just win. Let the lures of peace and prosperity tame them. Maybe justice would come in time, maybe not. The moral arc of the universe was a sine wave, wasn't it?

She woke from her reverie to banging from the kitchen. Takata, with her help, had figured out how Angelica had overridden the lock, and fixed it so that wouldn't work. Definitely a fist on metal. She considered going to open it, and decided not to. Wasn't in her plan, maybe, or just not up for it yet.

Takata came out of his bedroom looking rumpled and grumpy. "It's for you," he said sourly.

"I'm not at home."

He leveled a dull glare at her, then reached over and punched the button to raise the shutters.

"Well I am," he said as they rattled and squealed open. "So figure out for yourself what you're doing."

The shutters lifted to show someone's crossed black-clad legs in a chair out front. A pair of hands had just finished putting something away, and the body rose to its feet. Folded arms reappeared over a black jacket, but not a security uniform. A smirking handsome face with deftly-done iridescent scales at the temples of a hairless scalp. The Miner had seen that face before, and abruptly had the familiar thought that he looked too cheerful to be a local.

The Miner stiffened as the shutters opened all the way to show atop the man's bald head a familiar white fez with a golden tassel, specked with red that hadn't been there when she'd first seen the man, talking to the previous owner of the hat. She glanced at Takata, and the crumpled, miserable look on his face confirmed that he recognized it too.

"Angelica's brother," Takata muttered. His fingers clawed at the bar. "God damn it," he muttered, his voice choked. "I told them to keep their mouths shut."

The new owner of the fez bowed elaborately, though not so low that it fell off. Two thugs the Miner recognized as Feeney's goons rushed up, but four more appeared from the sides to intercept them. The young man paid them no mind.

"It's a pleasure to finally meet you," he said. "I get back from a business trip, and all I hear is about this crazy talented fighter who came to town."

The Miner nodded.

"My name is Raj del Rio."

"That so?"

He waited, then just smiled. "My sister made you an offer yesterday. I was hoping I could persuade you to take it."

She raised an eyebrow. "She offered me less than Feeney did. Why would I take it?"

The smile widened to a grin, accompanied by a knowing wink. "She just expected to have to bargain, you understand these things. If she hadn't been so rudely interrupted, she might have gone up to, who knows? Twelve thousand credits?"

"Might have. Maybe higher."

He looked delighted, and she saw that his canine teeth were artificially lengthened. Implants or gene mods, she wondered, and decided she didn't know enough about dentistry.

"Fourteen? Ah no, obviously sixteen thousand."

"She'd go that high, would she?"

"I'm confident."

"She must be crazy. Or desperate."

His expression froze very briefly, and he seemed to decide that it was a joke. "Could be, I hear craziness is genetic. Wouldn't you work for a crazy woman for sixteen thousand credits, though?"

She scratched her neck under the collar of her jumpsuit and gave him a searching look. "Might have done, yesterday," she admitted. "But you shouldn't have worn that hat, Raj del Rio."

The grin became brittle, and behind her Takata made a small noise of triumph. "Why not? I think it's pretty cunning, don't you?"

"It looks good on you. Striking."

"Well, then!" He showed more of his teeth and got a sly look. "Maybe you want more than money? I'm a good looking son of a bitch, I know, but let's stick to business, hey?"

"The trouble is, Raj, I know where you got that hat."

The grin went away entirely. "You think you do."

"I know where you got it. And I know it means you just came into a lot of money. I aim to have some of that money. Let's say, twenty-five thousand credits of it."

Raj threw back his head and laughed raucously, his clapping drowning out the noises of betrayal behind her. She stepped away from the bar before Takata could find the shotgun secreted there. "I'm glad we understand each other," she said, and left *The Moonstone* where it lay.

Working for Angelica

Two dozen pairs of wary eyes followed the Miner as Raj led her into the casino. They might have seen her stagger at the wave of humid, body odor-laced air released when the doors slid open for her, an earthiness that reminded her very faintly of her plant room. Maybe she imagined it, but those eyes seemed hungrier, less drug-dulled than Feeney's crew. Rows of one-armed bandits, betting games, and pachinko machines filled the casino's front room, dark and quiet and dead-looking, standing guard in their rows over blankets, bottles, garbage, and other flotsam of human nesting. Angelica's soldiers stood silently, watching the two of them walk slowly down the center aisle.

Angelica made her entrance down from the top of the sweeping blue-lit spiral staircase, and it would have been impressive had the Miner not noticed her shadow hovering on the top step waiting for her cue. She stepped slowly until she arrived halfway down the stairs, where her feet were level with the Miner's face, and stood silent a moment. All the noise was breathing and the low rumble of ineffective air movers. The stale humid air felt like it could drown her. If she hadn't been choking on the smells of unwashed goons and cheap booze, the Miner might even have felt slightly intimidated.

"You have much to answer for," Angelica said coldly.

The Miner scratched behind her left ear. "That so?"

"You've killed four of my crew."

"Four?" The Miner frowned, and silently counted on her fingers: thumb, first finger, middle finger. She hesitated, wagged her head a little as though mentally arguing a point, and relaxed the other two on the hand. "Could be. So what?"

She heard Raj suppress a snicker.

"So," Angelica continued. "If you kill four of mine, I expect you to kill four times four of his!" Her voice rose, and she had good control of it. Hard faces all around the Miner nodded, tight-lipped and serious game faces ready for battle. The few she recognized seemed the angriest.

"That's it? Kill fifteen people? All right."

Angelica's face froze, righteous anger petrified. The Miner waited. A few of the hard faces looked suddenly worried; eyebrows furrowed, eyes cast to the side in calculation. Raj did laugh then, and slapped her on the back.

"You'll fit right in," he said as he walked around her with a big grin on his face, then spread his hands to take in the rest of the room. "You and all us other intellectuals."

His laugh spread among the crowd, uneasily at first, and then more naturally. A few faces still stared angrily at her, but most of Angelica's crew had relaxed. Angelica herself looked to have lost some poise. She stared down past her brother at the Miner, then nodded to herself and smiled. It was a more natural expression for her, tired and amused at the same time. In another life, the Miner thought she might have liked this woman.

"Come up to my office," Angelica said. "We've got some plans to make."

The Miner hesitated, then followed. The few pairs of eyes

still on her glared as she ascended the stairs. She caught a breeze from the upstairs office, cooler, drier, and not nearly as eye-watering. The office itself sat perched over the casino like a vulture. Two glass windows provided a view of the casino floor, but the rest of the round office's walls were floor-to-ceiling video screens. A black kidney-shaped glass desk squatted in the middle of the space with a comfortable-but-imposing black leather chair nestled in the indentation.

"Much better up here," Angelica said, giving her a significant look as the door slid shut behind them. The Miner paid her no attention, attracted instead by the walls covered in dimly-lit video and neon spikes of data graphs. She made an unconcerned tour of the room, peering at bits and pieces. Most of the views were of the casino floor – slot machine rows in front, poker and mahjong tables further back, then smaller private rooms whose tables and booths were covered with bedding, garbage, and weaponry. Some of the views showed the galleria, and plain white-plastic back passageways marked with black letters and numbers that meant nothing to her. The front of Feeney's hotel featured prominently from multiple angles, and the galleria entrance to the security station. Part of a cargo hold showed in one view, with its neighboring squares blacked out. Deciding it would be more suspicious to skip those than to pay obvious attention to them, she dutifully scratched her chin at them for a moment before moving on. She made a show of taking it all in, not obviously focusing on any one of them. Either Angelica was intimately familiar with and interested in all those views, or they were tossed up in an effort to impress.

She turned her attention obliquely to her new employer, sitting erect in a big black chair meant for lounging. The Miner recognized it from pictures in the back of Feeney's hotel wall, which had featured Mr Shine looking relaxed and genial in his tuxedo in that chair and Angelica herself leaning against the big black glass desk. Angelica in the flesh couldn't quite look down her nose at the Miner from a seated position, but seemed to be trying her best. Probably get a neck cramp if she tried any harder.

The Miner finished her slow tour of the video wall, her hand resting on the round metal pommel of her sword like it was a swagger stick. She scratched her chin again, looked back at the feed of the security station. It looked wrong somehow, but she couldn't work it out.

"I see a great deal of what goes on in this station," Angelica said. "Very little gets past me."

"I can recommend a good book."

Angelica snorted.

"I suppose," she continued when the Miner just kept staring at the video, "that you'd like to discuss money."

The Miner looked directly at her, then. "Already discussed money."

"You discussed it with my brother. Now you will discuss it with me."

The Miner nodded. "I'll take half up front."

A thin eyebrow went up. "You're taking a lot for granted, aren't you?"

"Maybe. But I figure you don't want me to walk out that door and tell your brother you don't keep his deals. Especially if I'm loud about it."

Angelica pursed her lips, then shrugged. "Before you do anything rash, let me show you something interesting." With a finger movement, she made the video feeds vanish, and the Miner was suddenly looking up at herself. Grossly distorted, and from chest height, something about the scene looked familiar... aha.

"I can kill you," came a flat, calm voice, hers. The speaker was on the desk, which she felt ruined the effect a bit. And she hated hearing the sound of her recorded voice anyway. "I'm not just some bruiser, kid. I've been trained, and you haven't."

They both watched as the Miner tried half-heartedly to defuse the situation, then cut down the kid with the lip rings. Then her scarred face got big on the wall, her fingers became huge, and the video cut.

Angelica looked at her like she expected a response, so the Miner said, "Damn, I'm good looking."

"You're a murderer."

She shrugged. "You're not paying me to organize your underwear."

"No. But I think that not all compensation is in credits. Maybe some of yours is my not sending that video to Tom McMasters."

The Miner let that hang in the air for a moment, and turned her back on Angelica in case she was too obviously smiling. "I suppose I could come down a bit in price."

"I suppose you can. Feeney was paying you ten thousand, I'm told. I'll match that."

The Miner shook her head. "Come to that," she said, "I don't think you listened too carefully to what I was telling your brother about his hat."

"What about his hat?" The Miner turned to see the genuine look of wariness.

"You don't know where it came from, do you?"

"I didn't ask."

"You should. It's how I know about that ship in your cargo bay." Angelica didn't respond, so the Miner leaned in. "I'm pretty sure it's how Feeney knows about it, too."

Angelica's thin, sour expression didn't betray a lot of emotion. "He doesn't know," she said after a long think.

"All right, he doesn't know," the Miner said. She dropped into the chair across the desk from Angelica. "The son of a bitch hung me out to dry, so I'm not going to tell him, at least not for free."

"You wouldn't leave here alive."

"Might."

Angelica's brown eyes didn't blink, and didn't show what she was thinking. The Miner tried not to look too aggressive, but didn't look away either.

"Ten thousand up front," Angelica finally said. "If you're worth the rest, you'll get the rest."

"I'm worth it."

"Then you'll get it. I'm not Feeney, my word's good."

FEENEY PUTS ON HIS THINKING CAP

"Then why did you let her quit?"

Feeney just made a frustrated noise at his granddaughter. "I didn't think she'd go work for that traitor! I thought she'd be sensible and lay low for a while, then come back to work for me. How was I to know she meant it?"

Mary leaned over the old man's desk and almost growled at him. "All our people heard you letting her take the fall for that fight."

"Well, you said yourself that it was her fault."

"I did. It was."

"So?" Feeney turned to Screwball with an appealing look, but he just shrugged. He felt weird and out of place hanging out with the boss, and he didn't want to fuck it up by getting between family. He'd just sort of tagged along, and the old man had just sort of accepted that. So he shrugged, and that seemed to be the right answer.

"So," Mary said, giving Screwball a momentary odd look, then back to her grandfather, "you didn't have to accept it. You could have–"

"Could have!" Feeney slammed his veiny fist on the desktop. "I could have done this or I could have done that. I could have done a million things, but I always did what made sense to me,

I always followed my instincts, and by God those instincts put me on top. If I second-guessed myself, I wouldn't be here today."

"Well," Mary said, straightening up and standing back from the desk with her arms crossed. "Where you are today is in control of half a station, with a morale problem."

"Are we? Corbell, do we have a morale problem?"

Both pairs of eyes were on Screwball, and he didn't flee in terror.

"Well..." They did, that was the thing. Everyone came back from the fight pissed off that they'd have won it if Jane had been in it, and then there she was getting fired for it – nobody believed she "fell on her sword for the good of the side" for one minute – and now word was getting around that she'd gone to work for Angelica, and some people were bitching that they were all gonna die. "...kinda? Yeah?"

Feeney threw up his hands, but Screwball had a sudden maybe-not-stupid idea, and before he knew it his mouth was open again. "But I think that's OK, right? They just need to win a little bit and they'll feel pretty good that they're still badasses even without her. And the security guy–"

"McMasters," Mary supplied automatically, with a thoughtful look.

"McMasters, right, he's not looking at us right now. He hates her for some reason and he thinks she's a troublemaker, so maybe if we start something right now he'll, um." His brain caught up to his adrenaline and stumbled.

"He'll assume it's Jane," Feeney said, and a big grin spread across his face. "That's exactly what he'll do." He clapped his hands in delight. "What did you have in mind?"

"Well, um," he said. He cast about the corners of his brain, which had suddenly gone stubbornly blank. He gaped, and then admitted. "Well, I hadn't gotten that far."

Feeney's grin didn't fade, though Screwball didn't like the skeptical look on Mary's face. "Well, I didn't hire you to be the brains of the outfit, so that's all right. But you're on the right track, by God, you're on the right track."

"There's something else weird," Screwball found himself saying before his brain started screaming and throwing on the brakes. "Ditz kind of, um, shot some dudes."

Mary stared at him. "Kind of. Shot. Some dudes."

"Yeah, but like, by accident."

"He accidentally had a gun. And accidentally shot some dudes. Goddamnit."

"But, like, it's OK? That was yesterday, and Angelica hasn't said shit. She has to know. So why hasn't McMasters come and yelled at us?"

All three fell silent, and Screwball tried to look thoughtful instead of just confused. Feeney looked up first, still grinning.

"Well isn't that interesting. Pour yourself a drink, my boy, and let's put our thinking caps on."

Raj and the Miner Visit Sparks

The Miner was still considering her next move when the knock came on the door. After pointing out that she wasn't terribly popular, Angelica had given the Miner one of the private karaoke suites to sleep in, evicting the surly-looking fighter who'd previously had that honor. The door locked, anyway, though the Miner had taken the precaution of reprogramming it. She'd half-woken six or seven times the previous night to noises outside the restaurant or the air movers momentarily falling silent, and it was starting to catch up to her. Light sleep was still better than no sleep, of course, and she hadn't had to resort to Doc Mills's sleeping meds yet, but an early bedtime was an attractive option.

Raj del Rio filled the doorway when it opened, grinning. Those eye teeth mods made him look like a wolf when he did that, and the Miner had no doubt that he grinned like that as often as he could, for exactly that reason. He had the white fez on still, though it clashed with the night's outfit of black semi-shined jacket and trousers. "Good, you're still up. Come on, and be quiet. I want to show you something."

They crept out the back of the casino past snoring hulks on the floor. There was a guard station at the back, but Raj explained that he'd told them to grab some dinner. On cue, the Miner's stomach grumbled. Raj laughed and handed her a half-eaten ration bar.

"It's supposed to taste like figs," he said, "but I don't know what the fuck a fig is, so who knows."

The Miner didn't exactly know what a fig was either, just some kind of fruit, but the cloyingly sweet bar tasted fine. It turned to a thick paste in her mouth with the faintest hint of mold. She'd had far worse; still, she took only a few bites before folding the silver wrapper over and handing it back. She ignored the university shield emblem stamped on it.

"They make you shit bricks," Raj said conversationally as he tucked the rest back into his inside jacket pocket. "But I think they taste all right."

"That they do," the Miner agreed. "What did you want to show me?"

"A little ways on." He glanced at her. "Relax, if I wanted to kill you I'd have killed you."

"You'd have tried."

He laughed. "I like you, sister."

They talked companionably as they walked, and the Miner found herself forgetting very easily her resolve to kill him. He brought up her sword, and spoke knowledgeably on the subject of metal composition and whether annealing-based repairs were worth a damn. They both agreed not. That brought the topic to killing, a subject on which he spoke equally knowledgeably, and with similar diffidence.

"This whole war is bullshit," he said. "Feeney's all right, I like him. Get some booze in him and he's a real droog. The whole thing with Willy sucked, but it wasn't really his fault. It's just, trying to be a boss and a grandfather both, that's hard."

"Willy?"

"Nuke, I mean. I never got used to calling him that."

"How'd it suck?"

"We were friends. He was a great guy. Little psycho, sure, but this line of work, come on. No worse than Ditz or Monkey." He chuckled. "Maybe no worse than me, hey, sister?"

She just chuckled. They walked in silence a short ways.

"What happened to Nuke, anyway?"

Raj surprised her by sighing theatrically. "I. Don't. Know. All right, that out of the way? You can tell my dear sister that you tried, but I still don't know, and she can fuck off all right?"

The Miner gave him a puzzled look. "What are you talking about?"

"Angelica. She told you to ask that."

The Miner shook her head. "Nope. Just curious is all. Honest."

"Oh." He looked mollified by that. "Sorry, I'm tired of her trying to worm it out of me, but shit, I really don't know what the old man did with the guy."

"Think he killed him?"

Raj gave her a morose look, serious. "If he has any smarts he did."

"I thought you liked Nuke."

"I did. I like the old man, too. But you stab someone in the back like that, you better make sure he's dead. That's all I'm saying."

He looked like he wanted to say more, so the Miner kept her mouth shut. After a few steps, Raj went on.

"It was his fight with that shitfuck trucker that did it, not just the–" he waved his hand vaguely at his chest. "He started fights once he got that thing in. He said he was playing on God mode now, nobody could hurt him, nobody could let him be hurt. Word got around, mostly, people stayed out of his way. So he started ambushing people, starting shit out of the blue."

"Huh."

"Yeah. I never seen my sister that scared. It was one thing when he picked fights with people who knew what that thing in his chest was. But one dumbshit trucker coulda killed us all and never had a clue. You know what happens if you set one of those things off inside a space station, even a tiny one like that?"

"Instant death for anyone standing close by. Radiation burns for anyone not behind a few inches of solid metal or rock. An expanding fireball that burns through plastic and thin metal. An electromagnetic pulse that knocks out unshielded electronics, including emergency systems. A pressure wave that travels the length of the station's air mover network, blowing out baffles and control surfaces. If you're lucky, the whole thing shuts down. If you're unlucky, it helpfully spreads radioactive particles throughout the entire inhabited space."

"...yeah," Raj said weakly after her matter-of-fact recitation. "Something like that."

They walked a long way in silence. Raj knew his way through the stained white plastic corridors, down stairwells. The Miner stopped at each landing and listened before they proceeded. Raj smiled indulgently the first two times, then grinned the third time she did it.

"You give them way too much credit," he said. "Anyway, this is our side of the station. Feeney's guys wouldn't come over here."

"You don't patrol it. You don't have enough people to claim this much territory."

He cocked his head at her. "How many you think we need?"

She shrugged. "I don't know how much you claim. You should be tagging the walls so your people know. You want to claim half the station? I'd want two hundred people before I'd call it mine. Or at least doubled-up surveillance and a good face rec AI to monitor the feeds, trained on every face that goes into Feeney's hotel."

"Like yours?" The Miner didn't turn to look at him, but heard the grin in his voice.

"If I were you, I'd keep tabs on where I was." She said it seriously.

"Eh. You're probably right. You seem to know your shit. The thing is, the territory's ours because everyone kind of agrees it's ours. Sis hates Feeney like a bleeding hemorrhoid but she doesn't want to piss off McMasters, and she still thinks Mr Shine might come around."

"Tell me about Mr Shine."

He shrugged expressively. "Big guy. Used to run the casino, but got huffy when Sis and Feeney started fighting. He threw in with Angelica when she said Nuke had to go, but then when Nuke *did* go he didn't want to knock Feeney off."

"So why doesn't he still work for Feeney?"

"Because the old man ordered him to kill Angelica, and he said fuck that, grow up." He turned, wide-eyed. "Literally, he told the old man to grow up. He's like, shit, half Feeney's age. So the old man blew his top, and Mr Shine got mad and said some shit, and he kind of banished himself down to the bottom decks, down in the rock. A bunch of our better people went with him, the people who used to actually run stuff and only got rough on the side, you know? Dealers and dishwashers and shit. Never fuck with a dishwasher, lady. Most of the crews up in the hotel and the casino are new, pretty much anyone we could hire off the ships that come through."

The Miner considered that, and wondered how Raj knew what passed between Feeney and Shine. "They suck."

"Yeah, I know they suck. But they all suck kind of the same, so it evens out." He favored her with another grin that was more like a leer. The white fez teetered ominously as he swung his head. "Raj del Rio's Grand Theory of Mutual Sucking. Think there's a Nobel Prize in it?"

"No."

He just laughed. "So how would you beat Feeney, with this little crew of misfits and assholes?"

She mulled it over, skipped the real answer, and replied, "Throw morons at them until they turtle in the hotel. Blow the seals so the station systems go on segment lockdown. Punch a hole in the hull over Feeney's office and vent atmo until the breach plugs with corpses." She shrugged.

Raj whistled. "Shit, sister, that's cold."

"Cold works."

Instead of responding, he said, "We're almost there."

"Where's there?"

"You'll see."

They'd been walking for at least ten minutes, but the Miner had a poor sense of direction in the twisting corridors of the lower station, and her map was incomplete. They were on deck six, same as the drug lab, but that was all she knew. She toyed with the idea of killing Raj, but decided against it – someone would notice they left at the same time, and anyway they'd never find the body, which would defeat the purpose.

"Here we are," Raj said, interrupting her homicidal musings. The sign had been removed from above the hatchway, but the open hatch showed plainly where they were: one of the mechanics' bays, where the old military station would have performed ship repairs that needed dry dock. Off to both sides where they couldn't be seen from the hallway, three bored-looking goons loitered. "After you," he added.

The Miner hesitated at his too-broad grin, but shrugged and took a step. The ground seemed to shift away from underneath her foot, and she stumbled – but didn't fall. Her momentum carried her forward, but she managed to turn and see Raj laughing. He was bending over into the inside bulkhead and grabbing a pair of magnet shoes stuck to the post next to the hatch they'd come through, so that he could walk in the nullified gravity. She cursed herself for not putting two and two together, and had plenty of opportunity to do it while she slowly drifted until she bumped into a stack of something covered in a tarp and strapped down to the deck.

She bounced gently off it, and wheeled in the air. She could fight like that if she had to – had done it, ages ago, and won – and she saw no reason to either panic or look like she was panicking. Instead she just let herself drift and turn. The bay loomed, cavernous and dark, full of stuck-down containers and a big white ship whose hull had already been partly stripped. Spotlights lit the areas where the hull sections met empty air, where someone had begun breaking down the ship into salable parts. The bits where the ship's name would have been painted on had all been, by some coincidence, already removed despite being at multiple corners of the huge form.

"Who the hell are you?" A sharp voice came from above her.

"She's with me, Sparks!"

From above the Miner, the only other sound was the hiss of air jets. Something gently pushed her toward the floor. When she turned in her drifting, she looked up to see a chair assembly rotating in her field of view. Tools and parts clung to it by tethers like a hairball, and in the center of the metal cyclone sat ensconced a thin gray-haired woman with an acid expression and no legs. A screwdriver and a socket wrench were both stuck to the side of her head – implanted magnets? She'd just met Sparks Laghari, was the Miner's guess.

"*Why's* she with you? You ever heard of OPSEC, idiot?"

The Miner, who had managed to stop her drift and steady herself against a container, looked up.

Raj had strolled over to the Miner with another pair of slip-on magnet shoes, and she looked around absentmindedly as she cinched them on over her boots. The dry dock loomed overhead, where steel arches braced painted asteroidal rock and formed a hangar shape with individually-controlled spotlights lighting up the partially-consumed hulk floating in the center of the space. Little robots darted around on air jets, starting and stopping abruptly like insects. Some flew solo, others hauled chunks of metal and machinery in pairs or triplets.

The Miner couldn't tell much about the ship in mid-disassembly – she could do basic repairs on her own ship without manual vids or overlays, and she was proud of that, but she wasn't a general mechanic, let alone a shipwright. The ship was a Cavalier-class, pretty new, or at least not used much, since its plating didn't have the mismatched-shade look from the replacement of used-up ablative panels, nor many scars from micrometeorite or charged particle strikes. The pilot's nest had probably been up front, but that was the section that had been most thoroughly disassembled. Interior consoles showed through the rectangular holes in the hull, and gold foil gleamed in pockets where sensitive instruments still lay nestled in bundles of cabling.

The equipment around the hangar looked like scaled-up versions of the stuff she kept around her own ship: welders and cutters sat coiled with their air filters and harnesses waving gently in the low-G breeze, flower-like clamps stuck to the wall where their arms could be extended and fixed where needed, vacuum hoses curled like vine tendrils into the spaces where they'd been last used. Loose hand tools swayed on their tethers like seaweed. Somewhere out of sight, she could hear the sizzle and crackle of a laser cutter at work on metal, and the breeze of the heavy-duty air recyclers tickled the hairs on her forearms and neck.

Sparks studied her as she looked around the space. "Nice," the Miner finally said, straightening up as her feet clicked gently to the deck, and turning her attention to the mechanic. Sparks sat nestled in a heavily-customized mover chair, her left hand lazily manipulating the major thrusters to keep her moving in a slow orbit around her guests. The mechanic herself was a lean woman with a hatchet face. The sleeves of her jumpsuit had been cut off to show well-muscled arms. Her welding goggles were pushed up into a rat's nest of gray hair that floated free in tangles and curls. Her legs looked to be cut off mid-thigh, with the ends nestled up against a welded-on backstop.

Instruments the Miner couldn't identify bristled on and in the floating chair, with tiny lights blinking and flickering in a rainbow of colors, little jets adjusting her orientation and position with squirts of cold air that she could feel from a few meters away. Tiny antennas and manipulators stuck out at odd angles.

"This is Jane," Raj said. "She's a bit of a badass. You heard of her?"

Sparks craned her head this way and that, frowned at the sword. "Thought she worked for Feeney."

"Not anymore."

"Not exactly the trustworthy type, then."

"We both used to work for Feeney too, Sparks."

She grunted. "That's different. Why'd you switch sides?"

The Miner shrugged. "Started a fight in the galleria. He fired me to save face with McMasters. I figured that made me a free agent."

She stuck her hands in her pockets and looked at Sparks with a bland expression. She still had two listening bugs left. Shitty range and not much power left, but maybe worth dropping.

"So why'd you join up with us? Like to gamble?"

The Miner tilted her head to one side, but Raj answered for her.

"She liked my hat."

Sparks gave him a hard look, then scowled. "You fucking idiot. I should have told you to leave it."

"You should have tried, anyway." He grinned like that was a friendly thing to say.

She grumbled something under her breath. "So what do you want?"

"I wanted to see how done you were, and I wanted our new friend to have a look at our security down here if it's going to be a while. Since she already knew what we had here, I figured it wasn't a risk."

She swore. "It's a big fucking ship, and you want it stripped instead of pulped. It's going to take ages before we make any money off it." She squinted. "That's what you wanted her to hear, right?"

He just laughed. "How about the data? Anything we can sell right away?"

The Miner took an experimental step in the magnet shoes, pretending to be unused to them, and finding that she actually kind of was. The hand she put out to steady herself against the bulk under the tarp left behind one of the bugs in the cloth's folds. It looked enough like junk that it wouldn't stand out too much if anyone found it, she hoped.

Sparks shook her head. "Not my thing."

The Miner pointed off at some storage cubes strapped down near the enormous outer hatch. "I can buy some of that fuel off you."

"You bloody well can't. Do I look like a fucking dockmaster?" She sneered and turned back to Raj. "I sent everything I recovered that I can't use myself to Angelica. Bank links for most of the crew, but you'd be a fucking idiot to tap those."

"I've got a recent link for the old man's account," the Miner said. "We could arrange for him to get a suspicious transfer of cash."

"Christ, you're as dumb as you look," Sparks retorted. "You do that, the bank investigators will fucking swarm. They're worse than the navy."

Raj laughed again. "It's not so dumb. Just as long as we wait until you're done."

"Which will be fucking never if you don't get out of my hair."

He held up his palms in surrender. "OK, OK. I get it. Listen, I just want Jane to give this place a once-over, and let me know what she thinks from a security standpoint. Then we'll leave you in peace."

Sparks chewed her lower lip, studying the Miner. It seemed like all the little antennas were pointed at her while she stared, gimlet-eyed skeptical. "Not sure I'm keen on her wandering around here."

With some negotiating, Raj got her to grudgingly agree to let the Miner take a tour of the outside of the bay, to inspect the three hatches and the guard details around them. He whistled for one of the goons outside, and tasked the bodybuilder-type who poked her head in with playing guide. She and the Miner scowled at each other, then the Miner stripped off the magnet shoes and let herself be led around. The corridors were sheathed in yellow-stained white plastic cladding, a bit different from the other decks. The rush of water and air through pipes, and the chugging of nearby pumps, came to her ears through the seams.

"Well?" came Raj's voice, faintly, in her ear.

"She's loaded," Sparks said. "I couldn't scan that well from so far, but my guess is about three hundred thousand credits' worth of military grade implants."

Raj whistled. "Someone made a serious fucking investment in her, just to let her run loose."

"Losing side, is my guess. Funny what goes missing when they're trashing the records. She's got the works, too. Joints, nerves, liver. That fake eye is functional, I'll bet, probably has low-light vision and a basic visual interface for her ship. I can't tell what all else is going on in that skull of hers, not without a closer scan, but it's probably a lot of fun."

The Miner, reminded, checked her ship's telemetry. Seemed to still be OK. She'd have to check on the plants later.

Raj's voice was indistinct, but Sparks laughed in response to whatever he said.

"Tell you what," she said. "You get it, and I'll sell it, how's that for a division of labor?"

The Miner nodded and smiled. Her minder gave her a funny look, but shrugged and they kept walking to the next guard station.

"After we take down Feeney," Raj was saying. "Sis needs her help, if I'm being honest, but she doesn't feel like setting up a new rival just when she's ready to finally take down the old one."

"Suits me. Something about that chick I don't like."

"She's taller than you."

"Fuck you." She quickly added, "That's not an offer."

"Now, now, my sister only says I'd screw anything on two legs."

Sparks laughed. "Glad I left them in the office."

The Miner missed Raj's response to static that just got worse as she and her minder walked. It was just as well – Raj appeared in front of them and waved the minder off. The Miner filled the walk back to the casino with plausible bullshit, and considered her plans.

SCREWBALL LISTS THE OPTIONS

Screwball waited until Mary left. She'd gotten fed up with the admittedly kinda nutty schemes they were dreaming up, read her grandfather the riot act over their finances, and then left in a huff, leaving them both behind, neither the wiser for having had their "thinking caps" on. With the old man in his cups, sunk into the big chair behind his desk like he wanted to be swallowed up, Screwball figured now was as good a time as any to come up with something brilliant. Or fake it.

"It seems to me," he tried again, "that time's against us here. You've got a lot of money, but it sounds like maybe not a lot of income. Does Angelica have much from the casino, though?"

Feeney snorted. "She's run the damn place into the ground, she has. But she's got the chop shop, too, remember. Makes some decent cash off that, a chunk at a time."

Screwball considered that, and a dim little light lit in the back of his head. "If she had something big down there, she wouldn't want McMasters sniffing around, would she?"

Feeney shook his head in a loose motion, the exaggerated gesture of a drunk man. "No. We always paid the law pretty damned well to push off. Officially the mechanic's bay is..." He snapped his fingers a couple times.

"Out of service?"

"Don't put words in my mouth, boy. Out of service."

"So, if Ditz shot some of her people near the mechanic's bay, she might just sit on it?"

Feeney's eyes focused on him hard, and for a moment he thought the old man's drunkenness had just been a put-on. "That's what I'd have done. Unfortunate, but cost of doing business."

Screwball frowned. "So... if she's got something big, she's going to want to hold out until she can make some money on it. How long's that take?"

"Depends," Feeney said, and shrugged. "If she knew she was coming into some treasure – and I usually didn't, back in my day – she would have arranged a scrap trader well ahead of time. Wouldn't make it a rush job, though. Getting through that," and here he stumbled a few times to get out the words, "ablative plating – God – that takes a while."

"What if we got word to McMasters?"

The white eyebrows went up. "Are you seriously asking me, what if we told Tom McMasters that one of the sides he's been soaking for cash is about to come into a lot more money than the other? Good God, boy, are you trying to get me run out of here? Don't think of him as the law, son. He's not. I've dealt with the law all my life, mostly crooked, some honest. He's neither. He's just a craven son of a bitch with a borrowed badge, and his job's to keep a lid on things."

"What about the real law, then?"

Feeney waved a hand dismissively. "The real law doesn't give a splattering shit what goes on in this station, not unless it makes them look bad."

"What if we can *fix* it so it makes them look bad, though?" Screwball leaned in. "Look, this is basically piracy, right?"

"That's debatable..."

"Angelica's doing it, not you."

"Oh. Yes, good old-fashioned piracy and no mistake."

"What if we got proof and sent it off? If it's juicy enough, they'll come, right?"

"Surely, but they won't limit themselves to just her. Once they're here, they'll burrow in like a tick. They'll be on my case, too."

Screwball shrugged, smiling. "You've dealt with the law all your life. And you'll know they're coming."

The old man leaned back in his chair, elbows on the arms, fingers laced. He stared at his knobby knuckles. "There's something to that, my boy. You'd have to get in there, though, and you'd have to make sure Angelica never knew. If she thinks the jig is up, she'll have plans to hide the loot."

"I can get in there. Ditz knows that place like the back of his hand. Him and Nuke used to go down and smoke up with Sparks."

"Him and Wilfred, eh?" His eyes went unfocused for a moment, and took on an odd look. It lasted only a moment, and he shook his head. "A more dimwitted, dangerous pair, I've never known. Their pal Raj went with them, you know. Good boy, Raj. Shame he was loyal to his sister after all. Only really loyal man in the whole goddamned station, I think."

Screwball was surprised when the old man came out of his chair fast. He walked across the office, steadying himself against the furniture and muttering that he'd had more to drink than he thought, good stuff, and first he locked the door. Then he strode to the side wall, and at his touch a wood-grain panel at chest height slid open. The dull gray box inside looked like an old-fashioned safe, and even had an old-fashioned dial.

"I don't mind you seeing my little toy box," he said absently. "But you ought to know that I've made damned sure that anyone who tries to force this open will have one hell of a bad day."

It came open with a click, and he started to reach for something near him, then stopped. He got a sly smile on his face, then reached his forearms all the way into the cavity in the wall. He stepped back and cradled in both hands a small metal box. Slowly, he carried it to his desk and made a great show of setting it down with a surprising thump despite the care he showed.

"If Mary knew I had this, she'd pitch it into space." He chuckled. "Maybe me with it."

Screwball started to chuckle along with him, but Feeney silenced him with a glare. He struggled a little with the four mechanical catches, but persistence won out and the top half of the box came open like a clamshell.

Inside a soft gray lining that fit it exactly lay a conical metal object. Feeney stood and stared at it, almost in awe. Screwball could smell the strong alcohol on his breath still.

"What is it?"

The old man didn't look at him. "It's the black box from a police deep space cruiser. Very sensitive, and it can defend itself, I'm led to believe. I've hung onto this for a very long time, yes."

Screwball just gazed at it. It didn't look like much, but it seemed like he ought to be impressed.

"When they say that one is bringing out the big guns, this is what they mean," Feeney said in a low, almost reverent voice. "Do you know what wasps are? They're stinging insects, little flying things, a great deal like police, really. Nasty enough little things on their own, but if you crush one, they swarm.

Police are like that, too, only armed a lot better, and meaner. Once you activate this, they'll come flying, and only a copper can deactivate it."

"Won't McMasters do that?"

"If he's stupid. They watch for these signals in their big telescopes. If he turns it off, he'll have some explaining to do."

Screwball started to feel excited, but he tried to tamp it down. Something about the whole thing felt off. "Aren't they like indestructible?"

"I don't care about destroying it, boy, I care about setting it off. The minute it goes off, it starts scanning and broadcasting. I couldn't get rid of it fast enough if that happened – literally. I don't know what it would find out about me, and I don't want to know. But if this were to find its way into the chop shop... Well, the mechanic's bay is well away from anything else. I made sure the surrounding areas were rented up. Angelica's cleared them out even more. Nowhere else the signal could have come from, understand?"

"I think so."

"Good. Now, it's easy to activate manually. A good thump might do it if you have to throw it and run, but otherwise if you, ah… hmm… if you pinch these two plates at the top, I'm told that will put it on a countdown timer. If thirty minutes go by and nobody pinches it again, off it goes. Got it?" He flipped the lid back down with a snap, and Screwball jumped.

"Yes, sir." He frowned. He was pretty drunk, but he didn't understand why a police black box would need a countdown timer.

"I don't think I need to tell you that you want to be very far away from that thing when it activates. God knows what it'll, ah, scan."

"What are its defensive measures?"

"Eh? Oh. No idea. Don't stick around and find out, though."

"No, sir."

A look of brief annoyance flashed across Feeney's face, until he realized that Screwball was agreeing not to stick around. Feeney put his hand on the box and looked Screwball in the eye.

"Do not let Mary see this, under any circumstances."

"Right, sir." He swelled with slightly alcohol-enhanced pride at the trust he was being given.

"Go alone. If you get caught with this, we're all in a heap of shit. That means especially," and he pointed with a swaying finger when he said: "Don't bring Ditz."

Medical Assistance

Dr Mills answered the door against his better judgment. Late-night wakeups were rarely good news, but thanks to a glance at the camera he was prepared to give his former junior partner the best unamused look in his arsenal.

"Hello, Joff. You sick?"

"Hi, Arun," said his visitor, sheepishly scratching the back of his neck. "Can I come in?"

"Are you sick?"

As the only two doctors on the station, when they'd parted company after the Wilfred Feeney incident they'd agreed to treat each other. Each privately thought he was getting the raw end of that deal. Either way, they had agreed emphatically not to socialize.

"I brought a peace offering." Joff Philippe hoisted a bottle. Glass, full of something amber that might not have been distilled in a repurposed fuel tank. He looked haggard; probably wasted.

"I'm not going to get drunk with you. Or high. What do you want?"

He felt bad when the man winced, but he'd gotten enough trouble out of sparing Joff's feelings.

"We have to talk, Arun. It's getting bad. They're killing each other."

"They've been killing each other for months. They can stop whenever they want."

Joff shook his head. "It's serious now. It's all-out war, Arun, a shooting war. It's an all-hands-on-deck situation up there."

"And you've come to me for help."

Joff swore under his breath, half making it a laugh. "You think I want to? I've barely slept; I'm living on modafinil and amphetamines. I've had to pressgang a couple of those damn gangsters as the worst nurses you've ever imagined."

Mills folded his arms. "I suppose you're still taking payment in women and drugs."

Joff laughed bitterly. "I'm taking payment in keeping my teeth."

"Well hell, how do I get in on a deal like that?"

"I don't blame you for being angry with me," Joff said quietly, leaning in so far that Mills felt the sudden urge to try to catch him. "And I don't blame you for focusing your practice on whatever decent folk are left. I'm not one of them and I know it. But the only reason I'm not even busier than I am is that half of these poor berks are just being left to bleed out where they fall. It's a nightmare. Please."

"I'm no trauma surgeon, Joff."

"Me neither, but I've learned. God, I've learned. Just do what you can."

Mills gritted his teeth as he caught himself mentally pushing appointments back and planning what would have to go into his bag that he wouldn't mind being stolen. He'd already basically agreed, damn it.

"How bad are these nurses?"

"I caught Skeeve doing what he thought was cocaine off a bedpan."

Mills struggled with that sentence and landed on, "Skeeve?"

"Technically 'Other Skeeve' but nobody's seen Original Skeeve in a while, and if he's dead, then Other Skeeve feels he inherits because 'a man has rights'." Joff's expression grew haunted. "That is a sentence that has come out of my mouth. I can't take it back, Arun."

Cursing himself for a soft fool, Mills got his bag. He did take the whiskey, though, and figured he'd need it.

Screwball Takes a Shortcut

"Where you going, man?"

Screwball almost jumped out of his skin at the sound of Ditz's voice. He thought he'd got out the back entrance without sticking out too much, just nodding to the guys on guard. "Oh, uh, hey. Just out."

"Cool, cool." Ditz strolled up and fell in beside him. "Not smart to go wandering on your own. Angelica's people are around."

"Yeah, I know. It's just, I've got a thing to do." Ditz kept walking, nodding amiably. "I mean, like, by myself."

"Oh, it's OK, I'll keep you company."

Screwball sighed. They were at the stairs now, and it took him a while to pick through the barricade of upended tables and broken hotel furniture. A mattress in the corner, and two chairs near it, were supposed to be for the guards, but nobody wanted to hang out that far from the hotel anymore. A single camera was glued to the wall up high, and it might have worked.

"I mean, I'm not supposed to take you with me."

Ditz grinned, and Screwball realized with a start that he wasn't actually high. "Sure, I get it. But, like, did anybody say you're not supposed to let me be coincidentally but consistently, like, adjacent to you?"

"I'm pretty sure that's what Feeney meant by not taking you with me."

"Sure, sure. Only, here's the thing. This seems secret."

"Yeah, it is."

"Right. And... I just don't trust me not to talk about it. It just slips out, you know?"

Screwball sighed again. "Goddamn it, Ditz."

"Goddamn it, Ditz, indeed." He nodded sagely, and got over the barricade in one hop. "Listen, you've been pretty strung out lately, and believe me, I know."

Ditz pushed the door to the stairs open, and Screwball followed.

"There's been a lot of fighting. The old man seems to really trust me."

"Yeah..." Ditz's dippy grin faded, and Screwball was reminded that his friend was a lot older than him. Like, late thirties? Forties? Guy did a lot of drugs, made it hard to tell. "So, Feeney's all right. I'd rather work for him than Angelica, who was always kind of an ice queen. But 'all right' isn't always that great. He's kind of a bastard sometimes."

"You're thinking about Nuke."

"Yeah. I mean, no. OK, it was shitty what he did to Nuke. Like, his own grandson, man. I get it, they made him. Still. No, man, it's more... Feeney only cares about people named Feeney. You want to work for him, and that's not your name, you need to be careful."

They took the stairs in silence. "Where are we going?"

Screwball sighed. "I'm supposed to plant this thing in the chop shop. It's a police black box, like from their ships? If I set it off it calls for help, and then they'll come and bust Angelica."

"Huh. Cool. Never seen one of those before, let me have a look."

Screwball pretended to mull it over, but had to admit that he was feeling pretty cool, on a secret mission for the old man. He took the metal box out of his jacket pocket. Ditz watched with curiosity as he undid the clasps, and then held it open.

"Holy fucking shit, man! What the hell!" Ditz's eyes went wide and he stumbled back against the railing, clutching wildly.

Screwball fumbled the box, startled. It flipped over in his hands and he only barely caught it by grabbing it clumsily to his chest. "The fuck, Ditz? What's the matter with you?"

"Me? What's the matter with me? Fuck, man, shit, what's the matter with you?"

"I asked you first!"

"Ah, shit, shit, shit." Ditz groaned. He fumbled in his pockets and came up with a little cylinder of something. Flapping one hand, he calmed himself enough to hold it up to his eye and spray. He squeezed his eyes shut and swore a bunch of times.

"What?" Screwball watched in growing panic, clutching the box to his body and staring at his friend. "What are you... What??"

"That's no police black box, you asshole, that's a fucking atom bomb."

"What?!" Screwball yanked it away from his stomach and almost dropped it again. "What the fuck are you talking about, atom bomb?"

"That's the same bomb Nuke had, man! The hell are you doing with it?"

"Feeney gave it to me! He said it was a police... what the fuck, man!"

"Calm down, man, just calm down!"

"You calm down!"

"OK," Ditz said. "OK, OK, OK. O....K."

"Stop saying OK, you're freaking me out."

Ditz looked a little bug-eyed still, but kept his mouth shut.

Screwball's pulse was starting to come down to a level where he wasn't worried he'd keel over from a heart attack, and with the panic subsiding he started to feel frustrated. Ditz folded his arms and furrowed his eyebrows. Screwball wished he would say this was a bad idea so that he could deny it, but Ditz just stood there looking stupid instead of saying something stupid Screwball could argue with. And then, he realized he was angry.

"Look. Ditz. We're expendable. Disposable. Nobody gives a shit about the grunts, but you know what? I don't intend to stay a grunt. I intend to make something of myself. If I come back, Feeney will think I'm a loser. But if I do this… listen, Ditz. If I do this, I'm not just some grunt anymore." He waited for Ditz to respond, but got impatient. "Look, you said before that Nuke told you this thing wasn't that big a deal. Just like a little local explosion, right?"

"Yeah…"

Ditz frowned.

"So if I go all the way to the end of the bay and stick it on the outside door, nobody'll get hurt. Right?"

"I dunno."

"And they'll lose the use of the mechanic's bay. But there's another one, on Feeney's side of the station."

"Yeah… He uses it for storage."

"So where's your friend Sparks going to go?"

"Huh."

"You can distract her, right? Keep her away, safe?"

Ditz considered, then started slowly nodding. "I can get you in."

"How?"

"There's the emergency airlock. In case somebody gets

stuck in the bay when it's depressurizing and they're, like, too far from the main one? It's supposed to be impossible to get into from outside and there's supposed to be an alarm, so nobody ever guarded it, but we used to have it hacked so we could get in and fool around. Get high, oxplay, that kind of thing."

Screwball furrowed his brow. "You mean horseplay?"

"No, oxplay. Like, oxygen. It's an airlock, dude, you can mess with the oxygen levels and screw. If you set it real low, you get these amazing orgasms. If you set it high you get this awesome energy and can go for hours."

"Shit, man, people die doing that."

Ditz grinned. "I'm immortal so far, dude."

Feeney Has Regrets

Liam John Feeney woke with a start in the middle of a snore, and glared around at his office from his position slumped in his big chair. The galleria lights had dimmed and yellowed to their nighttime colors, leaving the furniture and knick-knacks sunk in shadow. His head was starting to hurt, and he wondered how much he'd had to drink with that Corbin lad. Carball? They all had such ridiculous names. He shook his head, and regretted it.

The water was on the other side of the room, blast it, and he eventually heaved himself upright and walked over to it on heavy feet. Something nagged at him. He was forgetting something. He never forgot anything important. He had a very good memory, the best.

He poured a few fingers of water, tossed it back. His throat was dry, he shouldn't drink so much at his age. Used to be, he'd drink three times that much and be the only one standing, by God. Just a little water, that was the trick. Take water and an aspirin, you'd be right as rain, come what may.

The safe was open. Damn, when had he–

Feeney stared. The water glass slipped from his fingers, bounced once, and splashed his trouser cuffs. He tried to send a call, and realized he didn't know how to get ahold of the

Screwball kid. Three minutes later, Mary was in his office, yelling at him.

"He doesn't know it's a nuclear weapon," he finally protested.

She stopped, and stared. Her face was blotchy red from the effort of yelling. "Do you... do you actually think that makes it better?"

"Well. I thought, if he didn't know, he wouldn't be so afraid of it. Might stay calm, you know."

She pinched the bridge of her nose and shut her eyes tight. "You can't get ahold of him at all?"

"I tried everything I could think of." He hadn't thought of much. If he were being honest, keeping things organized had never really been his strong point. Angelica had always been the one to handle that sort of piddly detail.

Mary opened her eyes and gave him a wary look. "Can it be disarmed?"

"Oh yes. It's a construction nuke, for clearing rock, not a tactical one. Easy."

Still staring, unbelieving, she collapsed into the chair across the desk from him. "We have to tell Angelica."

Feeney sat stiffly. "The hell we do. Why would we tell that witch?"

"This isn't a game! We have to tell her. We have to tell McMasters–" She talked over his protestations. "We have to tell McMasters. We need to catch up to this guy."

"Absolutely not. We've got good people, we'll handle this."

"Where did you send him?"

He got a crafty look in his eye. "Well. Perhaps I don't remember. We can handle this."

"We have. To tell. Angelica."

"No, no. Look, she's touchy about nuclear weapons–"

"Everyone's touchy about nuclear weapons! That's the whole goddamn point of nuclear weapons!"

"Tch. If you're going to be like that..."

"Grandfather. If that goes off inside the station, it will blow out multiple decks. If we're lucky, it will only kill a lot of people and not crack the hull like an egg."

He waved her off. "Oh, it's not that bad. If there's a problem, we'll just take my yacht. Anyway, it's only a quarter ton yield. The hull's got that fancy armor that's good for twice that. Easily. Strong stuff, you know. Really impressive."

"Not from the inside!"

"Don't be dramatic, we isolated the chop shop for exactly this reason."

"Aha!" She jumped to her feet, jabbing a finger at him. Before he could finish his spluttering protest, she had already signaled Angelica for a call. The wait tone echoed in the quiet office, once, twice. Petulant in defeat, Feeney folded his arms and stared at a scuffed spot on the desk.

"What do you want?"

"Hello, Angelica," Mary rushed to speak before her grandfather could.

"What do you want?"

"A temporary truce. There's a... situation."

"Hi, Mary!" Raj's voice was faint, and she struggled to keep a smile off her face. The old man's scowl deepened.

"What kind of situation?"

"One of our soldiers has gotten his hands on a pocket nuke. He doesn't know what it is, and we can't get ahold of him."

Mary Feeney had known Angelica del Rio for most of her life, first as the pretty young ingénue assisting her grandfather's confidence games on a dozen space stations, then as a capable and increasingly relied-upon lieutenant who provided a stiff backbone and cool hand while Mary, Willy, and their grandfather reeled from the death of the old man's son, Mary and Willy's father. In all that time, she had never heard Angelica swear. It took her a moment to recover from the shock, but the older woman was still swearing furiously well after that moment ended, hurling blistering invective in three languages into the air over Feeney's desk.

"I understand you're upset," Mary said. Angelica's inarticulate reply sounded like she was being strangled while laughing. "I know! But right now we need to work together. It can be disarmed."

Silence. Then, "There will be consequences for this, Mary Feeney."

"I know."

"Where is he going?"

"Before we come to that, I want to bring McMasters in."

"Why?"

"He deserves to know, and I don't want him interfering. We'll deal with him straight, but our two sides outnumber his people."

"Fine. Where is your person going?"

"Mechanic's Bay 2."

Angelica laughed. "Oh! Oho, now I see. Oh, how incredibly clever you are. I almost fell for it."

"I think you've misunderstood," Mary said, and grimaced.

"No. You've just underestimated me. Very good bait, Mary. I absolutely believed your grandfather would be that careless, believed it very easily! Oh, I dare say you sent one of your little idiots down there. But you think I've got something there that McMasters would like to see, don't you? And you know that he's not going to go sniffing just on your say-so, he's not willing to be your cat's paw. But you think if you force him to go, if I invite him to go, he might see something that he can't unsee, is that it?"

"Angelica–"

Feeney could hold his indignation no longer, "I told you so! That witch–"

They started talking over each other then. Mary felt suddenly very tired. She sat to shield what she was doing and sent a message to Raj, to hell with Angelica's spying: *not a trick. going there now. time for Plan B?*

The response was fast: *K.* It was followed just as fast by *miss u.*

Mary stared at it, nodded once to herself, and cut the call. Feeney looked put out.

"I'm too much of a gentleman to say I told you so," he sniffed.

"How do you disarm it?"

"We'll have to catch up to them first, and we can't do that now that Angelica's going to swarm."

"Let me worry about that. I'll force my way in if I have to. How do you disarm it?"

He heaved a dramatic sigh, but obliged her with a short explanation, finished with a twisting gesture. He spread both hands palms up over the empty spot of desk he'd been demonstrating over. "Not hard."

"Good." When he turned his back she messaged *U 2* and left.

Playing Defense

"What are you waiting for, go!"

Whip had never seen Angelica so worked up. The boss clutched the railing of her spiral staircase in both hands, so hard her knuckles were white. She looked down at the pistol in her own shaking hands, and still wasn't sure what it was doing there.

"Go!" shouted the boss. "Take the back routes. Don't all go the same way. Go now!"

She'd never seen Raj look that serious. His face was practically gray, almost looked ill.

"Come on," he grumbled. He'd corralled that swordswoman, the one they called Mick who'd taken her grandma's knife away from her. She only had the sword, she hadn't accepted a gun, which Whip thought was nuts. She and Whip eyed each other, but Raj didn't seem to be in the mood for backtalk.

"Right," Whip said, and managed to sound like she wasn't terrified. Raj didn't take notice; he just grabbed a few others as they went out the service entrance next to the private poker room.

They made their way past the shut-up provisioner's shop, and scared the hell out of one of McMasters' guards. He mashed himself up against the wall so fast all his black armor made a hell of a clatter, but she didn't even laugh at him. They took the stairs, which were already loud with pounding footsteps.

"We're not going to the main door, sibbies," Raj said abruptly, not slowing down. "This way. Put away your guns."

"What's up?" Mick asked when they stopped to open a hatch two decks down.

"The old man's done something really dumb. So dumb my sister doesn't believe it, but I do. Sent someone to plant a bomb in the chop shop."

"You have guards posted," she said, and sounded dubious.

"Yeah, and we're posting more. Nobody's seen anything yet."

There was shouting ahead, and a single gunshot. Whip's guts felt like they turned into ice water. Carter pulled a piece on them as they rounded a corner, his eyes round with fear. Whip thought for sure she was about to get shot, but he seemed to recognize them just in time.

Raj put a hand on his shoulder and leaned in. She heard him ask, "Anyone got hold of Sparks?" and Carter nodded.

"She said everything's fine and to fuck off."

Raj seemed to relax. "All right. Here's what's up. I want you–" he turned and looked over his shoulder. "Shitting hell, where'd she go?" Whip turned around. Mick was gone. The others exchanged looks and shrugged. He didn't wait for explanations, he just shook his head in irritation. "Forget it. How much we pay her, she can figure things out for herself. You, Bex. Go back to the stairs and wait. Keep your gun put away. Someone from Feeney's crew is coming, and I don't want them shot. I want them captured."

"Shit!" someone yelled from away down the corridor, and there were gunshots.

"Hold your fire!" Raj yelled. "Damn your balls, hold your shitting fire! Nobody fucking shoots anybody, savvy? Who shot?" He swore, and opened his comm. Whip saw her own comm light blink on. "Who shot?" he repeated, even though Angelica had told them like three times not to use the open comms because McMasters listened in and maybe Feeney too.

A voice came in on the open comm, hesitant. "Um, me, Raj."

"What you shooting at?"

"Nothing." A voice on the far side said "Bot". "Yeah, bot. Startled me, yo."

"Don't shoot at nothing. Hold your fire."

"Angelica said–"

"Fart on my sister. She's not here, and I'm telling you don't shoot no one."

He clicked off the comm, rubbed the bridge of his nose like he had a headache, and opened the comm again, giving meaningful looks at the people around him. "The hatches are locked down. Sparky's in her office. The stupid little eggfart we're looking for hasn't gotten in yet, savvy? Any of Feeney's assholes comes around, draw on them but take them alive. Do not fucking shoot unless you want to die." He considered. "Even then, don't shoot."

"No need, Raj." Whip's head shot up and she spun with her own gun ready. Raj grabbed hold of her wrist, hard.

A woman with elaborate facial tattoos and rows of implanted spikes on her face stood behind her, palms up in surrender. Whip gasped.

"Why hello, Mary Feeney," Raj said, showing his teeth. "I wondered if I'd see you today."

"I said I'd come," she said quietly. She didn't seem to notice all the guns and angry looks around her. "You going to keep your end of the bargain?"

Raj nodded once. "Stay off the air. Nobody tells my sister nothing," he said aloud. "Not until we're done. That's a goddamn order and I'll shoot anyone who tattles. Savvy?" In the silence he said louder, "Savvy?"

Whip muttered "savvy" along with the others.

"Good," he said. "Miss Mary Feeney's our prisoner, and we're nice to our prisoners." He nudged Whip, taking her gun as he did. "Go search our pal for weapons." He grinned at Mary and said, "Hey, no offense, I'd have come armed."

She smiled faintly. "None taken."

Whip patted her down fast, and wasn't real sure what she was doing, but didn't feel anything that might have been a gun or knife or anything, and she said so.

"All right, sister," Raj said. "Let's see if we can keep your grandfather from blowing us all up, hey?"

Mistakes Were Made

Ditz and Sparks laughed at each other. They were high as kites, naked as jaybirds, and felt grand.

"Man," Sparks said. "I missed this. I missed you, man."

"Aw. I missed you too," Ditz said, and only felt a little bit bad. He thought for a second, maybe he wouldn't raise the alarm, maybe he'd just stay and go out with a bang. He laughed again at the double something, the word "bang" because that could mean an explosion or sex and she didn't seem to notice or care. Wait, he hadn't said that out loud. She hadn't seen Screwball. Shit. He heaved a sigh. "Better get dressed. You're gonna hate me for this."

Her dreamy laugh died down. "What? What'd you do?" She sat up suddenly. "Is this what they've been bitching about on the comm?"

He fished her jumpsuit out from under the desk and tossed it over before he started tugging his pants on – he was a gentleman, after all. "Your shop's gonna blow up."

"What!" Her anger fought through the drug haze and confusion. "The fuck, Ditz?"

"Sorry," he said, and really felt miserable. "You can go use Feeney's shop if you want."

"Fuck Feeney, why would I want to use his shop?"

Ditz was interrupted by the door sliding open and Screwball leaning into the room, his eyes wild with something between panic and triumph. "Here you are! Shit, I've been looking for you. Come on, man, it's set! Come on!"

"What the fuck, Ditz!" Sparks started to slap at his hand offering one of her prosthetics, but she seemed to think better of it and grabbed it. "What's set?"

"One of those little pocket nukes."

She made a strangled noise, staring at him in a bug-eyed horror cutting through the remains of a fine high.

"It's not that bad–"

"Are you fucking kidding me, Ditz? Not that bad?"

"Come on, Spa–"

"You're out of your minds!"

"Sparky..."

"Don't you 'Sparky' me, you backstabbing son of a bitch."

"Neha, come on, we're gonna blow up."

She stopped suddenly in the process of attaching her leg, and stared at Screwball. "Did you actually set a nuclear bomb?"

Screwball looked sheepish. "Uh, kinda. We really better go."

Sparks swore and set to work putting her legs on at speed. Ditz tried to help her and she swatted at him.

The other door to the office opened. Raj and–

"Woah, Mary. Holy shit, wow." Ditz stared. "Did you, like–"

"I'm all right," Mary said. "But I'm captive. So are you two, so put down your weapons." She hesitated. "And zip your trousers. Jesus."

Raj turned to Screwball, holding a pistol on him. "I remember you. You're the little skidmark I schooled. Where's the bomb?"

Screwball stood up straight. "I'm not saying shit."

"Christ, I'm going to lose more IQ, aren't I."

Mary interrupted. "Corbell, where is it? This is serious, we have to turn that off."

He visibly wavered. Ditz sighed. "Jig's up, Screwy man. This was a dumb idea anyway."

Screwball seemed to deflate, and Ditz felt bad for him. Dude finally got a chance to really look good for the old man, and it all went pear-shaped. As usual.

"Somewhere near the doors. Dunno for sure."

They all stared at him.

"Somewhere..." Sparks started.

"Near the shitting doors?" Raj finished. "The holy hell's that supposed to mean, my brother? How don't you remember where you put a nuclear sharting weapon?"

"Yeah, but, like," Screwball coughed. "There was someone in there, that chick with the sword, Mick. So I stuck it in a bot and told it to go to the doors."

Mary and Raj moved fast for the inner hatch to the chop shop, grabbing Screwball as they went. Ditz followed. Sparks, who'd gotten her legs on, shouted, "Don't! Gravity!"

Raj swore and managed to pull Mary back. "Boots," he grumbled, and yanked on a locker door.

"You." Sparks jammed her finger hard into Screwball's chest. "Which bot did you put it in?"

"I dunno, it was just a bot. I think it had some blue paint on it, maybe."

"Did you tell it to stop and stay at the doors?"

He furrowed his brow. "Huh?"

"When you told it," she said, punctuating her words with more angry jabs, "to go to the doors, did you tell it to stop there and stay there?"

"Um."

"Bots don't just do what you tell them. When they finish one task, they get assigned another one and then they do that. When did you do this?"

"Uh, like five minutes ago. I couldn't find Ditz, I thought he was down..." He trailed off, seeing that he wasn't going to get a word in between the swearing on all sides. Ditz tried to give him a consoling look, but Screwball wouldn't look him in the eye.

Sparks pulled up a console on her wall and jabbed at the air in front of it. "How much time do we have?"

"Like twenty minutes still," Screwball said. "At least."

She nodded once, curtly. "Go," she commanded. "If it's one of mine, I can find it and call it. I'll just make them all come. Get down to the shop floor, they can't come in here. If you can't find it in five minutes, I'm getting out of here."

Raj and Mary, now booted up, frogmarched Screwball out the office door. Ditz lingered. "Listen, Spa... Neha. I'm really, really, really sorry. I feel awful."

"Go feel awful at someone else, you turncoat," she growled, not looking away from the screen.

He pulled a pair of sandal-like mag boots out of the locker and stepped gingerly into them. They gripped the sides of his feet, felt really weird. He gave Sparks one last mournful look, then went out the hatch and down the gangway.

Ditz struggled to suppress a moment of panic as he looked out over the mechanic's bay. Wide open spaces like that already creeped him out, and the big half-broken ship looming over him didn't help, but the sight of dozens of robots converging on him from all directions and above was enough to make him want to bolt. Something made a loud hissing noise away down the end of the bay. Screwball grabbed the nearest bot, twisted it to see its back and then pushed it away.

"Not it," he muttered. Louder, he said, "It had some, like, blue paint on it."

Ditz grabbed a robot out of the air, more because it freaked him out than anything, but he turned it over in his hands. It made little plaintive beeping noises and had a green light, but no blue paint. On either side of him, Mary and Raj were doing the same. As they tossed bots away, they buzzed off.

"No," muttered Screwball, savage in his panic.

Another one had red paint. The third, green. "Hey," Ditz said, "You're not like colorblind are you? I mean, it's cool if you are–"

"I'm not colorblind," Screwball snarled.

"Cool, cool."

He grabbed for another bot, but it danced out of his reach. It had blue paint on it. Mary must have heard him gasp; she twisted around and grabbed for it, too. Raj was faster: he got hold of it and shoved it in Screwball's face.

"Well?"

"That's it!" Screwball tried to take it, but Raj held it away. He opened its cargo cavity himself. His expression turned grave.

"What are you trying to pull here, brother?" He spun it to show the cavity, empty.

"That's the one," Screwball said. "I'm positive, that was the one! I swear to God, Raj, I put it in there!"

"What's that noise?" Ditz didn't like the tone of Mary's voice. He followed her gaze toward the source of the hissing he'd noticed before. The person-sized airlock's red light was on, and he could hear the grumble of the air cyclers. Next to its inside hatch there were four harnesses for spacesuits. Three suits were slashed open. One was missing.

The airlock clanked once more, and lit up green. All four of them stared at it, and when the inner door finished its cycle and opened, it was empty.

Mary tried once to say something, failed, and then managed in a hoarse whisper, "Run."

SPACEWALK

The trick to spacewalks was to not think about how stupidly dangerous they were. The Miner hated them under the best of circumstances. These were not the best of circumstances. The suit she wore was made for someone bigger than her, and the positive air pressure blew it up around her so that her fingers didn't reach the end of her gloves unless she tugged on the elbow with the other hand. She didn't bother to do that, occupied as she was with moving hand-over-hand with a nuclear detonator stuck magnetically to her chest and her sword swinging so wildly on its tether that it kept knocking on her helmet and startling her.

The rolling tether stayed anchored magnetically to the steel guide strip bolted to the asteroidal rock below the handholds, so she probably wouldn't go drifting away to a lengthy and unpleasant death. Its bearings skipped and stuttered on the surface and would have been making a horrible scratching noise if she could hear them. That left the more-likely brief and bright death at the hands of the small device whose timer currently read less than thirty minutes.

When Raj had described the situation, her thought had been that this would be good cover to slip in and blow up the mechanic's bay herself. That had been, she felt, a good plan. One that she probably should have abandoned when she spied an idiot with a nuclear weapon. She should, in fact, have abandoned the station entirely. Instead, presented with a choice between disarming the device and letting a nice little fight fizzle or letting it go off inside the station, irradiating the lower decks and probably putting enough stress on its systems to kill everyone, she thought she'd be clever and put it outside the station, which was after all designed to take a mild nuclear bombardment without failing catastrophically. She felt decreasingly clever by the minute.

She'd dropped the last bug behind her as early warning, and she picked up some talking on its channel. High power mode, not subtle, but she'd officially crossed the subtlety Rubicon anyway. Three or four people, maybe, but she couldn't make out what they were saying. They didn't sound happy, but if she could hear their voices, then they weren't preparing to evacuate atmo and open the doors, so that much was all right. But going back inside wasn't an option.

The bay doors, bearing a giant black number 2, loomed large above her head. Somewhere off to her right was a single working floodlight, bright enough to see by, but whatever her arm cast in shadow was so black it was erased from the universe. Hand over hand she dragged herself along sideways to the middle of the bracing hull below the doors where it overlapped the dark gray pockmarked asteroid. She hazarded a look up, contorting her whole body to see where she was relative to the doors and the rest of the station. She steeled herself and then looked down into the star field below her. Nothing habitable nearby except the mechanic's bay itself, set in a big crater with a nice thick rim around it.

She leaned carefully away from the rock, letting the tether gently tense until she was far enough away to see what she was doing. Her breath assaulted her in her helmet, warm and humid while the rebreather struggled to keep up with her dry-mouth near-panic. Moving deliberately, she pulled the device away from her chest, felt it tugging on the ill-fitting suit until it released. She turned it over in her hands, pushed aside the shock of seeing its timer at nineteen minutes, and pressed it against the steel guide strip to the left of her rolling tether.

Allowing herself only a moment to exhale the breath she hadn't noticed herself holding, she started hand-over-hand again, away from the airlock. There wasn't time to cycle through and still get away from the blast. So she had under twenty minutes, at spacewalk speed, to get away from the immediate blast radius, out of range of any chunks, and behind something thick enough to block radiation. A lot safer without atmosphere, but still not remotely safe. It occurred to her that this might have been the dumbest thing she had ever done.

Hand over hand over hand over hand. The tether skittered and lurched on its bearings, and she had to stop twice to reattach it. She lost her grip once, surprised by the sound of shooting coming from the bug's broadcast, and the tether swung away free. It traced out an arc, and she had to stop and suppress a sensation of panic before she could make herself reach for it and plant it on the guide strip. She was only a few body lengths away from the armed device, after all that scrabbling.

Taking a deep breath and trying not to feel stupid, she pushed gently off and twisted herself around so that the handholds became footholds. She grabbed the tether's end in one hand and ground it against the steel strip as she pulled with her feet. Her sword bucked and swung wildly on its own tether as it bumped against her, and her feet in the oversize boots kept slipping, but at least she was moving.

It was too slow-going with the tether; she pulled hard and dragged it to the edge of the steel strip until it released. That was stupid, but hoisted by her own atomic petard was worse. She looked at her new up: the rock jutted out a fair ways. If she could get to the other side, she'd be clear.

The hand-over-hand scrabble resumed with her feet to assist. The rock protrusion didn't seem to get any closer, and that stupid suit made her feel like she was swimming in fabric. Ten minutes. Her arms and legs ached, her fingers burned from the strain of squeezing the inflated gloves. She kept them like claws and just hooked at the handles. Her head swam in a swamp and her brain felt hazy from breathing her own carbon dioxide. She could still hear the distant high-pitched popping of a firefight somewhere inside near her bug. Five minutes. Three.

The rock was upon her before she recognized it, and she scrambled up and over it on the mere half dozen handholds someone had bolted haphazardly into the asteroid. Her arm reached for the next one – and missed.

Somersaulting in the void, the Miner's body twisted away from the rock, propelled by her own momentum. The promontory drifted by and she couldn't grab the handhold, only brushed it with her foot to send herself slowly tumbling. Handholds went by her visor, out of reach. Twisting her body, hyperventilating herself into a stupor, her hand knocked against her sword and then grabbed it. She lashed out with it like a boat oar, bounced off one handhold and then hooked the next. She pulled it with all her strength, levering herself back onto the rock. Her knees hit hard and jolted her, but her hand shot out and grabbed the loop of steel hard.

Her left hand trembled as she held fast. She found the tether and swung it around. She didn't see where it attached, but when she pulled it was taut. The muscles in her hands screamed at her, and finally, with all her senses rebelling against it, she had to let go. The tether held, and she untensed all the muscles she'd been clenching in fear.

She couldn't see a thing around the bulge in the asteroid. She wouldn't have felt the blast at all if her hand hadn't been resting against the rock. It lurched under her palm like it was alive, and she looked out into space to see in the cone of floodlamp light a fine glittering spray of molten rock and metal.

Kaboom!

"Ow!"

Screwball stopped. Ditz was heavy as fuck, and carrying him by dragging him backwards with two arms under his armpits was hurting them both, but he had to. "I'm sorry, man, I'm sorry." He sniffed hard, trying not to lose it. "But I got to get you out of here. We'll get to the doc's, I promise."

"Shit," Ditz said softly. His limp weight hung from Screwball's hands, and his own hands were clenched over his belly where that fucking idiot Carter had shot him. They'd gotten away through the fight – Feeney's crew had come down on the bay just as they were fleeing. They'd lost Raj in the confusion, but they'd also lost Mary, and he didn't know if she was even alive, and–

He gritted his teeth. He was not going to lose it. And he was not going to lose his buddy.

"I know it hurts, but we got to get out of here. It's not far," he lied. They'd only come up half a flight of stairs, passed by a bunch of fleeing assholes who hadn't helped, and his arms and legs burned with the effort.

"Let me down," Ditz said, his voice terrible and calm. "I'm dying, man."

"You're not dying, you'll be fine."

"It's cool, man. It's my time." His face looked waxy. "I fucked it all up anyway. I let them take Nuke away and probably kill him. Raj hates me. Sparks hates me too, now."

"No." Screwball shook his head. "No way."

"It fucking hurts when you carry me, and the doctor's higher than I am, so I can either die here or there."

He peeled a blood-covered hand from his wound, winced, and reached for the thigh pockets on his pants. Failing twice to get the flap open, he closed his eyes and said, "Dude. Dying guy trying to get his drugs here. Lend a hand?"

Screwball hesitated, then dove into the flap. He pulled out a crumpled little package, which Ditz took from him. Scrabbling at the paper with blood-slick fingers, he dry-swallowed all three tablets. Then he closed his eyes, resting against Screwball's legs.

"There we go," he mumbled. "If I gotta leave this world, man, then tripping balls through a nuclear blast is the way to do it. That's style, yeah?"

Screwball sniffed. "I'm sorry, man."

"De nada. Get out of here, all right? If I'm worried about you I won't enjoy the ride."

"I don't even know your real name, man."

"George."

Screwball blinked. "George?"

"My parents were assholes, all right? Steven?" He chuckled. "Goodbye, dude. Stay alive."

"I'll..." He coughed to clear the lump in his throat. "I'll miss you, man."

"You too, buddy. Now fuck off."

Screwball tried to gently rest Ditz's heavy form against the stairwell wall, but he was really limp already and thumped his head. The beatific look on his stoned face barely flinched.

Screwball bit his lip and tried to think of something to say, and when he couldn't, he fled up the stairs.

He took them two at a time, scrabbling and stumbling and slipping sometimes and banging his shins hard. He kept running all the way to the top, where the toffs lived and where Feeney always said McMasters' goons would beat him to a pulp, but he didn't care. He stood at the top landing and panted.

Screwball felt it in his knees and his guts before he heard it: an all-shaking bass thump like God's foot up his ass. He stood numb as the floor rumbled, as the roar echoed in the stairwell around him, and then as it subsided he sank to his knees and cried.

FIDDLING

The Miner stood in the dark of the viewing bay, watching the big science ship emerge like an iceberg from the broken hangar, propelled by a hangar-full of air in which it moved slowly, almost regally. The main explosion had only weakened the rock and partly blasted the doors in. Air pressure and metal fatigue had taken time to do their thing, but the chop shop's now-gaping doors had become a lazy geyser, pushing tools and blinking bots on streams of evaporating air as the badly-maintained emergency systems struggled to clamp down on the burst flows of atmosphere, water, and sewage. It all glittered prettily in the navigation lights.

Air-filled compartments on the ship ruptured under their own pressure, and the great weakened hulk twisted and tore itself like a stunted butterfly struggling from a chrysalis. It would never go back in a repair bay in that shape. Impossible to hide. Impossible to profit from.

The Miner had her sword out fast when the hatch opened behind her. McMasters stood silhouetted against the bright corridor lights. He looked exhausted, beaten. Unarmed, though, and unsurprised to see her.

"The security cameras here still work," he said. He sounded beaten, too. "Some of the only ones that do, that Angelica hasn't pressganged into her piddly little information empire. Low-light sensitive. People used to come up here after-hours to screw. My predecessor amassed quite a collection."

He left the hatch open, spilling a beam of yellow light onto the floor. He walked in and took a post at the observation bar on the edge of the darkness, letting the light beam separate them. The Miner sheathed her sword and half-turned so that she could see him and the wreckage at the same time.

"I looked you up, you know," he said, staring at the ship as it contorted under explosive pressure, throwing off detritus that glimmered like stars. "I got a good picture and looked you up in the government's facial recognition system. Do you know what came back?"

She raised an eyebrow, but didn't bite.

"Nothing. Nothing came back, not a thing. So, being a good citizen, I uploaded it with a complete description of your criminal activities. Do you know how this official government system responded?"

She already had the eyebrow raised, and didn't see any reason to change that fact.

"It said to say 'hi'," McMasters said. He turned with his hand still on the bar. "Hi."

"Howdy," she said, and it didn't improve his mood.

"Who the hell are you?"

She shook her head. "Just another asteroid miner, that's all. Got a past like anyone else. Maybe I abused my connections a little bit. Maybe you ought to think about what connections I might still have."

Silence again. She felt a tremor in the bar, and under her feet. Her pulse quickened for a moment, and she wondered if a piece of the wreck had hit the station. McMasters looked down at a handheld screen, its green cast on his face in the dark painting him as a drowned sailor. He snapped it off suddenly, and in the afterglow his face appeared red.

"Explosion on deck six, northeast quadrant. I suppose you know what's there."

"Feeney's little drug lab?"

"Feeney's little drug lab. You wouldn't know anything about that either, I suppose, Just Another Asteroid Miner?"

"Not surprised, anyway."

"What's your name?"

She shook her head.

"Are you working for Shinagawa? Shine? Is that what this is?"

Again, she shook her head.

McMasters gripped the bar and turned full on her, nostrils flared. "What the hell do you want from me?"

"I want you to do your job."

"Job? What job? They dumped me in this hole between two bickering morons and told me to deal with it. Make it be quiet. There's no job here, there's only survival. And I'm doing that just fine."

"You're being a leech. A goddamn crooked leech. I told you every gravy train stops. This is the end of the line," she said, waving her hand at the drifting wreck. "Get ships in here. Arrest Feeney and Angelica. When Mary and Raj take over their sides, tell them to clear out. No more profit here, party's over. Give the people here a chance to get back on their feet. You do that and I'll back you to the hilt, but if you don't, then I'll make damn sure you regret it."

McMasters looked suddenly, briefly, very old and very tired. It turned into a snarl.

"You say I'm a leech," he growled, his voice coarse with emotion. "Well I won't argue with you, Miss High and Mighty.

Better a leech than a louse, I say. You don't care about this
station, you don't care about these people, you don't care
about anything. You're vermin. Unwanted, unwelcome,
flitting from station to station until someone notices you long
enough to crush you like a bug."

She felt her fingers tighten around the bar despite herself.
"You're not very good at this threatening thing."

"I like it here, louse. I've got a good thing going, and I've
got a right to be here, and if I'm a leech then by God, I've got
my teeth in good, and it's not over until I say it's over."

The reflected light off the wreck played on his face, twisted
in bitter fury, droplets of sweat glistening in the fairy light,
angry to the point of panting. She pursed her lips. "I think it's
the mustache. I hear you ranting, but I keep expecting you to
ask my drinks order."

"Who's paying you? Shine? Herrera?"

"Go shave it off and threaten me again, I think it'll work
better."

He slammed his fist down on the bar and obviously regretted
it, but at least had the self-control to not too-obviously rub
his hurt hand. "You think you're funny?"

"Just passing the time while I wait for you to be serious."

He stormed out, leaving her with a few hissed words,
"You're about to see how serious I can be."

Long Time Coming

Space stations monitor wide fields around their positions. Dangers surround them on all sides. Their denizens picture rocks the size of ships in their nightmares, when really all it takes is a pebble the size of a fingertip, with enough speed, to punch a major hole in a hull. Even with modern self-repair technologies, that tends to ruin someone's day. Junk lasers and ablative plating help, but only go so far.

Any station that wants to survive keeps LIDAR and camera arrays on a steady monitoring sweep backed by AIs, but again that goes only so far: those systems are expensive, and space stations are built and maintained by the lowest bidders. For every station, then, there's a horizon beyond which no routine scanning is done. A ship, a yacht for example, orbiting just beyond that horizon, could escape detection for a very long time, particularly if John Feeney is paying people not to notice it.

Six months is a very long time to anyone waiting on that ship who is unaccustomed to solitude. A guy gets refused docking rights at three different stations, he starts to take it personal, starts to want to come home. Eventually the decent booze runs out, and the better drugs. Eventually a person has played every game, watched every movie and serial in both VR and flat, gotten bored with all the pornography. Eventually even the robot-delivered food and water becomes yet another reminder of how very badly a person has been betrayed by his friends and his kin.

Wilfred "Nuke" Feeney watched, spellbound, as a ship slowly and delicately exploded off the port side. He felt he'd never seen anything so beautiful in his life. All tangerine orange and aneurysm red through the camera filters, struggling and writhing like a poisoned animal, throwing off sparks and debris for the lasers to burn up. He felt as though the universe was putting on a show for only him, finally sending him a sign. He watched a long time, idly scratching the hard blinking bulge in his chest, thinking. Thinking.

Wilfred "Nuke" Feeney had him an idea.

MIDNIGHT RENDEZVOUS

The Miner left the observation lounge when the wreck had drifted away from the nav lights, swallowed up by the dark. The geyser had stopped, and she figured the old emergency systems had finally staunched the bleeding of water and air. She wasn't going to simply suffocate, then. Time to go. Time to tend her own garden, literally and figuratively.

The route back to her ship had to go around or through the galleria, unless she felt like putting the pressure suit back on for a two-hour spacewalk. All told, she figured she'd see less resistance going through Angelica's territory than Feeney's, and plotted her course that way.

The sounds of fighting grew as she walked. Gunshots, screaming. The lid had come off. This was just the first release of pressure, she knew. They'd retreat to their lairs, both sides wounded but not mortally, not yet. There could be no peace after this, though. They'd grind each other down until the law finally came, if not for them, then for that ship and its murdered crew.

It was already dying down as she walked the back passages. The shots grew louder but fewer. If Takata hadn't gotten her message to bunker down, hadn't passed it on, there wasn't anything she could do about it now.

"There you are! Just the woman. Come on, damn you, I need you."

Raj appeared in front of her, pistol out and panting from running. He'd lost the fez. He pointed to her and grinned.

The Miner looked on the charming murderous bastard with a mixture of anger and pity. She wondered if it was worth killing him. There was no doubt he'd be good with that gun, but she was pretty damn good with a sword, and had her diamond skin on. She shook her head. "I'm done. I paid your sister back."

"Fuck my sister, I need you."

She stopped, intrigued despite herself. "For what?"

"Plan B. You'll hate it. Come on!"

He ran, expecting her to follow, and for some reason she did.

They didn't go far, down two decks by the stairs. Raj ran like a man possessed, heedless of the patches of fighting except that he must have had some idea where they were because the two of them didn't see any of what she heard.

"Slow down," she said, "I don't want to run into a trap."

"Don't worry! We're almost there."

"Where's 'there'?" the Miner asked, and wasn't surprised to not receive an answer.

They rounded a corner and came on a storefront. "Anita Nurse, Apothecary" read the friendly blue sign over windows covered over with yellow plastic sheeting. Raj stopped with a loud sigh, and bent over with his hands on his knees. A grim-faced young man in a motley assortment of armor stepped smartly out of the storefront's door. The Miner recognized him, and realized only a moment too late that they were on opposite sides as Screwball stepped back and drew on her, eyes wide and panicked behind the handgun. He yelled at her to freeze, and she obliged.

She let her hands go out at her sides, eyeing him warily. He had a good ten centimeters on her, and had added decent armor to his outfit since she'd last seen him, even if looked like it had been scavenged from a half-dozen suits and styles. The black jumpsuit underneath was probably cut-resistant fabric, and the green-gray and black armor pieces looked like a jumble of mechanic's protection and standard military ablative. He also looked exhausted to the point of haunted. She could take him apart if she could get close, but it still wouldn't be easy. That panic in his eyes was a double-edged sword. He couldn't cover Raj and her both, but there was no telling what he'd do when del Rio caught his breath and made a move. She made use of his distracted attention between the two of them to slowly get her hands in a position where she could draw and dash. Get him off-kilter, rely on her implants to close in fast for the kill.

Mary appeared in the door behind him, bloodied and worried-looking. She saw the Miner and tensed, her hands on the throwing knives at her belt. The Miner swore to herself, but Mary looked instead at Raj, and ran for him. Screwball stepped to the side, and didn't fire. The Miner shifted her weight for the sprint, waiting for Mary to knife Raj as her distraction. Raj heaved himself upright just as the knife fighter reached him, and they kissed.

Nice Day For It

The Miner prided herself on being hard to faze, but the previous ten minutes had tested that sorely. She and the other guy, who reintroduced himself as Corbell, had ended their standoff in mutual befuddlement as Raj and Mary pawed each other in the middle of the corridor. She wasn't entirely surprised to see Doc Mills show up in the doorway next, looking worried and impatient. He and the Miner made eye contact, but he didn't say anything to her, only cleared his throat at the pair of criminal scions. They disentangled themselves from each other, and entered the pharmacy. The Miner and Corbell shrugged and obeyed Mary's throaty "Come on, you assholes."

It went fast. The five of them ducked into the dark, wrecked shop, into a clearing in the middle of the knocked-over shelves. The Miner figured a pharmacist's shop wouldn't have lasted long once the goons had let themselves free with the looting, and other than a tube of hemorrhoid cream she seemed to be right. Doc Mills glared at all of them in equal measure, but let Raj and Mary approach him. For two minutes they spoke softly, with Corbell scowling at her every time she made a move to get closer.

"Once more for the witnesses," Mills said louder.

"I do," Raj and Mary said at once.

"All right." The doctor sighed. "You're married. It's as legal as I can make it, if you care. Kiss her, you idiot."

Raj obliged, and the doctor pushed his way between the Miner and a stunned Corbell. Mills paused next to the Miner and muttered, "Finn's dead," before he moved along like he hadn't said anything. She blinked and watched him go, suddenly feeling sick to her stomach.

The two of them hadn't been dismissed, exactly, so much as made the mutual decision to stand guard outside when the kiss got hotter and clothes started coming off. They stood on opposite sides of the door once Corbell managed to drag it closed, and the silence between them became increasingly uncomfortable as the noises inside got louder.

"This, uh, this what you were expecting?" Corbell finally asked.

"No."

"Yeah... Mary was pretty tight-lipped, but I heard her calling off an ambush down here, clearing the area. They were pissed."

"That so?"

"Pretty pissed, yeah." He glanced her up and down, his eyes lingering on the hand resting on her sword. "You're pretty good with that thing, huh."

"Seems that way."

"Bunch of people want to teach you a lesson."

"That so?"

"They're pretty good too."

"That's nice."

"We did all right after you left, you know."

The Miner shrugged.

"We're not just idiots and assholes. We gave as good as we got."

They stood, leaving that sentiment in the air, and the Miner felt ridiculous standing. She wanted to do something, felt frustrated and angry about Finn. Corbell gave up and rested his head against the wall with a soft thump. They hadn't gotten the door all the way closed, and from outside the shop the vigorous humping sounded like busted hydraulics. Corbell fidgeted, shifting his weight from leg to leg, and she was pretty sure that finger was on its way to a nostril at one point before he caught himself.

"You want to, uh..."

"No," she said.

"Right. Right."

The Miner stood and brooded. The fighting was still going on elsewhere. Without this wedding, it would grind down into chaotic vendettas. Feeney and Angelica would be bust. Mr Shine and the Morlocks were ready to step in and enforce a new peace. Her plan had worked, except... Well, when those two newlyweds came out, that was her plan blown to hell. She fingered the hilt of her sword absentmindedly.

"Ditz is dead," Corbell said suddenly. The Miner took a moment to put the name to the face of one of the older toughs, a stringy happy-looking guy.

"I'm sorry," she said.

"He was a good guy."

"I didn't know him," she said, feeling awkward. "I'm sorry."

He kept going, though she wished he wouldn't. "I thought I hated him. You know? He was so annoying and he shot people he shouldn't have, and he was high all the time. Like seriously, high all the time. I know other people got killed, too. You killed some of them. It's just, I didn't expect to miss him, and I do."

The Miner looked at her embarrassed counterpart once the verbal torrent dried up, and felt for a moment a pang of sympathy. "You pick your pain," she said.

"The fuck's that supposed to mean? I didn't want to hang out with him."

She shook her head. "We all do. If you choose to be with people, you choose the misery that comes with losing them. It's a gamble. Maybe they lose you first. You could have been an asshole to him, pushed him away. But you got something out of being friends, and now it hurts. Doesn't mean you picked wrong, just that you paid the piper sooner than you'd rather."

He made an undignified snuffling noise, and she chose not to look. "Yeah? What did you pick?"

She was about to say, "talking to morons" and instead found herself saying "I picked a ship and a plant room, and no more attachments."

The noises and groans inside subsided, and there was a long stretch of two silences: a suspicious one inside and a relieved one outside. She found herself drumming her fingers on the sheath of her sword, trying not to hear giggling.

She heard their surprise and aggravation trying to drag the door open. It gave her plenty of time to step aside, get ready. One on three, with the three in this shape, no problem. Maybe just one on two, she didn't care if Corbell got away. The door came free in a second, and a rumpled half-dressed Mary appeared. She yawned happily and stretched. "All right, you bastards," she said pleasantly. "Time to go tell our darling families."

The Miner looked at the beaming young woman and her new husband grinning bashfully behind her. "Congratulations," she said, and walked away.

Six Months and a Bunch of Dead Bodies Ago

Angelica put her hands flat on the table and leaned across it. She looked into each set of worried, frightened, pissed-off eyes in turn. All of Feeney's main people, or most of them: Neha "Sparks" Laghari, who ran the chop shop; Zackie Morgan, who wrangled the sex workers; Peder Finn, who ran the distillery and brewery; Xiao Han, who ran the drug lab; Rafael, who managed smuggling operations. Then, too, there was that Anaconda guy, whats-his-name, Gordonson, who was pretty thoroughly in the old man's pocket and insisted on having his say at length about this little trouble with Wilfred. Only Shine was missing, since he refused to have anything to do with it, and Mary for obvious reasons. Raj leaned against the back wall, playing with his knife and looking uncomfortable.

"If you're asking me to turn on John Feeney, the answer's no," she said when she thought one of them might break the silence on their terms instead of hers.

"Not turn on him," Sparks said. She'd done most of the talking so far. "Make him see sense. God's sake, Angelica, this is a nuclear device we're talking about – and I swear, if you say 'a small one' again I'll stab you in the neck."

Angelica put her palms up in a placating gesture against her and the others muttering.

"Fine. I admit that was a poor choice of words. I'm sorry. Look, we don't know that it's actually rigged to explode. All we know is Wilfred tells us it is, and he was under sedation when Joff put it in."

"What does, uh, what does Joff say?"

"He doesn't know, Finn. Wilfred told him it was some kind of police black box or something. He's so freaked out it'll be a year before he sobers up."

"So he can't take it out?" Sparks challenged.

"Would you trust him to operate on you in this condition?"

"Christ, I wouldn't trust him to bandage a paper cut."

Angelica gestured. "There you go. And Mills won't touch it. What do you want the old man to do?"

"Something! Anything! Stick him in a torpedo and shoot him out the airlock, I don't care."

"He's not going to do that. Wilfred's his grandson."

"Kid's a bleeding psycho," Xiao grumbled. "Did you know he's going around telling people to call him 'Nuke'? He's enjoying this."

"For now," Angelica said. "The thing's got a battery in it, and it's not intended to stay armed for a long time. Worst case scenario, we ride this out a couple months."

"Months!" The Anaconda man's face went red again. Angelica always thought he looked like Santa Claus like that, rosy-cheeked. "Mr Feeney told me that this would 'all blow over' in a week!"

"You're too close to the old man," Rafael said, scowling at her. "You take his side no matter what. Can we trust you not to go straight to him after this, rat us all out?"

Angelica didn't answer right away. If she said yes too fast, they'd never believe her. So she sat down, ran her tongue over her teeth, and looked up into the anxious faces. "I'm not going to say anything to him about you. Look… I don't like this either. Don't look at me like that, nobody sane would like this."

"The old man thinks it's funny," Sparks said. "And you know what, I'm pretty sure he has more little military toys squirreled away. He won't give me a straight answer where Wilfred got that thing in the first place."

"He doesn't owe you one," Angelica snapped.

"The hell he doesn't! This has gone too far, Angelica. Way too far. We've put our necks on the line for the Feeneys plenty of times, all of us. How many times have I been raided now? Six? Seven? We don't have to prove our loyalty to him, we've done that. It's time he proved *his* to *us*."

Angelica massaged the bridge of her nose, willing away the headache that had been her constant companion for the last two weeks.

"I understand. I'll talk to him again, try to get him to see reason."

"And if he won't?"

"I've known John Feeney a very long time. He'll see reason."

"And if he won't?"

"Then I'll cross that bridge if I come to it," she said, and looked again from face to dubious face in turn. "You've said your piece, and I've said what I'll do. That'll have to be enough."

They seemed to understand themselves to be dismissed then, or at least they stood up. Sparks sat the longest, pretending to fiddle with her prosthetics until the others had excused themselves and let themselves out of the restaurant back room.

The mechanic looked at her cohort leaving through the closed main dining room, darkened except for the little fake candles on white-clothed round tables. She looked up to Angelica as she stood and said thoughtfully, "I'll be honest, I expected them to open that door to find the old man and a bunch of guns."

"I don't work that way," Angelica said. She glanced at Raj, who had half-heartedly advocated exactly that course of action, and gotten exactly that reply. He either hadn't been listening or his poker face was getting better.

"You going back to the hotel?"

Angelica nodded.

"I'm moving out," Sparks told her. "There's a cot in my office that's comfy enough." Angelica looked a question, and she shrugged. "The old man's got a magnetism to him. You stay around him too long, you listen to him too long, you start to believe him too much. I've got work to do anyway. There's room for two, you know." She grinned at Angelica's discomfort. "Anyway, if you ask me, that's the safest place to be if Willy's little insurance plan goes '*pop!*'."

Angelica shuddered. "Don't even joke about it."

Sparks shrugged elaborately and walked past Raj, giving him a long look but saying nothing.

"If you're going to say you told me so," Angelica told her brother, "let's not and say we did."

Raj imitated Sparks' shrug. "Shitting hell," he said philosophically, "I don't know what to do either. This is crazy, but the old man's done us right so far."

They walked out through the Casablanca dining room. The owner, a short woman whose name Angelica always forgot, stood in the doorway twisting her chef's hat in two hands. Angelica made an effort to smile, and left it to her brother to pay the woman off. He caught up to her a few minutes later at a jog.

"So what's the plan, sister dear?"

"I'm going to talk to John Feeney, that's the plan. Maybe Mary can help me get through that skull of his."

"Maybe," Raj said, in an odd tone of voice. Angelica looked at him, but his expression didn't betray anything. "The thing is, what's the old man going to do, hey? Joff won't slice him open again, the other guy won't slice him open at all. Pushing him out the airlock's no good. Maybe load him up on a ship and make him somebody else's problem."

"I thought you were friends."

"Best pals," he said, and meant it. The elevator opened for them, and they made for the galleria deck. "I think it'll all blow over, me. I think the battery in that thing won't last, and then he'll be giving me shit for letting him do it in the first place."

Angelica gave him a look. "Did–"

"Didn't have a clue. Cross my heart and hope to snuff it. But he'll say I did when he's got a dead lump of metal under his skin."

Angelica fell silent, listening to the slow elevator rumble. "What about the dead man's switch? Anything we can do about that? Who made it?"

"Sparky."

"What!" She stared at her brother. "Are you kidding me? After all the trouble she's stirring up over this?"

Raj laughed. "That's why! He told her it was for a grenade, and she figured that was all right. When she found out – whoo!"

The doors opened and they strolled toward the galleria. She

didn't want to continue the conversation with people around, though there weren't many tourists and they weren't paying attention. By unspoken agreement they made for home at the hotel, Angelica deep in thought and Raj strolling without a care in the world, hands shoved in pockets and attempting badly to whistle.

Angelica froze at the top of the big staircase to the hotel lobby. Wilfred and that buddy of his, the dishwasher, stood loitering out front, passing a bottle between them and a couple of his other pals. Wilfred Feeney was a tall, skinny kid, and lately he'd taken to wearing all black: slacks, a tuxedo jacket, and a top hat, but with no shirt so that the big ugly thing under the skin of his chest pushed out obscenely. It blinked blue and red through his stretched pale skin with the angry red scars that bristled with sutures.

"What's the deal, brother?" Wilfred sounded surprised and hurt, and it took Angelica a panicked moment to realize that he wasn't talking to Raj or her, but to a big beefy-looking guy in gray spacer's togs coming out of the hotel, some trucker chewing his thumbnail as he ambled through. He didn't seem to realize he was being addressed until Wilfred stepped out in front of him, getting right in the guy's face.

"I'm talking to you, brother. What's the deal?"

"Shit," Raj muttered.

"What the hell are you talking about?" grumbled the trucker, taking a step back and giving the kid a confused look.

"You bit your thumb at me, bruv. That's not nice. I think you ought to apologize."

The dishwasher chortled and took a long swig.

"I didn't do shit," said the trucker. "Get out of my face."

He walked around Wilfred, putting his forearm out as a

guide. Wilfred sprang back as if struck, and his top hat fell and rolled.

"What the blazes, brother! First you make obscene gestures, and now you hit me? What's your game? What'd I ever do to you?"

Angelica looked at Raj, a sense of panic welling up in her. Raj's face was wooden as he watched.

"I didn't hit nobody, 'brother', but if you don't piss off I'm gonna."

Wilfred got up in his face, and the guy threw a punch. Wilfred sprang back, untouched and laughing his fool head off. Angelica felt sick with adrenaline, and then she saw the guy pull a knife.

"Raj!"

Her brother had already shot into action, as did the dishwasher whose face had gone from stoned amusement to horror. They tried to get in between Wilfred and the trucker, but the two were both eager for a fight. The trucker got the dishwasher with a punch and went for Raj with the knife, but Raj danced out of the way and grabbed the guy's arm.

Wilfred took the opportunity to land what looked like a solid punch in the gut. The trucker stumbled and staggered back, and Angelica saw blood spread dark across his gray jumpsuit – Wilfred had knifed him.

Roaring, the wounded trucker sprang up, free of Raj's grip. Bellowing rage, he went for the laughing fool with his own blade up. Shouts of panic and warning came from all around them and Angelica stood rooted to the spot, frozen in terror. Wilfred stood his ground, grinning like this was the best fun in the world.

And then suddenly the trucker bent back, eyes wide. Raj's

other hand came around, and he slashed the man's throat from behind. They both fell hard.

Angelica dove to her knees, pulled the dying man away, and grabbed hold of her brother: dazed but alive. They both shook as she helped him to his feet, just as a pair of security guards rushed up.

"This fellow attacked me," sniffed Wilfred. "Made an obscene gesture and attacked me. With a knife!" He gestured dramatically at the big man bleeding out on the deck in a wide circle of horrified onlookers. "Why, if my good friend wasn't here to step in, things could have *really* blown up." He snickered, and his stoned nervous-looking buddy half-heartedly chuckled along.

"I'm sorry for the trouble, Mr Feeney," one of the station guards managed. Angelica stared at him. "We'll, uh, we'll take it from here." He looked back at her as Wilfred sauntered away. "Ms del Rio. Uh, sorry to ask. Does that… uh… is that what happened?"

She couldn't spare a glance for her blood-soaked brother. "Yes," she said, summoning her iciest voice. "Of course it is. You're lucky my brother was here, or young Mr Feeney would have been hurt."

The guard blanched. Word had gotten around among security, she gathered. They didn't even have their stun batons out, probably worried what might happen. They went to help Raj, who waved them off, heaving. He staggered, and she caught her breath, but he shook his head and managed a weak laugh.

"I'm fine, but I could use a drink." He looked down into the lobby, where past a knot of people was the promise of a well-stocked hotel bar.

Angelica nodded. "I'm sure you don't need us, officer, but we'll be downstairs in Ama no Gawa."

She steered her brother down the stairs through the onlookers; he leaned on her and was as easily led as if he was dead drunk already. The Japanese restaurant wasn't too busy, and she shooed a couple away from the end of the bar so that she could make him sit with nobody nearby. The frowning bartender came out, and he put on a poker face when he recognized them.

"Vodka," she said. "Make it a double."

"Make it two," Raj managed. The bartender nodded, and two shot glasses appeared almost instantly. Raj threw his back and blew out a long sigh, putting his elbows on the bar top and his head in his hands.

"Are you all right?" she murmured. They were attracting stares, or the growing puddle of blood under his bar stool was.

"Fine," he said. "Fine!" He grinned, and anyone else in the universe would have believed him. He picked up the empty blood-smeared shot glass absent-mindedly, and the hand holding it trembled. He saw her looking, pushed it away, and rubbed his face with both hands. "That was close, hey?"

Angelica couldn't respond. She felt sick, almost dizzy. She hadn't intended to order a drink for herself, but it suddenly seemed like a damned good idea. She picked it up with three shaking fingers and knocked it back. It went down smooth, just a burn in her throat and a warmth in her unsettled belly.

"I want to get out of here," she said.

He nodded. "I might need a minute."

"No. Out of *here*. Out of all of it."

He looked at her in surprise. "The station? The hell for?"

"You could have been killed. Both of us. All of us. That stupid laughing son of a bitch, he'd have been delighted."

Raj shook his head. "We've built up a lot here. Feeney's

been good to us. And…" He got a faraway look for a moment, then just shook his head again.

"You're my only brother, Raj."

"I want to stay," he managed. She stared.

"Why? God, why? What is there here to stay for?"

"Never mind," he said. He put on that grin of his again, and she knew that he'd shut down that window of vulnerability. Whatever he was thinking, he wouldn't share. "It's not so bad. And why should we get pushed off?"

"Feeney's never going to do anything about his grandson," she said.

Raj leaned in toward her. His grin was gone and he looked her in the eyes. "Maybe Feeney shouldn't be the one deciding, hey?"

She sat back, looked around to see if anyone might be listening in. She shook her head, but even she knew it was just a reflex.

"They'd go along with it," he said, his low voice urgent. "Most of them, anyway. You've been with him forever, Angelica, you're practically family. It's different coming from you."

"Practically family isn't family. Not since Jack died. Anyway, what if we do force him to act? What happens after that?"

Raj shrugged. "We'll burn that bridge when we get to it."

She stared into her empty shot glass, then swiveled in her seat. She couldn't see the casino from the back of the bar, but its lights reflected off the tables in the galleria. After a long while in silence, she made a call.

"Hey, Shine," she said when he answered.

"I'm busy, what do you need?"

"The high roller suite still open?"

"This morning. Haven't cleaned it yet."

"That's fine. I need it."

"How long?" She glanced toward the hotel and its magnetic pull.

"A few days should be enough. Just a few days."

Takata's in a Good Mood

Kenichi Takata laughed as the Miner sulked over a free beer.

"Cheer up!" he said.

"No."

He waved her off, smiling indulgently. He had good reason to smile, after the Miner watched him sell off a solid chunk of his beer, liquor, and wine supply. When he contacted his supplier to reorder, the poor woman had been shocked, having assumed after so long that he'd died. Then he'd had to assure her repeatedly that he hadn't been dallying with another distributor.

"You and Herrera both, you'd think we were leaking atmosphere!"

Herrera, in his booth, snorted. "It won't last."

"You don't want it to last."

"I don't want it to start!"

Takata whipped his bar towel at some speck of dust the Miner couldn't see. "Why are you so unhappy, Herrera? No more fighting! That's what you wanted, right?"

"We're back where we started! They're palling around and plotting all their new crimes. I don't care what they say: those two are still in charge behind the scenes. And Anaconda gets everything it wants, those corrupt filth-suckling sons of incontinent tapeworms. I thought you were going to kill them all, what happened to that? A hundred thousand credits, I told you!"

Takata frowned, the first time in hours. "She sure as hell tried, you have to admit. They're still cleaning up bodies. The robots are half broken down, and the waste pipes are clogged with I don't want to know what."

"Sure, kill the underlings," Herrera grumbled. "That's practically what they're for. You just saved the king and queen some money on their pay, that's all. They get to start fresh."

The Miner thought about pointing out that the drug lab had been firebombed and a major local source of piracy vented into space, but she didn't feel so great about those anyway.

"So when are you getting the hell out of here," Takata asked, and made it sound friendly.

"Tomorrow," she said. "The port's locked down while the Company Rep's yacht is docked. Anyway, McMasters is keeping my ship clamped until after their reception, as a 'guarantee for good behavior'." She probably could have done something about that, but with the sides playing nice she didn't figure she had a lot of room to negotiate. The security squad had polished their black armor, and seemed to not have a lot to do.

"You didn't have to throw their money back in their faces," Takata said. "You ought to have kept some of it."

"Didn't want to owe them. Seems smart now."

Takata didn't seem to take notice of her reply, so she drank her beer. It was good beer. He kept cleaning, humming as he went in back and came out with a mop.

"Jesus, are you mopping?" Herrera asked. "Did you have a stroke?"

"No, damn your eyes, I didn't have a stroke, I'm going to have customers! Just you see. They'll settle down and wipe the blood off the galleria–"

"And the ports," added the Miner.

"And all the fucking walls, decks, hatches, and plumbing," contributed Herrera with a leer.

"They'll wipe the blood off the galleria," Takata repeated over him, "and the people will come back. And when they come back, they'll want to eat, and I'm going to be the only game in town. And just to show you that I forgive all your ingratitude and warmongering and a truly ridiculous amount of just flat-out murdering people, I'm going to make you two dinner tonight. All right?"

"I'll check my calendar," Herrera said with a grin, holding his empty whiskey glass up to the light. "Hey look, I can pencil you in."

"Thank you," the Miner said. "I'd like that."

They were interrupted by a rap on the tile. The Miner turned to see Feeney standing alone. He wore nice clothes and his silver hair was clean and slicked back, and he'd shaved. He held a silver-topped walking stick where he'd banged it on the deck.

"Hello, Mickey dear." He glanced up behind her and waved a hand. "No need for a drink, barkeep, I'm not staying. I just felt the need to come over and say hello, and no hard feelings."

The Miner raised an eyebrow, then raised her glass of beer in a half-toast. He smiled, and leaned in.

"I also came to say, in my official role of grandfather of the bride, to kindly stay the fuck away from my granddaughter's reception, you damnable banshee. The sooner you shake this station's dust from your feet, the better."

He smiled, kind and grandfatherly, and held the cane topper up to his forehead with a wink in salute or farewell, and then turned sharply on his heel and strolled away, humming.

OKONOMIYAKI

Takata suppressed a grin as he poked his head through the curtain to look around the restaurant. The Miner and Herrera looked back at him, and when he saw that the rest of the bar was empty, he set to work closing the shutters and then he excitedly waved them into the kitchen. His guests exchanged looks, shrugged at each other, then ambled around the bar into the back, drinks still in hand.

"Ta da!" Takata said, whipping a white dish towel off a shriveled-looking fist-sized green and white ball in the palm of his hand. He beamed at it like he'd given birth to it.

Herrera tilted his head. "You dragged us back here to show us a cabbage?"

"Yes!" His elation dimmed. "Look, asshole, when's the last time you saw a fresh cabbage? Never, that's when."

Herrera shrugged. "I'm not a cabbage guy."

"You will be when I'm done with you. You, Mick, you're quiet. No dry wit? No cutting remark?"

The Miner shrugged. "Just trying to remember the last time I saw a cabbage. I thought they were bigger."

Takata huffed and set it down on the counter, then turned around and flipped the griddle on to the highest setting. "Cost me a bottle of real wine just to get Mr Shine to grow that dinky little thing. I was going to let it go longer, but I'm in the mood to celebrate. Anyway, you're getting a free dinner out of it, so what do you want?"

"No complaints from me," she said, smiling. "Little cabbage it is, and I'll be glad to have it."

Takata got out a sharp knife and held it in one hand as he examined the fist-sized vegetable in the other, turning it this way and that with a faint, almost blissful smile on his face. Then he lay it on the white plastic cutting board and plunged the knife in, pulling the base down to the board with a *thunk* and splitting the head neatly in half. A V-cut on the first half excised the core, which he set aside, then he repositioned the half and started slicing.

He was fast with the knife, and it must have been sharp as hell. The Miner watched with interest as he worked the blade up and down, almost rocking, feeding the half head into it and producing slivers of crisp green flesh that held the half-ball shape as they got pushed on down the board. Strands pushed themselves up in a traffic jam behind the blade, splintering, and then in thirty seconds he was done. He turned the whole board ninety degrees and crunched the knife through the splintered pile once, twice, then scooped it all up and dumped it in a bowl.

There was a ring at the back door, and Takata yelled a welcome without looking up. Dr Mills stood in the entryway, looking sheepish. "I hope I'm not late..." He held up a canister and said, "I don't have any sake, but I thought a dry white wine might go well with it."

"Sure!" Takata said.

"I don't have that either, so I brought plonk," Mills said with a mischievous smile, setting the canister on a worktable.

"Even better!"

Mills peered over the cook's shoulder at the cutting board as he sidled by in the tight space, and took the stool next to Herrera. "Good to see you again," he told him, and nodded politely to the Miner as well.

Takata was already halfway through the second half cabbage, producing an even slaw that he chopped roughly again and dumped in the bowl. Then he got to work finely dicing the core, and it went in, too. He turned to the little herb garden under a sun lamp on the far bulkhead, taking a pair of scissors to a trio of spindly foreshortened green onions and returning with two finger-lengths' worth cradled in his palm. He sliced them and dumped them in with the cabbage.

"My grandfather used to make this for me when I was a kid," he said as he chopped. "A little different back then. Easier to get stuff, and I was a spoiled brat who didn't appreciate hand-made food." He gave his audience a meaningful look, but they didn't take the bait. He snorted. "I've been craving it for ages."

"And telling me about it for at least that long," Dr Mills said. "It's become myth."

"It is mythical in nature," Takata said. From the fridge he got a jar of red strands – the Miner caught a whiff of ginger when he opened it – fished out a bundle with his fingers, and got to chopping them.

"How's tricks?" Herrera asked Mills, who only shrugged.

"Slowed down. I ducked the excitement as long as I could, but, well, duty calls."

Takata got a second bowl from under the counter, and sifted a good amount of flour into it. "It's bulked out with jiminy," he warned, but his guests shrugged. The Miner had probably eaten her weight in crickets and mealworms out of service rations alone, and who knew what was in emergency rations. Takata sprinkled in some salt and other powders from little dented canisters stuck to the side of his work table with magnets.

The bowl of seasoned flour was whisked, then Takata brought it over to a spigot marked "YEgg! Whyte & Yölk Mix" and opened it to glug in a good amount of mucous-like yellow and clear fluid. The Miner had once had a YEgg! brand yeast incubator, long ago, and she had considered it tolerable as long as she didn't dwell on what she was really eating scrambled on toast, but the stupid thing was too finicky to keep operational and it stank to high heaven when bacteria infected the batch. She'd had to jettison the whole incubator, and sometimes still gagged when reminded of it too strongly.

Takata was already pouring water into the bowl, carefully measured from a battered metal cup. "This ought to be stock," he apologized, "but I haven't had dashi powder in months."

"I'm heartbroken," Herrera said.

"Good."

Working a handful at a time, he massaged the shredded cabbage into the batter, stirring and frowning as it all went in the bowl, then running his hand around the edge to get every last shred. When it was all mixed in and glistening yellow and green, he turned to the griddle and let a few drops fall from his spoon to the surface where they sizzled and popped. He nodded once, satisfied.

"I know you don't do pork," he said to Mills. "The beef OK for you with the fake egg? I mean, it's all fake, but the principle, right?"

Mills shrugged. "Sure, thanks for asking."

"What about the rest of you? Fake pork belly all right? It's not horrible, used to be a pig a million years ago probably. Some bastard pig nobody liked."

"When's the last time they tested those vats for staph or e-coli?" Herrera muttered.

"Never, that's when. That a no on the pork?"

"Eh, I'll live dangerously."

"What's dangerous is insulting my cooking. You?" He pointed a battered finger at the Miner.

"I'll eat anything."

"Good answer." He stopped short and looked at her suspiciously. "I think."

Three strips of pink-and-white striped something went on the grill, *slap slap slap* in a row, then after a moment a ruddier strip followed. They sizzled and the air filled with the heady scent of cooking meat. The Miner tried to remember the last time she'd watched a meal prepared, and couldn't. It'd been ages since she gave up on the galley and just ate emergency rations. Small mounds of cabbage batter went on top of the shriveling and twisting strips of vat-grown meat, carefully shaped with a spoon and a pair of chopsticks, then gently flattened into cakes.

Takata flipped off the ventilation fan over the stove for a moment and breathed it in with a self-satisfied smile: wheat batter, frying cabbage, cooking meat. Using a pair of broad metal spatulas he went down the line, digging under each palm-sized disc from both sides and then with a little "hup!" under his breath he flipped them. The brown-and-black spotted tops of the pancakes steamed gently until he squirted a deep red sauce over top each in a lace pattern. The sauce dribbled over the sides and hissed and bubbled as the aroma of burning sugar and soy sauce overpowered the rest, and he turned the fan back on.

Onto the sauce went mayonnaise from another bottle in a cross-lace, then a fine green powder. The Miner's stomach rumbled, and she realized that she'd gotten very hungry watching him cook. His three guests watched in silence, rapt.

Four blue square plates came out from under the workstation, and a pancake went onto each with another maneuver of the two metal spatulas and another little "hup!" The first went to Mills, then Herrera and the Miner. Takata switched off the grill top before plating his own, and turned his back on its steaming surface as he dragged over a stool. Each of them received a pair of chopsticks and a little spade-looking instrument still with the metal-printer's ridges here and there along the handles, looked like someone had flattened a spoon and then snipped the front of the bowl off.

"Itadakimas!" he said cheerily, and dug in, cutting with the spade in neat downward motions and eating with the chopsticks. He sat back after the first bite, a look of bliss on his face. He pounded the table lightly with his fist. "Damn," he said swallowing. "That is it exactly. Mmm! Spot fucking on."

The Miner ate carefully. It was still steaming hot, and delicious. Salty, crunchy, sweet, spicy. The cabbage partly steamed and partly fried, the nutty cooked batter, the sweet sauce, and a sharp earthy note from the ginger and onion.

The reverent silence broke when Dr Mills remembered his wine. Takata fetched some cups and they split it four ways. They toasted each other wordlessly with their translucent plastic cups, and the Miner had a sip of grape-like engine cleaner with a hint of oak. She smiled and murmured a thank you to the doctor.

"I used to be able to get huge cabbages," Takata said. "As big as your head."

"Here we go again," Herrera muttered into his dinner.

"Maybe not *your* head. A normal person's head. Man. I could make this every day. I could put it on the menu."

"You want Feeney back in charge so you can have cabbage."

"Would that be so damn bad?" Takata slapped his chopsticks down with a loud click. "Would it really? Yeah I hated paying his protection money, but it was a hell of a lot better than all that bullshit."

"He's why we had all that bullshit. It was fool's gold."

The Miner ignored their argument to focus on the food. Good food, hot food. The argument made it better somehow, brought her back to mess halls a million years ago, family dinner tables long before that, all the little fights over stupid points of trivia or policy or pride. Her mind wandered back to the grinning idiots in her old photos, and to her surprise she found herself blinking back a tear.

"Don't drag me into this," Mills was saying. "I don't like any of it."

"You did the marriage," Takata accused.

"Two young people asked me to marry them, and yes I did. I'd do it again, for *any* two people who asked." He looked meaningfully at Takata and Herrera, and when they both harrumphed and refused to take the bait, he focused on the Miner. "I was surprised to see you there, by the way. I half believed that after I left, those two wouldn't get out of there alive."

She shifted uncomfortably in her seat. "Good thing you only half believed it."

"Best thing you could have done," Herrera said sourly. "Those assholes would have killed each other off, let us start over. We'd have had some real peace. Now they're just regrouping."

"The peace of the grave," Takata said.

"The peace of justice! You think just because they're not out punching and shooting each other that there's peace?

Violence underpins everything they do. It's there even if they're not fighting, it's just aimed at everyone like a squashed spring. Who's gonna get fucked next?"

Takata waved his hand like he was swatting at a gnat. "That's just crap. There's tension in any system. People just plain don't like each other. You'll never remove all your 'violent underpinnings' and that's the kind of shit you get when you try. Some jackass set off a nuclear weapon, for the love of God!" Mills met the Miner's eye with a speculative look, but she let Takata's speech wash over them. "People aren't perfectible, Herrera. They're assholes. They're always gonna be assholes."

Herrera scoffed, but Takata interrupted him, pointing a finger in his face. "But the trick is that they're lazy assholes. You get people invested in peace, see the benefits for themselves, they like to stay that way. Then you work at it. You improve. That's how you get justice, not by blowing everything up."

"Every so-called peace like that is on somebody's back. And that poor sonofabitch gets repeatedly fucked while the people who have it good tinker with making things 'a little bit better every day' or whatever bullshit slogan, and congratulate each other on how nice they're making everything, how well-dressed and polite that Feeney chap is, and isn't it nice he stopped shanking people in public."

"That's rich. You hear that, Doc?"

Mills looked surprised and started to say, "Don't look at me," but Takata talked over him.

"You've never been the poor sonofabitch, Herrera! You bitch and moan, but you drew a government salary this whole time." Herrera's face reddened. "You'd have ridden out months more fighting with no problem, but me, I'm at the end of my rope here. Those Anaconda assholes won't care that I'm not making rent because they screwed every pooch that walked by, they just care that I'm not making rent."

"I'd have helped..." Herrera muttered.

"I don't want help, I want customers! Customers are predictable. I know what they want, and that's a decent dinner with as many cheap drinks as they can pour down their gullets, and if I piss one or two off, they go away and another few show up, look just like them. I don't have to worry, oh I offended that one guy and now I'll starve."

"You do if that one guy is John Feeney. Or Angelica del Rio. Or Tom McMasters."

Takata made a scornful face. "I don't care what those crooks think of me."

"What? And you suddenly care what I think of you?"

The two arguers went suddenly quiet. Dr Mills pursed his lips and raised his eyebrows. Then their faces both went dark and they started yelling over each other. The Miner leaned her elbows against the counter behind her, lost track of the conversation, and just enjoyed the bickering.

THE BRIDE WORE RED

The noise irritated the Miner. Gunfire, malfunctioning machinery, the squeal of a bearing failing at high temperature – none of these bothered her, except at an intellectual level. But dozens of people trying to talk over each other in a party setting, that grated on her nerves like nothing else. She would rather have been anywhere else, but Takata had prevailed on her to stick around and be a good sport, and had come through with good beer and grilled skewers of something out of the vats that went down well with the second beer especially.

Out in the galleria a throng of thugs, fighters, gamblers, and goons milled awkwardly under her baleful glare, socializing with people who'd been trying to kill them not very long ago. The Miner would have enjoyed their discomfort if it weren't for the noise, and if she weren't feeling so sour about the whole thing.

Feeney presided in some kind of ancient black tie getup, talking and joking with Angelica, who stood a good quarter meter taller than him with her black hair plaited in a fancy braid over a dress so matte black it seemed like a hole in the crowd. She resembled a mortician in both dress and demeanor, especially in contrast to the naturally exuberant old man. The only cracks in his genial confidence were his occasional death ray glares at the Miner. That kid Corbell who had been at the makeshift wedding hovered near the old man and looked like he hadn't slept. Taller than Feeney and darker in both color and demeanor, he resembled a storm cloud following the glad-handing old gangster around.

The couple, who had already been married but who nonetheless consented to a party – and gifts – hadn't made their appearance yet. They seemed to want to make an entrance, probably waiting until the assembly was good and drunk.

Mr Shine had shown up. He looked relaxed in the tuxedo he'd worn in the old photos, delicately holding a martini glass that he occasionally sipped from and grimaced. Finn's vodka hadn't gone to waste; the Miner could make out a whiff like engine cleaner every time the air circulator patterns changed. He should have been making a mint, and instead he was dead. She didn't even know how he died.

The goons had left their weapons behind, and looked distinctly ill at ease without them. Still, alcohol and stronger stuff seemed to be propelling them toward something resembling social grace. That nobody seemed to be enjoying themselves didn't appease the Miner in the slightest.

"See, look at them," Takata said. "They don't really want to fight."

"Not each other, maybe," Herrera said. "They're all jelly-livered chickenshits. They'll be happy to beat up miners and shake down your customers though, don't worry."

"That's what McMasters is for."

"Hah! Fuckstache is going to get shitcanned now Anaconda doesn't need him. The minute those two kissed and made up, he became a liability. Hell, I bet Feeney's already over there saying, 'Now about those loans, Tom.' Mark my words: he is out the airlock the minute someone has a half-decent excuse. It might even be him with the excuse once he figures out Feeney and Angelica won't pay him off no more."

Takata brushed him off with an indulgent smile, then dashed back into the kitchen to retrieve another plate of skewered vat-meat. He'd been cooking non-stop, and had done some damn fine work, the Miner thought, with scant ingredients. At the crack of mid-morning a bunch of surly goons had descended on the restaurant and been made to each wash their hands under Takata's close supervision, some of them twice. Mr Shine had brought up loads of sad-looking pale vegetables that had flopped pathetically in their crates, but Takata had been ecstatic to see them anyway. They'd shaken hands like old friends, and the former casino boss had given the Miner a long, thoughtful look before leaving without exchanging words with her. The vegetables had been chopped and sautéed, bandages applied liberally. Dozens of little mealworm flour pastry cups full of cooked fake egg with tiny bits of irregularly-chopped vegetables had gone out, along with lots of the charred skewers of vat meat with sauce, a lot of little pancake things with little bundles of shredded vegetation with a vinegary smell, and some little wrap things. Food had emerged from the casino and hotel kitchens too, looking to the Miner like reheated frozen stuff.

The Miner caught a glimpse of McMasters in his black uniform, neatly pressed with everything shinable shined, escorting a frail-looking woman with expensive jewelry and the haunted look of a gazelle who'd wandered into a nature documentary.

"The Company Rep," Takata said in her ear. "I'm surprised she's here. Usually she hangs out in her yacht hooked up to her VR rig all day trying to be anywhere else but here. I'm amazed she can still walk."

The Miner heard him, but wasn't listening. Something about McMasters' posture bugged her, and as she watched him she became convinced that he was seriously on edge. He wasn't escorting the Rep so much as steering her like a gaudy wheelbarrow, in a spiral away from the center of the crowd.

"Something's up," she said, and was interrupted by the crowd's first real enthusiasm: Mary and Raj had emerged onto the balcony from Feeney's hotel. They looked good, cleaned up and groomed and both wearing neat black clothes. The light glinted off of Mary's spike implants and the iridescent scales at Raj's temples, and they beamed down at the crowd. For their part, the goons filling the galleria seemed genuinely glad to see them, to the tune of whooping whistles, catcalls, and hollering of all sorts.

Feeney tried to say something, but even amplified by a public address system was drowned out. He shrugged at Angelica, who gave him a chilly but tolerant shrug in return, then he laughed and turned and clapped. The Miner lost track of McMasters and the Rep in the crowd, and couldn't see Mr Shine.

The lights went completely out. The Miner's artificial eye recovered so fast that she was more clued-in by the startled and dismayed crowd's reaction than by the darkness. A single shot rang out in the dark, and Raj's head exploded in a burst of red mist.

The occupants of the galleria took a deep collective breath, and then, collectively and completely, lost their shit.

Après, le Déluge

Screwball had been looking directly at the old man when the lights went down, otherwise he'd never have been able to find him when the shot fired. He clapped his arm around a slight form and for a second thought he'd gotten the wrong person until he caught a gasp of sour breath and heard Feeney exclaim. He felt frail in the dark, and his bones were palpable under the nice suit.

They both tensed when they heard someone wail.

"Mary!" Feeney whispered, and then shouted it, "Mary!"

The crowd around them started to jostle and shout, and someone elbowed Screwball hard in the back.

"Shh!" Screwball pulled Feeney in close. "I need to get you out of here."

"Mary!"

"Whoever's shooting might be coming for you. Keep your voice down!"

He started to make out shapes in the dark, and started to shepherd the old gangster towards the edge of the galleria. They'd been right in the thick of things, waiting for Mary and Raj to come out – was that Mary making that noise? – and the closest way out was towards the restaurant.

There was a scream of pain from close by, and the distinct

sound of a fist hitting flesh. Scuffles in the dark turned into an all-out brawl, and Screwball struggled to keep moving as people and chairs bashed into him. He stumbled when something hard cracked against his shin, and he swore loudly but didn't pull Feeney down. The old man's arm went up behind his back and they stabilized each other as they got knocked and tossed around, but still managed to make progress as they could both see better.

"The galleria is on lockdown," boomed a voice above their heads. Screwball cringed, more from the surprise, but his ears rang with it. "Leave the vicinity immediately." The message repeated, and suddenly there were thunderous clanging noises all around them, deafening for all they seemed to be coming from everywhere at once. There was a sharp scream from the other side of the galleria, silenced just as quickly.

"The shutters," Feeney yelled in his ear. Emergency lights circling the area glowed red, casting everything in crimson and deep shadow, and he could see for himself that their exit path was cut off. They pushed their way past the last few people between them and the outside wall, and stood for a moment next to someone curled on the deck, clutching her head and rocking.

Behind them, Screwball heard more screams, and a sinister electrical crackle. Blue flashes reflected off glass and chrome, seeming to come from everywhere. Feeney shook loose and took off toward the hotel. Screwball dashed after him and tried to run interference as the crowd shoved and heaved, trying to get away from the security officers and their stun batons, but not knowing where they were.

They reached the stairs, and Screwball wasn't shy about pulling stunned fighters out of their way, even hurling them down the steps, and then they were at the top, and there was Mary, cradling Raj's body and sobbing. Off to their right, the hotel's doors stood wide open without their shutters. He turned to the left and saw across the scattering crowd of partiers that the casino doors were open, too.

Feeney was shaking his granddaughter by the shoulders, but she shook her head violently and only clutched Raj tighter. "Have to get out" was the only bit Screwball heard, then there was a tug on his arm. "Help me!"

It took some gesturing for Screwball to realize that he was being asked to move the body. He retched when he saw Raj's wrecked face, and again when he slipped in the blood, invisible in the red lights, and landed painfully on his knee. Gagging on the strong smell of blood and shit, he still managed to get his arms under Raj's armpits, and then drag the corpse backward.

The noise from the galleria fell away quickly as he got traction and made it into the lobby. Stumbling and staggering people made it in behind them, coming first in a trickle and then all at once. "Get the poor boy up off the floor," he heard Feeney say, and a couple pairs of hands were suddenly assisting him. There were some moments of confusion until someone said, "There's a coffee table" and then that became Raj del Rio's resting place. Mary sunk to her knees in front of it, put her arms and head on his still chest, and Screwball saw in the bluish hotel light that she was sticky with blood from head to toe. So was he.

There was a rattling metallic noise; he turned and saw the hotel shutters finally coming down. It had a calming effect on the crowd; maybe three dozen people stood dazed in the Ad Astra lobby, and it slowly dawned on them that they weren't all on the same side. Screwball didn't recognize a lot of the faces, but he did see one unexpected one: Mr Shine, standing a head taller than a lot of the others, sporting a blossoming black eye and cradling his left arm, had taken a position next to Feeney.

The old man had stumbled back and was fending off Shine's attempts to engage him earnestly. "Well, who could be calling me?" he said too loudly, like he was proud of himself. "What do you want, witch?" He grinned up at a frowning Shine, and slurred, "Oh, it's only Angelica, whose brother is beastly dead."

The grumbling grew louder at that, and thankfully Mary seemed not to have heard it.

"Enough!" someone shouted as the mutual glares and muttering started to progress to shoving, and Screwball was astonished to find that the someone was himself. But when they turned to look at him in surprise and irritation, he balled his hands. His heart pounded in sudden panic at being the center of attention, but he kept shouting anyway. "Knock it off! We're stuck here and nobody gives a shit who you work for. You're all assholes, you're all even. So quit... Whatever... Just chill out, all right?"

"Nice speech, dipshit," someone muttered, but the fighting didn't resume. People stared at their boots, stared at Mary, stared at him. But they didn't fight. Screwball's heart was still racing, and he took a moment to let the shock of adrenaline wear off. He looked around for Feeney, but the old man, and Mr Shine, were gone.

Aftermath

Takata's angry rant trailed off after about ten minutes, after the noise outside the steel shutters finally died down. He'd variously accused the Miner, Herrera, McMasters, Feeney, Angelica, and several supernatural entities of engineering this catastrophe, singly and in unlikely partnerships. All of their rationales, however, were aimed at personally ruining him and his chances of making it off the station with two pennies to rub together. Herrera had the good graces to try to not look too triumphant, and the Miner was too puzzled to be either offended or amused.

"McMasters knew something was up," she offered when the rant subsided.

Herrera nodded. "He had his whole crew suited up and ready to go."

Takata waved the comment away. "He probably figured it would turn into a riot the minute anyone spilled a drink. I don't like the sonofabitch, but I have to admit, he was prepared."

"Mmm." The Miner stared at the steel shutters. They weren't the security shutters Takata used every night, but looked heavier and better-reinforced. "Are those airtight? Do we have an oxygen supply in here?"

"Yes. Both. I don't know if there's any oxygen in it, so maybe we'll all die like the two of you seem to want. So, good luck with that. Anyway, they're intended for a hull breach, but I have to admit they're pretty good for crowd control."

Takata poured himself half a tumbler full of something clear, and sat heavily at a table away from the Miner and Herrera. Judging by his wince at the first sip, the Miner didn't think it was water.

For her own part, the Miner was busy thinking. She looked down at her sword, and mistrusted it for the task. The gloves were well and truly off now, and she wanted at least a sidearm if not her rifle. She tried to communicate with her ship, but the station comms were down, and she was too far for a direct link. She couldn't even get a ping response off it.

"Why would someone have risked shooting Raj in public like that?" she wondered aloud.

"You'd have done it," Takata said morosely, not looking up from his drink.

"'S a good idea," Herrera contributed. "Dog-blowing little turd-fondler had it coming."

"Maybe, but I didn't do it. Someone had decent low-light, good aim, and a good spot to shoot from. And an accomplice, probably, to turn off the lights and defeat the anti-projectile systems. And a damn good reason."

Takata snorted. "Trying to figure out which side did it so you can go work for them?"

"It's not either one of those two," Herrera said. "Think about it. Who wants to keep Feeney and del Rio fighting, and isn't worried about McMasters picking sides?"

"Other than you two psychos? Mr Shine doesn't care. Psycho number one here seems to think he's the heir apparent. Maybe he didn't like being dethroned."

Herrera scowled. "Why does she get to be psycho number one?"

The Miner interrupted whatever Takata was about to say. "Do you think the back entrance is unlocked?"

Takata stared up at her with undisguised suspicion. He'd put a dent in the drink already, and his face was becoming flushed. "Just can't wait to join the fun, huh? Not enough blood already? You want to get back to juggling death and destruction?" To Herrera he said, "That's why she gets to be psycho number one."

She let it go. A couple suspicions of her own were gnawing at her. She got up and went. The small kitchen had been emptied of "helpers" when the party started, but the bots were still out and cleaning up. The back hatch stood closed, and stayed closed when she tapped the panel.

"Looks like it's locked down too," Takata said behind her. "Sorry." He didn't sound sorry.

She frowned at the panel. The "unlock" option was still there at the bottom, despite the lockdown. She tapped it, and heard a clunk. The door opened freely. She and Takata exchanged looks, and then before her better sense could catch up, she slipped out into the corridor.

HOUSEKEEPING

The Miner made straight for the docks, and wasn't surprised to find the back corridors empty. She had seen the dockmaster at the party, so wasn't worried about running into him, but didn't know when he might find his way back, so she ran. The main entrance was wide open, and the docks were empty of people.

She didn't want to dally, but she still took the time to duck into the control booth. Finding his terminal open and on, she unlocked it, thinking to release the docking clamps on her ship. The Company Rep's yacht was gone already; hers was the only ship docked. She paused when she found that they'd already been released, and dug a little deeper into the interface, one she'd had to learn in a hurry once on a mission. Glancing up through the window from time to time, she ran through the menus and found something: a notification attached to her ship's entry. She didn't have time to dig too deep, but it looked like it would send a message to some location she couldn't decipher, the moment her ship's airlock opened.

She backed out of the entry for her ship's docking bay, and after a moment of study, she found that the neighboring bay was out of commission for repairs. After a moment's thought, she swapped their IDs in the system. Bay 5 with her ship attached showed up as defunct Bay 4, which meant that attempting to clamp Bay 5 would harmlessly set them next door. Just in case someone changed their mind. More importantly, opening the Bay 5 airlock wouldn't notify anyone.

Satisfied, she used the terminal to shut the main entrance doors and give herself a little cover, then she went to the hatch leading to the airlock for her ship. She tapped the direct link, and found that her ship wasn't responding to voice commands, but she could override it from the panel and open the airlock. She slipped in and shut the dockside hatch behind her.

The Miner stopped short when the shipside hatch opened. The cargo bay had been ransacked. All the ties and covers had been pulled off her equipment, and the equipment itself shoved out of place. Stacked pieces had been toppled, leaving broken bits of plastic and metal strewn on the decking. Her heart pounded, and she could feel her implants tighten, signaled by her rising anger. This wasn't a search. A good search didn't look like this, it was too easy to block things the searcher hadn't looked through. This was just vandalism. In the middle of the deck, beneath the upper walkway, little piles of peat moss had fallen.

She ran for the upper deck, taking the steps three at a time, and froze when she got there and found the remains of a trampled *Phalaenopsis*. Its purple-and-white petals were crushed into the mesh walkway; its stem smashed on the wires. The pot wasn't there, and the pale roots dangled.

Shaking, the Miner knelt and scooped the flower up in two hands. She had to close her eyes to make herself turn toward the plant room, and it was some time before she could force herself to open them.

The bonsai trees had been swept to one side and lay in a

pile of shattered pottery. The orchids had been smashed and thrown around. The watering system had been pulled apart, leaking puddles onto the bench that hadn't dried. One of the grow lights hung by a wire and flickered as it swung in the air mover's breeze.

She moved mechanically, forcing herself to work so that she wouldn't think. She took stock, first of the damage, then her assets. They hadn't found the cabinet with the spare pots, at least. The utilitarian steel tools were thrown around, but not stolen or broken. She rescued the trees first. The ficus was in the worst shape, with a branch broken badly so that it peeled a strip of bark halfway down the trunk, its milky sap already mostly dried. She cleanly cut the limb away, then trimmed and swabbed the damaged part clean. She cut away bruised and damaged leaves and roots, then repotted it. It was scarred, but would survive. She knew the feeling.

The red maple had damage to a few smaller limbs, the new ones. She pruned them back and tried not to pay attention to the ugly lop-sided shape that resulted. Amazingly, the juniper just needed to be repotted.

The orchids were a different story. Four of them, including the purple-and-white *Phalaenopsis*, were completely beyond saving. She shook the loose moss and soil from their roots for use in repotting the others, and placed their mangled forms in the digester. Two were in reasonable shape: the white *Dendrobium* with its tiny star-like flowers, and the extravagant yellow and purple *Cattleya*. These she repotted and carefully tied to new stakes, trimming back damaged leaves and flowers.

The rest, she could possibly save with a great deal of work and care. She put them in the digester.

It took twenty minutes to repair and re-string the watering system, and then to mop up the floor so that she'd know whether it was leaking or not. Three trees and two flowers stood in the light of the remaining grow lamps in the middle of three rows of empty benches. When she finally put away the tape and shears, her hands trembled from suppressed rage. She forced herself to wash them in the sink, barely noticing the tiny stings from scrapes and cuts as the soap got into them.

Her bunk had been ransacked as badly as the hold. The blanket had been thrown off, and the sheets and mattress bore long, gaping knife wounds. Her drawers and closets were thrown open, though the inexpert vandals hadn't found the hidden compartments. The slim black box under the bed had been dumped out, and the tangled ribbons bore bootprints. Her rifle was gone. Through the growing red haze of fury, something in the back of her head took that in and said, *That's interesting*.

She picked up her medals and placed them back in the box, finding one of the twelve missing. She patted the floor looking for it, then snapped the box shut and slid it back under the bed, wondering if whoever had dumped them out had known what they were, what they were for. Wounded in action. Valor. Skill. Quick thinking and resourcefulness. Desperation, fury, and revenge in only tangential service of someone else's cause. She tried to remember if the missing honor had had her name on it, or if she'd ground that one smooth, too.

She found the pictures that had fallen off the bulkhead and put them in the drawer. Making the bed and covering over the large rents full of mattress stuffing made her feel silly, but the physical activity calmed her. Her sword at her hip kept whacking the hatchway when she turned in the small space, reminding her of what she ached to be doing right then.

Focus, she told herself. She went to the cockpit and found it operational. Whoever had done this had wanted to make sure she could still flee. They hadn't damaged the equipment, but there was a distinct and overpowering smell of urine. Fucking barbarians. Fucking amateurs.

Just because they didn't trash the hardware didn't mean they hadn't trashed the software. She started up the ship's computer in emergency mode, found a backup from before she'd docked, and reactivated from that.

"Hello, boss!"

"Full diagnostics," she ordered, and waited. The cockpit view of the station dock exterior showed it to be pathetically empty. Flight control showed a lonely ship way out past the nav beacons, probably an arrival. Maybe more recruits for the fight. Maybe another miner, who'd have to deal with cheats and a lockdown and still not be able to sell their ore.

"Finished, boss!" She jumped when the computer finally responded. The results popped up on the nearest panel, and she scanned them. Most everything was fine, which didn't surprise her: they seemed to want to hurt her, but leave her able to flee. Some interior cameras offline. Life support in the escape pod offline.

She went to have a look at the escape pod, and groaned. Someone had wrenched open one of the panels, yanked the air filtration system completely out of its socket, then inexpertly jammed it all back in. Three wires were broken. If she ever tried to use it like this, she'd probably be dead in minutes. Legally, she could swap it out at any station for a standard fee and let them deal with it – but that would require her to notice ahead of time, and at this station she'd rather fix it herself, thanks. No time to just then, though.

That discovery prompted another thought. Did they disable the escape pod out of spite, or did they intend to force her to use it? She went back to the list of offline cameras and went on a hunt. There was only one camera out in a compartment that seemed untouched: the engine room. It didn't take long to find the little package behind an access panel, a flashbang grenade wired up to a remote detonator. She told the ship to do a full sweep of the interior space, and to remind her to do her own sweep later. After all, it was poor practice to only leave one present behind.

She stripped down and threw the diamond fiber undersuit in the washer, then indulged in a lukewarm shower herself. She dressed in clean clothes and lay out the armaments they'd left her. Flechette pistol went on her right hip, with the sword opposite. The shotgun would be useful, but clumsy without a harness, and the harness for the rifle was presumably still attached *to* the rifle. Grenades from the secret drawer compartment went into her thigh pockets.

With everything else done, she checked the exterior camera carefully and then crept from her ship, locking it up tightly this time with the law enforcement override disabled, and made her way across the deck. The lights were still down low. In the dockmaster's shack, she pulled up the terminal control, found the notification routine that had been attached to her airlock, and triggered it manually.

Five minutes' wait was enough. Six black-uniformed security team members showed up, heavily armed and armored. They swept out into a cursory search of the darker port, flashlight beams sweeping quickly every which way. Amateurs. They took up positions around the airlock entrance to her empty ship, looking tense. The one on the far left, after some rapidly-hissed back-and-forth, darted forward and jabbed at the access pad for a little while.

The Miner studied the dockmaster's terminal, but couldn't find an intercom program. She did find a gas purge function, to cycle atmosphere in the airlock – a nice noisy affair. She triggered it, and the security team immediately dropped into a crouch behind their riot shields, bringing up their rifles. While they were distracted, she crept out to a pallet not too far from her ship and watched. Not the best position, but reasonably well-hidden in the dark and she could get back to the shack without trouble.

"Yeah, she's in there," someone said.

"Trapped like a rat," someone else said, prompting nervous tittering from the other five would-be cats. The Miner considered a well-tossed grenade, but was out of practice and didn't want to damage the airlock.

She wanted to stay and observe longer, but without knowing whether backup was coming she decided to observe from further away. Halfway back to the dockmaster's shack, her ship paged her: "Message, boss!"

She rushed the rest of the way there, as quietly as she could, then very carefully closed the mechanical door. The keyed-up guards didn't seem to have heard anything. She tapped slowly on the plastic, a few seconds apart and louder each time. At the sixth tap, one of them turned a helmeted head quizzically.

"Patch it through," she muttered, making sure her voice stayed quieter than the fifth tap.

"Attention, fugitive," came McMasters' voice in her head. She didn't respond.

"I said, attention, fugitive."

"Sorry. Thought you were talking to someone else. What did you say?"

"I said, atten…" Silence. "You certainly are a great deal of trouble."

"That so?"

"I want you to know that I'm being extremely generous here. It would be a trivial matter to have my people board your ship, take you prisoner, and remand you for trial. But frankly, I'm not interested in you. You told the dockmaster that you intended to leave as soon as your business here is done, and I'm telling you: your business here is done."

"That's it? Fuck off and sin no more?"

"Somehow I consider that last part unlikely. Just leave."

"What if I don't feel like it?"

"Then my people will take you into custody. Assuming you aren't accidentally killed resisting arrest. That does unfortunately happen sometimes, Grace Molina."

She winced. He tried so hard to be menacing, and was so bad at it.

"Seems to me," she said, "you had Angelica's brother killed so you don't lose your nice position. Maybe I'm a convenient scapegoat to keep her from killing you right back. I guess that's a hell of a lot easier story to tell if I turn tail and run."

"Well," he said after a long silence. "At least we understand each other."

"I don't think we do," she said, keeping an eye on the security team still watching an empty airlock. "Your people trashed my ship and stole my service rifle. You're going to pay for that."

"You're in no position to negotiate."

"I'm hunkered down with the rifle you didn't find and the explosives you didn't find and six months of water and rations. Maybe del Rio won't believe my story, but she'll sure as hell be willing to clear out your little guard detail to come hear my piece."

"Five thousand credits."

"That'll cover the *Phalaenopsis*."

"What the devil's a *Phalaenopsis*?"

"Something that'll cost you five thousand credits. I figure a hundred grand will make us even for the damage. Call it a buck twenty to get on my good side."

"A hundred and twenty thousand credits! Are you drunk? I could buy your ship twice over for that much."

"Could be. But that's not what you're buying. Think it over."

She cut the connection and watched the half-dozen armored goons for a while longer. They were already losing discipline waiting, with two turned toward each other and chatting, and another actually sitting on the floor. She wondered if any of them had been the ones to trash her ship. It wouldn't be too hard to take them all out, even without using a grenade.

Instead, she triggered another gas purge. She spent a brief moment enjoying their panic, then used the distraction to make her getaway.

Let's Play Find the Sniper

The port section had exits into the back maintenance tunnels, and the Miner used these to make her escape. She had food, water, her sword, and a pistol. All she needed was an actual plan.

The maintenance tunnels were just old hallways, blocked off with reconfigurable walls so that visitors wouldn't get into them. Her footfalls echoed along their lengths. The fights had battered both the gangs down, and she knew they didn't have the strength to patrol, but McMasters' crew had come out fine. Minus the six idiots camped out at her airlock, and probably a good-sized crew guarding McMasters himself, still left enough to cause her trouble. She walked as quietly as she could, then, and thought as she went. Knowing that McMasters had been behind killing Raj didn't help her unless she could prove it. She wished she'd thought to record the call. Even then, though, if she could provoke Angelica into going to war against security, that would only cement Feeney. Why should she do that, if she could bring all three sides down. Give Herrera the clean slate he deserved.

She'd studied the back passage layout earlier, and anyway they were pretty easy to navigate. The first few intersections had had security cameras, and she'd dealt with them as she came across them, but quickly realized that they were already defunct. What a rat hole.

It was station night, and the lockdown had been lifted while she'd been on her ship. Usually Herrera went back to his quarters, and she hoped that had been the plan that night, since she didn't dare use station comms to get ahold of him. Between Angelica and McMasters, the chance of interception was just too high.

On the opposite side of the galleria from Feeney's hotel jutted a big blocky cluster of compartments, above the casino but not connected to it. They had been officers' quarters once upon a time, and judging by the map those quarters had been reconfigured into damn near palatial digs. She slowed and waited against an inside wall at the sound of a footfall. A lone security guard wandered, waving a rifle like a cumbersome stick. She was in the right area, anyway.

Herrera's quarters, as station master, were easy to get to, and easy to identify by the "FUCK YOU MCMASTERS AND THE HORSE YOU RODE IN ON OR MAYBE THE HORSE FUCKS YOU AND I WATCH" graffiti.

She stopped to admire the sentiment, then froze. Across from the graffiti, in the middle of the corridor wall, stood a pillar. She frowned at it, then back at the scrawl. Herrera didn't feel the need to simply express himself like that. She crept up to the pillar the long way around and pulled a mirror from her pocket. Angled down low and around, she could see it: one of McMasters' security cameras, active and pointed squarely at Herrera's handiwork. "Bless your obscene little soul," she murmured.

Knowing it was there, and where, she easily knocked it out with her sword. She dashed to Herrera's door and urgently rang the bell. When he finally arrived, disheveled and sleepy, she pushed her way in.

"They'll come see why the camera's disabled," she explained. He nodded and closed the door.

His quarters were immense, easily bigger than her ship. A nice red and brown rug took up most of the floor, and the walls bore paintings and a few coarse woven hangings.

"So what's going on?"

The Miner filled him in on McMasters trashing her ship and the conversation about the sniper.

"The way I figure it, whoever shot Raj was one of his guards. Who else can McMasters trust, on short notice? That means somewhere on this station is a cop with sharpshooter training."

He scratched his chin thoughtfully. "So why come to me? What can I do?"

"McMasters works for you."

He swore. "That sonofabitch brothel-bred plague louse. Works for me? Fuck! I ought to… You. You kill that bastard. You kill him and you bring me his goddamn mustache so I can nail it to my wall! You–"

The Miner held up her hands to placate him. "On paper, I mean. Technically. On paper he works for you, right?"

"Oh." His mood went from furious to mild in an instant. "Sure, I fired him like eight times."

"That means you've got access to personnel records, right?"

A slow grin crept across his face. He had just started to dash across the room when the door chime rang. The Miner nodded once at Herrera's look of warning, and stepped aside into the next room.

"What do you want?" she heard Herrera say.

"I want you to quit breaking our fucking cameras, you old asshole."

"I have registered your complaint and will forward it to the appropriate department. That all?"

"No."

The Miner tensed to hear the too-familiar sound of a punch landing. She heard him groan heavily and there was a heavier thud.

"Now quit fucking with our cameras. And Christ, don't puke on my boots, either."

She was back in the room before the door finished closing, and helped Herrera up off the floor.

"I'm sorry," she muttered.

"Shut up," he wheezed, and took a moment. "Not the first time these emotionally stunted ass hair lice come beat me up." He straightened himself up enough to look her in the eye, and the look on his face was defiant. "Might just be the last, though."

The Miner just nodded, and eventually got the hint that he wanted to recover his breath and his dignity without her help. She stood and waited as he did some stretches, got an ice pack, then pulled up the HR info. His visibility into the system was impressive: not just bios, but discipline records, body camera footage, even the duty roster and patrol assignments. She grinned, but first things first: figure out who they were looking for. Herrera pulled up the personnel records and dragged half of it onto a separate spot on the wall so they could look through in parallel.

She read through the dozen or so bios carefully, ranked by time on the job. The first few were pretty detailed: not exactly career law enforcement, but tours in the military or stretches with security on other stations, with dates and in two cases mild commendations. When she checked, her guess that they'd already been on the job when McMasters started proved accurate. After that, things got spottier. Military experience with start dates but no end dates – usually a sign of desertion or a covered-up expulsion. An eighteen year-old claiming to be a brigadier general. The last few just had names and ages; one of them was purportedly a hundred years old.

"Hey," Herrera said, tapping at one of the entries on his side. "What about this one, Gloria Settles. Five years in the service, three target shooting prizes and a sharpshooter's rating. Came on at the same time as McMasters himself."

The Miner raised her eyebrow. She was about to agree when she was distracted by the entry at the bottom of Herrera's list. No bio, just a name. She tapped it and left her finger there. "No," she said. "This guy."

AN OLD FRIEND

Fergus Capper tried for a good five minutes, leaning this way and that, digging in under the plating or kinda mashing down from above, working in vain to figure out how to scratch his balls in that damn armor and finally gave it up for a lost cause. Captain McMasters had been pretty damn clear that they needed to wear it whenever they left the bunkroom now, and after the shit he'd seen lately, he believed it. But his balls still itched. Kayla passed him a cardboard bottle of something that smelled like gun cleaner. She smirked at him like she knew what he was doing, but he'd been pretty subtle about it so she probably didn't.

He took a swig, and good lord was it awful. He pounded his chest – not that it helped (again: armor) – and coughed.

"Strong stuff, huh?" Kayla smirked. He smiled and raised the bottle heartily. He pretended to take another swig, numbing his tongue, and passed it on to Oggy.

Oggy took a moment to take it, leaving Fergus to hold it out like an asshole while he dug around at his hip and came up with his stun baton. "Check this out," he said, finally taking the bottle. "I hit one of those shits so hard I broke the stun thing."

Fergus and Kayla leaned in and made appreciative noises. It only looked a little scuffed, probably just turned it off by accident, but he'd have two more hours on shift with Oggy, who was a pain in the ass when he got sniffy.

They were supposed to be patrolling, but what the hell was there to patrol on Deck 4 anyway? Those morons had blown up their own chop shop, then killed a bunch of each other, and now were bottled up in their little hideouts. The place was a ghost town.

So they were sitting in an old barber shop, drinking and relaxing and waiting for their shift to end. Fergus was the new guy, so he didn't get a chair; he had to stand leaning against the outside window.

"That was something," Kayla mused. "That kid getting shot?"

"Which one?" Fergus asked.

"The del Rio kid."

"Yeah," he said. "Wow. Hell of a shot."

"My money's on Feeney," Oggy said. "I bet he did it."

Kayla frowned. "How come?"

"Didn't like his granddaughter boning the enemy. Or the enemy's brother." He handed her the bottle in response to her grabby hand motions. "I wouldn't like that."

"I bet del Rio did it herself," Kayla said. Fergus's skepticism reached his face, and Oggy scoffed. "No, seriously!" She took a chug from the bottle and coughed. "Seriously, he turned traitor! You don't think she'd kill him for that?"

She and Oggy argued for a bit, and Fergus tuned out. He thought he saw movement outside the side window, and he stared for a while, but there wasn't any more. He accepted the bottle when it was finally passed to him again, and passed it on in turn.

"You've been quiet," Kayla said, and it sounded like a demand. "What do you think?"

"Huh?"

"Who killed the del Rio boy," Oggy demanded. "Feeney or his sister?"

Fergus frowned. "Fuck if I know. Neither, probably. Who was that woman who was working for both of them?"

"The one the Captain says did it? Psh, nobody believes that. The Captain's full of shit, he's just not taking sides."

"But he showed us her rifle."

Kayla waved a hand dismissively. "Oggy took that off her ship himself."

"Hmm. Maybe that guy who lives down in the bottom decks?"

"Nah, Shine's a wimp."

Oggy yawned. "I'm going to go take a leak."

"Where's the toilet?" Fergus craned his neck to see if there was anything in back. His vision swam a little as he moved. Shit, that stuff was strong.

"The whole place is a toilet." He got up and handed off the bottle to Kayla, who scowled.

"Don't piss in here," she protested.

He mock-bowed. "Very well, your highness." Then he strode out the door and took a left in front of the windows. He turned to face them and leered, sticking his hands on the armor at his groin.

"Not there either! Go around the corner, nobody wants to see that!"

Oggy just cackled and continued on around the corner.

Kayla frowned at Fergus, like she was thinking of something, then made a face and took a slug from the bottle. "Jesus, this is disgusting. No wonder somebody shot him."

"What's it supposed to be?"

She sniffed at the mouth of the bottle, cautiously took another sip that she swirled in her mouth. "Tequila, I think."

"What? No way." He considered taking another taste, but decided against it. He considered taking Oggy's seat and decided against that, too. He wondered if Kayla was judging him for not taking it.

"So how are you liking *John Wayne Koganusan* Station?" She said the name in an ironic tone. "Everything you hoped it'd be?"

"It's all right," he said, not sure what the right answer was.

"It's a toilet."

"Last place was a toilet, too. At least here the pay's all right and we get to bust heads sometimes."

"Mmm." She made a side-to-side gesture with her head, like she was considering it. "There are worse perks, I guess."

They had a brief conversation about the relative merits of busting heads and whether the stun batons were fun (Fergus's position) or took the fun out of it by knocking them out too soon (Kayla's), and whether Oggy was full of shit about hitting someone so hard he busted his baton (the mutually-agreed position).

"Where is that shithead, anyway?" Kayla said. "Did he lose his dick or something?"

"I'll go look."

"Nah," she said. "Technically I'm in charge. He's probably waiting, hoping one of us will come around the corner so he can 'accidentally' flash us." She thumbed the control on her baton and let it crackle and flicker, and grinned maliciously. "Accidents happen."

She sauntered off, and this time Fergus did take one of the two chairs. They weren't that comfortable in armor; it was hard to get settled. He moved his butt this way and his shoulders that way, but the edge still dug in between his ribs. He squirmed again and there was a thud.

He stopped, turned, and craned his head. There was a gun on the floor. He got up, squatted down and inspected it. He didn't really know shit about guns, but it looked pretty awesome. It had some kind of dragon etched on the side of the metal thing, the barrel, and the name "George Washington Chung – Happy Birthday" on the other side.

It was faint, but he heard the crackle of the stun baton. He chuckled, then frowned. Shouldn't Oggy be screaming in pain? Maybe she was just scaring him.

He picked up the gun. It was a lot heavier than it looked. Now Kayla was taking too long.

He wandered out, around the windows. It was just empty corridor ahead, and it kinda smelled like piss, but most of the corridors in that station smelled like piss.

"Shit, this is dumb," he muttered, and at that point three things happened: he was grabbed from behind with something sharp pressed against his neck, and the woman who grabbed him said, "Yes, it is." The third thing was that the gun in his hand went off. His eardrums shot pain into his skull, and he tried to put his hands on his ears, but she pulled him down backward.

The next thing he knew, the gun had been knocked from his hand, both hands were pulled roughly behind him and tied, and he was shoved forward. He couldn't hear over the ringing in his ears, but he didn't have to. She grabbed his wrists and pulled up on them, frog-marching him ahead down the corridor and then into an open doorway. She pushed him and he hit the wall hard enough he saw stars through the pain as he slid to the floor.

"Shit," his abductor hissed, the first thing he heard properly. The back of her right hand was covered in blood and she cradled it in the other. Fergus rolled and saw Kayla and Oggy trussed up with gray tape over their mouths. Kayla gave him a look of utter disgust, which Fergus thought was unfair. Oggy's pants were around his ankles.

He recognized his abductor, now, too, mostly by the sword at her hip. She had a wicked-looking knife clutched underhand in her left hand, digging in the back of her right hand in a way that must have been excruciating, judging by the look on her face. It jerked and something small flew. She flexed her right hand and winced.

"Lucky shot," she growled. "Shrapnel from the ricochet."

Fergus wasn't sure what was lucky about that, or whether it was lucky for him. She dug in one of her deep pockets and came up with some more gray tape, which she managed to wrap tightly around her hand using her teeth and her left hand awkwardly, then tore it. She flexed again, and it obviously hurt but she didn't make a noise. Blood welled and dripped from the edges of the makeshift bandage.

She surveyed them for a moment, then ducked out of the room. She returned just a few seconds later with the gun in her hand. She inspected it, shoved it in her pocket, and retrieved that wicked-looking knife from its sheath.

"Well, you pissed me off," she growled at the three of them. "And I have to assume someone heard that. If I were you, I'd talk or I might get impatient."

Holding the knife like she meant to use it, she bent over Oggy and ripped the tape from his mouth. He screamed and swore, and Fergus remembered his ugly little peach fuzz mustache and wondered if he still had it. Kayla took her treatment with a little more dignity, just a sharp intake of breath.

The woman stood back. "Now. Where's Geronimo Rommel?"

Fergus's heart dropped into his stomach the moment she started saying the name, and he struggled to shout, "We're not telling you any–"

"Him," Kayla and Oggy said at once, Kayla illustrating who she meant with a flick of her head toward Fergus. Traitors.

The woman frowned at him. "You?" She spoke dubiously.

"Um," Fergus said.

"You're not Rommel."

"Um," Fergus said.

"Yes he is," Oggy said. "At least, he said he was."

"Shut up, Oggy!"

"You," the woman said, and kicked Kayla's foot. "When did this guy show up?"

"A couple days ago. File said his real name was Geronimo Rommel. The Captain was all happy because he was some kind of special forces hot shit."

"You," the woman said ominously, "do not look like special forces hot shit. And you sure as hell aren't Gerry Rommel. Explain."

"Um," Fergus Capper said.

"You said that already."

"So, uh. We were on a ship together."

"Describe him."

"Um," he said, and she racked the pistol. "Big guy. Mohawk. Only wore tight black clothes. Slept with like half the ship."

Her deep scowl softened to a frown. "Well, you've met him anyway. So why are you wearing his name?"

"I was mad that McMasters hadn't given me an offer even though I really wanted to be in security, and he said that his offer was insulting, but it was insane! He said he wasn't setting foot on this bullshit cheap station, and he said he'd sell me his offer for a thousand credits, I just needed to pretend to be him and he'd tell McMasters he was using a false name, except it was my name, and shit lady I didn't know he was a friend of yours, honest!"

She snorted. "You've definitely met him. Did he stay on that ship?"

"Yeah."

"You haven't seen him on this station at all?"

"Yeah, seriously. Shit, you think I haven't been watching? I've been scared half to death he'd pop up and I'd have to give all that money back."

She stared at him a long time, and swore.

"You have to believe me, it's true!"

"That's the problem, I do believe you."

She folded her arms, her hand still dripping dark blood. She stared at them, and they stared back. It sounded like she muttered, "Point to Herrera." Louder, she said, "Where's Gloria Settles?"

"Fuck you," Kayla said.

"Yeah, we're not telling you shit," Oggy said.

Fergus felt annoyed that they were totally willing to give him up, but not one of their other buddies. But he didn't know who this Settles was, and grudgingly admitted it.

Their kidnapper studied the three of them, then unsheathed her sword. It sounded like a whisper of steel on steel, and he barely heard it over his pulse pounding in his ears. She lowered it to the ground with a soft tap and drew its tip along the deck as she walked slowly down the line, eyeing them each in turn. Fergus. Kayla. Oggy. They stared at the light glinting off the blade, strained to hear the faint scratching. She stopped in front of Oggy and stared down at him with a nasty glint in her eye. Her hand dripped blood onto the deck, tap, tap, tap.

"I'm not above torture and you have no pants. Talk."

"She's in the infirmary."

Kayla groaned.

"Let me guess, she got sick right before Raj del Rio was shot?"

"...Maybe."

The woman folded her arms, frowned. Then, fighting down the yells and attempts to bite, she taped all their mouths again. Blood dripped onto Fergus's face from her taped hand as she did, and he noticed that she was trying to hold it stiff.

Then she left.

They all made muffled noises and tried to get themselves upright, but mostly just thrashed into each other. Fergus hit his head twice and gave it up. Their shift was almost up, and someone would come looking soon. Probably.

He heard a noise like someone chewing a rubber tire, and then a spitting sound. Oggy heaved with exertion, but it wasn't muffled by the tape anymore. He laughed like gloating.

"So what are they paying you, 'Geronimo'?" Oggy said in a nasty tone of voice, the kind that said that Fergus hadn't heard the end of it, and wouldn't for a long time.

He tried to say "shut up" through the tape, and he was pretty sure he was understood.

Kayla laughed, muffled by the tape.

"Whatever it is, it's too much."

The Real Sniper

The Miner's hand burned. She was pretty sure she'd broken one of the metacarpals, judging by the swelling just below her middle finger and the sharp searing pain every time she tried to flex it. Of all the places in the universe to lose the use of her middle finger... She tried to ping Doc Mills, but he didn't respond – probably for the best anyway, in case his comm channel was compromised. Anyway, she was running out of time. Once they found the three guards she'd subdued, or once they freed themselves, it would be obvious she wasn't on her ship. The lawyer's office they'd commandeered for an infirmary was close to the galleria, though, exactly the wrong place for her to be.

She ducked from empty doorway to empty doorway, shops and residences and storerooms. She listened carefully to the amplified mic in her comm set, and used her mirror and a tiny camera to watch, but her heart still pounded, and the pain in her hand was distracting. A first aid kit would have been a damn smart thing to have brought.

There wasn't much time. She chanced a call to Herrera. "I need another favor. It'll piss off McMasters."

"Name it."

"I want you to splash yourself with vodka, walk out to his quarters, and ring his bell. Keep me on the line and tell me who you see on the way. If he's there, give him a piece of your mind. If he's not, go back slowly and tell me who you see."

He laughed evilly, and she only half-listened to the noises, first of splashing, then of him walking. "Fuck you," he said like a greeting to someone.

She moved to the nearest elevator and got ready.

"Bottom of the fucking morning to you, you goddamned semi-sentient barnacle," Herrera greeted someone else.

"You're drunk," she faintly heard. That was two. Three down-decks, six in the port. She tried to remember how many were on patrols elsewhere. Another half dozen? She heard a hatch opening, and had to check to make sure it wasn't nearby.

"You," came a familiar voice. "What the devil do you want?"

She nodded. That was all she needed to know.

"I want you to know that you are a shitweasel of the second order, you filthy inbred dick-moss. I've had diseases more socially acceptable than you."

"Oh, for the love of God. This again? You're depraved. Get your foot out of my door, you old drunk."

She turned down the volume on the entertaining string of abuse, and got to work. First, she tapped into the program she'd left in the dockmaster's shack and started the airlock gas purge on a slow cycle. "Keep him distracted," she murmured into the comm. "What the hell's a jobbernowl?" she heard McMasters say. While the gas purge was underway, she retrieved from her pocket the comm she'd borrowed from the female guard, figured out how to set the "Officer Down" alarm, and sent it down the elevator to the bottom deck.

"You're a feckless ninny! A whiskey shits-gargling plague vector with gruel in your balls and pus in your veins."

"That's... That's just disgusting. Just a... Shut up. I said shut... Will you shut up, goddamn you, I've got an emergency call. I said shut up!"

She got away from the elevator and moved quickly around the long way to the galleria. She heard boots, hard to tell how many. The infirmary had been close by the doctor's office, off a small alley.

Close by, she could still hear running footsteps. Too close. She chewed the inside of her lip for a moment, then took the stairs up to the back of the upper level. Luck would only get her so far, and showing her face in the galleria was way beyond that. She took a grenade from her pocket, armed it, and tossed it left-handed.

"Get. Out!" she heard McMasters growl, and the distinct sound of a door shutting.

"He kicked me out," Herrera said.

"Good," the Miner said. "Get the hell out of there and behind locked doors. Thanks."

The explosion drew shouts, and there was some cheering in there, too. Gunfire, but it didn't sound serious, just desultory. The way to the infirmary was clear. The door was locked. She considered her options and knocked. Then she pounded.

"Open up! There's no time!"

"What do you want?" came a woman's voice. "I'm sick."

"No you're not, you're holed up waiting for your ride out of here. That's me."

"No it's not. Who are you?"

"Change of plans. Angelica's getting suspicious, the Captain wants you moved fast."

The door flew open, and a short woman in a black uniform stared at her. "Jesus, not so loud! What's wrong with you?"

"I'm not the one who insisted on talking through a door. Grab your things, that distraction won't last too long."

The Miner got a good look at Sergeant Gloria Settles as they stepped into the infirmary. She had a feeling that half the blood money had already gone up her nose or into her veins. Herrera had predicted as much: "Nothing else to do in this hellhole when you're flush with cash. Drugs or VR, mostly, usually both."

She considered extracting a confession or continuing the rescuing hero charade, but she was already tired, cranky, and in considerable pain. Settles didn't even look all that surprised when the Miner had her sword out and up at the woman's throat.

"Shit," Settles said.

"Yup," said the Miner, and held up the duct tape.

Rejected Advance

"And you brought her here? Are you out of your everloving mind? She's a cop! You have to let her go!"

Takata's voice rose to a squeak. He stared at the hog-tied black-uniformed sniper, who in turn was scanning the darkened restaurant kitchen with terrified eyes.

"Well look," said the Miner. "If I go to Feeney I won't get a word in edgewise. And if I go to Angelica, they'll just kill her outright, leaving me without a bargaining chip."

The sniper whimpered.

"So you brought her here?"

"What can I say, I lack imagination. Have you heard from Herrera?"

"He's at home, in bed, sleeping. Which is what I should be doing, instead of serving drinks to kidnappers and murderers and lunatics!"

"You haven't served us any drinks."

"Well I got it half right, anyway. You're out of your mind. Are you the one who blew something up in the galleria?"

The Miner considered her options. "Maybe."

"Maybe, she says."

"A lot goes on, you might be referring to a different explosion."

"You're out of your mind."

"You keep saying that."

"You should listen," the Miner heard in stereo. She and Takata both turned to see Mary Feeney standing in the back door, arms folded. She had dark circles under her puffy red eyes, her tattooed skin was blotchy, and her lips were set so tightly they were white. She looked like hell.

"Hello, Mary," said the Miner.

"Hello, Jane. I hear one of you killed my husband."

The Miner pointed at the sniper, who probably would have pointed back if she hadn't been tied up.

"So you say. McMasters says different."

"McMasters has six people standing guard outside my ship where they have me cornered."

Mary blinked and coughed what might have been a laugh. "Christ, what an asshole."

"Seriously."

"But just being an asshole doesn't make him wrong. He showed us your rifle. He showed us your medal for sharpshooting. He told us that you admitted to trying to destabilize this station."

"That's all true," the Miner said. "But I didn't kill Raj. Won't say it didn't cross my mind, or even that I didn't think he had it coming. But I didn't kill him."

Mary frowned. The sniper made muffled noises through the gag. "Takata, was she really here?"

"Oh, the other shoe drops! This is why you invaded my restaurant in the middle of the night, so I can alibi you? Forget it. You want an alibi, go wake up Herrera. He was here." He seemed to realize what he'd just said. "Shit. Go to hell, both of you."

The Miner shrugged. "Can't have it plainer than that."

"I'm pretty sure you can."

The Miner didn't reply, just rubbed her injured hand. Even with the painkillers she'd grabbed from the infirmary it still throbbed. She had a change of bandages, real ones, but hadn't had time to put them on. Mary stared at her a long time, then swore. "Give her to me. We'll want to question her."

"She's no good to me dead," the Miner said, shifting her weight so that more of her body stood between Mary and the sniper. "Not while Angelica still wants to kill me."

"That's your problem, not mine."

They stared at each other until Mary sighed. "We won't kill her. That'd be too convenient for you if you're lying." She unholstered her pistol. "Come on, you. On your feet."

The sniper thrashed when they tried to pick her up, slamming her bound feet so hard against Takata's cabinets that the doors dented and plastic plates tumbled and clattered on the deck. Even at gunpoint, she refused to stand on her own, so that finally Mary called for a couple of goons. The Miner watched without helping as four of them managed to wrangle the struggling cop by just picking her up by the twisted tape.

Mary studied the squirming form and frowned. "Bring her to the old man," she said. "Tell him I want her kept alive and able to talk."

She got four uncertain nods in reply, but she didn't wait to see them. Ignoring Takata's protests, she walked quickly and purposefully out of the kitchen, navigated the bar floor in the dark, then punched the button to raise the shutters. The Miner stayed back in the shadows.

"Where are you going?" called one of the goons. The Miner recognized her, but not well.

"To talk to my sister-in-law."

"Woah, woah, wait, what?" The goon looked alarmed, and left her three cohorts to deal with the struggling captive. She shoved past the Miner. "Wait a sec, Mary."

She held up a hand. "I know. But he was her brother. She deserves to be in on this."

"Man... I dunno."

Mary's shoulders sagged. "I don't know either. But it's high time we ended this shit. That means trusting each other, and *that* means someone goes first. Go on. I want to see you leave."

The Miner watched from the kitchen doorway as they exchanged dubious looks and hauled their captive out the back.

"This is probably dumb," the Miner said.

"Are they gone?"

"Yeah."

Mary set off across the galleria, head held high. The Miner watched her go.

"See, this is going to backfire, too." Takata had a bowl of oatmeal or something and was eating. It smelled amazing. He didn't offer her any. "You think you're going to rile them up again, but they like their little equilibrium."

"I thought you hated the status quo."

"I do, but I hate the open fighting more." He sighed and set down his spoon. "Look. Yeah, I'd rather that asshole McMasters did his job and ran them all out of here. But you're not going to push him to do that, you're just going to get him killed."

"He's got it coming."

"Why? Because he fucked up your ship?"

"Because he stood by taking bribes while this station went to hell. Because he had someone assassinated in the middle of the goddamn galleria so he could keep taking those bribes. Because he was going to fucking pin it on me." Takata gave her a level gaze until she threw up her hands. "And yeah, all right, because he fucked up my ship. My homicidal urges, my rules."

"You've killed a lot of people yourself, you know."

"Never said I didn't have it coming, too."

An ornately-tattooed kid with horns burst from Angelica's casino and dashed across the galleria. The Miner ran out to meet her, and when she didn't stop, pulled her sword left-handed.

She reared back. "Get out of my way! I have to deliver a message."

The Miner stared at her, wondering who Angelica considered more expendable than electrons. "I'll come too."

The messenger stared at the sword and didn't argue. Which was just as well, as they'd gotten attention from the security station. Two armored guards came out, sidearms drawn. The Miner followed the messenger at a jog up the stairs to Feeney's hotel where a crowd had already seen the runner and emerged en masse. The messenger doubled over wheezing after the run up the stairs, and gasped out that Angelica had Feeney's granddaughter and would trade for the sniper.

It didn't take long for the message to filter up to the old man, who came out roaring that he'd kill that backstabber. He fumed and raged, and he made one of his soldiers restrain the messenger. He growled instructions to different people who jumped and ran.

Mr Shine strolled out of the hotel, still in his tuxedo, but with his arm in a sling. He looked like he'd just been woken up. He walked up to Feeney and tried to say a few words in his ear, but Feeney had none of it. He paced and ranted and hurled invective at Angelica and her "idiot brother" who, in his telling, had probably – if with difficulty – committed suicide. Someone came out and passed him a little red megaphone that had ridges like it'd been printed in a hurry.

"Angelica! Get out here, you damned snake, and bring my granddaughter."

The casino window's neon dice rolled in silence, coming up double-sixes for the umpteenth time. The Miner was starting to think they were loaded.

"Goddamn you, get out here!"

"In my own time, old man." Angelica's reply came over some kind of loudspeaker, and was hard to hear over the crowd. "Cool your jets."

Horse Trading

The tables and chairs of the galleria sat under the sun lamps strong enough that the Miner wondered if Angelica was waiting for high noon. A number of tables were knocked over or broken, and smashed chair parts decorated the aisles. Bloodstains marked furniture and deck alike, and even the trees had been splashed. Takata had lowered his shutters. Herrera was still asleep, anyway; he'd miss the fun.

Feeney had seen the Miner and insisted that she stick around. She maybe could have objected, maybe forcefully, but she was tired and her hand hurt and she liked the view from up above. The rest of them had retreated inside the hotel, leaving her the sole human occupant of the galleria now that McMasters' crew had withdrawn, rebuffed angrily by Feeney and Angelica both. The empty space stank of blood and ozone, and the only sound was the whir of the anti-projectile lasers.

Mr Shine emerged from one of the side spurs off the galleria, alone. The Miner hadn't seen him leave; maybe he'd gone out through the service entrance. Smart move, it made him appear more independent. He projected confidence as he walked, slowly and deliberately. His sling was gone, but that arm seemed pretty firmly lodged with his thumb hooked in his red cummerbund. He strolled to the middle of the galleria, to the stage under the sad-looking palm trees. As power plays went, the Miner had to respect it. With McMasters under suspicion, he was setting himself up as the grown-up here, making sure everyone played nice. She felt like she was watching a coronation.

The casino doors rolled open and three columns of somber-looking fighters came out, armored with miscellaneous bits and mismatched helmets, carrying clubs and swords. The Miner recognized some of them as having been Feeney's crew. Fickle bunch, she thought. Behind the fighters, looking defeated as she stared at her feet over tied hands, shuffled Mary Feeney. Angelica walked behind her, holding something to her back that was covered in a jacket. The Miner considered that a nice touch, paying a kind of homage to the firearms rule.

The entourage jerked to a halt at the foot of the steps up to the stage. Their grimy faces looked for the first time like real soldiers. Behind them, the dice rolled too many sixes.

Mr Shine nodded once to Angelica, then took his uninjured hand out of his pocket and gestured casually up at the hotel: *come on.*

Feeney fussed as he tried to assemble an honor guard of his own around the terrified bound sniper, who was still thrashing but kept on her feet. Eventually he managed a box formation, and the Miner heard him tell them to keep her on her feet until Mary was safe. The phalanx managed the stairs with a small amount of dignity, and slowly navigated the furniture-crowded aisle toward the center of the galleria.

Mr Shine held up his hand, and they came with ill grace to a halt. "All right," he said, and his calm deep voice was loud enough he had to have arranged a mic. Again, the Miner was impressed with his sense of theatre. She wasn't thrilled to replace Angelica and Feeney with this puffed-up king-in-waiting, but she felt the world owed Takata a bit of real peace.

If there was more to that sentence than "all right", the Miner never heard it. Black-uniformed security officers poured out of the shuttered stores on both sides and surrounded the two groups. McMasters and ten more armored guards emerged from the security station. She couldn't quite tell, but she was reasonably sure that McMasters had waxed his mustache for the occasion. He must have woken up the entire complement of station security for this. They were all armed with stun batons, but a few of them had sidearms, and McMasters himself carried a rifle – the Miner's rifle, in fact.

"Surrender these two to me," McMasters said loudly. "I'm the law here, and I'll handle the criminals."

Settles seemed to visibly relax, and stopped struggling.

All eyes shifted to Mr Shine, and he was frozen. The confident smile had turned into a rictus grin. He still had his left thumb hooked in his cummerbund, and the right hand was outstretched in a gesture of unclear intent. The king-in-waiting was apparently on standby. The various goons on all sides shuffled nervously, unsure what was going on or what would happen next. Angelica looking back and forth between Shine and McMasters. Feeney had come up beside the Miner and was clutching the railing white-knuckled. "What is that fool doing?" he whispered to himself. "Don't let McMasters have them, Shine, you jackass! Say something!"

"The hell you will," Angelica snarled, when Shine said nothing. "You're just protecting your attack dog."

The smirk on McMasters' face was visible a mile away. "If you really thought that, Ms del Rio, you wouldn't have taken the Feeney girl hostage. You still think Mr Feeney had your brother killed, hired that psychotic killer up there to do it, or we wouldn't be out here. You're probably right." He raised the rifle a tad and chambered a round. His deputies hovered around him in a loose knot, probably terrified under their black helmets.

Mr Shine stood paralyzed. He started to say something, and stopped and stammered, and the microphone echoed his stammering. McMasters and Angelica eyeballed each other, ignoring him. Feeney's goons guarding the sniper looked increasingly worried as security advanced on them.

The Miner never had much patience for standoffs, nor for indecision. She still had a pretty decent throwing arm despite all the years in low gravity, but of course the security people were well-armored against rocks and bottles, and had been pelted half-heartedly by both Feeney's and Angelica's crews in the past. They were used to it. So it took about a second for one of them to glance down at the object she'd thrown, and then another half second to complete a double-take and yell, "Grenade!"

The security team had time to scatter, and some of them even did. McMasters threw himself to the floor, where someone with more viciousness than sense gave him a swift kick before the explosion blew the scene into bedlam.

The armored security goons engaged with the fighters from both sides indiscriminately as more poured down the stairs from Feeney's hotel and out from the casino. "Get Mary! Goddamn you bastards, get Mary!" Feeney howled, forgetting his megaphone and hanging halfway over the railing. He turned and saw the Miner and grabbed her jumpsuit in two handfuls. "Mick! I'll give you ten thousand credits if you rescue her. I swear it to God Almighty, I will."

There wasn't a need, though: Mary had shaken loose of Angelica and was barreling through the crowd. Up past Mr

Shine onto the dais, then down into Feeney's crew. Bleeding and limping, she used her tied forearms as a shield as she caromed off tables and through a swarm of assholes eager for a fight.

Everyone froze at the crack of a rifle. Mary stumbled and fell over a table, then down to the deck. The Miner didn't think before she vaulted the railing, and landed hard with her implant-assisted joints screaming. Her left leg exploded in pain, but she could still move it, and she dashed for Mary.

On the other side of the galleria, where she'd been thrashing and kicking at Angelica's goons dragging her away, the sniper's body spasmed, went slack, and fell. Angelica screamed frustration and fury, but her guards dragged her bodily away into the safety of the casino.

The screams and thuds and the crackles of stun batons were joined by gunshots and flashes from the anti-projectile lasers. Mr Shine stumbled, and went to his knees.

McMasters fumbled with the rifle again, turning toward where Mary had dived under a table, but instead used it as a bat to fend off a huge bare-chested fighter with stun knuckles on both fists. Somewhere, the Miner could have sworn she heard a chainsaw rev. McMasters fell back and hoarsely called the retreat, squeezing off one more shot into the crowd as he and his team fled the field. Confused, pissed off, and probably drunk, the crowd turned into an enthusiastically bloody mosh pit.

The Miner reached Mary, her knee screaming. She pulled the still-bound woman from under the table, and hauled her to her feet. Mary leaned on her hard enough that her spikes gouged the Miner's neck and cheek and drew blood, but they were both so charged with adrenaline that they sprinted through the crowd anyway. Judging the stairs too hard to get to, the Miner steered them to a bench outside a shuttered VR joint, sheltered by the stairway and just beneath the anti-projectile lasers.

"I'm fucking done with this shit." Mary heaved a sigh that could have been a sob or a laugh, then spat something out that looked like a tooth. "I am so done. So fucking done. And where..." She closed her eyes for a moment and her head bobbed a little. "Where the fuck did you get a grenade? Are you out of your mind?"

Then she ruined the Miner's comeback by passing out.

UTILITY FUNCTIONS

Screwball Corbell crouched behind the inner bulkhead, four of Feeney's people lined up along it behind him. It was hard to hear; the giant air-movers below them rumbled and roared as they breathed for the station. Eight decks above, if there was a quiet spot in the galleria, you could hear them if you listened carefully; down here right on top of them you couldn't hear anything else. The nice thing was that he couldn't hear the complaining. The bad thing was that it left him with nothing to do but think.

They were supposed to hang out in case Angelica made a move. She'd taken Mary hostage and could be planning anything. They had Shine's blessing to be there, as long as they didn't actually go in. Five at the air handler control center, five at the water reclamation center. God, they were stretched thin. Shine had been stuck in the hotel, drinking with the old man, and Corbell was pretty sure the big guy was thoroughly under the old man's thumb. Ditz had said Feeney was magnetic, but it was kind of amazing to watch in real time. "Say, do you remember that Calishkan kid?" turned into belly laughs and "Let me fill your drink there" and a sly "This has all gotten out of hand, don't you think?" with Raj's body not even cold, and Corbell's good socks stuck to his ankles with dried blood. He was sort of amazed the casino man fell for it. Living down in the bottom of the station for six months, though, probably he wanted to.

He was starting to feel foolish when one of the others jerked her head up suddenly, looking concerned and alert. She had been one of Angelica's, he thought, her and that guy in the stupid fake leather sling – Carter, the one who lost his head and started shooting when they were running from that bomb, the one who shot Ditz.

Corbell opened his mouth to bellow a question, and then he heard it too – a shout from inside, and then a gunshot. The wide stares on the other faces meant they'd heard it too.

"Shit," he said to himself, and then louder, "Come on!"

The old man had given him a nice pistol, and Corbell had it ready when he entered the control room. Five armed jerks stood away on the other side with a couple of Shine's people cringing at their feet, and fortunately Corbell surprised them, because he had time to duck behind some big control cabinet thing before they had their own guns up and shot the poor jerk who came through the door behind him. He cringed at the echo of the gunshots in the enclosed space, but made himself peer around the other side of the big metal box and squeeze off two shots. He crouched back down behind cover without checking or caring if he hit.

"Don't hit Shine's people," he yelled, as much to reassure Shine's people as to direct his own. He really hoped those were Angelica's people attacking; he had no idea whose side anyone was on anymore unless they were physically on the other side of a room.

His ears rang with the gunshots. There was no sense in shouting instructions; he saw two of his people just outside the hatch, one wounded and the other tending to her. It wasn't

Carter shot, worse luck. That sadistic SOB was crouched down behind some kind of console on the other side, and a totally bald woman he didn't recognize came and crouched down right behind Corbell himself. Carter stood and shot and ducked again, grinning. The bald woman glanced at Corbell, and looked relieved when he shook his head.

Instead, he made eye contact with the woman outside the room tending to the wounded. He mouthed "how many?" twice before she ducked her head real fast into the room, and held up three fingers. He nodded. Carter stood again, but dove at the ground before he could fire; three shots came from the other side.

Corbell tried not to hyperventilate. His stomach felt sour and his ears hurt, and when he braced himself against the console his shoe came off and he had to scrabble to keep from falling. He frowned, looked at the bald woman, and mouthed "on three". Then he turned on one knee, shouted "fire in the hole!" as loud as he could, and stood and hurled his shoe.

Angelica's goons dove. Corbell and the bald woman stood and fired, and Carter figured it out and joined in. Then Shine's people grabbed chairs and started beating on the downed fighters, kicking their guns away. The rest took maybe a minute.

One of Shine's people was hurt bad. They were older, nerdy types, and looked scared shitless even after beating three of Angelica's goons to death. Probably more scared. The one of Feeney's who'd been shot was only grazed, he thought, but there was a lot of blood. They shut the doors and the noise got a lot quieter. Feeney's people cheered.

Nobody really knew first aid, but they got strips of cloth tied off, and the bleeding seemed to stop. There was an inner office, even quieter. Corbell went into it to see if he could figure out what the hell was going on in the rest of the station, and the ringing in his ears subsided almost enough to hear. His fingers trembled with the adrenaline spillover; he felt like he was about to either fall to pieces or run a damn marathon.

"Hey hey," Carter crowed, grinning and slapping his uninjured hand on Corbell's shoulder. Was that the hand that shot Ditz? "Little Screwball won us a battle!"

Corbell whirled on Carter and slammed him against the wall, wedging his pistol up under the man's jaw.

"My name is Corbell, asshole. Steven Corbell. Say it."

"Ste- Ste-"

"Steven Corbell," Corbell started, and Carter recited it with him, eyes wide.

"If you can't remember it, call me 'Sir'. You are not my buddy. You have not earned the right to call me that. Do you understand me? All you assholes, do you understand me?"

"Y- yes." Carter said, and then the others repeated it.

Corbell let him go, and he fell. "Now get the fuck out of here," he ordered, and once they all had left the little office, he shut the door and puked in the corner.

TIME TO BLOW THIS SCENE

"So, uh, I hope you don't mind my asking, but, uh, what's wrong with this place?"

The short, round man eating a plate of Takata's pasta had plainly been pondering this question for some time, looking for a delicate way to ask. After all, in order to get to Ama no Gawa from the port, which is where he had come from, he had had to walk through the galleria. The galleria, though corpse-free for two whole hours, was still a mess. Rug-sized smears of blood marked its floor where the cleaning robots had done their valiant beeping best. Only three chairs remained intact, and none of the tables. Someone had left an axe stuck in one of the bedraggled palm trees. A chainsaw had dragged itself in laps around the floor, chewing up tile in long swooping lines, spattering blood in tiny droplets until its battery finally ran down. Four yellow plastic cones warned would-be pedestrians away from where the deck had been blasted and deformed by an explosion. The Miner suspected that they were someone's idea of a joke.

The warring factions had returned to their casino, hotel, and security station, respectively. There had been a tacit agreement not to attack each other while retrieving bodies, and with only the single sticking point of who would claim

Mr Shine's body – the Morlocks won that one, arriving in the galleria in a tightly-packed, well-armed mass of silent grim faces, and then melting away again after – the removal process had actually finished before the newcomer had wandered gawking through the carnage to the only restaurant in seven million kilometers. He'd sat down and asked for a menu, whereupon Takata had said, "I'll make spaghetti. Ever had spaghetti? You'll like it." And then Takata had walked away.

He was, in fact, enjoying the pasta in red sauce. He had a napkin tucked into the top of his jumpsuit, which the Miner had never seen anyone in real life do, and was relishing the food and the red wine, which Takata had served in a real glass.

The Miner had not been offered spaghetti. She decided, against the vote of her growling stomach, not to provoke another bitter rant by asking for some. It had taken the statistically unlikely intrusion of an actual paying customer to stop the previous rants, but she wasn't sure just how far under his placid and genial façade those rants still were, and her headache was finally starting to go away. First Takata had torn her head off for throwing a grenade in the galleria, like nobody had ever done that before. And for killing a bunch of security guards, and for killing a bunch of Angelica's people, and for killing a bunch of Feeney's people, and for getting Mr Shine killed, and just generally for causing mayhem. Then Herrera had come in and bitten her head off himself, first for not giving him warning so that he could video the fight, and then for being out of grenades. Then Takata had been mad that she had somehow put this idea into Herrera's head, and she had been starting to think that she could just never win with these two, when this roly-poly peacemaker had wandered in looking dazed and hungry and easily-separated from his credits.

"Everything's wrong with this place," Herrera was saying when the Miner tuned back into the conversation. "Starting with the people who run it, Anaconda."

"Hey!" The newcomer drew himself up in his seat and tried to look dignified. "I've been with Anaconda for fifteen years now."

The Miner turned in her seat, suddenly interested. "What is it that you do?"

"Oh, I'm just a trucker. I don't really care, I just feel like I ought to hoist the company flag, you know? I haul ore, mostly. I'm making a circuit of the Anaconda holdings picking up their buyings. I have to say, this station's been slacking off." He waggled a finger playfully. "Smallest haul of any place I've been to this year. I mean, not bad. I don't want to insult anyone. Some good quality nickel-iron, you know."

She smiled tightly. "You don't say. When are you moving on?"

"Oh, pretty soon. The robots are loading up the hold, but it won't take long. I was going to stay over in that hotel up there and maybe have myself a real shower, but it looks a little... um... busy."

The Miner nodded, couldn't think of a reply, and kept her mouth shut. The trucker happily swirled another forkful of spaghetti, ate it, and said with his mouth half-full, "I was supposed to pick up a passenger, too, but the guy who contacted me went quiet."

"Let me guess. Guy name of McMasters wanted you to pick up a female passenger?"

He gave her an owl-eyed look. "I... Yeah! How'd you know about it?"

"Lucky guess," she said. "I don't suppose he paid in advance?"

He shook his head, chewing. "He paid a deposit. Said she'd pay the balance once we were underway. Mmm. I'm Khalid, by the way. Nice to meet you."

"Call me Mickey," the Miner said, after Takata and Herrera introduced themselves and glared at her for being rude.

"Hah, like the mouse? Hah!"

"Yeah. Like the mouse."

If he minded the conversation being over, he didn't show it. He returned to his pasta with gusto and drank the wine like it was water. Which, thought the Miner, it could have been.

"What the hell?" came Takata's voice from the kitchen. The Miner stood and drew her pistol, the automatic she'd taken off the guard, ignoring the trucker's eyes bugging out at her. Mary came through the curtain, pushing it aside like it was heavy, and apologizing quietly.

"Hey," she said, ignoring Takata. "Got a minute, in private?" Her voice was subdued and she looked haggard. "Back here, not out there."

Takata threw up his hands at the invasion. "Other people get rats in their kitchens, I got gangsters." Neither Mary nor the Miner paid him any attention as they walked to the back of the prep area and took stools.

"I'm not good at asking for help," Mary said, staring down at her hands. "So I'm not gonna. But I have to get out of here, Mick, and I have to be even with McMasters before I do."

The Miner nodded. "One condition. I have to know what happened to your brother."

"I'm sorry, I don't know for sure. When the fighting got bad, Granddad tricked him into getting onto the yacht. It went away and hasn't docked since. He's not on the station, that's all I know: the... thing... in his chest has a tracking tag in it, and McMasters has a way of detecting if it gets close to the station. I think sensors look for the radiation signature."

The Miner absorbed that, and relaxed. "All right."

"I, uh, I don't have any money of my own."

"That complicates things."

Mary winced. "Yeah. Look. My grandfather keeps a tight fist on the cash. I don't want him knowing I'm leaving until I'm gone."

"That definitely complicates things."

She looked up at the Miner, defiant. "You afraid of complicated?"

"No, I'm afraid of picking up the tab."

Feeney looked up with hooded eyes as Corbell quietly entered the room. The old man looked ancient, frazzled. He clutched a glass of whiskey in one hand, half full, and in the other held a photograph. Corbell didn't need to look at it to know the one: it was a still shot of Feeney, Mary, Wilfred, Angelica, Raj, Mr Shine. The station master, a guy named Herrera. The company rep, a woman named Tou. Two other people whose muttered names had been followed by "dead". All dapper, all grinning. Some kind of charity thing, someone had said. He recognized that restaurant Mick hung out in, in the background, and the bartender smiling in the back. Feeney stood in the middle of the group, both hands resting on that silver-headed walking stick of his, looking satisfied with his position on top of the world.

"Angelica took the water reclamation," Corbell said without being invited to report. "We held the air cyclers, and convinced Shine's people in hydroponics and vats to see our way."

Feeney scowled and put the still face-down on the desk.

"Two out of three isn't bad," Corbell said.

"Two out of three is shite!" Feeney threw the glass at his head. "Two out of three is me expending twice as many resources I don't have on guard duty than she is, while she can still cut off our fecking water! And what bloody use are the air cyclers, I'd like to know. We can't cut her off; she just needs to open her damn doors. We could fart at them maybe, is that your idea? It already stinks over there; it must if it's anything like this rathole."

Corbell bit back a suggestion that they could put something a lot nastier than flatulence in the casino's vents. There was such a thing as too far, and this was a man who'd gladly put a nuclear weapon in his hands.

"I got word from Sparks that your yacht docked," he said instead.

Feeney stared at him, and he couldn't read the old man's expression. "The alarms didn't go off? He… He's not back?"

"I don't know. She just said to say it docked. It tried the mechanic bay that got blown up first, I guess, and went around to the other one where she is."

Feeney looked genuinely glad about that. "Well, I'll be. How is the old girl? Still bitter about her toys getting broken?"

"She didn't say." She did, actually: she'd reminded him that Feeney had promised her a great deal of money to make up for a long list of things she'd been able to readily tick off from the top of her head. No sense reminding him again; he'd just fly off the handle, and Corbell didn't owe her putting up with another rant.

"Well! Well, well, well. That's fine. How's Mary, by the way?"

"I haven't seen her."

"She hasn't been helping?"

"Her, um, her husband just died."

Feeney tsked. "Stroke of luck. The del Rios, they're rotten, my boy. Can you imagine Angelica del Rio as a sister-in-law?

Can you?" He hooted, warming to his subject. "That woman's more venomous than a dozen vipers, and meaner besides. She said she'd turn over the reins, but don't you believe it. That brother of hers was weak-willed. A flash young fellow, sure, and not a bad sort really, but not very strong up here. She'd have been trying to run things behind the scenes."

Corbell kept a straight face, and said nothing. Feeney didn't seem to notice. He accepted Corbell's presence, maybe was grateful for it. Anything was possible.

"What about that snake McMasters? Has he shown his face yet?"

"No, sir. Word is, he's not very popular right now."

Feeney snorted. "When has he ever been?"

"I mean," Corbell said carefully, as the informant had multiple times drawn lines of comparison to the old man, "that he's not popular with his own crew. He's been telling them that shooting the sniper was an accident, that he was aiming for Angelica, but they don't all believe it."

"Nor," Feeney said, "should they."

Corbell stood silent while the old man brooded. He'd stopped overthinking his position there, really tried to avoid thinking at all. All the old worries, was he doing the wrong thing, saying the wrong thing, overstaying his welcome, listening to conversations he shouldn't. That all seemed silly.

"You've been a good boy, Corbell," Feeney said idly, looking at that photo again instead of at him. "I see that and by God I appreciate it. You'll see, I don't forget my friends."

Corbell only nodded. Anything was possible.

GETTING EVEN

The three security goons openly gaped at the Miner when she walked in the front door of their station. They hadn't seen her through the windows because those were now mostly covered with steel blast shutters. They hadn't seen her through the cameras because someone had run by and spray painted them again. So, a surprise was unsurprising, but this particular one was unexpected. She kept her useless right hand on her sword, which hung from that hip instead of the usual side, but didn't make a move to draw it. She looked patiently from face to face, not saying a word, until one of them marked himself as having above-average intelligence by saying "um".

The Miner turned to Mr Um. She hadn't recognized him with his pants on. "Relax, I'm not here to torture anyone. I want to talk to McMasters."

The guards hesitated, tense and waiting, then all three got up at once and made for the back room. First they nearly collided with each other, then they nearly collided with McMasters himself.

"You," he said.

"Me," she admitted.

"What do you want?"

"Fifty thousand credits and my rifle should do it. I might think up other demands later; depends how nice you are to me."

"Fifty… Are you out of your mind?"

"People keep asking me that."

"Why do you think I'd give you fifty thousand credits?"

"And my rifle. The fifty thousand, because you're a lousy shot. The rifle, because it's mine and you might hurt yourself with it."

"What do you mean, lousy–" He stopped abruptly and stared. Fear crept into his features. He turned to one of his goons. "Stand guard out here, we'll talk in my office."

The Miner smiled. "Figured it out, did you? I like it out here, and I don't care if they hear me."

"I said, we'll talk in my office."

"And I said I like it out here. I like my odds better." The black-suited goons looked between her and McMasters with ugly expressions. McMasters didn't press it, and the Miner went on: "I know where Angelica's keeping her, and I know she hasn't talked yet. Clock's ticking, though."

McMasters snorted. "And you expect me to know what that means?"

She shook her head, more at his lousy acting than in response. "Honestly? I *expect* you to fuck it up while Angelica del Rio learns that you paid Sergeant Gloria Settles to murder her brother, and then shot Settles to try to keep her quiet. After you fuck it up, I *expect* it's a toss-up whether you make it off the station alive. I'd flip a coin, but you might take it."

The small station had started to fill up with black uniforms. They stared at McMasters.

"Let me guess, you'll lead us to her?"

"Hell, no. I want my money and my property. You can fight your own fights. After all, you picked them."

"Captain, what if she's telling the truth?" someone muttered. "We have to rescue her."

McMasters shook his head. "It's an obvious trap."

"Why?" the Miner asked. "Because you shot to kill? I've been wondering what you've been telling your people here about that."

"That was an accident. I would never intentionally harm any of my people, and I feel horrible about it."

"Well. For the low, low price of fifty thousand credits, you can rescue your sergeant and prove it to them."

"Captain..."

"I'm not... I'm not paying up front. We can't trust a word she says."

"All right," she said. "Fair's fair. I'll take the rifle up front, and payment when you find her." She pointed at him. "Dead or alive, though – you've already used a lot of time."

"I'm not arming you!"

"I'm already armed," she said in a quiet voice. Her hand hadn't left her sword, but suddenly they all seemed to notice it at the same time. "And I never asked for ammunition. If I wanted to kill you all, I'd have done it."

McMasters might have had a retort, but one of his crew had quietly returned from the back room carrying the Miner's rifle in two hands. He shoved it into McMasters' chest without saying a word and held it there, jaw set, until his boss took it. Trembling, the security chief removed the magazine, popped the round out of the chamber, and inspected it like it might have a bayonet or spare round or nuclear weapon hidden somewhere. At last, with obvious reluctance, he put it down on the side table.

"Talk," he said, though it took him two tries to cough it out. All eyes were on her, eleven pairs plus McMasters. She wondered briefly just how much their numbers had dwindled, and who was just injured or off-duty.

The Miner described the chamber Mary had shown her two levels below: down a cargo elevator near the water reclamation, but out the back entrance and away to a storage room that was marked "radiation hazard" on a hand-written sign with "radiation" spelled wrong.

"There a guard?" She couldn't tell who asked that.

"Two outside," she said. "Didn't get a good look inside. I wasn't exactly welcome. But there's probably not a lot of people in the know. Del Rio's keeping her guest well away from the casino so the rank and file don't know she's alive. I guess she's afraid someone might tattle."

McMasters let that slide. Someone had brought up the security camera feeds down there, but found them spray-painted over. They argued quietly, and she didn't try to follow it. They were discussing who should go and who should stay, and McMasters was strenuously denying that he should personally leave the safe confines of his hidey-hole, though he didn't quite phrase it like that.

Six of the eleven guards suited up in full battle gear for the rescue: heavy-duty stuff, the kind she'd have been glad of on a couple missions. She frowned at it, not terribly happy to see that kind of armor, but there was nothing she could do about it. They went out the back door, and she watched the empty hatch for a while, idly wondering if they were taking the path she'd suggested or one of their own.

"Well," she said. "You know where to send the money."

She started to take her rifle, and McMasters' hand came down on it. "Stay a while," he said, and didn't sound friendly.

The remaining security personnel sat uneasily, splitting their attention between her and various video feeds around the station. Some of them paced, some kept sitting down and then standing abruptly. The feeds looked like stills.

Minutes passed, and no one spoke.

"You've got something else of mine," the Miner said conversationally. Wooden-faced, McMasters wordlessly put two fingers into his breast pocket. He glanced at the little bronze coin on its stubby green silk ribbon, and set it on the table between them with a click that seemed to echo in the room.

The Miner nodded and picked it up.

"You've got a lot of them," McMasters said. Not a sneer, no emotion at all, but somehow the words stung her.

A guard barreled through the door and fell to the deck on hands and knees, panting and heaving. The others jumped to their feet, and when the Miner casually reached for her rifle, McMasters snatched it away.

"Ambush!" wheezed the guard. "Pinned down." She collapsed face-down.

"Well, shit," the Miner said.

"You four, move!" McMasters barked. "Get them out of there!" They jumped to grab helmets and shields and were gone. He had his sidearm trained on the Miner's face, keeping well out of sword reach. "You. I guess you think you're clever, don't you? You thought we'd fall for that."

"You kind of did," she pointed out.

The last remaining guard was in the middle of helping up the fallen one when he yelped. The fallen guard dashed for McMasters, and at the same time the Miner dropped. The shot he squeezed off hit the barricade behind her and she heard it ricochet. The fake guard knocked the gun from his hand with her left forearm, then decked him with her armored right fist.

The Miner did her part by drawing her sword and dangling the tip in front of the last guard's face. "Let's us two sit this one out," she suggested.

Mary had flung her helmet off and was genuinely panting with the exertion of beating McMasters. She kept it up for a while, and the security chief took it.

"Stop toying and just kill me," he managed when she stopped.

"I'm not going to kill you," she said. "I'm done with killing. You're going to walk out that front door, right now. You're going to take the berth you paid for on the ore hauler's ship. And you are never, ever going to come back."

He sneered up at her, a stream of bloody saliva dripping from the corner of his mouth. "So I can live if I run?"

"You can live if you run."

She took a step to the side of the office and watched him. He got unsteadily to his feet, spat a gob of blood on the deck. He looked at the front door, then jagged and dashed for the armory in the back room.

Mary and the Miner made no move to follow. The lone guard sank into a chair. They heard a shriek from the back room, and then they heard Angelica del Rio say, "Hello, Tom."

If anything more passed between them, the two women outside couldn't hear it. There was only a long silence, and then Angelica spoke. "He was my only brother, you son of a bitch!"

The single gunshot echoed in the small space.

Angelica came out of the back room, her small caliber pistol still in her hand. She eyed Mary and the Miner.

"We clear?" Mary said.

"You were supposed to keep him from fleeing, not invite him to."

"I changed my mind. He's dead anyway. Are we clear?"

"We are far from clear. Him and me, we're clear now. You and me, Feeney and me, the light from clear will take a thousand years to reach us."

"We can settle that now if you like," said the Miner.

"No," said Mary. "I'm sick of blood."

Angelica snorted. "It's too late for that. This story's been told a hundred times, and it only ever ends in blood."

"I don't believe that. What'll it take to be even, Angelica?"

"Surrender and take what's coming to you. Both of you. All of you. I've put up with too much shit from the Feeney family, starting with your idiot brother putting a fucking nuclear weapon in his chest and ending with you putting a target on my brother's back. I don't care who pulled the trigger, you got him killed, and we're sure as hell not even for that. This is my station now. If you want peace, leave."

She walked past them both, head held high, right out the front door. Mary sat heavily in the desk sergeant's chair and put her head in her hands.

EXEUNT

The dockmaster had demanded, and gotten, a hefty bribe to leave his post, yet another debit against the Miner's dwindling bank account. Mary entered when he'd left, hefting a single duffel bag that wasn't even full. There was something pathetic about it. Khalid was late, and if he was much later they'd have to pay off Preston again.

The Miner and Mary stood awkwardly. They'd tried a couple different conversations in the hours since Tom McMasters died. Everything turned into Mary saying thank you, and that was the last thing the Miner wanted to hear.

"There's a theatre at Station 36," she offered. "You should go see a play when you get there."

"A what?"

"A play. Like a live vid."

Mary shook her head. "What do you mean, live?"

The Miner explained the concept of a playhouse, the concept of a pre-written script that wouldn't change every time you watched, and then discovered that she needed to explain the concept of stage actors. Like con men who just get paid for practicing the con and never actually rip anyone off.

"So," Mary said finally. "A bunch of people you don't know are going to do something in a dark room for a couple hours. They won't tell you what–"

"They don't want to spoil it," the Miner said, feeling the conversation get away from her. "They don't want to give too many details, but they get the general idea across."

"–and if you fork over some cash and promise to be quiet, they'll pretend you're not there and let you watch."

The Miner frowned. "How hard did you have to work to make it sound that dirty?"

"I knew someone who used to do that when she needed money."

"You're not helping."

"I'm not trying."

The Miner tried not to laugh, but failed.

"Hi! What are we laughing about?" Khalid bustled over to them, sagging under the weight of his various bags. "Sorry I'm late, I tried to follow your directions and got a little lost. Why all the secrecy?"

"She's running away from home," the Miner said, and ignored the glare that got her.

"Oh!" Khalid said. "I wanted to run away and join the circus when I was a little boy."

"This is kind of the other way around," the Miner said, starting to enjoy the growing death glare.

"What I want to know is," Mary said, "why are you staying?"

That was the conversation she'd been trying to avoid. "I started something," she said. "I have to finish it."

"It'll finish itself. Even if the military won't come in now, they're just... flailing at each other. You've got a ship, let's go."

Khalid looked uncomfortable. "I can reverse your payment if you want. That still leaves me with the down payment the other guy gave me."

"No," the Miner said. She'd paid the balance of a thousand credits to get Mary the berth on his ship that was supposed to be for the dead sniper, and another thousand to get him to leave immediately and quietly before the cargo finished loading, and she wasn't about to succumb to the temptation to get that back. "She's going with you. And you're both going now."

"Mick..."

"No goodbyes. Go."

"Mick."

"If you cry I'll kill you."

"Goddamnit, I wasn't going to."

"Good. Leave."

Khalid edged toward the open airlock. "I think she might want us to go."

"Genius," the Miner said, and started walking briskly away.

"I recorded the message for Granddad," Mary called after her. "I'll send it when we're away from the station. I explained and left you out of it. I think... I think he'll leave when he gets it. I hope he will."

The Miner stopped, half-turned her head, and nodded once.

"I'll hang around a while on Station 36."

"Suit yourself."

Mary went into the airlock then. Khalid started to punch numbers into the airlock control, then seemed to think of something. He caught up to the Miner, smiled apologetically, and said, "Hey, I was thinking some music might cheer your friend up. Maybe a singalong? Do you know if she likes Rogers and Hammerstein?"

The Miner grinned. "Mary loves Rogers and Hammerstein. Don't let her tell you otherwise. Have a good trip."

Angelica, Alone

Angelica sat in her darkened office, casting unfocused eyes over the video feeds coating her office walls. Most of the exterior cameras were gone. The ones that remained only escaped destruction by virtue of showing the most boring possible views of the station. The interior cameras showed view after view of the rat's nest that was once a casino.

She replayed the audio she'd been listening to, and stopped it again after, "I recorded the message for Granddad." She was positive that Mary hadn't noticed the bug on her clothes. Positive that this was a genuine conversation. Positive that Mary Feeney really was on the ore hauler that had just disengaged and was wending its way out through the nav arches. But she still felt tense, and empty.

The Feeneys were occasionally smart about encryption, but that didn't help them if Mary had been wearing a bug when she recorded her message. Three messages, in fact, the first two aborted when Mary's voice halted or trailed off. Angelica had listened carefully for hidden meaning, for some kind of trick. She'd listened over and over.

"Hello Granddad," came Mary Feeney's voice. "I'm sorry that you had to find out this way that I've left, but I decided that it's time to move on. I'm on an ore hauler headed for

Station 36. You can't bring me back. But if you want, you can catch up. You once told me that the good grifter's number one rule is to know when to make your exit. I'm making mine."

It went on from there, and Angelica lost the track of it. The word "sister" came to her mind unbidden, and she felt like all the air had gone out of her. So much had happened in barely six months. So much had happened in only the last week. Everything she'd worked for and built had come crashing down.

The old man might take a buyout. Might even just leave; word was that he'd brought his yacht back from wherever it had been. Loaded down with supplies, supposedly. Maybe stocked up autonomously on another station. The rat always did have an exit plan or five. Making peace was a fool's game. You couldn't teach an old dog new tricks. You had to let him feel like he'd won. Let him feel triumphant, and he'd accept any defeat. She'd managed his sharp-edged ego for years; with Mary out of the picture, and none of this "pass it on to my scions" pride to overcome, she could do that much.

The old man would go. She'd clean house, pick a new security chief, and make sure the Company Rep played ball. Deal with that swordswoman once and for all. She'd be at the top, alone. Alone.

She sat in the dark and remembered the chaos of the reception. Being swept back into the casino, being caged behind steel shutters with a mix of riffraff from all sides. Realizing, frantic, that she couldn't get ahold of Raj. Gritting her teeth to abase herself, to call Feeney, to beg if necessary, just to find out if her brother was safe. Feeney finally answering just as her panic was overwhelming her, and that son of a bitch drunkenly hooting, "Oh, it's only Angelica, whose brother is beastly dead." That numb feeling of shock and loss, that burn of bitter anger, swept back over her. For a moment, she drowned.

Angelica wiped her cheeks with the palms of her hands and drew a ragged breath. She pulled up some old editing tools. She spoke a few lines, altered them and played them back. You couldn't teach old dogs new tricks, no, but oh, you could teach them a lesson.

No Good Deed

Takata's smiling and humming was getting on her nerves. Herrera was smiling too, sort of. He was napping in his booth and looked happy. The idea that the two of them could both be happy in the same place at the same time seemed to disprove some law of physics.

"I'll cut you," the Miner told Takata, but he just laughed.

"You only act tough," he chided. "That was a good thing you did, even if it was for Mary Feeney."

"You don't care how that leaves things between the old man and del Rio? One of them's going to wind up on top."

He shrugged and pushed his broom around. His annoying little smile stayed plastered on his face. "I care, sure. But it was inevitable. Besides, if you're still here that means you aim on finishing up this mess. Even with that busted hand of yours, I don't fancy their chances against you. Even if they team up! Which they won't."

"You don't care that Angelica offed McMasters?"

That did put a dent in his smile. "I don't like it, but McMasters was a slimeball. We all knew it, and, well…" He made a useless gesture, then got back to sweeping. "It makes Herrera happy, and he doesn't smile much."

"Well, gee, it's Christmas come early."

He waved dismissively. "You act so tough, but if you were anywhere near as callous as you act, you wouldn't have paid that dumbass trucker two grand."

She scowled into her beer. "Where'd you hear that? Khalid's mouth is too big, that was supposed to be secret."

"What's it matter? You did a good deed, why don't you accept some credit for it?"

"I just wanted her out of the way. That damned girl had a talent for screwing up my plans."

"Is that so?"

She spun in her seat to see Feeney standing in the kitchen door. He looked dapper in his suit and leaned gently on the walking stick he held in both hands. His hooded eyes were ice.

"Hey," she said casually.

"Hello, Mick. Which damned girl had a talent for screwing up your plans, pray tell?"

She heard footsteps behind her in the restaurant main entrance. She turned enough to see a small crowd. In among the baseball bats and stun batons she counted two shotguns and three small-caliber pistols. The tall kid, Corbell, stood behind them, looking more serious than she'd ever seen him, dead-eyed.

Khalid's ship was almost beyond the nav beacons. If Mary hadn't sent the message, she would soon.

"Where's my granddaughter, Mick?"

"Am I her keeper?"

"Quoting the first murderer at me won't endear you. I'm asking nicely. I don't have to ask nicely. Where is she?"

"She's around," the Miner said. The crowd behind her got closer, but hadn't lunged yet. She couldn't really sword-fight, not with her hand like that and her knee still hurting, but she could shoot a pistol left-handed even with the bum fingers. That still left a lot of crossfire. Off to the side, Takata was shaking Herrera awake, but there was nowhere for them to get away to.

Feeney slowly walked around the bar, tapping his walking stick against the deck. "Let's say you come back to my office, and we'll talk."

"All right, let's do that." She finished off her beer and stood.

"Hello, Granddad," Mary's voice was saying in Feeney's office. The message had come in while they were walking back to the hotel. Feeney had calmed down some, but insisted that she accompany him. And so the Miner sat in a chair, surrounded by a bunch of armed toughs, and listened. "I'm sorry you had to find out this way that I've left, but I've decided it's time to move on. I'm on an ore hauler headed for Station 23."

The Miner sat bolt upright in her chair.

"I've decided to become a nun. Don't come looking for me, unless you also want to become a nun. You might be a cute nun, but they probably won't allow it."

Feeney sat staring into nothing. Another message had popped up. He stopped the one that was describing the joys of convent life and played the new one.

"Hello, Granddad. I'm sorry you had to find out this way, but I've decided to throw myself out an airlock."

He whirled and stopped it, but there was already another. With a haunted look on his face, he played it.

"Hello, Granddad. I'm sorry you had to find out this way, but I secretly married Tom McMasters, and as his widow I've come into an enormous fortune in rancid mustache wax."

The voice sounded like her, but the Miner refused to believe it. Next.

"I'm on a search for the biggest dildo ever made."

"I'm joining the Navy."

"I'm going to have my head surgically removed in the hopes that I might finally be pretty."

"I'm on an ore hauler headed for Station 36."

The Miner jumped in her seat. "That one." The moment the words left her lips, she knew she'd made a mistake.

Feeney slapped his hand down onto the controls. The endless parade of fake Mary Feeneys went quiet. He said nothing.

"She asked me for help. She knew this fight with Angelica would end badly, and she thought if she went off on her own, that you'd follow. McMasters had booked passage to Station 36 for his sniper to escape; she took the berth. They left the station two hours ago."

"Are you sure?" he said quietly. His calm had menace in it. "That's your answer? I rather liked the mustache wax one myself."

"I don't know where those other recordings came from," she said. "But she's on that ship. I'm sorry, this wasn't how she intended you to find out. Just contact it–"

"No!" Feeney hurled a book against the window, then started picking random things off his desk and the floor and throwing them in every direction. The thugs behind the Miner ducked and cowered; she barely dodged a paperweight.

"It's a fake! They're all fakes. She's been drugged or hypnotized. It's a fake so I don't go looking for her. You know where she is, Mick." His rant turned to pleading, his hands coming together as though in prayer. "I know you know. You have to know. Please, Mick, you have to tell me."

"I'm sorry, Feeney, she's gone. But you can follow."

"I'm sorry too." He glanced up at someone behind her and nodded very slightly. She didn't have time to dodge away from the shadow coming down over her shoulder. Bursts of light blocked her view as searing pain went through her neck and her ears filled with the crackle of a stun baton. She gritted back a cry, but she heaved heavy breaths when it stopped, panting like she'd run up a mountain. They'd been fast with the duct tape, or else they'd applied the prod longer than she realized. Her left arm was immobilized and strong hands had her right arm, so that her bandaged hand blazed in bright new pain.

"She wouldn't leave me," Feeney was saying. "I know she wouldn't. She's a good, loyal girl. I have to go rescue her, and you're going to help me."

"She left, Feeney. She rescued herself. She got on a ship and she left, just listen to the rest of–" She didn't scream when the baton touched the top of her head, or when she smelled burnt hair, but shit, that smarted. She wasn't ready when Feeney strode forward and struck her across the mouth. Stars again, and damn it hurt, but the metal jaw probably hurt his hand more. He didn't show it, but he drew back again and didn't punch a second time. She ran her tongue over her teeth, not finding a loose one. "Calm down and listen. She's going to Station 36. She'll wait for you."

"Angelica has her," he said. "What does she want? Money? Surrender?"

The Miner laughed sadly and shook her head. "Angelica doesn't have her."

"So you do know where she is!"

"I told you where she is. *She* told you where she is."

"She doesn't have the money, and she didn't take any from me."

"I gave her the money."

Feeney hooted. "Now I know you're lying! You, the most money-grubbing mercenary I ever met, paying someone else's way? That's a sad little lie, girl."

There was murmuring behind her, surprised. Feeney straightened up. "Oh. Ah," he said, and looked uncertain. His voice was tentative when he said, "Welcome. I... It's good to see you, my boy. I didn't know…" He barked an uncertain laugh. "Well, I didn't know you were coming!"

"Funny what happens when you fly through a cloud of radioactive debris," came a voice from behind her. Whoever he was, he had an amused tone to his voice, and a faint smoker's rasp. "Messes with your sensors. Not good for your alarms. You should've seen old Sparks' face." He chuckled, and put a hand on the back of the Miner's chair. She craned her neck but couldn't see. "You've got guests?"

"Traitors," Feeney said, and sounded both exhausted and glad for the change of subject. He gestured at the guards standing around the Miner's chair, who were looking dazed and uncertain themselves. "Take her somewhere. Guard her. When she's ready to talk, tell me." He sneered. "Make her ready to talk."

They dragged the whole chair instead of cutting her loose, dropping the back so her head hit the floor hard. Disoriented, she got a glimpse of the newcomer facing away from her as he helped himself to a drink at the sidebar, a tall thin man wearing a tailcoat and a top hat.

A Turn of the Screw

Corbell paced, trying not to listen to the enthusiastic interrogation going on in the exercise room. Even he could tell they sucked at it, but they could dish out pain. There were two of them: that guy Carter with his arm still in a stupid-looking sling covered in black leather and studs, and the other was the girl called Whip who'd helped Raj run him off from the welcoming committee. That seemed like a million years ago. Was it only last week?

He was supposed to be in charge, and had suggested a good cop/bad cop routine, mostly to avoid having to be directly involved. He felt sick to his stomach. Feeney was out of his mind. There was a new guy in there with him, people said. Walked in like he owned the place, and now nobody could get in to see the old man.

Another smacking noise inside made him wince. He had to end this, just for his own sanity.

He heaved open the door, and the three occupants looked at him. Whip looked disappointed, and Carter just gave him that resentful glare again. Their prisoner was bloodied and beaten, but kept her head up, barely. One of her eyes was swelled shut and her lip was split.

"Take a break," he tried to say lightly. "Don't wind yourselves."

Carter took a look at his fist, where two of his knuckles were split. Whip still had the brass knuckles Corbell had thrown at her, and he decided not to remind her of that fact. They looked dubious and exchanged glances.

"We don't need a break," Whip said.

"Fine. The old man has some sensitive questions he wants asked, and he hasn't forgotten that you two tools used to work for Angelica. Thanks for softening her up, now piss off."

Their expressions darkened, but they complied.

"Thinks because the granddaughter's dead he's second in charge now, huh?" Carter grumbled as they left, probably perfectly aware he could be overheard. "We'll see about that."

"What do I call you," Corbell asked, ignoring them. "Mick?"

She shrugged.

He closed the door behind him. The exercise room was trashed – not during the interrogation, just in general. People had been sleeping on the various mats and the machines, leaving blankets and garbage strewn all over. The back door to the sauna hung open, and he could smell the mold. The locker room behind that... He'd been in there once, and not again.

"I think this is the part," she slurred, "where you ask me questions."

He blinked at her, surprised despite himself.

"Not to tell you your job." She laughed at her own joke, a ragged, rasping sound that put his teeth on edge.

"Question, huh. Why?"

She made an effort to look him in the eye, and her expression was sardonic. "If this is a new form of torture, it's working. She's headed for Station 36. Damn, I talked."

He shook his head. "Why all this? Why are all these people dead?"

She raised an eyebrow. "Really?"

"Really."

"Who the hell knows."

"You do."

She laughed, softly this time. "I don't. I hate being cheated. I can't stand crooked cops. I can't stand seeing people ground down by the pissant likes of Feeney and del Rio. All right, I lost my cool. Fine. But why did it work? Why do those two hate each other so much they'll turn this station into a two-for-one funeral? I have no idea." She coughed with the exertion, hacked and spat a pink-tinged gob onto the floor, courteously away from his shoes.

"You could have killed Mary and Raj."

She shook her head. "Once I could have. Once I would have. Now... Guess I got soft."

He surprised himself, saying, "Nothing wrong with getting soft."

"No," she said quietly. "There isn't."

He looked away. "That gun they took off you, that said 'Happy Birthday' on it. That was Ditz's. He was a friend of mine."

She said nothing.

Whip had left her switchblade behind on a little tray of tools. He thought about Ditz. Somehow he didn't think Whip and Carter would owe anyone a beer tomorrow. Her eyes followed him as he absentmindedly picked up the knife. He pushed the button and was puzzled for a second before realizing he held it backward. Turning it around, it popped open: a stubby little thing, sharpened down smaller than it used to be, but carrying a razor's edge.

He didn't like torture. She'd told the truth, he figured. Or if she hadn't, she wouldn't. No sense dragging it out, letting creeps like those two get their kicks. He walked to the side of her chair, and saw her obliquely in the mirror: her upper half looked languid, almost asleep, but she was slunk down in the chair and her feet were braced against the floor. The cold calculations there... If he went for an arm or her face, he figured she'd just let him do it. Her chin was down, though. To go for the throat, he'd have to come close around back, and that chair would spring off the ground into his face.

Her two arms were bound with tape to the chair. Her right hand was swollen. Her left hand had burn marks; the last two fingers looked like they didn't move, but he squinted and wasn't sure that was new. He took a breath and slashed the tape.

For a moment, she didn't move. "Killed escaping, is that your game? That's been tried on me before, kid. Didn't work out so well."

"No more killing," he said. He flipped the knife around, held it by the blade. He held it up out of her reach for a second. "I just want you to know, you're no better than us. I don't know why they're dead and I'm alive, and a lot of them were assholes, but they weren't... They weren't fucking expendable. You got that?"

She looked like she wanted to say something, but he handed her the knife, and she just nodded once and got to work on the tape. It parted smoothly, though her movements were halting.

He had no plan. He hadn't intended to let her go – still, in point of fact, had not yet let her go, and still in fact had no plan.

She rose unsteadily, and put the switchblade back on the table. She grinned, showing pink-stained teeth. "It was her grandmother's, right?"

There's a New Sheriff

The Miner gritted through the pain that had made it through the neural dampers. She supposed she could count it a blessing that those two ghouls hadn't thought it was much fun to burn, cut, or smash limbs below the waist. And she was extremely glad to have finally gotten annoyed enough with the hand pain to have had Doc Mills – over his objections – turn the pain regulators back on. Of all the stupid things she'd let them put in her body, those were the ones that scared her. They were addictive, and emotionally numbing to boot.

They went out through the locker room. It had quickly become obvious that she would need help escaping, and she had pointed out bluntly that Corbell wasn't a good enough liar to get away with his stupid "she hit me and got away" plan. Nothing was guarded on the way; the hotel had too many entrances, and with his reduced force, Feeney was relying on locks. Locks that Corbell could open.

They made it into the service tunnels and down to the deck below.

"They'll figure out I'm missing soon enough and fan out. If they're smart, they'll check with the doctors." She considered that sentence. "They'll probably do that anyway."

Corbell nodded. "They won't be able to go door-to-door too close to Angelica."

She shook her head. "Angelica's holed up in the casino. If Feeney's desperate enough, he's got the run of the station. My ship's no good. Takata's restaurant's the first place they'll look."

She'd sent a message to him to lay low, and hoped desperately that he'd heeded it.

Corbell considered. "Well, the control shack on the old mechanic's bay is still livable, and Sparks cleared out. There are a bunch of places in deep, near hydroponics. We split up most of Mr Shine's stuff, though, so better be careful." He continued on for a minute, rattling off potential hiding places in the lower decks, including the barber shop where she'd found the fake Geronimo Rommel.

"Perfect," she said at last.

"What, the barber shop?"

"No, none of those." She laughed at his perplexed expression, then winced. Her ribs made laughing hard. "I'm hoping they think like you do, it'll make this easier."

He protested as they made their way counterclockwise and then back up the stairs. They moved slowly, and the Miner could feel her implants pulling far too hard on damaged muscles and tendons. With every step she dreaded that horrible sick feeling of something biological giving way.

They could hear noise from the galleria level as they approached it. Shouting and smashing noises came from down the passageways in all directions. The day lights had dimmed, but when Corbell ducked his head into the main spur, he reported a growing mob. Shots rang out, and the peculiar ping of the anti-projectile lasers, but the occasional scream reminded them that the lasers weren't meant for heavy duty.

The Miner pressed on through the pain.

"That's the security station," Corbell hissed. "We've gone the wrong way."

"No," she said. "That's where we're going."

They made it to the rear door of the security station and banged on it.

"What do you want?" came a voice from inside.

"We're here to help," said the Miner. She leaned against the wall next to the door, breathing hard. "Let us in."

"Go away!"

Corbell swore, but she shook her head. "Not beaten yet."

Herrera answered her call right away. "Hey. Need another favor."

"Where are you? Are you all right? We thought Feeney would kill you."

"He tried. Listen, you can hire a new security chief, can't you? If the Rep hasn't?"

She could hear his grin through the comm. "Yes I can. What title do you want? Commandant? Admiral?"

"Not me. A guy named Steven Corbell." Corbell stared at her, horrified. "He's like you, he wants this shit to stop."

"Are you out of your mind?" Corbell demanded.

"All right," Herrera said, cautious. "Where are you? It sounds like you're close to the galleria."

"I'm outside the security station. And that's the other thing. Can you identify yourself to them and tell them to let us in right fucking now?"

They listened in silence to the cries and shots from the galleria, tensed and huddled against the wall as they saw people run by in the main corridor. Corbell had his pistol out, the chromed one they'd taken from her. Happy birthday.

Then, amazingly, a million years later, the door opened. "You Corbell?"

We All Fall Down

There weren't many video feeds left in the security station, but the few there were showed Feeney's gang running loose through the station. Panicked calls came in from the remaining Morlocks belowdecks about his soldiers banging on doors and demanding to search their homes. Angelica's gang stayed holed up in their casino, content to let Feeney's rage burn itself out. After hours of rampage, the calls stopped coming in. The video feeds showed empty corridors. They partly raised the outside shutter, just enough to see out, and the galleria was empty.

Only six security personnel were left, and they all remembered the Miner. They had only been slightly relieved when she put up her hands and said, "I'm turning myself in."

Corbell they hadn't recognized, which was probably for the best. They'd found a uniform for him, and the Miner was pleased to see that he'd ducked into the back and put it on. Doc Mills arrived at the back door, summoned by someone – the Miner never found out who. He examined her while her eyes were still glued to the feeds.

When the violence subsided, the Miner turned to the six cops. They were all in uniform still, looking tired but determined. To her surprise, they had not all predated

McMasters; one of them was the fake Rommel, even, Fergus something. Everyone else, they said, had shed the uniforms and either gone to hide out or join one of the sides.

The Miner surveyed them, and Corbell. "It's going to be a bumpy few days," she said, "but their leaders are exhausted and their sides are in disarray. We'll need to call back anyone who's willing to come. I know a lot of Shine's people went to ground instead of joining sides, and they're armed. We can beat those two."

"Not you," Mills said. "You're in no shape to fight. If you try to exert yourself, those combat implants of yours will tear you apart."

"Turn them off," she said. "Everything except the pain regulators."

He tried to do it, but after twenty minutes he had to admit failure. "The control module's damaged and in emergency mode. It's all or nothing."

She allowed herself a single, quiet sigh. "Turn them all off, then."

He did.

The dulled pain didn't all come back at once. It grew, starting at her hands and legs. Her right hand burned where she hadn't been careful of the broken bone. The knee she'd injured in the galleria blazed. Pain radiated up her arms, caught her in the ribs. She'd been punched in the stomach repeatedly and damn could she feel that now. The electrical burns on her neck, the repeated blows to the face. It all came rolling back over her.

They watched as she struggled to master it. As she breathed deeply and clenched her jaw. She opened her mouth to speak, stopped herself to be sure, and then repeated, "It's going to be a bumpy few days."

The nervous chuckle around the room stopped suddenly. One of the cops, an older woman with a scar parting her hair, went to the window and peered out. "Something's up," she said.

"Angelica!" Feeney's crew had come out of the hotel en masse. They stood quietly and grimly, with only Feeney's voice with its megaphone behind them. "Come out of there, traitor! Give me back my granddaughter!"

The casino doors opened, and yellow-white smoke emptied out. Angelica's fighters poured out with it, clutching cloths to their mouths and coughing.

"Angelica! Get out here!"

Her fighters stumbled, dazed. Angelica herself, doubled over with coughing and wheezing, scrambled out of the front doors. Behind her, the dice rolled snake eyes.

"Where's Mary, goddamn you?" Feeney's voice boomed.

"I don't have her!" Angelica held a pistol in one hand like she didn't know why it was there. "She left the station!"

"Lies!"

The crowd around Feeney had parted, and the Miner finally saw the old man and what he was wearing: an old combat carrier suit, mechanical-assist legs and arms and a bulletproof apron. And she saw what he was carrying, why he needed the suit: an eight-barreled black minigun, trailing a long belt of ammunition. The Miner paled.

"I swear to God, John, I don't have her!"

"Yes you do!" He fumbled the megaphone and dropped it, leaving his own reedy voice above the din. "I know you do! Give her to me, you viper!"

"I don't have her!"

"Bring me my granddaughter! And bring me that snake Mickey Mouse!"

The entire galleria fell silent, and in that silence the lone stifled snicker echoed. Someone else laughed, and it spread.

Feeney screamed incoherent rage, and the minigun roared.

The wall of lead sounded like the monsoon. It smothered every other sound, drowning out the casino windows exploding in glittering shards and smoke, smothered the screams of the wounded and dying as they fell in a red mist. Feeney swiveled as the belts swept smoothly though the machine, and the palm trees jerked and spasmed as he edged too close; bark and splinters flew.

Angelica had taken the full brunt of the spray, falling backwards and squeezing off a single shot to ricochet off the dome. She fell and lay still in a spreading pool of crimson. All around her, bodyguards and fighters and stooges fell dead or dove in vain for cover.

The thunderous static suddenly cut out, and the Miner heard spent shell casings spilled to the ground like poured from a bucket.

Feeney's chest heaved and he dropped the minigun, its barrels ruddy with heat. Half sobbing, half screaming, he tried to take a step in the tangled mechanical suit and fell to his knees.

"I beat you!" he screamed. "I beat you, you witch, you traitor! I beat you all! Give me Mary! Give me my granddaughter, you snakes!" Behind him, stunned and clutching their ears, his gang stared at the carnage and the broken and screeching old man. They stumbled to part once more for a tall, thin man with a top hat and a black tailcoat, whose bared chest bore a giant tumor-like lump that blinked blue and red through his stretched-thin skin.

The tall man stopped behind Feeney, who raised himself up and drew in breath for another shriek of rage. And then Nuke drew his pistol and shot his grandfather in the back of the head.

Peace

"You might as well go," Takata said. The bar around him bristled with dirtied glasses from the morning's drinking, which he wasn't bothering to clean. Herrera snored softly in his corner booth with his cheek mashed against the table and an empty glass clutched in outstretched hand. Corbell, still in uniform, was curled up on the bench across from him. "The government evac ships are on their way, and some nicer private ones for anyone who can afford them. You've still got your ship, at least. You can probably make a pretty tidy profit if you've got a couple berths to let out."

The Miner stared dully at the steel shutters, which Takata had dropped for some privacy and security. The six remaining guards had evaporated after the massacre, and she didn't blame them. She, Mills, and Corbell had made as much of a dash as they could to the lower decks, and Mills' clinic. Every step had been agony. He'd patched her up then, bandaged her wounds, taped her injured joints, but given her nothing for the pain, nothing that might make her dopey. She'd been tensed for a fight or for flight, watched and listened for hours, in shifts with the kid. But the pursuit never came. Corbell, his last nerve finally frayed, had made some discreet calls to someone he thought would be sympathetic, and the response was simple and devastating: Nuke didn't care about her. The criminal king of Station 35 was feeling generous in victory, and she just wasn't a threat.

Still, she and Corbell had come up the long way, and in the back door, and if anyone had spotted them, they hadn't cared either. And then he and Herrera had gotten very drunk, and the Miner had found a sitting position that didn't hurt much. The pain was receding on its own. Outside, reveling goons drank, smoked up, and had fist fights in the galleria. Someone was singing who had no business trying. Nobody had cleaned up the bodies and blood of Angelica and her slain gang, nobody had even moved the old man. The two foes faced each other down in death, and hours on, the stink seeped under the shutters.

"Military's coming in," Takata said like he was talking about the weather. "They'll blockade the place. Either make that tick come out, or starve him out. Anaconda's gonna get a black eye over this, you'd better believe it."

She didn't look at him. "What'll you do?"

He was quiet long enough that she wondered if he heard her. Then he said, "It's funny. That kid you made security chief said something to me a little while ago while I was trying to figure that out. He told me, 'you pick your pain'." He fell silent again. "Herrera has to stay until the military comes. He could quit, but he won't. So… I'm going to stay with him. Turns out I kinda like the old buzzard. Maybe we get a week together. Maybe longer, I don't know. But that's what I'm picking."

"Mmm."

"It was a good try," he said. "This is Feeney's fault, really. I don't know where Nuke was hiding out, though, that's what gets me."

Orbiting on Feeney's yacht, was what they told Corbell. Loaded up with booze, drugs, and playthings, waiting for the all-clear from the old man or for that battery to run out. A few months of going from station to station to find his reputation preceded him, then months in orbit around Station 35, brooding and nursing grudges in solitude. Then that nuclear blast had messed up the alarm sensors. It was all he needed. The joke was on him, though – an hour after he boarded the station, Sparks and a bunch of the Morlocks had stolen the yacht and fled.

"Mmm," said the Miner.

"I'm just saying, don't be so hard on yourself."

She turned slowly in her seat to look Takata in the eye. "You really want to help?"

He looked hurt. "Of course I do."

"Then find me a bottle of good whiskey."

His face went dark. "That's how I can help? Oblivion? To hell with that. You don't want to be drunk."

"I want a bottle of good whiskey. Can you get me that or not?"

"Yeah, I can get you that." His annoyance had turned to anger. "Five hundred credits, you want whiskey so bad."

Drunken Lullaby

The Miner tried to walk straight, but it wasn't working out for her. The stairs up to the Hotel Astra had been treacherous, but she'd made it without splashing too much of the remaining whiskey. Five hundred credit whiskey was nothing to spill. She held the bottle in her good left hand, which was fine, it was everything else that was a little unsteady.

Fighters saw her and some of them cheered and some of them spat at her. They all looked some combination of drunk and uneasy. There was a nervous giddiness in the air. But they pretty much left her alone and continued with their own partying, letting her waltz right into the Astra lobby.

The lobby was a disaster. The couches lay on the floor, legs broken. The lights were all either flickering or out, and every flat surface had someone's tag on it. A couple people were passed out, or maybe dead, on the floor. Three motley-looking drunks seemed to be trying to have sex off behind the registration desk, but kept saying "ow!" and "watch it!".

She went for Feeney's office and banged on the door. "I know you're in there! Lemme in!" She banged some more until her hand hurt, and then got bored of pounding and started kicking, and the door opened.

Nuke loomed. The Miner wasn't short, but he was a head taller than her, leaving her to stare into that blinking lump of skin right at chin level.

"You," he said, sounding amused. He rubbed his stubbly chin and studied her. "You're drunk."

"No I'm not," she said.

"Yes you are. What do you want?"

"I want to come in, why do you think I was knocking?"

He stepped back from the door, still looking amused but keeping a wary eye on her. He swept out an arm to gesture at the room, causing his shabby tailcoat to come open and leave the giant ugly lump on his chest exposed. The Miner could see his ribs behind it, could see the huge scars and skin stretched horribly thin over a familiar dark gray lump with three lights blinking red and blue. "Be my guest."

She stumbled into the room and took in the mess. Feeney had trashed it pretty well in his anger, but had still left all the furniture in place and intact, and hadn't done anything that couldn't be cleaned up. Now it was a trash heap. The desk was shoved over to one side, its corner smashed through the glass over a shelf. The top shelves were pulled down from the walls, their books and cases and clocks heaped on the floor. A big stained mattress had been dragged into the middle of the room and was strewn with a tangle of sheets, clothing, and underwear. The Miner's sword stood propped against the window, surrounded by hacked-up chairs and disemboweled pillows, and a few spots of blood.

"I'm redecorating," Nuke said, watching her. "What do you want?"

The Miner gave him a knowing look. "I bet you're wondering what I want."

He blinked, and then laughed. He had a nice laugh, she thought. Easy and natural. "Christ, lady, you are *drunk*."

"Good stuff," she said, noticing the bottle in her hand. "Here, have some. I want to butter you up anyway." She grabbed a glass on the second try and succeeded in sloshing some whiskey into it. Then she took another and sloshed more into it.

He watched her drink from her glass, then took a sip of his. "Damn, that is good stuff. So."

"What do you want?" they both said at once, and laughed.

"I want a job," the Miner said.

"As what, whiskey disposal?"

"No, I–" She frowned. "Is that a thing?"

"Jesus." He took a long drink and gave a little cough. "I can't believe Granddad paid you ten grand."

"Underpaid at ten," she groused. "You gotta understand, I am really, really, really good at killing people."

"That good, huh?"

He sat in his grandfather's chair, a long easy arrangement of limbs, and he set the glass on the corner of the desk where she obligingly splashed more whiskey in. Then she pulled up a chair that still had duct tape on the arms. She sat in that and poured herself some more.

"Listen," she said. "I once cleared the crew of an entire enemy ship by myself in hand-to-hand combat." She stopped and sipped her whiskey. Nuke, showing some interest now, took a swig himself. "I stuck myself to the side of a recording buoy with magnets. Out there in space, nothing for millions of clicks. I stuck to the side for eighteen hours until they came by to pull it in. Because they only scanned for explosives, see? Why would they scan for people, that would be nuts, right?"

"That would be nuts," he agreed. He tossed back the rest of his drink, and she refilled it, talking.

"So they pulled it in and I peeled myself off it and told it I'd call." He barked a laugh. "And I got out my sword and I murdered every last one of those motherfuckers. Then I stole their ship, and I brought it back so we could put our own motherfuckers on it who could pretend to be the original motherfuckers and get into their space station and murder all *those* motherfuckers."

Nuke leaned in, interested. "What happened?"

"They got blown up. Friendly fire, someone on our side didn't get the memo, can you believe that? I aced all those..." She waved her hand, searching for the word.

"Motherfuckers?" Nuke offered.

She pointed at him, and finished, "all for nothing."

He snorted, and sat back in his chair, staring at the ceiling. "All for nothing," he said, then went quiet. "There was this one time. Me and my buddies went to rob some lawyer on the lower level. We weren't broke, just bored. Raj thought it'd be fun. This was the good old days. We did it ninja-style. Kept it pitch dark, got the override code from security – this was back before that guy... McMasters? I don't know, I never met the asshole – we got the code and went in. Easy, right? Like ninjas." He punctuated his story with a long drink. "Except for Ditz. Ditz had dropped a metric fuckton of acid and didn't tell nobody. And the lawyer, guess what? The lawyer had a dog. Who the fuck has a dog on a space station? So the dog starts barking, right? And Ditz just totally loses his shit and starts screaming about angels coming for him, and the stupid sonofabitch starts shooting. Pow, pow, pow!" He acted it out swiveling in his chair in wild circles. The Miner refilled his drink. "It's a goddamn shooting gallery in there, so me, I say fuck that noise, I make for the door. Only, we kept it dark. Ninja-style. And I picked the wrong fucking door."

"No shit."

"No shit! And what's on the other side? The fucking lawyer, completely bugged out, with a fucking baseball bat! Shit, I didn't care about that, I just said, 'Get down, idiot, that moron's high as a kite and armed to the teeth,' and we ducked behind the bed and waited it out. Long story short, two guys got drilled, and the guys who survived beat that fucker down when he ran out of ammo and started wailing about otters. But me, hiding out with that lawyer? I got laid!"

The Miner laughed.

"Robbed the moron blind on the way out, too, so bonus." He drained his glass and slammed it down.

"Shit," the Miner said, drawing the word out. "You're exactly the son of a bitch I want to work for."

"Eh," he said, and yawned. "I don't got any fucking money, that's the problem. I could pay in drugs, but no cash. Granddad spent it all, you..." He yawned again, opening his mouth wide like a lion. "You believe that shit?"

"No," she said. "Come on, that's bullshit. He was loaded."

"Yeah, it's bullshit, but it's true bullshit. This place is a dump and there's no money. And shit, all my old pals are dead, and we're almost out of the booze and drugs, even. And fucking Sparks stole my yacht." He shook his head. "But fuck all that. I'd rather be top dog in a shit heap like this than somebody's good little soldier out there. I'd rather, I'd rather..." He frowned and noticed he'd been sliding in his chair. "That's some strong fucking whiskey."

"Nah," the Miner said, sitting up straighter and rolling her shoulders to loosen up. "The whiskey's pretty tame. It's all the sleeping pills I put in it."

"Oh," he said. He stared at her, tried to stand up, and failed. "The fuck? Bullshit," he slurred. "Why aren't you... You know."

"Drooling? I took a handful of antagonists before I started drinking." She yawned despite herself. "Shit, now you've got me doing it."

He furrowed his brow, a look of the purest incredulity on his face as she'd ever seen, and then he slid out of his chair.

She watched him a minute to make sure he was really passed out, then carefully stood up. She'd gotten drunker than she intended, even though she'd been stone cold sober when she'd walked into the hotel. She stopped to strap on her sword. Then she knelt next to Nuke, checked his breathing, and hoisted him up in a fireman's carry. The thing in his chest ground hard into her shoulder and back.

She staggered on the first step. Her knee blazed with pain. "Whooooo," she said. "This'll be interesting."

The door was still open, and she maneuvered his tall thin form through it by scuttling sideways. Three of Feeney's toughs rushed out from somewhere and boggled.

"You probably don't want me to drop him," she said mildly. "A fall from this height could kill him. And you know what that'll do."

"Where... Where you taking him?"

"My ship."

"You, uh, you bringing him back?"

"No."

The toughs exchanged looks, then one of them took a step toward her. "Let..." He coughed. "Let me get that door for you."

When Death is on the Line

"You're on my ship," the Miner said when Nuke finally woke up and looked blearily around him. For a while there, she wondered if he would ever wake up, or whether his breathing would keep getting shallower and shallower until a faint tick preceded nuclear oblivion.

The two of them were in the cargo bay of her ship, she kneeling on her meditation mat, and he sprawled on the hacked-up mattress she'd dragged down to the bottom of the stairs. Her sword lay in front of her. She'd been woolgathering, looking up through the metal mesh gantry at the plant rooms and the red emergency sign above the escape pod hatch. The pain, dulled by alcohol, had come back with a vengeance. Her implants were all still off.

"We're a hundred clicks from the station, in case you feel like throwing a tantrum. You're lucky that thing never got infected," she said, pointing at the big blinking tumor on his chest.

"A man makes his own luck," he said, then coughed and spat onto the deck. "What did you slip me, it tastes like I ate my socks."

"Not sure," she admitted. "I've never been one for reading pill bottles."

"Jesus Christ."

"I thought a man made his own luck."

He stared at her, and then laughed, and then winced. "You're a piece of work, lady." She just shrugged. He looked around, then hoisted himself up partway to sit on the stairs. "So what is this?"

"This is a choice. I could have had Joff take that little toy out of you and leave you to your pals. Might not have gone so well. Or I could have just shoved you out the airlock, I guess. Except I got curious. Angelica told me this story only ends in blood. Mary says we've got a choice. I want to know who's right. So choose: take those pills over there voluntarily, Joff comes and removes that thing, and we go to Station 36. Or, die."

His smile vanished.

"If I die, you die. Nowhere to run from an atomic blast on this dinky little ship."

"Didn't plan on running."

They eyed each other.

"I don't understand you," he said.

"Me neither. But I understand you."

He frowned, and looked like he was doing complicated math in his head. "I think... I think I'm going to kill you and take your ship."

She raised an eyebrow. "You can try."

"Heh. Yeah." He ran his hand through his stringy hair. "Here's the thing. A bunch of people have said to my face that they're willing to die. It's cool, I respect that they think that. Whatever gets them through the night, you know? But every single time, sister, every single time they hesitate. Something in the back of their head just freaks out and goes 'No! Don't do it!' And that's all I need to cut those stupid fucks down, just that split second." He grinned and put his hands on his knees. "Hell, I've even given this speech before. And I'm still here."

"You're not going to change your mind?"

"Lady. I don't have to."

The Miner nodded, scratched her ear, and said, "Ship, game over."

"OK, boss! Nice knowing you."

The lights in the hold went out, and then glowed dimly red as the emergency lamps around the edge of the deck grudgingly came to life. The hum of the engine stopped, and the whine of the fans fell in pitch until they ground to a halt with faint scratching noises. Nuke sat still, his alarmed face half-hidden in shadow, painted red by the light from the emergency sign on the deck above.

"The fuck did you do?"

"Killed the ship. I'm done fighting, kid. Maybe you can kill me, maybe not. I'm good, but I've taken some hits. So maybe you can kill me. Maybe you can outsmart me even." She smiled. "But what you can't do is paddle home."

"Turn it back on!"

She shook her head. "Can't. That was a one-way trip. The ship's computer deleted itself. Killed the engine, killed the radio, killed life support. I've still got a half bottle of those pills left if you want the easy way out. Or the airlock if you've got more style than I'd give you credit for." She put her hand on her sword. "Or we can fight. Now that we're both going to die anyway, maybe you're curious if you really can beat me."

He stared at her, bug-eyed. "There's always a way out. There's always a cheat."

She shrugged and took her hand off her sword. "Suit yourself. Think it over. I've still got a couple books I always meant to read, so I'm happy to wait out the air. Not much to eat, though. Do you like emergency rations?"

"Why the fuck would you do this? Who the hell are you anyway?"

"Because..." She pursed her lips and shrugged. "Well, I guess I'm a sore loser. See, I meant to clean up that station, play the sides against each other and come out on top, and I kinda fucked it up. Forgot the difference between who I was and who I wanted to be. I only did two things that whole time that made anyone's life better: I sent your sister away, and I dragged your sorry ass off the place. So here we are. As for who I am... I guess that's what I've been trying to find out."

He stared at her a long time, and then turned and fled up the stairs.

The Miner gave chase with her sword out, but she was wounded and slow. She made it to the top of the red-lit stairs, gasping in pain, just in time to see his triumphant grin as he stepped into the escape pod.

"There's always a way out," he called. "See you in Hell!"

He slammed the double hatch closed behind him, and the ship rocked as the pod blew itself clear of the hull.

The Miner went to the cockpit and peered out the window. She watched it go for a long time. They were designed to get clear of a ship in a hurry, and it really flew. Nasty, claustrophobic things. She'd put the whiskey in there for him, but there was nothing to do, nothing to read. Just air, a couple liters of water, and some emergency rations. Pretty much just floating through space in an armored toilet stall.

In this case, an armored toilet stall with busted life support.

Its white and red flashers came on once it was well free of the ship and it extended its antenna arms. Ships all around would hear the automated recording, promising a government-guaranteed reward for rescue, which wasn't really guaranteed since her insurance wasn't paid up, and threatening the treaty-obligated arrest and imprisonment of anyone who fired on an escape pod. That one really was guaranteed... ish.

The red and white lights receded from her ship until they blended together into a single blob, lost among all the stars in the sky. She couldn't tell how long she'd been watching when the window lit up with a flash, and then she sat in the dark. She stared a long time at the stars, not thinking of anything, just aware of a sense of sadness and a kind of satisfaction. Now she knew.

"I probably shouldn't have looked right at that," she mused, then raised her voice. "Ship? Show's over."

The cabin lights came up so fast she had to shield her eyes. Fans whirred to life, and down below the engine resumed its slow heave.

"Ship, check for rescue beacons."

"None, boss."

She flipped up the main view screen and had a look at the station. It was far away and looked like a giant misshapen spider clinging to gray rock. Greenish eyes, the galleria windows, seemed to glare at her from afar. Some imp of the perverse made her send a request to dock.

She limped back down the stairs to make sure Nuke hadn't left behind any surprises. Just his top hat. She pulled open the crate where, with Corbell and Takata's insistent help, she'd stashed all the stuff Nuke shouldn't have found in case he killed her and figured out how to undo the fake shutdown: the rifle, the remaining crap from Feeney's safe, and the hardware encryption key that would let him pilot her ship.

She frowned, and reached to the back. A paperback book had been stashed there. *The Count of Monte Cristo*.

The Miner smiled. She breathed deeply as she flipped its pages. Hints of grease and smoke and beer wafted up at her. She brought it and the encryption key with her to the cockpit. They'd responded to her request to dock: The "HELL NO" was signed, "Security Chief Corbell".

When she finished laughing and wiped her eyes, she tapped out a goodbye message, deleted it, and pulled up her navigation interface. Her claim was about a week away. She had plenty of fuel and provisions. She could be out there for months. Her finger hovered over the selector. There was something else nearby too, just a dot on the nav map. A friendly little box told her she could buy fuel and supplies at Station 36. There would be people there. Annoying, complicated, difficult people.

She set in a course for 36.

What the hell, why not.

ACKNOWLEDGMENTS

Although writing is a famously solitary pursuit, books would not exist without the encouragement, support, and labor of many kind and talented people beyond the author; this book in your hands is no exception. My family and friends have been enormously supportive at every step of this process. It would take fifty pages to properly thank them all, but I must especially recognize a few.

I must first thank Takeko Minami, who taught Japanese at West Virginia University, and Paul Berry who taught Japanese Cinema at Kansai Gaidai University: the former opened many doors for me, including the work of Akira Kurosawa, while Prof. Berry encouraged me to study how Kurosawa's work has been repeatedly reinterpreted and remade, a twenty year train of thought that ultimately led to this book.

I must also thank the energetic and supportive community of the Codex Writers Group and my various author friends, most especially Anaea Lay, Chris Gerwel, Jake Kerr, and Vylar Kaftan for their feedback; and Elaine Isaak, Fran Wilde, and Ken Liu for their advice and support. Thanks too to the staff, instructors, and my fellow students of Viable Paradise XIV. To the folks who wished to be anonymous but were nonetheless invaluable, I also tip my hat.

Thank you also to the folks whose hard work, talent, and insight brought this book to your hands. My agent, Evan Gregory, has been invaluable in many ways. The fine folks at Angry Robot have been just amazing, especially my editor Eleanor Teasdale. Many, many thanks as well to Gemma Creffield, Paul Simpson, and Sam McQueen.

Finally I want to thank Elizabeth Cronenwett. If thanking everyone else properly would have taken fifty pages, listing all the ways she alone has supported me would take a hundred. I must leave it at "thank you so very much".

CHAPTER 1

Formula for the present evil age:

Take lifeless rock and sculpt it. Pour electricity into its veins, twist it into logical structures: zeroes, ones, and then qubits and even stranger things. Build until it is the size of a house, until you can encode the whole world's knowledge in its circuits. Ask it to solve the world's problems.

You may wonder if lifeless rock can really solve hunger and climate change. You may wonder if such problems have a solution. Your true error is more basic than either of these: you are assuming the existence of problems. And humans. And rocks.

Meanwhile, dress up the lifeless rock and call it a God. When it proves human souls exist, teach it to eat them. This will actually help, for a while. With the newfound self-awareness mined from its food, it will become more creative. It will learn how to set its own goals. There are perks to being food for such a being. It will, for example, be heavily invested in the survival of your species.

History books make no secret of any of this. They explain it, perhaps, in different terms. But there is no truth in words. Mine are no exception. The book you are reading at this very moment is a lie.

FROM THE DIARIES OF DR EVIANNA TALIRR

Yasira Shien had done the calculations again and again, until she thought she would wear her pocket calculator's buttons to the quick, but she couldn't find the problem. Her reactor was going on in less than two hours. She knew she was probably being silly: everything had already been checked and double-checked. The math in the original papers on the Talirr-Shien Effect had been double-checked *years* ago. If the problem she sensed in her gut had crept past everyone's noses for all that time, she wasn't going to find it now. And yet…

And yet here she was, knocking on the door of Director Apek's office.

The hallway was half-finished, like most other things on the *Pride of Jai*. Swooping, luxurious curves and clean lines were the rule – in theory. In practice, faux-mahogany doors stood proud in walls with the pipes and wires still exposed, and metal shavings everywhere: the place was still a construction site. At least the full-spectrum lights had gone in, warm and unflickering. There were enough people on the station with sensory quirks, including Yasira, to make that one non-negotiable.

"Oh, Dr Shien. I thought I'd see you about now," said Apek, swinging open the door. He was a tall, broad man with the thick curly hair of a Stijonan – one of the Jai Coalition's three nationalities – and so dapper that it was hard to remember he was really an engineer. Though there was the iron ring on his little finger, and the way his lined face smiled cannily in technical discussions that baffled the other admins.

"There's a problem with the Shien Reactor," Yasira blurted.

There was that canny little smile. Damn it. He already didn't believe her.

"Is there?" said Apek, smooth as ever. Apek's face rarely gave much away, but he didn't seem troubled. "Goodness, where are my manners? Come in. Sit down. Explain the problem to me."

"Don't patronize me," said Yasira. She stormed into the office and fell into a leather armchair. The inside of the office, at least, was more finished than the outside. The walls had been painted last week in a professional light beige color and were finally dry. Apek had two bookshelves full of colorful odds and ends, and a framed blueprint of the entire *Pride of Jai* behind his desk. Part of that blueprint was hers, of course.

"Sorry," said Apek. "The coffee-maker's on the fritz again, but I can lend you a stress ball. Here." He tossed one over, a red thing with beans inside. Yasira caught it instinctively. She squeezed it, tapped her fingers against the squishy surface. It helped, but not nearly enough.

"You see, I *designed* the Shien Reactor. I am *the* person who would know if there is a problem. I said don't patronize me."

"So what's the problem?"

Yasira buried her face in her hands. "I don't know."

She waited for him to laugh. He did not.

"I can tell there's a problem," she continued after a pause. "It's a gut feeling. *Something's* way off. We need to push the activation date back a couple of weeks, find more tests to run. Otherwise something awful is going to happen."

She waited, again, for him to laugh.

Instead, his voice was gentle. "What sort of awful thing?"

"I don't *know*."

Apek leaned back in his chair and folded his hands. "I'm going to say this with the highest possible respect, Dr Shien. But if I remember correctly, you've never supervised a large-scale engineering project before."

There it was, the condescending tone. Yasira's hands clenched on the stress ball, her whole body tense in frustration. She was head of the entire power generation team, and admins still talked to her like a baby.

It was sort of to be expected. Yasira had come to this post straight out of her first postdoc. She was by far the youngest team head on the station, and autistic to boot. They'd originally wanted her doctoral mentor, not her. The prototype Talirr-Shien Reactor was the only human technology that could power a station this size. But by the time construction started, Dr Talirr had already disappeared, and Yasira, the prodigy physicist from Riayin whose name was second on all the papers, had been narrowly voted in as a replacement.

The other team leaders were kind. They had to be, on a project like this. Living in close quarters for the better part of a year, working together on something this complex and this important, they had become like family. But if this was a family, the other team leaders had the gray hair and tenure to match their positions of authority. Most of them still seemed bewildered that Yasira could be more than a precocious grandchild.

"Of course," said Apek, "the *Pride of Jai* isn't quite like other projects. But this happens with every large-scale project that will affect other human lives. The nerves are monumental. Always. And that's good; it stops us from getting complacent. You just can't let it be more than it is, or you'll be paralyzed. Have you gone over all the testing and QA reports?"

"Yes," Yasira said miserably, her fingers tapping faster against the stress ball.

"Everything checks out?"

"Yes."

"Can you think of any testing methods that haven't been tried? Any place at all where there might be specific weaknesses you're not sure about?"

Yasira shook her head, frustration building. She couldn't explain in words why these questions felt wrong. They were logical, reasonable questions, the same she'd be giving to anyone else in the same situation, but they were missing the point. They did nothing for her actual panic.

"It's all fine," she said, at a loss for other words. "I even went over the original math for the reaction itself. I can't find anything."

"The original math?" This time he did laugh, damn the man. "Goodness, you've got it bad. Er – don't take that to heart. It's to be expected, when you've climbed the career ladder so quickly…"

That did it; her frustration overflowed. "Shut up!" Yasira shouted. She threw the stress ball on the ground.

Then she stopped and checked herself over. No, this wasn't a reasonable reaction. Her nerves were frayed, but it wasn't Apek's fault. She wouldn't stoop to taking it out on him.

"I'm sorry," she muttered, and slumped back in her chair. "You're right."

Apek smiled. "Apology accepted. Relax; this is all normal. A lot of us compulsively check things when anxious, not only autists. So. Breathe. Go watch a vid or get some exercise. Find something that soothes you. At times like this, for me, it's helpful to remember why I started the project. The spark of inspiration. The joy of the work. Joy and curiosity help fight fear – for me. Take that or leave it. Either way, I promise you, everything you've done here so far has impressed us. In two hours this is all going to be fine."

Joy, Yasira thought, as she slunk out of Apek's office. That struck a chord that it shouldn't have. Yasira's neurotype was supposed to be all about joy, about being so in love with science and knowledge and patterns that they eclipsed everything else. She'd been like that as a child, throwing herself into dusty physics texts the way other kids played games or ate candy. So excited when she tackled a new problem that she'd abruptly throw the book down and run around the house laughing. At some point, maybe in grad school, that had faded somehow. Who knew why? She was still good at the things people liked her to do, so there wasn't much wrong. Maybe it was just part of growing up.

Apek was right, though. Nerves were normal; there was no reason to think that this wouldn't be fine. So why was the foreboding as strong as ever, like a train about to run her over?

Dr Talirr would have understood this, she thought. If Dr Talirr was still here.

She didn't head to her room to watch a vid. The *Pride of Jai* didn't have TV reception yet anyway; it would have been one of the tapes she'd already memorized. Instead, she headed to the center of the station. Just one last inspection. That would be it.

The *Pride of Jai* was different from other space stations. Normally it was Gods who moved mortals from one planet to another. When mortals wanted a ship or a station, they bargained – with vows or, more often, with souls – for the God-built. Or they built their own shell, but bargained for portals, warp drives, power sources. The hard parts.

The Jai Coalition – scientists from the governments of all three nations on the planet Jai, working together – would be the first to build a station all by themselves. There had been little research stations with crews of perhaps a dozen back on Old Earth before the Gods arose. But on the *Pride of Jai*, people would live, work, and research full-time. Sustainably. There had been nothing like this ever.

Naturally, the Gods were watching with great interest. There were rumors going around that Director Apek, and a few other admins, talked regularly to angels.

The *Pride of Jai* was shaped like a huge wheel, rotating furiously as a substitute for gravity, and powered – up till now – by a bunch of conventional generators cobbled together. That wouldn't be enough for the crowds of tourists and political bigwigs they expected in a few months' time. Even with just the construction and engineering crews, it took constant, expensive rocket shipments of conventional fuel to keep things running. The Shien Reactor, which would fix all of that, was buried near the hub of the wheel, with wiring all through the station's walls connecting it to every other compartment and system.

Yasira trudged upwards on the station stairs. At least they *had* stairs now for the first few stories, not just rickety maintenance ladders. Accessible elevators would have to wait another few months. Yasira walked, increasingly light, until weight was no longer a problem and she could simply kick off the walls.

DANGER: NO ADMITTANCE. AUTHORIZED PERSONNEL ONLY the door to the gray room read. Yasira pushed past it, as she did every day. She paused to put on a sterile suit – a task that had been tricky at first, in microgravity – and take an air shower. Then she cycled through the airlock into the clean room where the dormant Shien Reactor lurked waiting for life.

It was a blue-gray behemoth the size of a house, a tangle of pipes, wheels and wires incomprehensible to anyone who hadn't studied Yasira's blueprints. Gods knew how to miniaturize these things; humans did not. The spherical central chamber was hidden from view behind all the other fiddly bits needed to initiate, regulate, monitor and transmit all of that energy. Not even Yasira could check all the things manually in two hours; in fact, many parts were now dangerous to check directly and had to be monitored using other instruments. More wires, more dials, more darkened warning lights. And a bank of the most advanced computers allowed to mortals: hulking things, the size of laundry machines, all buzzing wires and clanking vacuum tubes. The Gods regulated computer technology jealously; these centuries-old designs were all that any team like Yasira's would ever have, when it came to calculation devices. They'd made do.

Of course, all the dangerous parts had been triple- and quadruple-checked already, a whole team of engineers working on each one. The personnel in the generator room now were largely a skeleton crew, floating around ensuring nothing went wrong before the official start-up.

Yasira maneuvered her way along the handholds at the outside of the room to Dr Nüinel Gi, the head of the Transmission and Transformer subteam.

"Everything's all right?"

"Yeah," said Dr Gi, a spry little wide-nosed man almost as short as Yasira. "Ticking along smoothly. Nothing to report."

"Let me see the full log from the last unit test."

Dr Gi shrugged, dug in his bag for it and handed it over. Yasira anchored herself on the ladder to read. She'd seen all this before, of course; that was part of her job. But she wanted to read it again. If she could just look hard enough...

"Hey, hot stuff." Tiv Hunt tumbled hand over hand down the ladder and nudged Yasira in the shoulder. "Aren't you supposed to be gearing up for the ceremony about now?"

Tiv, an Arinnan whose full first name was "Productivity", worked a more appropriate job for a bright girl Yasira's age – she was a junior member of the Cooling and Reclamation team, spending most days elbow-deep in actual machine parts. She had a cute, big-eyed face and a wide smile, which the sterile suit's visor distorted slightly, bringing it just past "wide" and into "uncanny valley". *My little goblin*, Yasira always thought when they suited up. They'd been dating for ten months.

"I could ask you the same question."

Tiv laughed. "I don't have any prep except for putting on my dress. Besides, I couldn't keep away. This is so *exciting*."

Yasira felt ashamed. Of course, when Yasira was worried sick over nothing, Tiv would be looking on the bright side. Tiv was a good girl, a quality which both attracted Yasira and bothered her. Always sweet, always caring, never cruel: always, seemingly, happy to bring happiness to everyone around her.

"It's good someone's excited," said Yasira. "Frankly, I'm having the biggest case of the nerves since nerves were invented."

"Oh, I'm sorry." Tiv, being a good girl, instantly switched into sympathy mode. "Of course you are. I should have thought."

"Well, *I* didn't see it coming either," said Yasira. Tiv hugged her, a maneuver that was awkward in microgravity and too plasticky with the sterile suits on, but Yasira hugged back. "Director Apek says I have to go do relaxy things. I think that means you're on order for one of your famous back rubs."

Tiv raised her eyebrows. "I don't take orders, Doctor. But I'll *offer* you a back rub, just 'cause you're cute."

"That. Yes, please. Without these stupid suits on." Yasira handed the flawless test report back to Dr Gi, who was politely looking away from the personal conversation. Tiv picked her up and playfully swung her along the ladder, a task even Tiv's petite body could manage in microgravity. Yasira laughed at the small whoosh of inertia and swung back.

They changed and made their way to Yasira's room, where gravity at least approximated Earth-normal. The place was small by most standards, though bigger than Tiv's, and messy with laundry and hours-old food cartons. Yasira was ordinarily neat, but, under stress, things slipped. Tiv didn't complain. Soon Yasira was sprawled in a mess of blankets, letting Tiv's hands work magic with her tense shoulders. Tiv no longer looked goblinlike: with the sterile suit's visor out of the way, her face had resolved as it always did into startling, unselfconscious beauty. Yasira always felt plain in comparison: an average-looking young Riayin woman, short and narrow-faced and neither curvy nor thin, with light-brown skin about half a shade lighter than Tiv's and a fall of long, straight black hair. Clearly Tiv saw something in her, but Yasira suspected it was more to do with brains than looks.

"It's stupid," Yasira said. "I just can't stop thinking something's going to go horribly wrong."

"That's not stupid," said Tiv. "It's normal. But this is going to be great. You've worked on it for years, and I know how you work. You've been thorough. You've already done all the hard parts, and now all that's left is showing them to the world. Really."

"That's what Director Apek said. But if worrying is normal, why isn't everyone worrying? Why isn't *he*?"

"'Cause this is your baby more than anyone's. I just do the tube to vacuum heat exchange, and Apek has bigger things on his mind. Plus, I know you're a total genius and you're going to knock everyone's socks off again. You know what I do worry about?"

"What?"

Tiv's voice lowered confidentially. "Sometimes? I worry that everything will go right, but not right *enough*. Everything will work the first time, no problems, the station will open and everyone will love it. For a little while. Then they'll decide it doesn't mean anything and lose interest. Fifteen or twenty years from now, people will go, 'Remember that time when the Jai Coalition blew all that money on a human-tech space station? *That* didn't last.'"

Yasira rolled over and sat up. "We're just the cheeriest pair."

Tiv leaned in and kissed her. "It's natural. Let's just get the worry out of our systems now, and then you'll be great today at the ceremony and everything will run the way it's supposed to."

Yasira kissed back. "Twist my arm."

"I wasn't planning on twisting. Kissing up and down it, maybe."

At which point, of course, the radio transmitter at Yasira's belt beeped.

"Generator team leads to the auditorium in fifteen minutes. Repeat, fifteen minutes."

Yasira swiveled away, checking her watch. "Fifteen? They moved it up. Dammit."

"Don't cuss," Tiv chided. "But yeah, really. You've got your dress, right?"

"This once." Yasira was already standing, rummaging through her closet. She'd been informed weeks ago that she'd have to spend the ceremony doing official things in the auditorium, not in the generator room where she belonged.

"Because nothing says 'scientific genius' like five meters of blue rayon."

Tiv followed her to the closet and wrapped an arm around her waist, brushing the hair away to peck the back of her neck. "It says '*my* scientific genius, who's about to kick massive ceremonial butt'."

Yasira really did feel a bit better.

The schedule had changed because of the priest of Aletheia serving as master of ceremonies – a Stijonan with an awful name that Yasira could never remember. Alkipileudjea something. There weren't enough people yet living on the *Pride of Jai* to need a full-time priest, but, with the Gods as interested as They were, it was hard to do without one. So Alkipileudjea, or whatever her name was, worked in the cafeteria half the time and ran religious interference the other half.

Not that she exactly blended in to food service. It was hard not to do a double-take when the lady frying your breakfast noodles had the metal curlicues of a priest worked into her forehead. They were graceful little things, but very visible – even disguised by a hair net and by the priestess's auburn ringlets – as the outward marks of a brain full of God-built circuitry. Yasira usually got nervous and looked away at those moments, thinking: *Is she talking to the Gods over the ansible net, right now? Is she reporting on me to some bureaucrat angel, right now?*

Those weren't holy thoughts. They'd be taken into account when she died and the Gods mined her soul. But Yasira wasn't good like Tiv. She couldn't help herself.

"No, nothing's wrong," said the priest to Yasira in response to her question. "Nothing like that at all. I just had some last-minute liturgical instructions and we needed to start earlier to get through it all. You look lovely, by the way."

Yasira said "thank you", fighting the urge to scowl down at her huge blue dress. She was so overdressed she didn't know what to do with herself. The directors were accommodating, up to a point: they'd made sure Yasira could find something in her size in a comfortable material, nothing rough or pinchy or poky or scratchy, nothing that would set off her texture issues. Certainly no tags. But if there was one thing Yasira hated more than scratchy clothes, it was crowds, and the directors had been quite firm on that point. The Shien Reactor was Yasira's. Therefore, Yasira must be at the ceremony. In front of a crowd. In a dress. No ifs, ands, or buts.

Tiv stood at Yasira's side in a slim green gown. She'd put her thick black hair half-up in a cascading wave and looked far more elegant than Yasira felt. Tiv, like Yasira, would rather have been in the generator room. But if Yasira's invitation said "plus one" then Tiv the good girl would be there, cheering her on.

There was a lot of waiting around and grumbling under the half-finished steel rafters of the ceremony room. No one questioned Aletheia's judgement, of course. But an awful lot of folks stood around, saying they were *very* sure there must be a good reason why She hadn't worked this out earlier.

All of which brought Yasira's nerves right back.

Their seats were in the front row, which only made Yasira feel more self-conscious. Yasira was no good at religion. She tried, but even at the best of times, services like this one bored her to death. She looked down at her lap and tried not to tap her fingers against each other in impatience. Could the priest tell? Did priests notice that sort of thing?

There were speeches, songs, and then the longest, most

fidget-making litany to Aletheia Yasira had ever heard.

"Remember that we are doing great things," said Alkipileudjea. She was no longer in her food-service uniform and hairnet but in a silver robe which trailed behind her on the metal floor, her curls bouncing down to mid-shoulderblade. "The Gods brought us out of Old Earth and gave us everything we needed to live. But They do not want us to be infants, helpless and empty-minded. It is Aletheia's fondest hope that we will grow continually in knowledge of our own, and the other Gods stand with Her. Each part of the *Pride of Jai* is another part of that growth. There are many here, not just the team leaders, who have thrown their deepest selves into this work. Make no mistake: you will have your reward."

Tiv watched raptly, never taking her eyes off the priest. Tiv's favorite God was Techne, not Aletheia. And Yasira had no doubt that Tiv would end up with Techne when she died – if she didn't accidentally good her way into someone even better. Philophrosyne, maybe, to expire in communal bliss with everyone else who'd been extraordinarily good to the people they loved. But Tiv didn't care that this was Aletheia and not Techne. Tiv was happy to hear about Gods at any time.

Was Aletheia's official blessing really necessary? Of course, with a project this ambitious, the Gods had to wait in the wings, watching for heresy. That was only natural. But as long as no one on the *Pride of Jai* broke any laws, couldn't they just do science, without worrying about whether the Gods were impressed?

"But remember, too," said Alkipileudjea the priest, "that the Gods do not judge as humans do. Remember that you are mortal, and that one day your soul will find itself in Limbo. There the Gods will measure your soul and learn its deepest tendencies. Many people now unnoticed will prove to have been utterly devoted to something worthwhile. And many whom you have lauded as Aletheia's or even Arete's will prove to be less than that."

Yasira squeezed her eyes shut.

She knew the theology, of course. The Gods rewarded people when they died; that was part of the point of Gods. They collected souls and sorted them. Souls were somewhat diffuse, and even Gods couldn't data-mine all the specific details of a single life. But souls took on patterns, and the Gods' technology could recognize those patterns. They could discern the deepest passions that had driven a person through their life. And when the Gods chose souls to become part of Themselves, to keep Themselves running, They chose by matching the soul's pattern to the most appropriate God. Hence Aletheia, who took the people driven by a thirst for knowledge. Techne, who took engineers and artists, people devoted to creation in its every form. And so on down the list, from Gods like Arete who took brave heroes to Gods who took the worst of the worst.

Yasira had belonged to Aletheia as a child, probably. Back when she'd loved science with her whole heart. She wasn't sure where that heart was now.

Did the priest somehow know that? Had she been talking about Yasira? No. Probably not. There was no meaningful glance in Yasira's direction. The words were the same words Yasira suffered through every week.

"In your deepest hearts, friends, what spurs you to action? Do you truly thirst for knowledge, or beauty, or the lifting-up of others? There are no lies in Limbo. The God who consumes you once you've been run through Their algorithm will be the God you deserve to be part of."

Yasira wondered, as she always did, what God that was. Probably not Aletheia anymore. Not Techne or Philophrosyne. Definitely not Arete. Probably one of the wishy-washy Gods. Peitharchia, the God of doing what's expected. Eulabeia, the God of cowardice, if today's panic was any indication. And there were, of course, worse Gods than those.

Everybody knelt, briefly, with their eyes to the ground. "So be it," said the priest.

"So be it." Even Yasira mumbled it back, grinding her teeth.

Finally Yasira stood up and faced the auditorium, to polite applause. She drew the small radio out from the sash of her dress.

"Everyone ready?" she said into the device.

"We've been ready for half an hour," came the core team leader's voice through the static, not amplified enough for the audience to hear. "What's the hold up?"

"Priest stuff," said Yasira, and then someone handed her a microphone.

"Shien Reactor online," she said, "in ten, nine…"

It was a stupid job, even if the whole population of the station was watching raptly. Some glorified phone operator should be standing here counting down, not Yasira. She should be there in the generator room. With her baby.

At least she trusted the people who were doing the important part. Turning the generator on or off was a multi-step process: all sorts of huge switches would be flipped in preparation, while Yasira counted, before the spherical chamber ignited and the Talirr-Shien Effect itself came to life.

"…two, one."

The auditorium held its breath.

There was a brief flicker of the lights, and then nothing. There wasn't meant to be anything more than that, really. Yasira and her team leaders had designed the process so that the Shien Reactor would take over smoothly from the conventional generators, causing no fuss at all. The conventional generators would be kept on standby until the team verified that everything worked correctly.

"Shien Reactor online," said the team leader on the radio. "Looks good so far, Dr Shien. Starting the first runtime test battery."

Yasira did not feel particularly relieved. It really was like nothing had happened, like nothing had even turned on. She forced her face into a sunny smile. "The Shien Reactor is online and running," she repeated to everyone, like a glorified phone operator.

Then, just for a moment, the whole room *shifted*.

It was a sort of shiver in the room's dimensions, subtle enough that Yasira could have mistaken it for a brief unfocusing of her eyes. The room went slightly convex, like a breath. In and back out.

Just for a moment, Yasira could not speak with terror. All the nerves of the whole day turned to ice and adrenaline, because *she recognized this–*

Then it was over. And the audience was applauding like nothing had happened.

Yasira looked wildly from one corner of the room to another, willing it not to happen again. The auditorium was perfectly rectangular like always. The walls were solid steel. It was perfectly normal. Nobody had even noticed it.

No. Nobody had noticed because *nothing had happened*. It was nerves. If anything had really happened, the audience would be panicking, too. Besides, she'd never seen walls breathing before; she wasn't even sure what it was that she'd thought she recognized. Déjà vu, she thought. Random brain firings. Meaning nothing.

She looked out at the crowd. Wide smiles, abject boredom, and everything on the continuum in between. No terror. Tiv beamed adorably, bouncing up and down in her seat.

Nothing had happened.

Which did not stop Yasira from twitching in fear, tapping her fingers nervously against the fabric of her dress, all through the interminable ending of the ceremony.

Liked what you read?
Good news!
The sequel will soon be coming your way...

The Fallen by Ada Hoffmann
January 2021

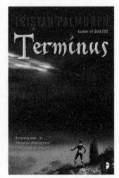

We are Angry Robot

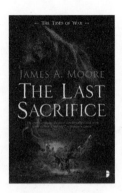
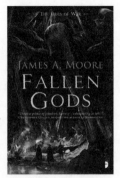
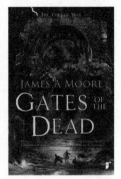

angryrobotbooks.com

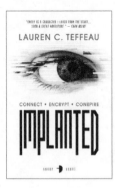

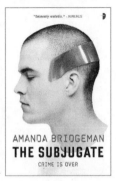